Exiled In Palestine

Peter R. Auer

ISBN: 0692767983
ISBN 13: 9780692767986
Library of Congress Control Number: 2016913427
Peter R. Auer, Washington, DC

This book is dedicated to all people who have been displaced from their homes due to circumstances beyond their control.

TABLE OF CONTENTS

FOREWORD

THIS STORY IS about Rudi and Lili Auer living in Palestine from July 1934 to August 1941. The book is the second in a trilogy. The first book, *Flight from Vienna*, details Rudi Auer and Lili Gruen's life, mainly in Vienna from 1932 to 1934. They would become my parents during their period in Palestine. If there are any resemblances of the minor characters to any living or deceased person, that is purely coincidental.

Much of this story comes from letters Rudi sent to his father that were kept and from what my parents shared with me during their lives. My father shared much more than my mother. She preferred not to talk about these years and several others following. I now believe that memories of those years were too painful for her to share, even with me, with whom she was very close. I became determined to write this story because of what I was not told, rather than because of what I was told.

First trained as a historian and involved in education for half a century, I decided to write this so that it may become a contribution to Holocaust literature. Holocaust literature needs to be as complete and comprehensive as possible to help curtail anti-Semitism, which again seems to be on the increase in Europe, reduce future Holocaust denial, and help prevent human beings in the future from committing major atrocities against other human beings.

I also wanted to write this story for my grandchildren in order that they might appreciate how their great-grandparents strove to live a normal life during a period of tension and unrest with the rise of Nazism in the background and in a milieu completely foreign to them.

Looking back to those years, it is with some consternation that one recognizes the relatively widespread undercurrent of animosities and hostilities during this period between 1934 and 1941 in Palestine. During this period there were hostilities between the British and the Palestinians, Arabs and Jews, and Jews and Germans, especially with the increase of Nazism in Europe and the concomitant anti-Semitism at a time of increasing Jewish immigration to Palestine.

Acknowledgments

I AM INDEBTED to my wife, Carolyn Schiller, who continues to help me appreciate the importance of historical fiction as a genre and who encouraged me to write the story of my parents, Lili and Rudi. I am grateful to her for listening each evening to the story of *Exiled in Palestine* as it unfolded and for providing invaluable, insightful, and good-humored feedback until the process had been completed. And I am particularly indebted to Carolyn for her meticulous editing and proofreading, without ever suggesting it to be a chore. She has been, throughout the entire process, a true comrade-in-arms.

To my family and friends who read *Flight from Vienna*, I owe thanks for providing me with invaluable feedback that allows this second part of the trilogy, *Exiled in Palestine*, to be an improvement on the first.

To our Jack Russel terrier, Charlie, I owe sincere gratitude for not complaining when dinner was served far too late due to her dad being busy at the computer.

CARGO HOLD

SITTING IN COMPLETE darkness on a hard wooden box in the cargo hold of that brightly colored ship, Rudi didn't know what to say. There were strong smells of oil, tobacco, leather, and grain and a continuous vibration that traveled from their backside to the top of their head. Lili stood up and walked around in a circle and sat down again while Rudi scratched his head.

Lili broke the silence with some sobbing. "Where are we headed, Rudi? Where are we…going? Why did we really have to leave Vienna? Did you tell me the truth, Rudi? Did you tell me everything? I couldn't even say good-bye to my mother," she said as she stood up, her bruised backside throbbing.

"I'm so sorry, Lili. I should not have written that article. I now realize those university authorities were determined to shut me up… even though they all knew that I was not making anything up…I didn't think."

"You didn't think, and look where it's got us." Lili's sobbing became ever louder. Rudi stood up and put his arm around her, but she pulled away.

"You got us into this—now you get us out of this. You're a fugitive from justice, a criminal. Do you realize…we are both illegally on a ship and don't know where in the world we are going? Where, Rudi, where?"

Lili soon became exhausted and sat beside Rudi, putting her head on his shoulder. The vibration from bum to brain seemed to awaken some remorse, as Rudi thought about how stupid he had been.

I didn't need to write that article. I should have known that the university authorities would have pulled all strings to shut me up and not further expose the anti-Semitism within that administration; after all, it had been entrenched for several years, if not longer. Eminent professors and citizens had tried to change the mind-set within the university, and they had no success. How the hell did I think I could have made a difference—just a second-year law student? Shit, I was arrogant. Shit, shit, shit! I know I'm not yet even twenty-one, and it's easy to make mistakes. Yes, it's easy to make mistakes, but I'm married and should have been more responsible. What a stupid arsehole! This will likely jeopardize my relationship...I'm so lucky to have Lili. She's twenty-eight and could have married any number of men well established and mature and who wouldn't make goddamned stupid decisions. What an immature idiot I've been. I let her down so badly. No wonder her mother thinks I'm a poor match, and neither her brother Walter nor her friend Hanna are over the moon about me. I should have been much more caring; I should have thought much more about Lili. In Villach, my mother and father, who love Lili dearly, will be furious. Tante Marianne, who adores her and is proudly knitting for the future, will never forgive me. We had such a good life in Vienna. Our apartment was small, but it was adequate, and my stipend was paying for that. And Lili earned good money, enjoyed her work, and loved her boss, Mr. Schwartz, who has always been generous, even to me. What an idiot...Christ, what will my flatmate Joseph think when he comes back, the apartment stone cold and all of Lili's and my things still there? He won't know what the hell's happened.

The boat began to pitch as it found the open sea, and some wooden boxes began to creak to the rhythm of the swell. Rudi started to feel a bit queasy, and Lili needed to go to the toilet, she told him.

"Go have a wee behind those big metal crates, Lili."

"I have a more serious need," said Lili, standing up.

"Perhaps we should have lunch now, and you'll have some paper then, Lili." They had lunch, and Lili went behind the big metal crates.

"How long will this journey take, Rudi?"

"I really don't know," he said somewhat sheepishly. "Some of the boxes are stamped Perishables, so it can't be more than two or three days."

"Two or three days, Rudi...how could you have done this to me? Are you out of your mind?" Lili burst into tears. "My mother knew best; your decision-making skills are lousy." Rudi felt really bad. "We didn't even have a honeymoon, and now we're on a ship to God knows where. Have you really no idea where we could be headed?"

"My geography isn't very good, but some of the cargo has Arabic writing on it; that probably means we're headed to Palestine or somewhere in Africa."

"I don't want to be in Palestine or Africa. It's so damned hot there and all that sand. Oh, Rudi, what have you done? You'll have no more schnitzel, *Kaiserschmarrn*...or Café Louvre...and I'll be without the opera, Café Demel...and all those nice shops on Kaerntnerstrasse. Won't you miss Joseph and any of your professors? Won't you miss your mother and father...and Tante Marianne? I so wish I were with Tante Marianne right now, watching her knitting." Lili's voice trailed off as she began to quietly sob.

Lili felt something rubbing up against her legs. She was momentarily taken aback and pulled her knees up. A black cat with luminescent green eyes looked up at her and let out several meows. Soon some scratching noises a little distance away distracted her, and she disappeared.

Just around to their left were dozens of Hessian sacks that Rudi thought contained grain. Rudi led Lili onto the sacks, and they lay down. Lili felt utterly disappointed with Rudi, and Rudi felt utterly disappointed with himself. They did not speak for a long time. Despite or because of the movement beneath their bodies, they fell asleep.

Rudi and Lili awoke to a shaft of daylight, as a metal hatch creaked open and a silhouetted figure carefully came down a set of steep steps and placed a bowl, with what appeared to be bread and milk, just around the corner from the steps. The cat meowed a "thank you,' and the hatch closed with a bang. Lili laid her head down again and fell back to sleep. Rudi stayed awake till he got restless and then got up to walk around the space he and Lili shared with the black, green-eyed cat and various assignments of cargo.

Upon examination it appeared that the most common destinations shown on cargo items were Jaffa, Haifa, and Jerusalem. Rudi did not mention this when Lili woke up for fear of another response of anger or dismay. He returned to his position to find Lili in the company of the meowing and smooching cat. He just sat quietly and reflected upon his own inadequacies till the cat moved over to him and distracted him from his own misery. There had been no other communication in the cargo hold, when the hatch creaked open again, and the same silhouetted figure came down the same steps and replaced the empty bowl with a full one.

The cat ran to the food, and her server said, "If I hear any rustling of mice or worse down here, you won't get your next meal, pussy, do you understand?"

"Meow," said the green-eyed black cat.

"Good," was the response, as darkness again descended with a metallic clang.

Rudi and Lili were both determined not to speak with one another, and they would take turns to climb down from the sacks and walk around in the semidarkness till boredom would overtake Rudi and fright would overtake Lili. Hours passed, and they both fell asleep despite feeling hungry and thirsty. Lili woke to the creak of the hatch being opened again and the cat being brought fresh food. Lili's throat was parched, and her stomach was growling.

"Could I please have the remaining apple, Rudi," were the only words spoken during a period of more than twenty hours. Rudi passed Lili the apple and headed to the cat's bowl, from where he had a sip of milk.

"Nice and sweet," he said to the cat. "Thank you." Rudi sat on the bottom rung of the steps, observing the cat's table manners and continued his conversation. "Caught any mice lately, pussy? Do you know where we're headed? Do we have much longer to go?"

Rudi and Lili were utterly exhausted and parched when they heard the engines of the brightly colored cargo ship power down and the vibrations of the engines diminish. Suddenly all was quiet. Where had the boat stopped? The engine noises did not suggest that the boat had docked at a pier. Lili accepted Rudi's hand as he led her to where the cat had been receiving her food.

"Wait a minute while I look up here to check out the situation," said Rudi as he began to climb up the steps and open the hatch. He looked around and climbed down again, leaving the hatch open to provide some light. He led Lili to the hatch on the opposite side, which provided the view of a shoreline. He estimated the shore was about two hundred meters from the boat.

Not providing Lili enough time to get overly anxious, he said, "Give me your shoes," as he put his own in the empty lunch bag together with a purse. "Jump," he said as he leapt into the water, holding the bag closed and above his head. Lili followed, her dress billowing before she reached the water. After the instant shock of hitting the water, the sea was quite warm, certainly by Ossiachersee (Austrian lake) standards. Without speaking, they swam beside one another, Rudi holding the bag aloft. The water appeared very deep, and they had to swim for quite a while till they found themselves wading. They reached the shore and fell into each other's arms. It had been some days since they had embraced one another.

"Where are we?" asked Lili. Rudi just shrugged his shoulders as he stubbed his foot on a broken piece of shell. They half staggered up a sandy and stony slope and were greeted by a sign in English. It read: THE PORT OF HAIFA.

It was Friday, July 27, 1934. Rudi and Lili were fully clothed and dripping wet. They now needed to drip dry. That would not take long, as it was becoming hotter by the minute, the sun shining fiercely from a clear sky as it was moving toward its zenith. Lili, with tears in her eyes, stumbled along, holding Rudi's hand and frequently trying to loosen her dress that seemed determined to cling to her legs. In a moment of frustration, she hitched up her dress a little with each hand and swirled it around, pretending to imitate Carmen dancing. Rudi and she both managed a bit of a laugh. They headed south and uphill into the town, all the while looking for a hotel where they could stay for some time and get some real rest before finding some more permanent accommodation.

IN THE MEANTIME IN VIENNA

ON THE TWENTIETH of July, 1934, around lunchtime, Mr. Schwartz anxiously listened to Lili relate the last conversation she had with Rudi, whom Lili hadn't heard from for more than twenty-four hours. Mr. Schwartz noticed Lili becoming red in the face and terribly agitated. She went to the bathroom, picked up her bag when she returned, and gave Mr. Schwartz an abbreviated hug. He gave Lili an envelope, said he was very sorry, and wished her much luck as she hurried out the door. *Will I ever see Lili again?* he wondered. He collected himself, took several deep breaths, and phoned Lili's mother.

"Hedwig?"

"*Ja.*"

"Schwartz *hier.*"

"*Ja*…I don't know how to tell you," said Mr. Schwarz.

"What is it?"

"Lili has just left the office and is about to meet Rudi, and they are leaving Vienna."

"What do you mean…leaving Vienna? What for? Where are they going?"

"They didn't say."

"Leaving the country? What? Where to? Why?"

"Rudi was arrested and locked up, and then he escaped. And now—"

"*Ach du liebe Zeit!* Locked up? What did he do? Where could they be going? Schwartz, stop them! Can't you stop them?"

"Not really! I wish I could, Hedwig. Lili was meeting him at the Hauptbahnhof. That's all I know."

"*Gott im Himmel!* What to think? What to do?" Lili's mother began to sob as she hung up the phone. *Why? Why? Why did she fall in love with that nobody...and marry him? That boy, that country yokel...and now...a criminal...a fugitive from justice? What did he do? Kill somebody...rob a bank? I never knew how he could afford to do what he was doing. Oh, Lili, Lili, why are you with this man—so far below your station? I told you—*

Hedwig's phone rang. "Schwartz here again. I'm off to the Hauptbahnhof to try and stop them."

"*Danke, Danke,*" she said as the phone clicked off.

Mr. Schwartz climbed into a taxi. "*Zum Hauptbahnhof, bitte. Schnell, schnell...*as fast as possible," he told the cab driver, who took the request seriously. The taxi sped between cars, overtaking traffic.

"Whoa," said Mr. Schwartz, as the car lurched from one lane to another, the driver really driving quite recklessly.

When the taxi arrived at the station, Mr. Schwartz pressed a couple of coins into the driver's hand, slammed the door of the taxi, and ran into the front entrance of the Hauptbahnhof. He ran onto several platforms and saw one train about to leave for Trieste, according to a platform sign and a whistle from the guard. He ran along the length of the train and with craned neck, looked anxiously into every window as passengers were quietly putting their bags and other items onto the racks above their seat.

"Lili, Lili," he called out a number of times. *No Lili. No Rudi... verdammt noch a mal. Where are they?* Mr. Schwartz ran onto another platform where a train was just pulling in. No Rudi and no Lili to be seen. On to another platform. No Lili, no Rudi. All other platforms were empty at this off-peak time.

Dejected, Mr. Schwarz left the Hauptbahnhof just as an Opel truck, with the signage Constantinople–Wien turned in front of him and disappeared.

Mr. Schwartz took a taxi back to his office and sat at his desk, head between his hands, preparing to phone Lili's mother again. He had found the earlier phone call with her very difficult, and he tried to imagine how difficult it would be for her to receive the news he now needed to share. He couldn't find Lili or Rudi. He was about to call her, when the phone rang.

"Schwartz?"

"*Ja.*"

"Walter *hier.* Mother just rang me…did you stop them?"

"No, I couldn't find them."

"*Ei yei yei*…she's hysterical…Mother's hysterical. What is this…Rudi a criminal…killed someone or robbed a bank or something…locked up and then escaped and Lili running off with him, police chasing after them?"

"Rudi was apparently taken to the police by the university administration for attempts to disturb the peace…actually by exposing the administration as working together with the Nazis."

"Stupid young man…wouldn't listen to advice."

"He was locked up overnight and escaped the next morning.'

"I will ring Mother back, Mr. Schwartz. *Servus.*" Walter ended the call with Mr. Schwartz.

"*Mutter.* It's Walter *hier,*" Walter said to his mother.

"Did he find them?" asked Hedwig anxiously. "No, he tried very hard…no sign of them," Walter said.

"Oh, Walter, that's terrible. What will happen? They are fugitives… from justice. Lili's a fugitive. She may not be safe with Rudi." She burst into extreme sobbing. "Oh, where is Lili? She can't just disappear. I may never see her again. I'm so frightened, Walter. And you're not here. Can you come to be with me? Oh, Walter…I feel faint."

There was some convulsive coughing, and the phone went dead. *She could be having a stroke,* thought Walter. Walter redialed; there was just an engaged signal. He took his coat and was about to head off for the train station, more than a little concerned for his mother. Surely, she couldn't be having a stroke or a heart attack. He phoned the Gruens' family physician and asked him to visit his mother pronto. Walter said he would be in Vienna in the morning.

In the meantime, Mr. Schwartz phoned Rudi and Maria Auer, Rudi's parents, in Kaernten. "*Gruess Gott.* Herr (Mr.) Schwartz *hier,* Lili's boss and friend of Rudi. Is that Maria Auer?"

"*Ja, ein* moment, I'll give you Rudi."

Mr. Schwartz could hear Mrs. Auer speaking to Rudi Senior. "Rudi, it's Lili's boss; something doesn't sound so good."

"*Ja*, Rudi Auer *hier.*"

"Herr Auer, this is Mr. Schwartz. Has Rudi called you this morning?"

"No, why?"

"We are not exactly sure—"

"Yes, yes, get to the point. Is there a problem?" asked Rudi Senior impatiently.

"Yes, your son was arrested, locked up—"

"What do you mean, locked up? Maria, the police have locked Rudi up. Mr. Schwartz, what happened? They must have made a mistake. Rudi is not capable of doing something that justifies being locked up."

"Of course not, he's a good—" exclaimed Maria Auer in the background.

"He was accused of disturbing the peace in Vienna, Mr. Auer," said Mr. Schwartz.

"What, by playing the violin?"

"Mr. Auer, he wrote this article—"

"Oh no, we told him to just concentrate on—"

"Yes, well, he didn't, Mr. Auer. Rudi wrote an article…accused the university administration of being in cahoots with the Nazis."

"Probably true."

"Yes, but it got him into terrible trouble. He was locked up last night and escaped from custody this morning…was obviously going to spend more time in prison."

"*Ei yei yei*…for telling the truth?"

"He and Lili were leaving Vienna…probably left by now. Lili's mother is terribly worried. Any idea where they might be going?"

"Can you imagine where Rudi might be taking Lili, Maria?" Mr. Schwartz heard Rudi Senior ask his wife.

"No."

"No, Mr. Schwartz, we have no idea. *Meine Guete!* Let us know, please, if Lili gets in touch with you." Rudi Senior hung up and wiped the sweat from his brow.

"*Ja*, Maria, where could he go?" Rudi Senior said. Mrs. Auer shrugged her shoulders and began to sob.

Perhaps Joseph is back and knows something, thought Mr. Schwartz. *I think I'll walk to the apartment and see if Joseph's there. Some fresh air will do me good.*

Nobody answered the door, so Mr. Schwartz quickly wrote a note and left it under the door. It read:

> *Lieber Joseph, please call or visit me as soon as you can.*
> *Schwartz*

THE GRUEN FAMILY doctor went to see Hedwig. He had to knock on the door a number of times before Hedwig answered. He was momentarily worried. She was very red in the face and was wiping tears away as the doctor entered. The tears soon reemerged as she related the story she had heard from Mr. Schwartz. The doctor, who had looked after the family for decades, fetched Hedwig a glass of water and sat opposite her in the living room. He had another thought, got up again, poured two glasses of cognac, and handed one to his patient.

"Hedwig," he said, moving his head from side to side. "Do not worry. They have just been married a month; there was some foolishness...just some foolishness...and now they will take a honeymoon. Don't worry, Hedwig, lots of lovers run away...that's why the opera and ballet are full of such stories. Just calm down, take these sleeping pills at nine o'clock, and Walter will be with you in the morning."

It was well into the afternoon when Mr. Schwartz decided he'd be in touch with the university administration to try to find out what had really transpired that sent Rudi fleeing. The phone was answered immediately.

"*Ja*, can I help you? Who am I speaking with?"

"I am Mr. Schwartz, and I am calling about Rudolf Auer, a student."

"*Ja, natuerlich,* I will pass you over to the *Ober* administrator."

A few minutes later, a different person came on the phone. "*Ja*, Mr. Schwartz, why are you calling?"

"I am calling on behalf of Rudi Auer's wife...she works for me... she is too distressed to make any phone call herself."

"Aha, yes, she is now the wife of a fugitive. Auer was on the way to receive his sentence of thirty days imprisonment when he escaped."

"*Ei yei, yei*...that's very serious. What did he do to receive such a sentence?"

"He was convicted of crimes against the University of Vienna—he had not obeyed instructions from the administration on several occasions before. He ran very fast, we are told, no one could catch him. He is now a fugitive, and police are looking for him throughout Vienna. Police are confident they will have him in their hands before the morning."

Mr. Schwartz, not being able to concentrate any further upon his work, straightened some papers on his desk and locked the door. It was a gray day, and the wind was still when he bought some flowers for his wife, as he regularly did on a Friday evening, and walked home slowly, exhausted and sad. *Where could they have gone?* he wondered. *Are they safe? Will I ever have Lili working for me again? She is such a good worker and a very nice person. Will I ever see her again?* After a fitful night's sleep, he was sitting at the breakfast table, poised to take his first sip of coffee, when the phone rang.

"Don't they know this is the Sabbath, even if we aren't practicing?" he said to his wife.

"Have you heard from Walter? He is not here yet," asked Hedwig over the phone.

"Who's that?" asked Mrs. Schwartz.

"Hedwig," answered Mr. Schwartz, hand over the mouthpiece. Then he said to Hedwig, "I haven't heard from Walter; the train from Paris is just due in now; I'm sure he'll be with you soon."

Mr. Schwartz had finished his breakfast and had just dialed the phone to speak with Hanna to see if she had heard from Lili, when there was some very loud rapping on the front door. Two uniformed policemen entered, somewhat agitated.

"Good morning. Are you Mr. Schwartz, the employer of Mrs. Lili Auer?'

"Yes, I am."

"Why are you here?" asked Mrs. Schwartz.

"Have you seen Mrs. Auer this morning…Mrs. Lili Auer?"

"No, of course not, it is the Sabbath. We do not work on the Sabbath," said Mr. Schwartz.

"We are looking for Rudolf Auer; he is a fugitive of the state, and when we find Mrs. Auer, we will find the fugitive. May we search your house, Mr. and Mrs. Schwartz?"

"Really! That is surely an unnecessary intrusion…do we have a choice?" asked Mr. Schwartz.

"No, not really."

"Then why do you ask? Go ahead. Mind, the beds are not made yet, and you will likely find some towels on the bathroom floor."

The police officers went straight upstairs and looked in each room, under the beds and in the armoires, and returned downstairs. "Thank you for your assistance. Should you see either Mr. or Mrs. Rudolf Auer, you are obliged to inform the police. If you were to fail to do that, you would be regarded as an accomplice. Do you understand, Mr. and Mrs. Schwartz?"

Mr. Schwartz quietly closed the door behind them. "Do you realize, darling, they did not ask you whether you were Mrs. Schwartz?"

The phone rang. It was Hedwig. "Hallo, Hedwig here. He has arrived. Thank you." Hedwig hung up.

Mr. and Mrs. Schwartz glanced at one another, and Mr. Schwartz dialed the number for Lili's friend Hanna again. "Schwartz here. Can I speak with Hanna, please?"

"This is Michael. Of course…I'll get her." The phone was silent for a moment.

"Who is that?" Mr. Schwartz could hear Hanna speaking to Michael in the background.

"Mr. Schwartz," said Michael to Hanna.

"Mr. Schwartz? What could he want on the Sabbath?" Hanna asked.

Hanna came on the phone. "Hanna here, Mr. Schwartz. Is something the matter?"

"Have you seen Lili, Hanna?"

"No. Why, is she in trouble?"

"Maybe indirectly, but Rudi certainly is."

"Oh, has he offended the university again?"

"Unfortunately, yes. He was locked up overnight...Lili was beside herself."

"That poor woman, I told her he wasn't right for her...sorry, Mr. Schwartz, I interrupted."

"He was on the way to his sentencing...got a thirty-day sentence... he escaped, ran away. He called Lili at the office, and she left in a hurry to meet him at the Hauptbahnhof. They were going to leave Vienna."

"*Ach du liebe Zeit.* Do you have any idea where they went?"

"No, I phoned you to see if you had heard from Lili. Would you have any idea where she might consider going?"

"No, I have no idea," she said as the phone was put down.

"That poor woman!" Mr. Schwartz relayed the whole story to his wife and after lunch, quite exhausted, took a nap. He had not yet completed his snooze, when there was another call.

"Mr. Schwartz, Walter here. I must speak quietly; I do not want Mother to hear. I am very worried. My mother is still beside herself, and I'm concerned she will have a heart attack or something; it's that bad."

"I'm sorry to hear that. I'm exhausted, too, I must say," said Mr. Schwartz. "I would have expected Lili to have contacted someone just to say she's okay."

"Yes, it's not like her to be inconsiderate...she has frequently phoned just to see that her dachshunds, Kafka and Bela, are okay."

"I can't imagine where she might be. I expect she'll contact someone soon," said Mr. Schwartz. "Sorry, I can't think of anything... remember, your mother is quite partial to cognac."

The Sabbath came to a close, and Mr. and Mrs. Schwartz had an uninterrupted Sunday. Hanna was furious with Rudi and couldn't imagine where her friend might be, while Walter was still trying to console his mother with the aid of alcohol. Joseph was on the train somewhere between Munich and Vienna.

———

MR. SCHWARTZ WAS approaching his office on Monday morning, wondering what tasks to tackle first, as he would be without Lili, when he noticed somebody sitting on his doorstep. He recognized Rudi's flatmate, Joseph, who stood up and let out a sigh.

"*Gruess Gott,* Joseph," Mr. Schwartz said.

"*Shalom,* Mr. Schwartz. What's happened? I got your note...on the train not far out of Vienna I had this bad feeling...I had a premonition that something terrible had happened to Rudi...and...then I arrived home...all their things there, but they had obviously not slept there overnight. And then I got your note."

"Come, we can talk better in the café."

"*Gruess Gott.*"

"*Gruess Gott...Kaffee,* Joseph? *Zwei Kaffee, bitte.*" Mr. Schwartz ordered as he and an anxious Joseph sat by the window, where they had sat before. Joseph looked nervously at Mr. Schwartz as the coffees arrived.

"Two brandies, too, please, Herr Ober...*Ja,* where to begin. But first, Joseph, are your parents out of Munich? Lili told me—"

"Yes, thank you, Mr. Schwartz...it was quite a month, but they should be in Lyon about now. And?"

"How to begin, Joseph. I presume you haven't heard from Rudi or Lili in a while."

Joseph nodded in agreement.

"They've run away," said Mr. Schwartz.

"What do you mean, they've run away?"

"Rudi was imprisoned and escaped, and he ran away."

"*Oy Gevalt.* Anybody know where they went? What happened? When?"

Mr. Schwartz ordered another couple of coffees and told Joseph all he knew.

— 15 —

Joseph became somewhat drained just from listening and rubbed his face with his hand. "That university administration is in cahoots with the Nazis, of course, and they obviously wanted to shut Rudi up for good."

"Well, they seem to have succeeded; they've chased him out of the city…if not the country. Do you have any idea where they might have headed?"

"Lili spoke of New York once, and Rudi has mentioned Australia and New Zealand a few times, but—"

Herr Ober walked quickly to their table and said to Mr. Schwartz, "There are three police officers at your office door."

Now what? thought Mr. Schwartz as he and Joseph walked back to the office.

"*Gruess Gott,* is Mrs. Auer here? Have you seen Mr. Auer—Rudolf Auer?" asked the officers when Mr. Schwartz and Joseph arrived.

"No, I have not opened the office yet."

"Yes. We can certainly smell that! Have you something to hide?" The officers were aware of the scent of alcohol in the air. "Who is this?" asked an officer, nodding toward Joseph.

"This is Joseph; he lives in the same apartment with Mr. and Mrs. Auer."

"Good. Stay with us, young man, but first, Mr. Schwartz, we will search your offices." The police officers briskly and wordlessly searched the offices.

"*Alles klar,*" said one officer to the other as they emerged on the front step. "Get in, Joseph," said the other officer as he opened a police-car door. "Direct us to your apartment."

"COME IN, OFFICERS," said Joseph when they reached his apartment.

The officers took a quick look around. "Sit down. We need to ask you some questions. How long have you been in this apartment? How long have you known Rudi? Lili? Have you any idea where they might have gone?"

"No idea, I'm sorry. I would like to know myself."

"Do they have a favorite uncle they may be able to hide with?"

"No, but their favorite auntie is a Tante Marianne; she lives near a lake."

The police officers glared at Joseph. "If they contact you, you are obliged to inform the police. Do you understand? Otherwise, you'd be an accessory."

Joseph closed the door after the officers left and watched the police car drive away. He poured himself a beer and sat in a chair at the table, leaving two chairs empty. It was deathly quiet, eerily quiet, except for a fly buzzing against a windowpane. On the table was a copy of the *Wiener Uni Zeitung* open on page two. He read Rudi's article.

Nothing untrue, he mused. *Mr. Schwartz had told me everything there is to know, but why has this all happened? I knew something awful had happened... that dream told me. How could the authorities have meted out such a heavy punishment? Is there no such thing as free speech at the university? How the hell did Rudi escape? Oy vey, all their things are here; they'll surely be in touch soon. Rudi will want his violin, Lili her wedding dress. Yes, I will hear from them soon.*

Joseph felt empty and unable to concentrate on any university work today. He poured another beer and wondered whether his parents had arrived at their destination in Lyon. He moped around the apartment a bit, threw out all perishables from the kitchen, took the unpacked bag he had brought back from Munich, and went to his girlfriend, Ester's, apartment.

Joseph phoned her at work. "*Shalom,* I'm here. Rudi and Lili have gone. *A feir zol sie treffen!*"

"Who? What? What happened?" asked Ester.

"The university administration...*a feier zol sie treffen*...they locked Rudi up...got a sentence of thirty days...he escaped, she went to meet him at the Hauptbahnhof, and they have not been seen or heard of since...since Friday."

"*Oy Vey.* Is it because of one of his articles again?"

"Yes, obviously determined to shut him up. They would never have predicted that he would escape...outran the police apparently."

"And outsmarted them, too," said Ester.

"I don't think it would be too wise to leave Vienna with Lili...she loves Vienna...she is so part of Vienna. If she weren't married to Rudi, she'd never leave Vienna," said Joseph.

After their conversation ended, the phone rang. It was Hanna. "Joseph, I just phoned on the off chance—"

"Who is it?"

"Sorry, Lili's friend, Hanna. Have you heard from them?"

"No." Hanna sighed, hung up, and phoned Hedwig Gruen.

"Frau Gruen?"

"*Nein,* this is Walter here."

"So sorry. I am Hanna, Lili's friend. Have you heard from them?"

"No."

Rudi Auer Sr. from Villach phoned Mr. Schwartz. "Mr. Schwartz, Auer von Villach here. Have you heard anything?"

"No."

And so it was for the next couple of days.

THE APPINGER HOTEL, HAIFA

NOW DRIP DRIED, tired, and running out of patience, Rudi and Lili walked into the lobby of the Appinger Hotel. It seemed a pleasant-enough place, with a couple of sturdy couches and a coffee table in the foyer, and it appeared very clean. A man and a woman were talking behind the counter.

The woman asked, "What have you done with your arm, Sahib? Did you break it?"

The gray-haired man, of small stature and a healthy, tanned complexion, said, "Yes, unfortunately, and now I'm a driver short. I need one straight after prayers, otherwise I will not get my consignment off the wharf in time...and I'll have to pay a fine."

"Oh, you'll be fine; everything will be okay, Sahib."

"*Insha Allah.*"

"Excuse me, sir, I couldn't help but overhear your conversation," said Rudi. "I have just come into town, and I can drive. Perhaps...you'll let me help you get out of your predicament?"

"Oh, excellent. *Alhamdulilla,*" said Sahib, giving Rudi the once-over. "I'll see you here in the lobby in one hour. I must rush off now."

Rudi and Lili were checked in by an elegant woman and walked to their second-story room.

"Will this be adequate?" the woman asked confidently in Swabian German—very different from Austrian German. Rudi and Lili's eyes met, and they both nodded in unison.

This certainly beats sitting for umpteen hours on the hard seat of a truck, bumping along roads halfway across Europe, or lying on top of sacks of grain patrolled by a black cat with green eyes in the blackness of a smelly, airless cargo hold, thought Lili.

"Thank you, madam...would you please be able to tell me where I might buy a few clothes this afternoon?" asked Lili, wanting to be a little more assertive.

"Of course. Go to Jaffa Street; you'll get whatever you could possibly want. It's easy to find," said the woman, frowning a little at hearing Lili's different accent. "Oh, and you can call me Gudrun."

Rudi and Lili went for a quick bite to eat around the corner just as the ear-splitting call to prayer summoned local Muslims and caught Lili and Rudi off guard. Cold stuffed vine leaves and lamb kababs were very good, though some spices smelled and tasted rather foreign. A liter of water was also well appreciated.

"It will be excellent to have work straightaway," said Rudi to Lili. "That was very fortuitous...overhearing the conversation. Would you buy me a pair of underpants, a pair or two of socks, and a short-sleeved shirt, please, Lili?"

— ∞ —

SAHIB MET RUDI in the lobby with hand outstretched, and they shook hands.

"*Salam Alekum.* My name is Saleh Abdullah, but everybody just calls me Sahib. What is your name?"

"Rudi Auer."

"You're neither Arab nor Jew...Christian? You look German. Can you drive a truck? Good. I broke my arm, so I can't do any lifting... building materials are to be transported from the wharf and taken to Akko. I'll take you for the first trip; then you'll be on your own."

They walked to a medium-sized truck seemingly without pedigree or name, and Sahib threw Rudi the keys over the bonnet as he said, "You drive."

Sahib, relaxed yet alert, instructed Rudi in brief sentences till they got to wharf 3B. Sahib jumped out of the truck, opened a large wire gate, and motioned Rudi to drive through. Sahib closed the gate, jumped in again, and instructed Rudi to drive another hundred meters or so to where there was a mountain of girders.

"These are for a warehouse. Um…load the longer ones first—these over here. Can you manage? Um…are they too heavy for you?"

Rudi managed, and Sahib smiled. "*Tamam,*" he said.

The truck was loaded in about an hour and a half, and Sahib instructed Rudi on how to secure the load with ropes that Sahib collected from the cabin of the truck. Rudi drove. Sahib opened and closed the gate behind him and proceeded to provide minimal instructions on their way to Akko, as they first swung east for a few miles and then north.

The road was of uneven quality, several areas rather rough and some winding. Rudi slowed down at the appropriate times to avoid losing the load. It was close to an hour's driving, and Sahib pointed to some concrete footings for a large construction. Sahib sat on the running board of the truck and passed a felt-covered water bottle to Rudi, who took more than a few gulps.

"Thank you,"said Rudi.

"*Afwan,*" replied Sahib, as Rudi started to untie the ropes that had secured the load. Rudi began to carry the girders to a place Sahib had suggested.

"Mister, here," said Sahib as he threw Rudi some gloves that didn't need wearing in. "Wouldn't want you to get blisters."

Rudi worked quickly, as he wanted to please Sahib.

"*Shwei-shweia,* Rudi; slow down; you'll burn yourself out."

Sahib continued to sit in the shade on the sideboard of the cabin of the truck, pulled up his not-so-white *thobe* to his knees, and lit a cigarette. He flicked the match away, blew a plume of smoke into the air, and watched Rudi methodically transfer the stack of girders from the truck to beside the concrete footings. Rudi was soaked in perspiration, his arms and face glistening, as he moved the last of the girders.

"*Tamam,*" said Sahib, looking at his watch. "I'll have plenty of time for *Isha* prayers. Rudi, you keep the truck at Appinger, and you do four loads each day till you have delivered all the girders… *capiche*? You understand Italian? No work tomorrow, though…start again Sunday."

Rudi smiled and nodded. He had a splitting headache, probably as much from lack of sleep as from a lack of water. As if Sahib were able to understand, he passed Rudi the water bottle as he was turning on the engine. Rudi, wet through, drove to the Appinger Hotel, where Sahib bid Rudi "*ma'a salama.*" Sensing the meaning, Rudi responded with a *ma'a salama* of his own. Sahib smiled and was gone.

WHILE RUDI WAS sweating and laboring, Lili was coping with one situation after another herself. First she went to a money-exchange facility to exchange Austrian schillings for Palestinian pounds. The teller, noticing that Lili was looking a little anxious, assured her that the rate of exchange was fixed, and she would not be cheated as long as she used only an official money exchange. Lili's level of anxiety dropped for a time, but she soon became a little concerned, as most conversations she heard on Jaffa Street were in Arabic, and her entire Arabic vocabulary at this time was *Salam Alekum,* and she was not exactly sure how to use it. There were many people shopping and walking and chatting on Jaffa Street, and Lili soon observed that *Alekum Salam* was the common response to *Salam Alekum.*

She walked up and down each side of Jaffa Street to check out the shops. The street was nothing like any of the shopping streets in Vienna. The fashions could not be compared. There were lots of stores specializing, it seemed, in various long robes and head coverings. Lili was admiring some very elaborate embroidery, when a young, veiled woman looked up at her.

"Can I help you, ma'am? I can help you...and I can learn me English. Let me come with you. I ask for no money."

"All right," said Lili after a brief hesitation.

"My name is Basmah...I just call you ma'am." Lili learned the difference between *thobes* or *dishdashas* (robes), cloaks, and coats and the difference in the way Muslim women wear scarves and burqas.

"Do you like this burqa, ma'am?" asked Basmah, pointing to a very elaborate and colorful face veil.

"Yes, it's very beautiful," said Lili with a smile. As Lili and Basmah walked along the shop fronts, Lili noticed that some shops were for women only, others were for men only, others seemed to concentrate on Middle Eastern fashion, and yet others seemed to carry European clothes. One shop window displayed clothes that were unmistakably German.

"For German colony," commented Basmah, as Lili admired some *dirndls* (dresses). Lili nodded at Basmah, and they entered a clothing store that seemed to have an eclectic collection.

"*Salam Alekum,*" said Basmah, whereupon the saleswoman said, "*Alekum Salam...Shalom...*May I help you?" in perfect English.

Wow, thought Lili, *three languages in a simple greeting.* Lili tried on half a dozen dresses, Basmah showing her comparative approval by the breadth of her smile and the number of nods. Lili walked out with two dresses.

"*Shukran,*" said Lili, which she picked up earlier, and "good-bye." The next shop added four pairs of less-than-sexy knickers, but at least they were pure cotton and looked comfortable.

"You want buy sandals, ma'am?" asked Basmah, noticing Lili peering at a variety of sandals while wearing midheight dress shoes.

"Yes, Basmah; is this a good shop?"

"Shop is very good, ma'am, very clean." Lili tried on several pairs and decided on a simple, brown pair, flat and comfortable with crossover straps and a low price tag.

"*Shukran,*" said Lili with increasing confidence. "You are a great help, thank you, Basmah," as they left the store.

"My English getting better, ma'am?" asked Basmah.

"Your English is very good," said Lili assuringly. Basmah was a little hesitant as she followed Lili into a men's clothing store. Lili soon found a khaki short-sleeved shirt in the correct size for Rudi.

"For husband or brother, ma'am?" asked Basmah.

"For my husband, Basmah."

"Is he handsome, ma'am?"

Lili smiled, moved a few feet, and selected two pairs of socks of unequal size, which caused a minor stir.

"Different size, ma'am…may I say?" said Basmah. The salesgirl giggled.

"One pair is for my husband and one pair for me," said Lili.

"Ah, *tamam*," said the saleswoman. Basmah smiled.

"*Shukran*, bye-bye," said Lili as she left the store. "Will you have an ice cream with me, Basmah? I would like to buy you an ice cream, and we could both sit and talk."

"Thank you very much, ma'am…I must go…my mother expecting me. Thank you for helping me with English, ma'am…*Shukran*…bye-bye," Basmah said as she skipped off.

Lili had no problem selecting an ice cream. She sat at a table under a palm tree, which provided shade but little relief from the heat. She had to focus to prevent drips from getting too far down the cone. Leaving the shade of the palm tree, she passed a shop where an item caught her eye. She stopped. It was a small cloth diary with two dachshunds on the front cover; they reminded her of her two dachsies at home, Kafka and Bela. She decided she'd buy it. She had been thinking about keeping a diary for some time; now would be a good time to start.

As soon as she got to her hotel room, she wrote the following:

> *Exhausted ! We are in Haifa…I had barely heard of it…what an ordeal. Rudi's already working. I wouldn't care if he were home very late. The weather is very hot. The smells here are very different to those of Vienna; it's very dusty, and there is a strong smell of the sea, strange spices, and sheep or camel manure. The call to prayer frightened us… I'm going to bed…good night.*

She hid the diary under the Koran in a drawer.

As RUDI CAME through the door, Lili was fast asleep on top of the bed in fetal position, only in a pair of fresh knickers. On a second bed beside hers, there were carefully laid out two summer dresses, one short-sleeved khaki shirt, two pairs of socks, one pair larger than the other, and a heap of less-than-glamorous underpants. A pair of flat, dark-brown, open sandals was on the floor partly under the bed.

Rudi quietly took a shower, as cold as the water would allow, and put on a fresh pair of knickers he deemed were meant for him. He carefully moved all the clothes onto a chair. A loud call for the *Isha* prayer blared through the open window and took Rudi by surprise. Lili did not stir. Despite being quite excited, he, too, soon succumbed to sleep. Lili woke first. It was already dark, as Lili whispered sweet nothings in Rudi's ear. As he was coming to full consciousness, Lili put on a newly purchased floral cotton dress, snug on top and full to just below the knee. An attempt at a cancan elicited a smile and brought Rudi to his feet.

"Very nice, *Schatzerl* (treasure)." She threw him a look.

"I see you had a most successful outing to Jaffa Street...thanks for getting the things I asked for," Rudi said. "Have you got a little money left over...enough for dinner perhaps?"

"Yes, we're okay...Mr. Schwartz was very generous. The notes are very dirty, and there are lots of different denominations of m*ils.* Anyway, Jaffa Street is much less expensive than Kaerntnerstrasse." Lili laughed as Rudi put on his trousers.

"You better get a new pair before you take me to a swish place tomorrow night. After all, it'll be Saturday," Lili said.

Rudi put on his new shirt to help his appearance a little. "Will you take me and my grubby trousers out to eat? I'm starving."

They left the key at the front desk, and the word *Dollfuss* in print in the *Palestine Post* caught Rudi's eye. He picked up the newspaper and read: *"Dr. Dollfuss, the chancellor of Austria, was murdered—" What is this?* He continued to read: *"on Wednesday, the twenty-fifth of July, by Austrian Nazis, who forced their way into the chancellery."*

"Ach, can't be true! How can that be? Do you see this, Lili?" Rudi and Lili continued to read together. Rudi's hand trembled while holding the paper.

For a time they held three ministers prisoner. Loyal troops surrounded the chancellery, and the Nazis were captured. Before the assassination, Nazis captured the Vienna wireless station and forced the announcer to broadcast that the Dollfuss ministry had been deposed, and that Dr. Rintelen, Austrian ambassador at Rome, was now in control. Dr. Rintelen was arrested on entering Austrian territory, and he later committed suicide. Italian troops move toward the border.

"This must be close to…war," said Rudi.

"Terrible, terrible, Rudi…that black cat was an omen," said Lili. "I hope Mother is okay…Mr. Schwartz, too. Those Nazis are like black cats, lurking in the dark and perpetrating evil…they are nothing but evil."

Rudi was momentarily dumb struck. Then, as white as a ghost, he again began to quietly speak. "I knew Dollfuss couldn't contain the Nazis… remember me saying so? As long as so many Austrians keep their heads in the sand and the government can't get its shit together, we'll remain in danger. I hope the people in Leopoldstadt will be all right, because the Nazis will probably gain a lot of confidence from this near success and go on a rampage." Rudi again fell silent and screwed up his face.

"You may want to write some letters tomorrow, Rudi…come, we should have some dinner."

They both felt sick to the stomach as they found themselves in a noisy café. They both ordered cabbage rolls with a vegetable filling of mainly rice, lentils, currants, and olives. The rolls were covered in a tomato sauce and were heavily spiced with cumin.

"Good, but not as good as the ones Ester makes," said Lili. Rudi nodded as he sipped on an *arak*, which helped with the digestion but not with his mood.

"I can imagine the Leopold sextet will be quite beside themselves with worry," said Rudi. "How can it be that a head of state can be murdered like that? There has likely been a very strong reaction from around the world…perhaps the evil designs of the Nazis will now be understood by more people," he said with some wishful thinking.

It was still hot and uncomfortable as Rudi and Lili walked uphill on Mount Carmel just to see what there was to see. There was a great deal to take in, especially the view looking back over the city. They also noticed a few signs at residences—Room for Rent or Apartment for Rent—and they looked at one another. They didn't say anything about this, their first day in Haifa, still perplexed as to why they were actually here. Rudi and Lili did admire the view over Haifa, and Rudi also admired some old, gnarled olive trees, while wondering what changes they had witnessed over time. They strolled downhill, hand in hand, and passed cafés with groups of people, large and small, just sitting around…some cross legged, eating with their hands from a large communal platter, others drinking tea, and some smoking a tobacco water pipe.

"Are they hubble-bubble pipes, Rudi? I think I've seen them in a movie."

"I think so," said Rudi, whose mind was in Vienna, still thinking about the Austrian chancellor's assassination. After several exchanges of Masaa el kheer, which Rudi and Lili believed meant "good evening," with some of the people at the café, they were soon back in the Appinger Hotel and quickly fell asleep, despite overwhelming feelings still of dismay and confusion.

As the wail for the Fajr prayer woke Lili and Rudi with a heck of a start, Rudi jumped out of bed and closed the window. It was pitch black.

"Only about four o'clock. Are they narrish?" he said, not expecting or receiving an answer. Closing the window had little effect, and they both pulled the sheet over their heads.

Lili had a wonderful dream that included dancing with a prince to the music of Strauss in the Vienna Stadtpark. Rudi was too disappointed with Austria and with himself to have dreamt about anything positive. The sunrise call to prayer, at least as loud as the earlier one, and well before six, was also not welcomed. Lili's dream continued with the prince dying in her arms and the music fading in a soulful dirge. When she woke, feeling unsettled, she wondered whether or not the dream was some omen. Rudi just tossed and turned between prayer times.

It was close to midmorning when a pair of warblers, singing to each other on the window ledge, woke them and brought a smile to both Rudi and Lili's faces. Rudi shook out his trousers, which he had washed just before going to bed, and he admired their improved lock. They left their room wanting breakfast and greeted Gudrun, the front-desk clerk, as they dropped off their key.

"Guten Morgen, Frau Auer, Herr Auer. Sleep well?"

"Yes, thank you," said Lili.

"Servus," said Rudi automatically, as he again caught a glimpse of the same newspaper that carried such disturbing news.

"We have a very good European breakfast here, and it's very reasonable," Gudrun said.

Rudi and Lili enjoyed a hearty breakfast, which included a soft-boiled egg, some sliced meats and cheeses, and a variety of bread, including semmel. Lili even enjoyed a piece of Guggelhupf. The aroma of Turkish coffee was sufficient for Lili to order an extra pot of hot water, and she was pleased that there was plenty of sugar on the table. While they were enjoying their breakfast, Rudi and Lili noticed that the interior of the Appinger Restaurant was indeed in a European pension style. There was also a disproportionate number of Germans dining, and Rudi and Lili exchanged smiles as they discerned the Schwaebisch that was being spoken. Lili suggested Rudi needed to write several letters, but both were distracted from that task when they went to the front desk to retrieve their room key.

"Hat's g'schmekt?" asked Gudrun. "You notice there are lots of Germans here. It reminds them of home...even if they have never been home." Gudrun chuckled to herself. "Many of them were born here, of course, in their own community."

"Their own community?" asked Rudi.

"Yes, they are Templers. You are at the edge of the Temple Gemeinde, the Templegesellschaft (Temple Society). You'll see the German-style houses with their red roofs and green shutters. Everything is nicely looked after...mainly an agricultural community with the best fruit and vegetables. I don't think their wine is very good, though...I hear lots of people say that. They first came here from Germany in 1868, I was told, for religious reasons...I don't understand exactly. They have their own school and community center...even their own bakery."

"Can anyone buy their bread?" asked Lili.

"Ja, they like to do business...like to do business, but it is not so good like before."

"Why is that?" asked Rudi.

"From last year, just after Hitler came to power in Germany, there were boycotts by some Templers of Jewish shops. Many Jews retaliated and no longer bought fruit and vegetables and milk from the Templers. The Jews are now generally very suspicious of the Templers and other Germans…even like me. They don't get on all that well with the Arabs, either. They fight over land sometimes."

"You are not a Templer?" asked Lili.

"No, my family is not religious…not at all. My father wants to believe in something, but he can't warm up to any of the three main religions here. They are always fighting, he says…he is reading about Buddhism," she said with a smile. "He also said to me…some Templers joined the NSDAP…that's the Nazis, *ja*? Some even ride around in cars with a little flag—the *Hakenkreutzflagge* (swastika flag)."

Lili and Rudi couldn't believe what they were hearing. They had hoped that Palestine would be free of Nazis, free of anti-Semitism. Gudrun noticed the look of near horror on Rudi's face.

"It is not really that bad, Mr. Auer…no, not really bad at all. We all get on very well, really. Look at the restaurant. There are Jews and Arabs—some Christian, some Muslim; there are British and Germans and Italians. Lots of Germans here. Most Templers and my father hate Hitler. Don't worry, Mr. Auer, life is good here. There is good work here…the food is good, and Haifa is very beautiful…and the weather…"

Rudi and Lili thought they had just been hit over the head with a brick. They forgot to ask for some writing paper and were certainly in no mood to write any letters at the moment. Rudi lay on the bed and reflected on the last week and beyond, and his thoughts were far from coherent.

What a donkey I've been. I was convinced I was taking Lili away from that anti-Semitism. I know she wasn't experiencing it yet herself in Vienna; she was in Austria, though, as we couldn't ski the Grossglockner together. But her life was good there with Mr. Schwartz, who provided her with work she liked. I wonder whether she'll get good work here? Of course she will; she is very experienced…look how friendly the people are here…I wonder what they smoke in those pipes? We are lucky…I already have work…I like physical work…I'm sure Lili will find work here soon, too…and with Dollfuss assassinated, Austria will only get worse, much worse. Yes, it is good to be out of Austria. We will have an interesting life here. I can feel it. I must help Lili feel it, too.

Lili's dream continued from where it had left off. An even more handsome prince swept her off her feet and took her for a driving vacation in a gleaming white convertible with a red-leather interior on the Amalfi Coast in Italy. Evenings were spent mostly in a bubble bath with a glass of champagne in her hand. She woke up with a big smile on her face, which was instantly erased by a searing hot breeze that invaded the room through the open window and the recollection of their conversation with Gudrun. Rudi took both of Lili's hands.

"It will be fine, Lili...I promise. I'm glad we are out of Vienna. Dollfuss's murder will only bring trouble. Let's get to the top of Mount Carmel and see how things look from there in the daylight."

IT WAS EARLY afternoon on Saturday, July 28. It was very hot, close to forty degrees Celsius, Rudi estimated, as they began in a fairly pensive mood, walking with measured steps ever uphill and seeking the shade of trees as much as they could. They reread a sign they had seen last night, advertising a room for rent, and were looking the building up and down, when a woman appeared with a garden hose.

"*Guten Tag.* I am Gudrun, remember? I do not work this afternoon."

"Oh, yes...hello, how are you?" said Lili, surprised, and Rudi smiled. "Do you live here?" he asked.

"Yes, with my father, my mother, and my two girls—Ilse, who is seven years, and Annemarie, who is five...she is a real devil. Mr. Auer, I am sorry I frightened you earlier today, telling you about the Nazis. I could see it in your face. There are very few of them, and most of the Templers are very nice and don't like the Nazis, either. People from all over get on very well in this town, really, Mr. Auer. Are you looking for a place to rent?"

"Yes, we need a place with a kitchen, so I can cook," said Lili.

"We only have a single room here, but I know a husband and wife on this very street who have a small apartment for rent. It has a kitchen and a very good view over Haifa. Would you like to have a look at it?

I'm sure Mr. and Mrs. Weber are home, and we could just knock on their door."

A couple of minutes later, they were in front of the Weber home.

"*Guten Tag*, Frau Weber. This is Lili Auer and her husband, Rudi."

"*Gruess Gott.*"

"*Gruess Gott.* Mr. and Mrs. Auer are presently guests at the hotel and are looking for a small apartment with a kitchen."

"You are from Austria; I can hear it. Please come in...you are welcome to look at it...follow me. Some painting has not been completed yet, but it will be ready in a few days...one more flight...here it is. You see it has a good kitchen with a good wood-burning stove...it's very economical...and a table for two. Four is possible, but you would all need to breathe in," Mrs. Weber said with a smile. "And here is the living room with a good view, we think. Yes? You can see all the way to the sea, and you get a very good breeze in summer. That picture of the crucifix will not stay...the previous tenant left it. We are not at all religious. Come. Here is the bedroom. It is a little small, but the bed is hard...good for your back. So there you have it. It is a wonderful spot...we have been here for more than twenty years and have not lost our accent." She laughed. "Felix will finish painting it in a matter of a few days. You can let Gudrun know if you are interested, and she will pass on the information. We will not let it to anyone else before we hear from Gudrun."

Rudi and Lili followed Gudrun down two flights without saying anything, thanked her for taking them to meet Mrs. Weber, and continued with their excursion to the top of Mount Carmel.

"What did you think, Rudi?"

"I liked it a lot."

"I did, too," said Lili with a degree of resignation in her voice. Despite the fact that the apartment, though small, was very nice, Lili couldn't come to terms with the fact that she was no longer in Vienna. She was perspiring heavily, walking up Mount Carmel with Rudi beside her. Given what transpired for Lili the last eight days, she was, at this time, not at all enamored by Rudi. She felt she was, after all, prized away from her environment, her work, and her life in Vienna, which she had been enjoying very much.

Lili thought about her recent dream and wondered about its significance. They looked at each other and decided to abort their quest for the top. It was just too hot. Back at the hotel, Lili pushed the urgency about writing letters with the view that she had to be prompt in thanking Mr. Schwartz for the money he had given them. To write to him was comparatively easy, because he knew most of what had transpired during their last couple of days in Vienna: he knew of Rudi's incarceration overnight; he knew of Lili's anguish being at home on her own the night of the nineteenth of July, and he knew of Rudi's escape from custody the following day. Nobody else knew that much. Mr. Schwartz had simply informed their parents that Rudi and Lili had left Vienna. And nobody at all knew where they were now and how they got there.

Lili penned a quick note to Mr. Schwartz, which included several sincere thank-yous, telling him that she and Rudi were healthy, hot, and in Haifa. The word *happy* was missing. She gave the return address as the Appinger Hotel, Haifa, Palestine. Lili then wrote to her mother, with tears in her eyes, explaining that it was necessary for her and Rudi to leave Vienna quickly and that they had traveled by boat to Haifa, where it was hot and they were healthy. She should follow events closely following the assassination of Dollfuss. Lili's third letter was to her brother, Walter, whom she also told they were healthy, hot, and in Haifa. Lili would write to Tante Marianne and to Hanna tomorrow. In the meantime, Rudi wrote to his parents:

Haifa, Saturday, July 28, 1934
Liebe Eltern,

I am sorry we did not contact you earlier. Mr. Schwartz will have told you that we had to leave Vienna in a hurry and under less than ideal circumstances. The assassination of Dr. Dollfuss since has reinforced the correctness of our decision to leave Vienna. You should know that we are healthy, hot, and happy in Haifa.

Please write c/o the Appinger Hotel, Haifa, Palestine
Viele liebe Gruesse,
Rudilili

Rudi also wrote to Joseph, providing the same meager information about the circumstances of their departure, knowing that Mr. Schwartz would fill in some of the gaps. He hoped that Joseph was able to safely see his parents leave Munich for France. He shared his deep concern for Austria, given the Nazis' murder of Dollfuss, and he hoped that Ester and their friends in Leopoldstadt were safe and that the *Juedisches Selbstwehr* was able to curb any increase in Nazi activities.

Rudi apologized for leaving so many of his and Lili's possessions in the apartment, and he requested Joseph to wait for his next letter before getting rid of everything, in case he wanted him to forward on some items—certainly his violin and some of Lili's clothes. Rudi wished Joseph well with his university work and with his life in general. He expressed the hope that their paths would cross in the future. He finally wished him and Ester *Mazel Tov*.

Lili burst into tears as she read the letter to Joseph. "How could you have done this, Rudi? I so miss Joseph…and Ester. I miss Mr. Schwartz…I miss my work…I miss Vienna. You didn't think of me at all…selfish, just damned selfish," she said with some anger and began to hit him several times on the arm with a clenched fist. "I'm homesick. I don't want to be here with all this heat, sand, and…I want to be back in Vienna."

Rudi's face turned all colors. He became very sheepish.

"*Bloeder Hammel*," she blurted out before quieting down.

"I'm going for a walk," said Rudi, as he got up and walked out the door.

"*Gut*," said Lili. While Lili was slowly composing herself, she reflected on how much she had loved Rudi since they had first met in Annenheim, but how, more recently, she had developed doubts. She'd been so often warned about his poor decision making, it had begun to have an effect. She opened her diary and wrote:

> *Why on earth do we find ourselves here? I feel I was torn away from Vienna…ripped from her breast. Yes, I do blame Rudi. What did he do that necessitated our running away like scolded cats? Cats…oooh, that black cat in the cargo hold…sends shivers down my spine.*

And here we are...Haifa. Haifa is a hellhole...hot...oh, so hot, sandy, dusty, camels and camel dung, sheep and sheep shit, flies every-where...and the call to prayers...even in the middle of the night...can't sleep even when I'm dead tired.

Some people, though, seem nice enough. No idea why they'd be here.

Rudi's doing his best to be nice now. He knows he's screwed things up badly. I'm still so angry with him...and he keeps writing we are happy. I'm not happy...oops, he's back!

Lili locked her dairy and hid it in her knickers drawer and hid the key in a singleton sock.

Rudi had been doing some reflecting of his own. Lili's recent out-burst had hit its mark. She had never referred to him as *bloeder Hammel* or anything similarly offensive before. She was right, he thought; he deserved it. He reflected upon how lucky he was...to have met Lili, fallen in love with her, and married her; that she was content to live with him in small, humble student digs and teach him a great deal about life in Vienna; and that his parents and Tante Marianne loved her and she them.

He would have to do the best he could. They could not return to Vienna; no, they could not do that—the Nazis, Dollfuss's murder, and all that. But he needed to try to do whatever he could for Lili here. He needed to have a good job...to be a good provider; they needed to have a nice apartment, and they needed to make some friends and help Lili find things to do to bring her satisfaction—be that work or something else. Rudi was determined. He certainly didn't want to lose her.

Lili, in the meantime, was thinking about the dream she had been having and was trying to interpret it when Rudi came back into their room, still a little sheepish and sweating. He sat beside Lili on the bed and said nothing. After a while, she rested her head gently on Rudi's shoulder, but neither spoke.

ONLY THE SHRILL call to the *Isha* prayer caused them to move. They wandered down to a restaurant they had seen before and entered the patio area. They sat at an outside table under a leafy trellis.

"Salam Alekum. You are German?" asked a waiter.

"Alekum Salam. No, we are British," said Rudi. Lili threw Rudi an inquisitive glance.

"From England?"

"Yes, from London."

"Hamdulillah! My brother and I have been to London. We come from Lebanon and now have this restaurant...for three years already; excuse me a moment."

"I hate to be mistaken for German...always have," Rudi said.

The waiter returned with two tall glasses of cold lemonade. "I am Hamoud, and my brother is Ibrahim."

Lili sipped and Rudi downed half the glass of lemonade, as music wafted from inside.

"Music is from Syria," said Hamoud, as he brought Lili and Rudi a menu. "No hurry, it is not yet nine, and most people don't come till after ten."

Rudi and Lili exchanged faint smiles. "It's certainly not Strauss," said Lili as they considered their options.

"Tonight we have three shawarma—lamb, chicken, and beef," said Hamoud, "or mixed...very good. You need a big tabbouleh tonight...excellent in hot weather."

Lili wanted to try the beef shawarma, and Rudi ordered lamb.

"Tabbouleh for both, yes...some Carmel wine...red? Lamb is very good; lots of sheep here; more sheep in Australia. Australian lamb tastes good, too, but all sheep are very dumb."

Lili had to bite her lip not to laugh as Hamoud disappeared. There was barely a breeze, and it was still quite hot, even under the grapevines covering the trellis. Lili counted only fifteen tables outside, and they were sufficiently well spaced on the wooden slatted floor to allow for a baby's pram to be navigated between. There was, indeed, one pram in the furthest corner, with a family of five enjoying dinner from a large platter. Two birds, with unknown intentions, sat on a vine directly above the platter.

The wine arrived, and two plates and cutlery were set before them. Without their eyes meeting, Rudi and Lili clinked glasses, took a sip, and made a bit of a face. The wine would taste better with the food, they thought. It did. It wasn't a Bordeaux, but it complemented the shawarma quite well, which they shared and enjoyed.

"Very tasty meat," said Lili, and Rudi nodded. They had never eaten tabbouleh before, and they quite enjoyed identifying the ingredients. The components of tomato, cucumber, onion, parsley, and garlic were easy to discern…so was the mint. They couldn't identify the grain specifically, but they thought it was like wheat, and they liked its nutty taste. Their second glass of wine tasted better than the first, and they sat back in their chairs as people began to drift in.

"*Masaa el kheer,*" said one of the waiters observing Rudi and Lili getting ready to leave.

"*Ma'a salama,*" said Rudi as he and Lili got up from their table, pushed in their chairs, and headed downhill toward the sea, hoping for a breeze.

Lili got a bit of the giggles as she thought about the sheep comment.

"Yes, I know, I'm a bit of asheep" Rudi said.

Lili took off her sandals when they got to the beach. The waters of the Mediterranean were lapping onto the sand as some water birds were rummaging for their supper, and several groups of people were enjoying a picnic of their own.

There was just the slightest breeze, but it was still quite hot, as Lili, holding up her dress with both hands, waded out knee deep. She looked out into the deepest blue and emptied her head of the travails of the previous eight days. She imagined bobbing down into a sea of bubbles with champagne in her left hand. The image brought a smile to her face as she noticed Rudi standing beside her, trousers rolled up a couple of turns but wet to the knees.

Rudi was about to take her hand, when Lili turned the other way, waded back toward the beach, and looked toward the harbor, where dreadful memories returned. *The bumpy, four-day truck ride was bad enough, but stowing away in a dark, smelly ship's hold without water or a toilet and not knowing where you were headed...well...and then jumping overboard— swimming and wading ashore, Rudi holding our little money aloft. We didn't know where we were till we read a sign. Terrible, terrible...what a nightmare.*

Lili brushed some sand from her feet, slipped on her sandals. and headed slowly toward the hotel. Rudi had burst into tears and was sitting beside his shoes, sobbing. She looked back occasionally but kept walking. Rudi wiped his face and caught up just before they entered the hotel and collected their room key.

RUDI'S WORKWEEK WAS, from now on, to commence on a Sunday, and he and Lili found themselves early in the dining room of the Appinger Hotel, not having been able to get back to sleep following the call to sunrise prayer. Lili waved to Rudi as he drove off.

Rudi readily remembered his routine and completed his four trips before the wailing call to the Maghrib prayer, despite the occurrence of a flat tire. He was exhausted due to the heat, the heavy girders, and his own feelings of guilt, which provided the only company he had all day.

Lili commenced her morning writing letters without Rudi locking over her shoulder. She decided to write to Tante Marianne first, as the very thought of her would be certain to bring a smile to her face. Instead, Lili burst into tears, so much so that a woman in the next room knocked on the door.

"Ist alles in Ordnung? (Is everything okay?)"

"Ja, Danke."

Lili worked hard to dismiss the thought that she might never see Tante Marianne again. She wrote that she and Rudi missed her very much, but that they could keep in touch with the help of the postal system. She explained that she and Rudi had seen a very nice apartment, and they would decide whether or not to take it by the end of the day. Haifa was a nice town. Rudi had already found work, but she was worried that he might hurt himself, as he had to schlepp very heavy steel girders. Lili explained that she would need less than half a normal wardrobe here, as the weather was much warmer than what she was used to. She promised to write again soon, and she sent a thousand Bussi.

Before she would write to Hanna, Lili decided to go back to Jaffa Street and buy Rudi a pair of khaki shorts for work and a pair of sandals and perhaps another shirt. She came home with shorts and sandals and another dress, as it cost very little, and she liked the way she looked in it. She bought some fruit from a street vendor on the way back and then set about writing to Hanna.

Hotel Appinger,
Haifa,
Juli 29, 1934
Liebe Hanna,

If you have not heard, you will surely get a fright when you see the address at the top of this letter. Yes, Rudi and I are in Haifa, Palestine. We arrived here by ship a few days ago. The circumstances under which we left Vienna were unfortunate and complicated and now infuriating. They were due to some poor decisions Rudi made. Perhaps I should have listened better to you and Mother.

Anyway, I had this dream, and it has been haunting me. I know its meaning is significant, but I am unable to analyze it clearly. I would like you to think about it and interpret what the meaning might be and tell me in a reply letter.

The dream begins with me dancing with a prince to the music of Strauss in the Vienna Stadtpark. Soon the prince is dying in my arms, the music fading in a soulful dirge. When the dream continues after an interruption, an even more handsome prince sweeps me off my feet and takes me for a driving vacation in a gleaming white convertible with a red-leather interior on the Amalfi Coast in Italy. Evenings are spent mostly in a bubble bath with a glass of champagne in my hand. I can't seem to get the dream out of my head for more than half an hour at a time. I look forward to your interpretation.

Best wishes also to your husband and children. Please remain vigilant now that Dollfuss has been murdered, and let me know all about what happens in Vienna.
Viele liebe Gruesse,
Lili

When Lili had completed her shopping and had written and posted her letters, it was only just after midday, as the call for Zuhr prayer had again given her a fright. All calls to prayer had done so. *Could I ever get used to such loud wailing?* she asked herself. *If it were at least musical, it might be more bearable.*

She walked outside for a break from her room, but the searing heat soon sent her back inside. *Phew, it's hot out there—not that much better in here... but better. I'm lonely...I miss Rudi, damn it...he made some terrible and hasty decisions. Bloeder Hammel! And apparently he didn't care much about me, either...me, his wife. Rudi, listen to me, I'm you're your wife. Damn it! Why don't you care? Oh, you do care now? Damned late for you to care now. What a mess...Rudi, I miss you. Why do I miss you? I don't want to miss you. I want to be in Vienna, my Vienna. Vienna and I got on so well together.* Lili dozed off with the hope that Rudi didn't find the work too exhausting. She wished he were home.

Rudi arrived home hot and hungry. Lili offered him a kiss and an orange. He happily accepted both. He showered and tried on his new shorts and sandals—both fitted perfectly. She had always admired his statuesque, athletic, and perfectly-proportioned body.

Lili did a few pirouettes in her new dress, which elicited smiles of approval. They each shared what their day had brought and decided to eat in the Appinger dining room, as it offered a mainly German menu prepared by two German cooks who had enjoyed a good reputation for German dining for decades, even before the family-owned pension was turned into the present hotel in the late 1920s, they were told.

The restaurant was about half capacity when Rudi and Lili were offered a typical German menu and were pleased they had several items they found enticing. Rudi ordered the fish of the day with a side salad for Lili and Bratwuerstel and potato salad for himself. Lili had a glass of house white wine, while Rudi started with a beer to quench his considerable thirst.

They didn't converse much, due to Rudi's tiredness and embarrassment and Lili's anger despite still caring for Rudi. Empty glasses were replaced with full ones before the food arrived, and when it did, Rudi and Lili were quite impressed. Lili's fish, served whole, was simply panfried and succulent and accompanied by an ample salad, dressed with a vinaigrette. Lili wasn't all that happy, however, about the fish's left eye observing her every move. Rudi was pleased his two sausages were oversized, and Lili offered him some of her salad, having just spied some good-looking desserts passing by. Among the few words spoken at the dinner table was a suggestion by Lili that Rudi should order his own slice of Schwartzwaelderkuchen.

BACK IN VIENNA

ON WEDNESDAY, JULY 25, everyone became too distracted to think about Lili and Rudi. There was major upheaval in Vienna and in much of the rest of Austria. In Vienna, particularly, there was a great deal of confusion and consternation, as people heard gunshots within the Austrian chancellery and within the radio building. There were sounds of hysteria on the radio.

On that day, more than 150 members of the Schutzstaffel (SS), disguised as soldiers and policemen, forced their way into the Austrian chancellery and shot Chancellor Dollfuss to death. The rest of the government was able to escape.

At about the same time, the radio building was overrun, and an announcement was made that Dollfuss had been replaced by Anton Rintelen. This led to armed skirmishes in many parts of Austria, including Carinthia, Styria, and Upper Austria.

The coup attempt was crushed by the police and the military, and when the smoke subsided, several hundred were dead—Nazis, government supporters, civilians, and many more hundreds were injured. At this very time, Dollfuss's wife and two of his children Hannerl and Eva, were in Italy as guests of the Mussolini family. The next day—Thursday, July 26—military tribunals were convened in Vienna, thirteen Nazis were executed, and approximately four thousand were detained.

Many Nazi supporters fled to Germany or to Yugoslavia. Kurt von Schuschnigg was sworn in as the new chancellor of Austria. Vienna had known Schuschnigg as minister of justice and minister of education.

Viennese society was shaken to the core. A couple of days later, approximately five hundred thousand Austrians attended Dollfuss's burial.

Viennese *Gemuehtlichkeit* had not, for a very long time, been so badly disrupted. Rudi Auer Sr. followed the events with great interest, including the events in his own state of Carinthia where Sankt Paul in the Lavanttal was a center of Nazi activity. His mind turned to Rudi and Lili, and he thought that perhaps it was a good decision for them to have left Austria...if they had, indeed, left Austria, because no one he knew, knew where they were, and no one had heard from them now for a week.

It was Friday, July 27, and Rudi Senior and Maria visited the Gasthaus in Villach as normal, and much of the talk was about the Nazis' attempted coup in Vienna and the skirmishes in their own backyard. Rudi Senior and Maria were hopeful for some news soon.

IN VIENNA, THE aftermath of Dollfuss's murder remained intense, as the Viennese tried to make sense of the events that had engulfed their city. Added anxiety remained, as there were daily phone calls between Mr. Schwartz and Walter, Walter and Hanna, Joseph and Mr. Schwartz, and Mr. Schwartz and Rudi Auer Sr. No one had any news—no news at all. Hedwig Gruen, despite the consumption of considerable amounts of cognac, became increasingly hysterical, as she envisaged her daughter in every form of danger imaginable, Maria Auer remained flummoxed that she had not heard from her beloved son, and Tante Marianne suspended all knitting for the future.

On August 3, nearly two weeks to the hour that Lili had left the office in a hurry, a letter from her arrived at the office. Mr. Schwartz read the contents, took a few deep breaths, and made a phone call.

"Hedwig, they are safe."

"Wonderful, wonderful...Walter...they're safe. You talk."

"Walter here, yes, Mr. Schwartz."

"Good afternoon, Walter. Yes, they are safe; they are in Haifa."

"Good God, in Haifa. In Palestine. *Mutter*...they are in Haifa."

"My God, Haifa…how could they be in Haifa?" asked Lili's mother as she began to sob.

"What are they doing in Haifa?" asked Walter.

"I have no idea. The note from Lili simply said it was necessary for her and Rudi to leave Vienna quickly, and they had traveled by boat to Haifa, where it was hot, and they were healthy. They were staying at the Appinger Hotel."

"Oh, all that sand…can you phone them?" asked Lili's mother between sobs.

"I will try," said Mr. Schwartz. Walter phoned Hanna, and Mr. Schwartz phoned the Auer household in Villach.

"Schwartz here. Is that Mr. Auer?"

"*Ja, Gruess Gott*, Mr. Schwartz. You have some news?"

"They are in Haifa."

"In Palestine? Maria, they are in Palestine." Maria burst into tears. Her son and Lili were safe. That was all that mattered to her at this moment.

"Why Haifa? How did they get there? When? Where do they live?"

"All Lili said was that they had to leave Vienna quickly and that they had traveled by boat to Haifa, where it was hot, and they were healthy. They were staying at the Appinger Hotel."

"Did they travel from Trieste, Mr. Schwartz?"

"Lili didn't say. I'm sure you will hear from Rudi very soon. At least we have heard, and they are safe. Lili also said we should follow events closely following the assassination of Dollfuss."

"Perhaps she is right, and perhaps it is not such a bad thing that they are in Palestine, where there are so many Jews and no Nazis," suggested Rudi Senior. He ended the call with Mr. Schwartz and called Tante Marianne, who had barely moved from the side of the phone for more than a week.

"Marianne, hallelujah; they are safe."

"Hallelujah. Where are they?"

"Palestine."

"Where?"

"In Haifa...in Palestine."

"*Lieber Gott,* all that sand...Lili will miss Vienna so badly...at least they are safe." Tante Marianne phoned half of Annenheim and began knitting for the future again.

Mr. Schwartz phoned Ester's apartment, wanting to speak to Joseph. Joseph was not there yet.

"You can tell me, Mr. Schwartz, please...have you heard from Lili?" Ester said.

"Yes, Lili and Rudi are safe. They are well."

"*Mazel Tov.* Wonderful! Where are they?"

"They are in Haifa."

"In Palestine? *Oy vey*...I'll get Joseph to call you. Thank you, thank you."

Ester phoned Moshe and Rachel and Benjamin and Rivka. Joseph arrived in a terrible mood. He had gone to the apartment with the hope of there being a letter from his parents and a letter from Rudi. There was neither, only a letter from the university administration telling him what he already knew—he was far behind with his university work, and he was to make an appointment with a counselor.

"Guess what?" said Ester excitedly before he had even closed the door. "They're in the Holy Land."

"Who? What?"

"Rudi...Rudi and Lili are in Palestine."

"How do you know?"

"Mr. Schwartz phoned. They are in Haifa. I told him you'd call back."

Joseph called Mr. Schwartz, with whom he had a lengthy conversation, and Joseph was soon in a very good mood and was sharing a beer with Ester.

———

WHAT A COUPLE of weeks it had been—an arrest, an imprisonment, an escape, police searches and warnings, missing fugitive friends, umpteen phone calls and distraught parents, and all that before the murder of the chancellor of Austria and the shattering of Vienna's *Gemuehtlichkeit.*

VIEW FROM MOUNT CARMEL

RUDI HAD TRANSFERRED all the girders from the B3 wharf to the construction site in Akko by the end of the workday of the first Thursday after he started. He was wet and weary and mopping his brow, when Sahib arrived on the back of a motorbike.

"*Salam Alekum*, Rudi. Good timing. I want you to meet Mr. Finkelstein…he is the owner of the warehouse to be built, and I told him you are good worker."

"Thank you, Sahib."

"You see, Mr. Finkelstein, he has good manners, too."

"Can you start on Sunday? We need to finish construction before end of summer…Sahib will pick you up on Sunday at seven, and we finish at four…bring your lunch."

—∞—

LILI AND RUDI had let Frau Weber know that they would rent the apartment on Mount Carmel, and on Friday morning at nine sharp, as had been requested, the Webers presented them with two sets of two keys—one for the front door and one for their apartment.

"You may want to open the windows to let out the paint smell or keep them shut to keep out the heat. Felix and I hope you enjoy the apartment. If you need anything, just—"

"Leave them be; they will be fine," said Felix Weber, giving Rudi and Lili the once over. He observed that they made a nice couple- Rudi quite tall with fine facial features with thinning blonde hair and Lili considerably shorter, pretty, and with very dark, wavy hair and black eyes.

"Thank you very much." Lili screwed up her nose and opened the window. She breathed in the already warm but fresh air from outside, and they both looked toward the sea. Rudi put his arm around Lili, and they took in the expansive view over Haifa to the Mediterranean. They could smell the quite strong scent of a flower they couldn't identify, but it was certainly more pleasant than the smell of paint.

The apartment, on the second floor, was facing mostly to the north, perhaps slightly toward the west, shielding it from the most brutal heat of the sun. It was well appointed and furnished with a wood-burning stove and craftsman-built, sturdy furniture, including a round kitchen table with two chairs and another couple of chairs in the bedroom. There was a sofa and two comfortable armchairs in the living room, one decent-sized bed, a chest of drawers, and an armoire in the bedroom—certainly superior accommodation to that which they had shared in Vienna and more than adequate for their present purposes.

Lili had, at least for now, resigned herself to staying with Rudi—even here in Haifa with all that sand, no Vienna Opera, no Musikverein, and no Demel. There was neither Viennese sophistication nor snobbishness, as far as they could tell. Rudi had work, they now had a very nice apartment, they had met some friendly people, and they were beginning to enjoy food hitherto unknown to them. Rudi was determined to earn enough money over the next couple of months to repay Mr. Schwartz.

This was to be a weekend of shopping, mainly for food, as Lili was anxious to cook. They first purchased all the essentials from a Jewish deli and an Arab grocer—potatoes, flour, rice, butter, eggs, cheese, olive oil, coffee, milk, confiture, and sugar. They went to the German bakery and purchased bread and several *semmels*, not all of which made it back to the apartment. On a second trip they purchased some fruit—oranges, a melon, and vegetables, including aubergine and zucchini...*kusa*, in Arabic, they were told.

Lili had Rudi hold all the bags while she ducked into a shop she had visited before and came out with a tablecloth, four serviettes, and a smile. They ate *semmels* with cheese for lunch, and Rudi couldn't resist trying a local beer. *Not bad,* he thought, and Lili agreed, as they used their serviettes for the first time. Rudi and Lili were having an afternoon *kip* when they were startled by the call to the *Isha'a* prayer.

"So bloody loud," said Rudi sharply, as he closed the windows. Lili made some lemonade, and they sipped till those soulful sounds suddenly stopped. They decided to walk the neighborhood while several Muslim men meandered to the mosque close by, though most people in this location were Germans and Jews. Ahmadi Muslim Arabs and Jews got on very well together here on the slopes of Mount Carmel, they had been told.

The same flower smell that had greeted them upon opening their windows earlier accompanied them again now as they walked. Some birds flew overhead and squawked their own call, while several children sped bikes up and back with the apparent purpose of making themselves hotter and the neighborhood dustier. Lili got a fit of the sneezes, and Rudi passed her a folded brown-and-white-checkered handkerchief. Most of the two- and three-storied dwellings in this neighborhood were oriented toward the sea as much for the breeze as for the view. Rudi and Lili tried to imagine who lived in which house. Who would live in the house with a pristinely maintained English cottage garden? Who lived in the house with a camel tethered in a front yard, with about fifty sacks, possibly of grain, stacked on the front porch and with fishing nets drying in the sun?

They wandered back to their apartment, settled in the kitchen, and after reading the paper, began to prepare dinner. On this, their first evening in the apartment, they prepared stuffed peppers, aubergine, and zucchini. The dish reminded Lili of Ester's stuffed cabbage leaves, and she wondered whether Joseph had yet received Rudi's letter. She began to wipe tears from her face.

Rudi asked, "What's the matter?"

"It's just the onions." But it wasn't just the onions, and Rudi knew, as the sobbing didn't stop with the onions being diced. Lili's thoughts had little to do with food. *Will we ever have dinner with Joseph and Ester again? Will we ever again enjoy their company? Will we ever see them again? And Moshe and Rachel and Benjamin and Rivka? What will happen to them... to all of us?* Lili put down the kitchen knife, wiped her face in her apron, went into the living room, and looked out the window. She composed herself in time to add the diced tomatoes, dried currants, pepper, salt, allspice, and dillweed to the rice and onions that Rudi was mixing.

Rudi opened another beer and handed Lili a glass. She drank it quickly, wishing it were cognac. When the dish was complete, the peppers were done just right, but the zucchini were a little mushy and the aubergine a little hard. *Nothing quite right*, she thought. She hoped she'd get over her predicament.

⁂

SAHIB CAME TO pick up Rudi with his lunch early Sunday morning and returned him in time to hear the call to *Maghrib* prayer. That became the daily routine. Lili would go each day to the Appinger Hotel to see if there was any mail, and on Wednesday, Gudrun asked Lili whether she could speak with her about a matter.

"Let's go and have a coffee and a little something," said Gudrun as she led Lili into the Appinger Restaurant.

"What a nice smell," said Lili as they entered and discerned the aromas of cinnamon and apple.

"They've just finished making the main dessert for the evening… they've just taken the *Apfelstrudel* out of the oven, in fact. Should we see if we can snaffle some?"

Lili just smiled as Gudrun disappeared into the kitchen. She returned empty handed but with a big smile on her face. She had barely sat down, when a chef, all in white, including his hands and some of his face, and with beads of perspiration, brought two coffees, two strudels, and a mountain of whipped cream. Lili smiled from ear to ear.

"We must do this regularly, Lili, it could do us good. Anyway, I wanted to ask you a favor: Would you be willing to help my daughters with their English…especially with their reading? We have plenty of books at home…the girls are just a little lazy, especially Ilse, and they would learn better from you than from a family member. I will pay you, of course. Well, what do you say?"

"I'm sure my accent isn't so good, but if they can handle Viennese English."

"Excellent. Come to my home…you know where it is, of course…on Tuesday and Thursday afternoons…say, at three. Wait one moment," said Gudrun as she disappeared into the kitchen and reappeared with a paper bag with two pieces of still-warm Apfelstrudel. "Take it home for supper; it will keep for days, and it's good cold, too. See you tomorrow, Lili…at three, if not sooner." Lili was very pleased.

Rudi was also pleased with the construction work he was now doing, working with two young Arab men who spoke very little English, putting together the frame of a large warehouse. Mr. Finkelstein checked in on the work's progress each day, arriving in a cloud of dust and soon thereafter disappearing in one.

Rudi began to enjoy Sahib for his clever and dry sense of humor. It made the journeys to and from work always pleasant. Rudi hadn't yet figured out the working relationship with Mr. Finkelstein, but Sahib was clearly involved with a number of his projects.

THE FOLLOWING WEEK started much as the previous one, when an incident driving to work one morning showed a different side to Sahib. They had just left Haifa, were picking up a little speed, and were about to pass a newish-looking car, when Sahib said, "Watch this," as he accelerated and purposely drove into the car in front, producing a considerable thud. To Rudi's astonishment, Sahib did it again and again, providing not inconsiderable jolts. Rudi became a little edgy and somewhat perplexed.

"What are you doing that for?" he asked, as Sahib smashed into the car again.

"Shut up and hang on tight around the next corner," Sahib said in a commanding tone. He accelerated and pulled up beside the car he'd been attacking. "Hang on," he yelled as he pulled hard on the steering wheel, smashed into the car near the front wheel, and sent it into a ditch. Rudi looked back and noticed the car roll over in a cloud of dust.

"*Ahamdulillah…hamdulillah*…the bastards," Sahib said, as a broad grin of satisfaction spread across his face and he looked excitedly at

Rudi. "Sorry, Rudi, I didn't mean to frighten you. These Germans…
they are Templers, and most of them are very nice, and we got on very
well with them. But there are some who want to take our business away,
especially since Hitler came to power in Germany. Since last year, they
sometimes boycotted businesses owned by Jews, and then the Jews and
some of us Muslims also refused to buy their vegetables. They had to
throw hundreds of tons away."

Rudi was trying to take all this in when Sahib continued. "And
then, Rudi, there are a few…very few…they are Nazis…you see they
have a Nazi flag—yellow and black, I think—with the Nazi swastika…
sticking from their car…we try to run them out of town."

"Or off the road," Rudi said.

"Yes, it is a sport…very good sport."

"What if they tell the authorities?" asked Rudi. A smile broadened
across Sahib's face.

"Ah, the authorities…they understand…they don't even go to the
authorities any more."

"And the damage to your car, Sahib?"

"There will not be much damage…all fixed by the time I pick you
up this afternoon…we have put on very strong bumpers…for bumping," he said as he let out a little laugh.

They had arrived at the work-site. "Out, Rudi…*Salaam*, boys. *Ma'a salama*, Rudi." He turned the car around and still laughing, drove off, waving
to Rudi and the two young Arab workers, and leaving a dusty trail behind.

———

AT THE END of the day, Sahib drove Rudi up the hill as the call to the
Maghrib prayer penetrated the whole neighborhood. Rudi was still
somewhat taken aback by the morning's adventure and decided not
to share it with Lili anytime soon. Rudi and Lili kissed without any
embrace, as Rudi needed to get into the shower.

"Guess what, Rudi?"

"Pardon?"

"We have two letters today."

"Who from? What did they say?"

"You should just read them yourself…one from my mother and the other from Joseph." Lili brought Rudi a large glass of lemonade as he began to read.

> *Vienna*
> *August 4, 1934*
> *Liebe Lili,*
>
> *I am very pleased that you and Rudi are safe. It was a terrible shock to hear what had happened and not to hear from you directly for more than a week after you disappeared. In fact I was very sick from it all and had to be treated by our doctor and have Walter come and stay with me. Without him I would have gone out of my mind. Rudi should be thoroughly ashamed of himself to put you through this ordeal. I presume you took the train to Trieste and the boat from there.*
>
> *If you wish to return to Vienna, we can send you the money for a boat journey back. Your room is always here for you. Bela and Kafka would love to have you home. They still look for you in your room. You must make whatever decision is best for you. Haifa, with all that sand, would not be my choice of place to live.*
>
> *Schuschnigg should be okay as the new chancellor of Austria. As I said, if you want to come home…*
> *Best wishes,*
> *Mutti*

"I would not have expected anything different from your mother…and I can't blame her," said Rudi.

"No, I'm sure she was very distressed and nearly drove Walter mad. He probably fed her lots of cognac or armagnac. Here, read this from Joseph."

"Did his parents get to Lyon?"

"Yes, Rudi…read it for yourself."

Vienna
August 4, 1934
Dear Rudi and Lili,

It was quite a shock to hear the way the university administration treated you and literally ran you out of town. I read your article, and you said nothing that was untrue or hadn't been said before. We hope you enjoyed the boat trip to Haifa; it must be a pleasant sight, looking back at Trieste. Just think of what you want me to send from the apartment, and I will pack it up properly and ship it off.

I was fortunately able to help my parents secure their papers in Munich, and they are now safely in Lyon. My mother is much happier now, too.

I came home just before the police searched for you and Lili at Mr. Schwartz's home, his office, and in our apartment, and they asked a whole lot of silly questions like, did I know of any favorite uncle you might want to stay with.

The murder of Dollfuss came as a great surprise in Vienna and has disturbed the city greatly... for how long... will remain anybody's guess. We had a suspicion all along that the fires and explosions in public buildings and public works and several mysterious deaths of public officials over recent months were the handiwork of the Nazis. That has now been corroborated. Schuschnigg, the new chancellor, is pretty weak, I think, and will not be able to maintain the same relationship with Mussolini as Dollfuss had. Only time will tell.

That alta Kaka-Hindenburg died a couple of days ago (Aug. 2), and Hitler is now president and has full control of the government. Things can only get worse... even if things are a little quieter right now.

Benjamin and Rivka and Rachel and Moshe send their best wishes. Moshe can't stop talking about you giving the cops the flick.

Ester and I will miss you both very much and hope an opportunity will arise sooner rather than later when we can break bread together. Mazel Tov to you both,
Joseph

"We should write back to him straightaway, and we can let him know what to send to us. I will really miss him," said Rudi. *A bit late now,* thought Lili but didn't share her thought as she had expressed it many times in recent weeks, and besides, she didn't want to start the weekend off negatively.

———

DURING THE NEXT few weeks, Rudi and Lili settled into their apartment, both getting used to their new environment and developing relationships with some of the people of the neighborhood. Lili enjoyed her English tutoring, and her students enjoyed her Viennese English Rudi was happy to be the main breadwinner and happy to invite Sahib in for a drink, time permitting, before *Maghrib* prayer.

"I go to pray two or three times a day, but I make excuses pretty often," he said to Rudi. "I'm not a good Muslim; I like a beer, as you have noticed, and I like to run Nazis off the road," he said with delight. "I don't believe in everything that I'm supposed to believe in, Rudi. I don't believe in God, really...in only one God...perhaps there are three; how am I supposed to know? Do you believe in God, Rudi?"

"No, Sahib, I don't. If there were a God, he wouldn't allow all that fighting among human beings."

"I'm with you, Rudi; he wouldn't allow those Nazi bastards, either...hope we find another one to run off the road again soon. *Ma'a salama,* Rudi." He also said, "*Ma'a salama,* madam," to Lili, who had been looking out the window and had not been listening to the men's conversation.

It was also a period of considerable correspondence—letters coming from Rudi's parents, Walter, Mr. Schwartz, Tante Marianne, Hanna, and from Rudi's high school teacher Mr. Birnbaum, all of which were answered. Two parcels arrived from Joseph, and Lili was delighted to get all the clothes she had had in the apartment and was surprised to find a silver candlestick she had given Rudi. Rudi was very pleased the shipment included his violin, and he wasted no time to play some melodies before he declared his fingers were getting tired from lack of practice. Lili's mother delayed sending Lili some clothes she had requested, with the hope that Lili would one day soon arrive on the doorstep to the welcoming barks of Kafka and Bela.

All the recent letters either said that the Nazi activity in Austria and Germany had subsided, or there was no mention made of any anti-Semitism at all.

People should not be fooled by any lull in activity against Jews, thought Rudi, *the Nazis' Judenhasse having been made abundantly clear in Der Stuermer, Der Voelkischer Beobachter, and other Nazi publications. How quickly people forget,* he thought, as he read an article in the *Palestine Post* of August 22 with the headline "I Saw Dollfuss Die," written by Major Emil von Fey. *Dollfuss's murder occurred only months ago, and people have forgotten already?* wondered Rudi. Most Austrians, it seemed to Rudi, were taken in by Schuschnigg, as they had been by his predecessor Dollfuss. Though less overt, anti-Semitism continued to flourish, especially against a backdrop of fractured opposition coming from Jews. A letter arrived from Mr. Schwartz that lent credence to Rudi's view of continuing discrimination against Jews.

> *Wien*
> *November 27, 1934*
> *Liebe Lili und Lieber Rudi*
>
> *I was very pleased to receive your recent letter and am glad to hear that you have settled in well, enjoying your apartment, and that you both have work. Speaking of work, I was finally able to employ a replacement for you, Lili, and I am pleased to say she is doing well.*
>
> *Also about a matter of work, a friend of the family was recently laid off from his position as a physician at the Vienna Hospital because he was a member of the now illegal Social Democratic Party. He had won many awards for excellent service. Many doctors who were Jewish have been dismissed, while non-Jews, who had also joined the SDP, were able to retain their positions. There was no apparent reference to this in any of our local newspapers. I am now beginning to agree with Rudi's understanding of the pervasiveness of discrimination against Jews both in Germany and now here.*
>
> *Thank you for the money you sent. Please stay in touch.*
>
> *I wish you much success and happiness,*
> *Viele liebe Gruesse,*
> *Schwartz*

Rudi and Lili were sad, though not surprised, to hear of the continuing discrimination against Jews under the new Austrian chancellor. They noted that Mr. Schwartz was only now able to perceive the extent of the anti-Semitism when persons close to him had been affected. That there was no reaction in the Vienna press to such blatant discrimination was also a great disappointment but no real surprise to them.

"It's hard to believe that the press didn't disclose this scandal," said Rudi. "I'd love to have access to all the papers I read at Café Louvre; perhaps the story was covered in one of them."

"I'd love for you to have access to the papers, too, Rudi. You could also enjoy your overflowing schnitzel there occasionally," said Lili as she threw him a look. Lili was, however, coping quite well now, living in Haifa, but her thoughts still returned frequently to Vienna, and she became particularly homesick with the arrival of letters from family and friends. She missed Mr. Schwartz, as he had become rather more than a boss to her over recent years, especially with her father being no more. Lili also had no idea where they should go to celebrate Rudi's birthday on the eighth of December. It was, after all, his twenty-first. Rudi wanted to celebrate at home, so Lili cooked his favourite Wiener schnitzel and *Kaiserschmarrn* with *Apfelmus*. Rudi had, weeks ago, lamented that he didn't have any coloured pencils when he was sketching the view from the living room, so Lili bought him a box of colored pencils and a good-quality sketch book. Rudi had always liked to draw, and he was delighted with his present.

Within a couple of weeks of hearing from Mr. Schwartz, a lengthy letter also arrived from Joseph.

Saltzgasse, Wien
December 15, 1934
Dear Rudi and Lili,

Thanks for your Happy Hanukkah wishes. We enjoyed the holiday without any harassment of any sort. We hope you are happy and well.

I became rather dismayed during the last few months at our inability—the Jews' inability—to work together in a united way to resist the anti-Semitism that still lurks around every corner, though in a more covert way than it was following the period of Hitler's rise to power. It just doesn't seem possible at the moment for the Zionists to cooperate with the integrationists or the Orthodox Jews to work together with the more liberal. So I decided to join the Bund Juedischer Frontsoldaten (League of Jewish Front Soldiers), where there seems better cooperation. I am still a member of the Selbstwehr (Self-Defence Force), but the Bund is more active in trying to keep official-dom, including government, accountable in responding to anti-Semitic behavior. I will be taking an active interest in responding to breaches by institutes of higher learning. I'm sure to be thinking of you often, Rudi.

I have been trying to convince Moshe to join because of the intel-lectual contribution he could make, but he refuses to join any organi-zation that has a uniform and emphasizes military virtues such as discipline, obedience, and physical fitness. I'll keep trying.

Ester and I are doing well, but she worries for my parents in Lyon and hers in Poland.
We wish you a very Merry Christmas,
Ester and Joseph

SAHIB WAS SITTING in the living room having a beer with Rudi and Lili as he frequently did, waiting for the call to the *Maghrib* prayer, when he had a surprise for Lili and Rudi.

"You know Ramadan starts on the twenty-fifth of December, and not much work happens here in the Holy Land for four to five days from the twenty-third of the month. Do you have anything planned, Rudi?"

Rudi looked at Lili, and neither thought they'd be doing anything there, except that Lili would be wishing she were with Tante Marianne.

"You don't have a car, do you?"

Rudi shook his head.

"What if I lend you mine for a few days over the holidays, and you could get to know Palestine a bit better. That'd help me, too, actu-ally—as a part of Ramadan, I need to do some charity. Offering you my car for a few days would fulfill my *Zakat* charity obligations. That'd be a win-win situation, right?"

"What a very generous offer, Sahib. Won't you need your car?"

"No, I don't plan to drive, and anyway, I'd still have the truck if I needed to. The kids love it in the back of the truck as you know.' The wailing of the call to prayer abruptly interrupted the discussion.

"You can think about it overnight. I'll pick you up as normal in the morning, Rudi. *Ma'a salama. Ma'a salama,* madam."

———

EARLY ON SUNDAY morning, December 23, Rudi picked up Sahib's car as had been arranged. It was a yellow, two-door, four-seater. Sahib said the chassis was a Fiat, but the rest was anybody's guess. He wasn't even sure whether all wheels were the same make. Lili and Rudi threw in their bags, including lunch, and with a map on Lili's lap, they headed for Jerusalem.

This was the first time they were together on their own in a car with Rudi driving. They enjoyed the intimacy of the situation as they motored toward Jerusalem. It was quite warm for December, so they pulled off the road and stopped under an old gnarled olive tree for lunch. They didn't linger, due to the many flies and the increasing heat. It was not long before they found themselves at what turned out later to be the periphery of the Old City. They stopped by a sign that said European-style Hotel—Moderate Rates.

They were told, in perfect English, that they were lucky to get a room at all at this time. A couple had just canceled, and hence the last room had become available. It was clean and had its own bathroom, so they did not hesitate to book the room for two nights.

It soon hit home how lucky they actually were to get a room, as the streets were very crowded. This was, of course, the time of year when many made their pilgrimages to this holy city of three major Abrahamic religions of the world—Judaism, Christianity, and Islam. Rudi and Lili were both taken by the cosmopolitan nature of the crowd and the excitement in the air. They walked for most of the two days they were there, exploring the different sections of the city and navigating some very narrow lanes and some marketplaces where the majority of smells were foreign to them.

They entered and exited most of the major gates leading into the Old City, and they joined the throng of people visiting the most important holy sites. They visited the Church of the Holy Sepulchre, where Rudi admired the old architecture. They marveled at the intricate blue tile work and the brilliant golden dome of the Dome of the Rock. They stopped and stood for several minutes to look through the archway leading to the al-Aqsa Mosque.

Lili retied her scarf to better cover her hair, and they both removed their shoes as they entered the mosque. It was difficult to find an empty space for their shoes, and they wondered how people didn't get shoes mixed up. A man trying on several pairs of sandals didn't provide any great confidence as they left their shoes on the third shelf, to the extreme left and one on top of the other. Lili moved to the women's section, while Rudi stood at the very back of the main prayer hall. They stayed only a few minutes before putting their shoes on again, thankful that no one had mistakenly taken the wrong ones.

They looked around at the Temple Mount and headed for the Western Wall, where they just observed from afar hundreds of men, with heads covered, in prayer. There were some women, but there were fewer women than men on the extreme right of the wall. Rudi and Lili walked southwest and left the Old City via the Zion Gate.

That evening they found themselves at a small, cosy Jewish restaurant, where Hungarian and Viennese dishes were prepared alongside more traditional Polish cuisine. Rudi and Lili ordered borscht to start, then duck with apple for Lili, and Rudi had *cutlet de volaille.* A bottle of light red wine from Burgundy lasted more than an hour, and then they shared a slice of poppy-seed cake. Complimentary chocolate-covered plums came with coffee, over which they lingered for quite some time. They wandered back to their hotel, weaving between revelers, and they soon wished each other a Merry Christmas with surprise gifts. Lili unwrapped a hand-held fan to better cope with the heat, and Rudi got some hand cream to help repair his laborer's hands.

On Christmas morning, their curiosity took them a few miles to Bethlehem, the birthplace of Jesus and the Church of the Nativity, which was crowded with worshippers and tourists. Rudi became sick of the crowds and wanted to leave. He had heard of the special qualities of the water of the Dead Sea, and he didn't need to convince Lili of it being worth a visit.

They headed east and were soon near the beach, the vast body of water on their right. They drove north to where it was easy to pull the car off the road near the beach. The weather was warmer here than it had been the previous couple of days, and the area was really desolate. They changed into their swimming costumes and were soon floating on their backs.

"I don't think you could sink in this even if you wanted to," said Lili.

The lake, well below sea level, is so salty that animal life and vegetation are nearly nonexistent in and around it. Being in the water was very pleasant as they stayed afloat without any effort, and the water temperature was higher than the surrounding air temperature.

"This is like a bath," said Rudi. "I don't think I've ever been swimming in water anywhere near this warm at Christmas."

Lili nodded as she floated about, head held high to avoid any water splashing up her nose or into her mouth. They very quickly drip-dried, as the air was dry, and with their bodies salt encrusted, they headed northwest for the destination of Jaffa, where they hoped to enjoy some aspects of the Mediterranean.

They found a tiny hotel room with very meager amenities, but it had a small balcony with a wonderful outlook over the harbor. Rudi and Lili explored the harbor, and Rudi wondered how old many of the interesting buildings might be, and they soon found themselves back in the water. It was much cooler—in fact, quite bracing. Lili stayed in barely long enough to wash the Dead Sea salt from her body before wrapping herself in a towel. Rudi went for a lengthy swim, not finding the water temperature any colder than that of the Ossiachersee that he was well used to.

They walked around the old town of Jaffa till dusk and picked up some shish kebabs and a bottle of wine, which they shared on their little balcony overlooking the harbor and the Mediterranean Sea. The red-and-yellow sunset over the water was quite spectacular, and the rattling of ships' masts and the occasional squawking of birds flying home to roost offered the only distractions.

Rudi and Lili spent the next morning walking along the beach, and Rudi had a swim. Towel and sun dried, he returned to the car with Lili. The wailing of the call to *Zurh* prayer sent them on their way, windows wound up, as they had not been able to really get used to the loud calls to prayer. They enjoyed traveling by car together very much as they headed to Haifa. Lili, though, did a little daydreaming on their way home. She wondered about how different the trip might have been with the prince of her dreams driving along the Amalfi Coast in that red convertible as she spent the evenings mainly in a bubble bath with a glass of champagne.

Rudi soon pulled the car up by a service station, filled it up with petrol, and very thankfully dropped it off at Sahib's house, as four playful children greeted them both. Sahib introduced his wife, Amelia, who, in perfect English, invited them to help break their fast on Friday evening. They were to come half an hour after the call to the *Maghrib* prayer. Rudi and Lili walked up the hill and decided to have lunch at the Appinger Hotel before heading home.

Gudrun greeted them. "*Gruess Gott.* You've just come back from a vacation?"she said, noticing Rudi and Lili carrying a bag each. "My children are looking forward to you coming again on Thursday, Lili; they have so much fun with you. I have a couple of people I'd like you to meet. They have actually just come in."

She turned to a couple sitting at a table and said to them, "I'd like you to meet Rudi and Lili Auer. This is Dr. Arnold and Rebecca Knopfelmacher. They have just arrived from Vienna." Arnold and Rebecca were both comparatively tall, dark and slender. Arnold wore long cotton, khaki trousers and an off-white shirt with, rolled-up sleeves. Rebecca wore an autumnal-colored floral dress and brown, open sandals.

"*Gruess Gott,*" Arnold said.

"*Gruess Gott. Ja,* it's very nice to hear a Viennese accent again," said Lili. "What brings you to Haifa?"

"That's a long and complicated story. Why don't you join us?" said Arnold. "We haven't even got our menus yet. Gudrun said you have been here several months already."

"Yes, since July, and Lili is quite homesick. How long have you been here, Arnold?"

"We had a few days in Jerusalem and came here yesterday, as we couldn't get any more accommodation. It was really very crowded in Jerusalem."

"Where did you live in Vienna, Rebecca?"

"In the ninth district."

"Why did you leave Vienna? I miss it so much," said Lili.

"It is a little embarrassing to say," said Arnold. "I was laid off after working as a doctor at the Vienna State Hospital for over eight years."

Rebecca said, "He was always highly regarded…there was never any complaint about his work…no one ever died when he was on duty… he was just laid off."

"The reason is simple…I am a Jew," said Arnold.

"And we are highly integrated into the society," said Rebecca. "Even both our parents were born in Vienna. The government is so weak, it buckles under Nazi pressure, and there is a widespread movement against Vienna's professionals."

"That's terrible," Lili said. "We are so sorry…my boss in Vienna wrote a couple of weeks ago, declaring that the same happened to a physician friend of his…sacked just because he was a Jew…and he fought the decision with all the influence he could muster in Vienna… had no luck."

A waiter appeared before them. "No hurry, take your time; I'll be back momentarily." He was, and everybody ordered the house special for the day—goulash with baby potatoes. A bottle of Mount Carmel red wine was also ordered.

"What happened to Rebecca was just as bad and very telling," said Arnold.

"Yes, it's laughable, really, if it were not so serious."

Rebecca continued the story. "I was working at the *Kunstgewerbeschule* (a school of arts and crafts) and was reading *Moerder, Hoffnung der Frauen*, by Kokoschka at the time. Kokoschka had been a student there and was recently dismissed for producing *entartete Kunst* (degenerate art), the decision clearly made due to Nazi influence at the institute."

"How could that get you dismissed...because you were reading something somebody didn't like?" asked Lili.

"I was reading the book during my lunch break and left it on my desk while I went to the bathroom, and somebody noticed. I was dismissed the next day, being told that my job had been made redundant. If I knew who reported me, I'd go and ring his or her neck," said Rebecca, her voice trembling. Despite the pain of recounting such stories, the goulash and wine were much appreciated.

"That's why we are here, Lili," said Arnold. "The circumstances are far from optimal. We can understand you being homesick, and we will be, too, from time to time, I'm sure, but Palestine is now the best place to be for Jews of Europe."

"With sheep walking down the main street as we saw on our first day?" asked Rebecca.

"There's a real Jewish population explosion here at the moment," continued Arnold.

"And I hope we will add to it...*Ja*, Arnold?" asked Rebecca as she squeezed him on the arm. "We heard that there's a need for doctors in Haifa, so that's why we came specifically to this town."

Lili and Rebecca threw a glance at one another, as the waiter asked whether there was a preference for dessert.

"Three *Esterhàzy* slices and one *Apfelstrudel* for Arnold, please...and four coffees, d*ankeschoen*."

"You were just ahead of your time, leaving Vienna when you did, Lili," explained Arnold. "It became crystal clear with the attempted *putsch*, when Dollfuss was murdered, that the German Nazis will stop at nothing to annex Austria. They will take over Austria. There is nothing more certain. Hitler has written and talked many times about extending the *Lebensraum* (living space) for the master race."

"Do you not think that Schuschnigg will be more effective than Dollfuss was at repelling the Nazis?" asked Rudi.

"No, unfortunately, I don't," continued Arnold. "Schuschnigg seems to be liked by a lot of people because he is quiet and does not ruffle many feathers. But against Hitler's desires, he is no match... and he hasn't got the same backing from Mussolini that Dollfuss had. You know, Rudi, while there are fewer incidents of brownshirt hooliganism on the streets, there has been a slow but steady increase in Aryanization, especially in Vienna...in a few other towns, too...as Jews have been squeezed out of professional jobs or have not been employed where positions have become available. This has also been the case at the University of Vienna."

"What has happened there, Arnold?" asked Rudi with heightened interest.

"Some Jewish professors have clearly been shown the door, while replacements have generally been non-Jews and often not as qualified as many Jewish applicants. The word has it that the university admin wants to have the Jewish teaching staff reduced to the same proportion as Jews are to non-Jews in the Viennese population."

"That would reduce the quality of teaching terribly at the university, wouldn't it, Arnold?" asked Lili. Arnold nodded his head, as did Rudi. Everyone found this discussion quite tiring, and it was decided that it should continue at Lili and Rudi's apartment on Saturday night.

"Should we bring something, Lili?" asked Rebecca.

"No, no, please."

"And don't go to any trouble, Lili; we're sure your story will nourish us all."

"Anyone have anything against cabbage rolls? I can make them ahead of time."

"That would be perfect, Lili...they're our favourites."

Rudi and Lili were happy to be back in their apartment; they unpacked, showered to wash off the salt, and did some shopping. On Thursday, December 27, Sahib picked up Rudi with his lunch as normal, and Lili went to tutor the girls, Ilse and Annemarie, in the afternoon.

"See you tomorrow night, Rudi," said Sahib as he pulled up beside his apartment. "I'm sorry, I'd better not stop for a beer tonight. I have already too many sins for Muhammad, peace be upon him, to forgive me."

THE CALL FOR the *Maghrib* prayer was a call for Rudi and Lili to share a beer, as they would certainly not be having any alcohol with dinner this evening at Sahib's house. Rudi and Lili brought some dates and some baklava, which Amelia graciously accepted, and they were soon introduced to Basima and Erina, who were five and seven, and to Khalid and Muhsin, six and eight years old. The girls were beautifully dressed in ankle-length floral dresses, stockings, and closed shoes, similar to their mother, who also wore a scarf. The boys wore long-sleeved shirts and khaki pants—smaller versions of their father.

Rudi and Lili were led to an enclosed back veranda with a large oriental rug covering most of the floor. There was a large, low coffee table in the middle of the floor and a variety of soft and hard cushions for sitting at the periphery of the room. Rudi pretended to creak as he sat on a cushion close to the floor and beside Lili. The girls giggled as the children took their place on some cushions. Amelia came in with a dish of dates and offered them around.

"I like to include the children," said Sahib. "Firstly, I know where they are, secondly, it is so they can learn the way of adults, and thirdly, I enjoy their company...don't I, boys?"

"Yes, Daddy," the girls said.

"Mr. and Mrs. Auer are from Vienna. Can you remember where Vienna is?"

"Vienna is in Germany, isn't it, Daddy?" offered Khalid.

"It's in Austria, dummy," said Erina.

"Isn't that where the Danube River is?" asked Muhsin, proud because he knew he was correct.

Sahib asked, "What do you like most about *Iftar*, Basima?"

"The sweets, Daddy."

"Yes, all girls love their sweets, but the boys don't," Sahib said, teasing.

"Yes, we do, Daddy," said Khalid as Amelia came in with a large salad bowl that was placed in the middle of the coffee table. The children shuffled forward immediately, providing the cue for Lili and Rudi.

"We all eat with our fingers, Lili," said Sahib. "That's why the children are always careful to wash their hands before dinner. That's right, boys, isn't it?"

"Yes, Daddy," they said resignedly and in unison as they showed their confidence in eating from a communal bowl. Lili and Rudi found this way of eating a little awkward at first, as much because they weren't used to sitting on their haunches, as being without knife and fork. They also felt as if all eyes were on them, although they were not, as Sahib had sternly instructed the children not to stare.

"Amelia is from Egypt, Lili…Sahib told me," said Rudi.

"Yes, I'm from Cairo, and I'm still homesick for Cairo, Lili. I was a school teacher there. I was on a fishing trip out in the middle of the Mediterranean with my father when we sailed straight into Sahib's boat. I think I was the only fish he caught that day."

"Ha ha," said Muhsin as his mother disappeared into the kitchen, calling, "Basma, Erina, come help, please." The two girls left and came back with an armful of plates, which they distributed, and returned a second time with serviettes and two sets of cutlery that they set down in front of Lili and Rudi.

"It is not so easy eating rice with hands," said Basima. "I'm still learning." A huge silver platter was put before them. A mountain of rice was topped with a copious quantity of lamb with a variety of grilled vegetables around the base.

"Can we start, Mummy?" asked Basima. "We're starving." Basima, using an oversized serving spoon, dished out for Erina and herself, and they showed they were clearly hungry. Amelia offered to dish out for Lili and Rudi, who were invited to indicate what they preferred.

"We eat with our fingers, but feel free to use your knife and fork…that'd be perfectly fine." Lili took up knife and fork immediately, but Rudi observed from the others to see if he could manage with his fingers. He was struggling to eat the rice with his fingers, when he received an unsolicited lesson.

"Mr. Rudi, watch me," said Muhsin. "You make a bit of a rice ball with your fingers, and you slide it up to the first two fingers...look, and you pop it into your mouth with the help of your thumb...easy, right?"

Rudi smiled and learned quickly. "How am I doing?" he asked after a while, as if he were an apprentice demonstrating for his master.

"Don't worry if some goes on the floor, Mr. Rudi; there's always lots on the floor, isn't there, Daddy?" said Muhsin.

"And," said Sahib, "when it's all over, girls, we just open the back door, and birds clean it all up. That's right, isn't it?" The children all giggled. Rudi and Lili enjoyed their meal a great deal, and they ate copiously. The lamb was succulent, the grilled vegetables were very tasty, and the rice was done to perfection.

"This is the best part now, isn't it, Mummy?" said Erina. "It's time for sweets." The children all offered to clear the table, and Basima came running in with a table broom-and-dustpan set. She got the giggles when she came to clean in front of Rudi, and there were more giggles when she ran back into the kitchen.

Four coffee cups were rushed out from the kitchen, and the aroma of Turkish coffee soon filled the entire back half of the house. Amelia soon came out with a variety of sweet cakes and a large coffee can on a large platter.

"Will you fetch another can of just hot water, please, Sahib?" Amelia said, throwing Lili a knowing glance. "I've been here a dozen years, and it took me six before I could get my first cup of undiluted Turkish down."

"Thank you. Now that you are no longer teaching, Amelia, how do you keep up so well with your English?" asked Lili.

"I read a lot; my family sends me books from Cairo."

"What sort of books do you mainly read, Amelia?"

"Oh, I like a variety—some of Jane Austen, George Orwell, John Steinbeck. I loved Gertrude Stein's book...can't remember the name. It was all about Paris; I love reading anything about Paris...Sahib has to take me there when we can rake together enough money and before that Hitler idiot gets to take over all of Europe. Oh, and I loved *Murder on the Orient Express* by Agatha Christie…it only came out earlier this year. If you want to borrow a book, please don't hesitate to ask. We could discuss a book we've both read. You should come one day when the children are at school, and we could do lunch."

"That would be lovely…wonderful dinner tonight, thank you, Amelia, and your children."

Rudi and Lili walked the fifteen minutes or so home, and Lili made another coffee she could enjoy. Lili and Rudi were very pleased to have met Sahib's wife and family, and they both commented how delightful the children were. Lili reflected on how different this dinner had been from any dinner she had ever been to in Vienna.

I would never have been allowed to speak with adults as Sahib's children were able to do…and they were delightful…and not disrespectful. They were confident and happy. I can't imagine my mother ever sitting on the floor on her haunches eating salad with her hands from a communal salad bowl, either. This was such a nice relaxed dinner.

Rudi and Lili were getting ready for bed, when Lili burst into laughter. As Rudi took off his trousers to hang them up, rice kernels fell all over the floor, and more were dislodged as he examined his cuffs. He also couldn't help but laugh. "Do you want me to sweep them up and keep them for the cabbage rolls tomorrow evening, Lili?"

———✥———

SATURDAY EVENING CAME soon enough, and Rudi and Lili were looking forward to having Arnold and Rebecca Knopfelmacher over for dinner.

"It will be nice for the first time to entertain people in our apartment, Rudi."

"How are you going to entertain them, *Schatzerl?* Tap-dance on the table?"

"Ha ha. Why don't you open the wine to let it breathe? Does the whole place smell of cabbage? You might want to open the windows till they come."

"I'm sure the whole neighborhood knows we're eating cabbage tonight, Lili. Shall I pour you a beer?" Rudi and Lili sipped on a beer while they set their rather small table, and Rudi brought in two chairs from the living room. A few minutes later, Rebecca and Arnold arrived.

"*Gruess Gott*, glad you could come," said Rudi.

"*Gruess Gott*, these are for you, Lili," said Rebecca, handing her a bunch of flowers. Rudi, knowing there was no vase in the apartment, took a water jug from the cupboard and half filled it with water. *Perfect*, he thought, as Lili untied the flowers and arranged them within moments and brought them into the living room.

"Thank you, Rebecca. See how nice they look here."

"Glass of wine or beer, anyone?" asked Rudi.

"Nothing for me at the moment," said Rebecca, and Lili shook her head also.

"I'll have a beer, please, if I may, Rudi." Rudi poured Arnold and himself a beer.

"We told you the reason why we came to Haifa the other day, and we've been curious ever since as to what brought you and Lili here, Rudi."

"Do you want to hear the long version or the short?" asked Rudi as he threw a glance at Lili. "The short version is that I was a subeditor for the university paper and didn't abide by university administration demands that I stop exposing some of their anti-Semitic practices. They locked me up and promised thirty more days in jail for sedition…insurrection against the lawful authority of the university. So I escaped, and here we are."

"Wow, taking the boat from Trieste—that must have been nice," said Arnold. Rudi didn't correct Arnold, and Lili was in the kitchen out of earshot. She came into the living room, carrying a plate of latkes.

"They smell wonderful," said Rebecca.

"Just to get us started," said Lili.

"Would you like a beer now, Rebecca, or a glass of wine—white or red?" asked Rudi.

"A little beer, please, Rudi."

"I'll have the same, please," said Lili. They enjoyed their latkes and were soon feeling quite comfortable with one another.

"You know," said Lili, "we must have nearly been neighbors in Vienna…Rudi and I lived in the Saltzgasse, and you were just a little further east."

"Yes, not far at all. What is it you miss most about Vienna, Lili?"

"So many things…I had an excellent boss. I miss my work…I miss the opera, the concerts at the Musikverein, walks in the Stadtpark and the Burggarten and some favourite cafés—especially Demel and Landtmann."

"I'm sure we'll miss lots of things, too, Lili," explained Arnold, "but we are very happy to be out of Europe for the time being. Mind you, we would have preferred to leave under different circumstances."

Rebecca continued. "We have a number of friends who have been affected by changing policies trending toward Aryanization, and we think they'll also come here to Palestine. We never thought all this would affect us integrated Jews. Who do those damned Aryans think they are?"

"They think their shit doesn't stink," said Arnold so that only Rudi could hear.

"What was that?" said Rebecca. "How long has your family been in Vienna, Lili?"

"At least three generations…there are a lot of us there, as my grandfather was a rabbi, and he had thirteen children. I worry about those poor devils just across the Donaukanal from you…there in Leopoldstadt."

"There seems to have been less anti-Semitic activity there in recent months, I think," said Rebecca.

"I just think the Jews there have become used to regular infractions against them, and they just brush off daily incidents unless they are really egregious," said Arnold.

"Friends of ours tell us much the same," said Lili, "and we hear that the *Juedische Selbstwehr* does quite well now at defending the community."

"It's a scandal, of course, that the Vienna police cannot protect the community in the second district," said Arnold.

"Yes, don't let me start about the Vienna Police," asked Rudi. "Let's eat…they're enough to make anyone lose their appetite."

Lili placed the large dish of aromatic cabbage rolls in the middle of the table, having to remove the candle for the time being, and Rudi poured the wine.

"Lili tells me you are from Kaernten, Rudi," said Rebecca, "and quite a skier."

"Yes, I love the mountains. Did Lili tell you that we weren't able to ski the Grossglockner because of the Aryan clause written into the Austrian Ski Club charter?"

"Oh, you're quite a skier, too, then Lili." Lili just shook her head.

"Very interesting, after all these years of restrictions against Jews belonging to sporting clubs, there is now actually some pushback and copious arguments being presented against such regulations," said Arnold.

"Is that because of some opposition to Germany hosting the next Olympic Games?" asked Rudi.

"Yes, there is a little in the papers right now, albeit pretty buried, about countries possibly boycotting the Berlin games because of Hitler's policies," said Arnold. He thought for a moment. "I think I read recently that a Mr. Brundage…Avery Brundage, the president of the American Olympic Committee (AOC), went to Berlin to help him decide whether there should be a boycott or not. I have not heard about any outcome as yet. These are wonderful cabbage rolls, Lili."

"Would you like some more? I'll get them. Rudi, would you lift the candle off the table for a moment, please? Two or three?"

"One would be just fine, thanks, Lili."

"And you, Rebecca? Rudi?"

Few cabbage rolls remained, as they drank the last of the second bottle of Mount Carmel red. All returned to the living room for an interval, and discussions continued about matters serious and some trivial. Lili indicated that the interval was over and led the way back into the kitchen, where a large piece of *Apfelstrudel* soon occupied the centre of the table.

"From the Appinger Hotel," said Lili. "I couldn't roll out the dough on this small table. I hope you like it." Everyone took a piece, and Rudi's mountain of *Schlagobers* topped the others. A pot of coffee finished the evening, and Arnold and Rebecca promised to have Rudi and Lili over to their place soon, as they were confident of being able to rent an apartment within days.

Rudi slept like a log, but Lili tossed and turned, due either to the excitement of the evening or to the cabbage rolls. She took her diary from her knickers drawer, stole quietly into the living room, and closed the door. She started to write.

> *What a difference having good friends makes. Amelia and Sahib have a really wholesome family. They are just all so warm, competent, caring, and comfortable in their own skin. No one was ever so at ease at our dinner table when I was young. Arnold and Rebecca should make good friends, too, I hope so. What terrible experiences led them to depart Vienna. I still wonder if it is really that bad. It is amazing we lived so close to one another, and now they are looking to live in the same neighbourhood we live in here. Being away from Vienna might even become tolerable with good friends here in Haifa.*

THE HOLIDAY PERIOD lasted a few more days, and Rudi and Lili took some walks around the Mount Carmel area and along the water on warmer days. Rudi played some violin and did some drawing inside and out. New Year's Eve came and went, and on the second day of 1935, Sahib was waiting for Rudi at the normal time to drive him to work. Sahib's arm had been out of a sling for a long time now, and he had become the supervisor for Mr. Finkelstein's construction projects. Rudi was now working on a second project, also in Akko and not far from the first. Lili was still enjoying her tutoring but was interested in working more if she could find an appropriate position.

Two letters, other than from family, arrived in the middle of January; one was from Hanna, Lili's friend in Vienna, and the other from Mr. Henning, Rudi's art teacher at high school, who had not written before. Lili opened Hanna's letter first.

> *Wien,*
> *Dezember 26, 1934*
> *Liebe Lili,*
>
> *I trust you and Rudi received my Christmas letter in time and that this note finds you both well. I also hope you were able to have a pleasant vacation period together.*
>
> *I considered your dream many times over and also took the liberty of discussing it with a friend without divulging the origin of the dream. It was actually more than a dream, Lili; it contained a clear message for you.*
>
> *You have obviously been having second thoughts about having married Rudi, and you clearly see your home in Europe—probably Vienna, though there'd be nothing too shabby living somewhere in Sorrento. There's a wonderful song written about Sorrento, "Torna a Surriento," and it was sung by Beniamino Gigli. Can you imagine anyone writing a song about Haifa?*
>
> *I know you love Vienna; you have always loved Vienna. How could anyone be satisfied with all that sand with sheep and camels walking around the streets? And everybody misses you here, Lili. Perhaps you should give your situation a great deal of thought.*
> *Love as always,*
> *Hanna*

Lili shed a few tears. *It is often difficult to face reality,* she thought. *I certainly like it here better now than I did three months ago. Some of the people we have met are very genuine and interesting and have an open mind. But I do miss Vienna. Why can't Hitler just pull his head in and leave Vienna alone?* She read the letter once more and burnt it with the envelope.

It was a Tuesday, and she needed to teach reading to a couple of very nice girls in the afternoon. She turned the second letter over in her hand a couple of times and wondered what Rudi's high school teacher, Mr. Henning, had written about. She'd have to wait for Rudi to open it, as it was addressed to him.

Soon Lili poured two beers, as she heard Rudi talking with Sahib on their way up the stairs.

"I can't, Lili, it's still Ramadan…no, give it here as long as you don't tell," said Sahib. "Doesn't that taste good, Rudi? *Hamdulillah*…thank you, Lili." Call to prayer had sounded as Sahib took his last sip. "Thank you again, Lili. *Ma' a salama.* Same time tomorrow, Rudi. *Ma' a salama.*'

Rudi looked out the window and watched Sahib drive away. Lili stood beside Rudi and handed him a letter.

"From Mr. Henning…how nice," Rudi said. "I wonder what he writes; I haven't seen or heard from him for several years now. He was a very good teacher to me after Franz died, I remember. You know, I still think of Franz quite often…how we'd skip school and go skiing for the day. And the accident on that day…the tip of the ski pole through his heart…still makes me very upset. Anyway…"

> *Sattendorf am Ossiachersee, Kaernten*
> *January 10, 1935*
> *Lieber Rudi,*
>
> *I wish you and your wife a happy New Year and hope you had a wonderful Christmas. You will likely be surprised to hear from me, but Mr. Birnbaum mentioned you the other day, and I felt I wanted to write to you.*
>
> *As you and I both share a love of sport, I thought I might share my desire to go to the Olympic Games one day…and now the disappointment of not being able to go. It was too far and costly for me to go to the Los Angeles games in 1932, so I was looking forward to going to the Berlin games next year. I lost interest in that idea when Hitler came to power in 1933. With his ongoing violations against various peoples, especially against Jews, I find myself not able to support the games.*
>
> *It is a pity that the forces promoting a boycott of the games have not been strong enough or coordinated well enough yet to be successful. Avery Brundage, the head of the AOC, was obviously in some*

way influenced by Hitler when he visited Berlin last year. He said that German Jews were being fairly treated. He must have been blind and deaf not to have become aware of the discrimination.

In any event, he was able to convince the American Olympic Committee to send a team, but I'm sure the American Athletic Association will not automatically allow that to happen.

Brundage also said that he himself belonged to a sports club in Chicago that did not allow Jews. How can he be head of the AOC if he himself supports an anti-Semitic organization? And now he will have a very strong sway in the United States and in other parts of the world, too, I believe. Let's keep our fingers crossed that a boycott can still happen.

I'd be interested to hear from you, Rudi. Mr. Birnbaum sends his kind regards,
Best wishes,
Henning

Rudi smiled as he passed the letter to Lili. She was very pleased that Mr. Henning took an interest in writing to them, and they were both impressed that the discussion regarding the Berlin olympic boycott got as far as the provincial Kaerntner newspapers. Some of this discussion also made it into the *Palestine Post*, which Rudi and Lili now read on a near-daily basis. What was intriguing to both of them was the frequent news out of Germany about the support Hitler had been receiving. Newspapers had been applauding Hitler's policies for ending the depression, and polls seemed to show strong and increasing support for the fuehrer's leadership in general. He had apparently been giving major speeches extolling the virtues and superiority of the German people.

They'd love that, of course, thought Rudi and Lili. Hitler also spoke passionately about the importance of peace for Germany and the importance of good relations with all its neighbors.

"I'm surprised that people are so gullible," said Rudi. "They know that what they read from the press and hear from their radios is basically pro-Hitler news. Have they forgotten that all the newspapers and radio stations are now being run as a voice for Hitler?"

"Just propaganda machines," said Lili. "And he's supposed to be an excellent orator, able to fire up the people and get them behind him."

"Yes, not just fire up his own people...he seems to have gained quite strong support across Europe as well...especially in Austria, it seems."

THE ROUTINE OF each day and week and the distance from Europe gave the illusion of weakening waves of anti-Semitism, though they were really there, stronger in Germany, but also gathering momentum in European lands far from that epicenter in Berlin.

In late February, Rudi and Lili enjoyed dinner with Arnold and Rebecca in their apartment. Their apartment was a two-bedroom home, a couple of streets higher up on Mount Carmel than was Rudi and Lili's and with a similar view. They had it nicely furnished with their belongings from Vienna. Arnold had also set up his practice just off Jaffa Street, while Rebecca was still looking for work. Rebecca bumped into Lili as she was rushing off to her tutoring obligation and invited her and Rudi again to their apartment to meet Arnold's parents, who had arrived in Haifa, also under less than optimal circumstances, and they needed some cheering up.

"On the twenty-ninth...a Friday...Lili, at eight in the evening."

"Thank you, Rebecca; we look forward to it. Sorry, I must rush." Lili also had lunch with Amelia in early March, and they laughed till they cried. They both shared the stories of how they met their husbands. They also shared lamb, rice, and vegetables, Amelia having remembered how much Lili enjoyed this meal the last time they were together. They emptied a bottle of rosé from the Côte d'Azur.

"This is a lovely wine, Amelia."

"Thank you, Lili. I have another one if we need it...cheers."

"Cheers, Amelia."

"Remember I told you, when you were here with Rudi, that we sailed straight into Sahib's boat out in the middle of the Mediterranean.

Actually, the boat Sahib was on crashed straight into our boat. Sahib was hanging over the bow, untangling a fishing line, when their boat hit ours with an almighty thud. Their boat stopped abruptly, but Sahib kept going…flew straight over his boat's railing and landed in my lap. I kid you not, Lili…I was at that very moment relaxing in a chaise longue, quietly dreaming about something; the next moment, I had a stranger in my lap with some fishing line in his hands. He was so terribly apologetic and nice…he wasn't a stranger for long."

"That's very funny. How long ago was that, Amelia?"

"Must have been more than ten years ago, Lili, and he had terrible breath…reeked of garlic and cheap wine. I remember it as if it were yesterday."Amelia chuckled and shook her head. "He wasn't a good Muslim when I met him…he tries to set a better example these days because of the children. I'm afraid I'm really a terrible Muslim, Lili; I don't believe in any God. Reading Bertrand Russell and Albert Einstein when I was at university turned me off believing in God completely."

"Rudi and I don't believe in God, either, though Rudi would like to, I think."

"How did you two meet, Lili?"

"Oh, it was hilarious, Amelia. Do you remember Shakespeare's *Romeo and Juliet* from your school days?"

"Yes, I do."

"Well, it was like the balcony scene. Rudi climbed up a ladder to my first-floor bedroom, rapped on the window till I opened it, and then insisted I meet him the next day. I did, and the rest is history, as they say."

"You know, both our husbands have an adventurous spirit, Lili. They also have something else in common."

"Oh, what's that?" asked Lili.

"They both hate Nazis with a passion. Did you hear when they ran some Nazi's car off the road?"

"No, Rudi didn't tell me."

"Oh, I shouldn't have mentioned it, Lili. I'm sorry."

"No, not at all. You've got me curious now, Amelia."

"There is a small group of Nazis in Haifa, and ever since Hitler came to power, they have apparently been required to fly a Nazi flag on their cars."

"I haven't seen any, Amelia, though Gudrun from Hotel Appinger mentioned it, I think."

"No, there aren't many…might only be five or six altogether, Lili. Anyway, Sahib and a few of his friends love to literally run them off the road."

"Isn't that dangerous, Amelia? Couldn't they get into trouble?"

"Probably not."

"Probably not what, Amelia?"

"Sahib has had especially strong bumper bars put on his work car—the truck. When he sees one of these Nazi cars, he likes to follow it to where the road is a bit winding and at the right moment, drives into the car so that it rolls over."

"And he did that with Rudi in the car?"

"Yes, I believe so, one morning on the way to work."

"No wonder he didn't tell me."

"Don't worry, Lili. The Palestine Police would like to run the Nazis out of town themselves and would never come to their assistance."

"Really?"

"You must promise not to tell Rudi I told you. I'm sure Sahib is already looking forward to running the next one off the road. Don't worry, Lili. Rudi's in safe hands when he's around Sahib."

Lili wasn't so sure but was, for the present, willing to take Amelia's word for it.

"Lili, you should read *Murder on the Orient Express* by Agatha Christie…it's excellent. I won't tell you the plot or the outcome, but I will tell you I wouldn't mind Hercule Poirot taking me out to dinner."

Lili smiled and happily accepted the book and an invitation for another lunch on April Fools' Day…a Monday.

BEFORE THEN, HOWEVER, on Friday, March 29, Rudi and Lili arrived at Arnold and Rebecca's apartment with a bunch of flowers and a bottle of red wine from the Côte d'Azur, one of a dozen Sahib had provided. Arnold introduced Lili and Rudi to his parents, who had arrived from Vienna just two weeks ago.

"Lili and Rudi, this is my mother and father. They are staying with us until we can find a suitable apartment for them."

"*Gruess Gott.*"

"*Gruess Gott.* How was your journey from Vienna, Mr. Knopfelmacher?" Rudi asked.

"It was fine, Rudi, thank you," said Mr. Knopfelmacher.

"It was not...far too bumpy," said Mrs. Knopfelmacher. "And to come here to all this sand, more camels and sheep than cars, and oh, those calls to prayer...*ei yei yei*, is everybody deaf here? Haifa is not Vienna. Lili, I'm sure you agree."

Rebecca thrust a glass of champagne in her mother's hand and offered Lili one as well. The three women sipped champagne; the men each had a pilsner.

"Father, Rudi was at the university."

"What did you do there, Rudi? Why are you here? Arnold did tell me, but—"

"I was studying law, but that had nothing to do with us being here."

Rudi provided the complete account of his work as a subeditor of the university paper while Lili chatted with Mrs. Knopfelmacher and Rebecca about recent cultural events in Vienna. The three women loved the opera, and the two Mrs. Knopfelmachers were fascinated by Lili's experience, performing with her brother, both as extras, for several years. They agreed that performances of *Aida* over recent years were very special.

Rebecca, noticing mainly empty glasses, looked at her watch. "Please come to the table. Arnold, please seat people, but not all you men together; then come carry out a few things." Arnold brought a large bowl of potato salad to the table while his mother panfried the veal schnitzel.

"Help yourselves to the potatoes, and Rebecca...serve a little for me; the schnitzel are nearly ready."

"When Mother is here, she never lets me do the schnitzel," said Rebecca. "She thinks I'll burn them or something." The schnitzel arrived on a platter, piping hot with a bottle of Mount Carmel white, well chilled.

"You have to drink this very cold; it is not good enough to drink at room temperature," said Mr. Knopfelmacher. "We will have to import some good wine before I get much older. The schnitzel is excellent as usual, thank you, Mother." Everybody agreed. Rudi was about to finish his story, when Mr. Knopfelmacher suggested he wait. "I can only concentrate on one thing at once, and that's when I'm not eating schnitzel."

"If you haven't noticed, Lili, he loves his schnitzel." Rebecca said. "You can see, Mother, we all love your schnitzel."

"Now, Rudi," said Mr. Knopfelmacher, "you were about to tell me how you got to Haifa."

Lili emitted a little cough, and Rudi told a lie that included a reference to Trieste.

"Arnold tells me you have a very nice apartment," said Mr. Knopfelmacher. "Rebecca and Arnold have a nice apartment here, too, and we will also find a nice apartment, I am confident. But we had a beautiful...a really beautiful apartment in Vienna, and we should never have been compelled to leave it."

"Why did you feel compelled to leave?" asked Rudi.

Here we go again, thought the rest of the Knopfelmacher family.

"I was a professor of medicine and a practicing surgeon at the state hospital...for more than twenty years already...and then about a month ago, I was offered early retirement. When I told them I didn't want early retirement, a longtime friend of mine from the administration invited me into his office and poured me a glass of cognac. I knew immediately that the news would not be good. They had been instructed that they had to reduce the ratio of Jewish professors to non-Jews at the university to the same ratio as that of the Vienna population as a whole."

"Half the professors would soon be gone then," said Lili.

"Yes, many professors have been dismissed with lies...often terrible and incriminating lies...and even threats. I was at least told the truth, and I appreciated that. I was reminded of what Mark Twain once said: 'Never tell the truth to people who are not worthy of it.' Yes, I was pleased I was told the truth, but it made me very angry...very angry."

"Did you drink the cognac, Father? You hadn't told me about that before," asked Rebecca.

"Yes, it would have been a waste to throw it in his face, though I was tempted." Everybody felt sorry for the recently sacked professor, and there was an awkward moment of silence.

"*Kaiserschmarrn*, anybody?" asked Rebecca. "There's both *Zwetchken* and *Apfelmus*...I know that's both Papa and Rudi's favourite." Arnold opened a half bottle of dessert wine, and twenty minutes later there was not a drop remaining. Wiener schnitzel and *Kaiserschmarrn* had long been Mr. Knopfelmacher's favorite meal. That was not the only thing Rudi had in common with him.

"Did you read last week that Hitler has publicly repudiated the Treaty of Versailles and declared that he wouldn't adhere to the limits on the German military that had been imposed by the treaty?"

"Yes, we did," said Rudi. "It's an absolute scandal that Britain and France could not hold Germany to the terms of the treaty."

"The Germans loved Hitler for that, of course...standing up to those powers," said Mr. Knopfelmacher. "They could now again build a huge army to show the world their military strength. It's not a coincidence that there will be the Olympic Games next year for Hitler to use to show off the superiority of the German people—economically and militarily."

"Do you realize, Father," said Arnold, "that Hitler has also just decreed a law establishing compulsory military service."

"No, I did not see that, but it makes perfect sense."

"Half a million men, I think," said Rudi.

"I'm sure Hitler will build a far larger army than that," said Mr. Knopfelmacher, "and who knows where his ambitions will lead him."

"Unfortunately, I think we have a very good idea," said Rudi.

"Let's talk about something less stressful, please," said Rebecca.

"We could speculate as to where they'll run the camel races," said Mrs. Knopfelmacher. "On the beach or in the desert, do you think?" Arnold poured several cognacs to help people find the answer.

"I hope they don't run them on the beach," said Rebecca. "We'd need to take a shovel as well as our beach towels to do some sunbathing." Mrs. Knopfelmacher pinched her nose and smiled at Lili.

"By the way, Rudi, I just remembered. When we first arrived here, I thought I saw a car with a Nazi flag. Are you aware of there being any Nazis here?" asked Mr. Knopfelmacher.

Lili looked at Rudi, nodded, and answered. "There is apparently a small Nazi Party organization here, and Rudi and his manager do their best to put a dent in their numbers." Rudi turned red in the face, not from the cognac, but from the realization that Lili knew something he should have perhaps told her.

"I hadn't told Lili, but she obviously found out anyway," said Rudi "My manager, Sahib, who drives me to and from work every day, has a favorite sport." Rudi took another sip. "He drives Nazis off the road.. he literally drives his truck into them, preferably round a bend, and their car flips over."

"What if they got hurt?" asked Mrs. Knopfelmacher.

"They are not allowed to get hurt...they are Aryan," said Arnold flippantly.

"No, really?"

"Don't worry, Mother. The Germans here have a very good hospital."

"*Ei, yei, yei.*"

"With some luck they'll get gangrene in hospital...Nazi bastards! How can you have any feeling for them whatsoever?"

The Knopfelmacher apartment became quiet; the cognac glasses were empty, and the conversation for this evening had come to an end. Everyone wished everyone else good-night and thanked somebody for something. The parents retreated to their room, and Rudi and Lili meandered downhill, holding each other up.

"I SEE WHAT you mean about Poirot," said Lili, as she met Amelia for lunch, two days later, on April Fool's Day. "I haven't read all that far into the book, but I'm really enjoying it. He seems so gallant and intelligent, Amelia; I'd be nervous about my table manners, though."

They both smiled as Amelia ushered Lili inside to be welcomed by pleasant aromas. Amelia took out a tray of stuffed peppers, aubergine, and squash and put an open bottle of Côte d'Azur on the table.

"I couldn't resist having a glass to help me cook, Lili."

"Of course not."

"Cheers." The women clinked glasses.

"Have you thought of asking your mother to come here to Haifa, Lili? Your brother lives in Paris, you said. Just a moment, let me turn the radio down...this is Sahib's new toy. He listens to the news every evening, by shortwave from Europe...BBC Empire Service, I think. We get Radio Paris, too, sometimes."

"I have thought about it...yes, we've asked her to come join us," said Lili to Amelia's question.

"With the increase in anti-Semitism and Aryanization in Germany and Austria, Lili."

"Yes, only a few days ago, Rudi and I had dinner with a medical professor of twenty years standing who had just been dismissed from Vienna University...just for being Jewish. He was well established, highly regarded...came to him as a terrible shock. At least there'll be another good doctor here in town now. These vegetables are wonderful, Amelia, and you can see I don't mind the wine, either. We should do lunch at my place next time, Amelia."

"Oh, it's better for me here, Lili, in case one of the children comes home early...and they sometimes do. Would your mother like it here in Haifa, Lili?"

"She'd hate it here; she loves Vienna so much, she'd hate it anywhere else. After one day on vacation, she becomes homesick. She's just so at home in Vienna. She'd miss the opera, the Musikverein, the elegance of the city, the shopping, the parks, and the cafés. I'd be surprised if she ever left Vienna...maybe...if her very life depended upon it. Even then, I'd doubt she'd leave."

The ladies finished their lunch and vowed to meet again soon. Amelia turned up the volume of the radio again a little.

"Just tell Sahib when you've finished the book, and I'm sure we'll have lots to talk about...not that we can't manage without that, hey, Lili?" They both smiled, and Lili went to do some shopping on her way home.

There was joyousness in the air. School children were skipping about, some still trying pranks on their peers as Lili left Jaffa Street. The month of April was supposed to bring beautiful weather, and spring would soon be replacing winter. Lili was just putting away the groceries when she heard Rudi and Sahib come up the stairs. She gave Rudi a kiss and handed both men a beer, and the three chatted till the call to *Maghrib* prayer. Rudi jumped under the shower, and Lili prepared some items for the evening's meal.

"What's that melody you're humming, *Schatzerl?*" asked Rudi.

"I don't know, but I can't get it out of my head. It was playing on Amelia's radio. They are one of the few in Haifa who have a radio." "Did you have a nice lunch?"

"Yes it was lovely, but I don't know the song I've been humming these last couple of hours, and it's been driving me mad." Lili kept humming the tune all the next day till she went to tutor Ilse and Annemarie in the afternoon. On her way, the lyrics of "April Showers" came to her—well, some of the lyrics—she couldn't think of the first few lines. She began to quietly sing: "*And where you see clouds, up on the hills. You soon will see crowds of daffodils, so keep on looking for a bluebird and listening for his song, whenever April showers come along.*" The girls sang along with Lili several times before Lili sang it to herself repeatedly on her way home.

APRIL AND MAY did bring some showers but mainly beautiful weather—warm days and little rain, and May also brought about a major change for Lili. Gudrun had heard of a secretarial position at the local medical clinic that required both written German and English. When Lili applied, she was a little anxious about the standard of her written English, but that was short lived, as everyone was quickly pleased with her work. It was not quite a full-time position, so Lili could leave early on Tuesdays and Thursdays to continue tutoring Gudrun's girls. The work mainly required recording doctor's visitations, writing letters, filing, and answering queries in person or by phone in German or English; communications in Arabic, Hebrew, or Yiddish were being dealt with by a coworker sitting a few feet from Lili.

"Did you hear about Hitler's speech the other day, Rudi?" asked Sahib one morning as he drove Rudi to work.

"No...when? What lies was he telling this time?"

"On the twenty-first of this month, he apparently impressed Germans and most everybody else in Europe with a speech about the importance of peace."

"Hasn't anybody read *Mein Kampf*, Sahib? I have only read excerpts of it myself, and I suspect many have not even read that much...but I know what Hitler is about."

"He apparently talked a lot about peace—how Germany needs and desires peace and how Europe needs peace. He proposed a German navy of the size of thirty-five percent of that of the British Navy and declared he'd go along with a broad reduction of arms across Europe."

"Has he just decided to ignore the limits the Treaty of Versailles had imposed upon Germany?" asked Rudi.

"Even the *Times* of London," said Sahib, "seemed to ignore that, as they praised his speech."

"Did he make any reference to Austria?"

"Yes, something about Germany not wishing to interfere with the internal affairs of Austria and not having any intentions of any Anschluss with Austria."

"Bloody liar! And the international press are hoodwinked by such statements? Stupid bastards!"

"Rudi...out," said Sahib, as they arrived at the Akko construction site. "I have to drive to Tel Aviv to drop off some materials. I'll see you this afternoon. *Ma'a salama.*"

"*Ma'a salama*, Sahib; don't run anybody off the road."

DURING THE LAST week or so of May 1935, Rudi and Lili received a number of cards congratulating them on their first wedding anniversary. Cards came from Rudi's parents, Lili's mother, Lili's brother Walter, Tante Marianne, Onkel Julius, Joseph and Ester, Moshe and Rachel, Benjamin and Rivka, Hanna and Michael, Mr. Schwartz, Mr. Birnbaum, Mr. Henning, and the owners of the Gasthaus in Villach.

"Your father must have set the *Wirt* at the Gasthaus straight about our wedding date, Rudi," said Lili, as she and Rudi reread the cards several times. "You also have a letter from Tante Marianne, Rudi, addressed only to you. Can I open it it?"

"Of course, *Schatzerl.*"

Lili carefully opened the envelope with a letter opener and slowly unfolded the letter.

"Hurry up, Lili. What's taking so long?"

"Oh, Rudi, I really miss Tante Marianne and wish we weren't so far away." With tears in her eyes, Lili read the letter.

> *Annenheim,*
> *May 18, 1935*
> *Mein lieber Rudi,*
>
> *You know exactly why I'm writing. Your wedding anniversary is on the thirtieth, Rudi, and you need to think about it ahead of time.*
>
> *You also need to know that I have run out of space for the pieces of knitting for the future. Does the air, water, or wine not agree with you in Haifa? Do I need to send you some good chocolate, perhaps?*
> *Viele Bussi,*
> *Tante Marianne*
> *PS: a thousand Bussi to Lili*

Lili wiped tears from her face and put her arms around Rudi's neck. She just held him tight and said nothing. On Thursday, May 30, Lili was coming home from tutoring Gudrun's girls, when a post office delivery person met her coming up the stairs.

"Good afternoon, madam. You are not Lili Auer, by chance, are you?"

"Yes, that's me."

"I nearly took these beautiful flowers home; they need to be in water. They are from Paris, I think. And I left a small parcel at the door. Your landlady let me in."

"Thank you so much. *Ma'a salama.*" Lili opened the card that accompanied the flowers. It read:

> To my dearest sister, Lili, and to Rudi,
>> Happy Anniversary. May these flowers last for a week and your love last forever.
> Walter,
> Paris, May 30, 1935

Lili stood on a chair and took down the water jug that doubled well as a vase, half filled it, and carefully arranged the thirteen red roses, being careful not to prick herself with one of the thorns. She put them in the center of the kitchen table and smelled four or five of them in turn, as if each one had a different scent. Lili was about to open the little parcel, when Rudi came home with Sahib at his heels.

"What could this be, do you think, Rudi?" Lili said as she handed him the little parcel. "It's from Moshe and Rachel from Vienna."

They poured a beer, everyone admiring the roses, and Sahib congratulated Lili and Rudi on their anniversary. They passed the parcel to each other, turning it around in their hands; no one had a clue as to what might be inside. Lili opened it, and a broad smile appeared across her face. She passed the little box to Rudi, and he started to laugh.

"Cheeky buggers," he said as he handed it to Sahib for a look, too. Soon the three were laughing heartily as Lili held up a pair of baby booties.

"I think they're trying to tell you something," said Sahib. The call to prayer signaled Sahib's departure, as Rudi jumped into the shower and Lili put on her wedding-day ensemble. It consisted of a long and beautifully tailored rich-brown dress of midcalf length, with a camisole top and many round, dark-brown buttons down the front. A lightly scalloped, deep-V-necked jacket was draped loosely over the top. Lili admired how she looked and also admired Rudi's singing voice coming from the bathroom:

Wenn der lieber Flieder wieder blüht,
küßt ich deine roten Lippen müd'.
Wie im Land der Märchen, wurden wir ein Pärchen,
wenn der Flieder hatt geblüht.

"Have you changed the lyrics, Rudi?"

"Just the tense, *Schatzerl,* not the essence. You look wonderful…guess I can't wear my shorts," he said, as he took out his wedding suit and laid it on the bed. Ten minutes later they walked out the door and were greeted by their landlords, Frau Weber and Felix in the front garden who said, "You look splendid…as if you were getting married. Have a lovely evening."

AND A LOVELY evening they had. The Appinger Hotel was their choice for any special meal out, as it provided very good German-Austrian food, and the Mount Carmel wine wasn't bad. Rudi ordered *Gebackene Ente* for Lili and Wiener schnitzel for himself. Out of the blue, the waiter offered them a light red wine from the Côte d'Azur—the same wine they got from Sahib. *Haifa must have managed a special delivery,* thought Rudi.

"We save it for special guests celebrating a special occasion," they were told with a smile. Rudi and Lili held hands between courses and fed each other a little from their dessert—Lili with a slice of *Esterházy Torte* and Rudi with his *Apfelstrudel.*

"This is definitely one of my favorite desserts," said Lili excitedly. "I just love the chocolate buttercream. This Hungarian prince Esterházy apparently was in love with all Austrian pastries," she said, as she fed Rudi another piece. They lingered over a coffee and chocolate-covered dried apricots.

"When can we go and see Tante Marianne, Rudi? I just miss her so." Rudi was able to avoid answering, as the bill arrived at exactly that moment. His throat tightened as he, too, thought of how he missed Austria and Tante Marianne, but right now he had no answer.

They wandered home, arm in arm, beneath an umbrella, as it had begun to rain.

"Good for the plants," said Rudi, "and none too soon."

———

It was a dreary morning and raining quite heavily in early June as Sahib drove Rudi to the warehouse-construction site in Akko. Rudi was pleased that the roof had been completed just the previous week, and work could continue today out of the rain.

"Is that a Mercedes-Benz ahead?" asked Rudi. "I haven't seen a car like that before."

"Let me see," said Sahib as he wiped the inside of the windscreen with the back of his hand and sped up to get a closer look. "Yes, I believe it's a Benz—quite swish looking, too."

"Don't drive so close, Sahib, you never know—"

"Look, Rudi, is that a flag? Isn't that the Nazi flag?"

"Not so close, Sahib," said Rudi, pleading.

Sahib opened his window a little and wiped the windscreen again with the back of his hand. "Can you see, Rudi? He has a Nazi flag…yes, it is…I'm sure. Hang on, Rudi."

Not this again, thought Rudi, becoming a little anxious.

"He's speeding up…he knows we're on to him. Here we go…shit, he's fast."

The Mercedes began to pull away.

"He can't keep this up through the bends up ahead, though. Hang on to your hat, Rudi," said Sahib as he put his foot to the floor. "The bastard's fast, Rudi, I'll give him that."

Rudi grabbed each side of his seat beside his legs.

Around the first bend, Sahib had already caught up a little. "We'll catch him, Rudi, you'll see." Sahib changed gears, and the engine began to roar as the car tires screeched around a bend. Sahib glanced gleefully across to Rudi as he was beginning to catch the Mercedes. Rudi was as white as a ghost, speechless, and hanging on for dear life. He was sure something bad was going to happen today.

"Relax, Rudi, we'll catch him shortly."

That's what I'm worried about, thought Rudi.

"Hang on...here we go...we'll frighten the shit out of him first. Whoa—hang on, Rudi." Sahib rammed his truck into the Benz for the first time. There was quite a jolt. Bang, whack. Rudi couldn't believe this was happening again...he was paralyzed. Another jolt, and Rudi's forehead nearly hit the dashboard.

"Hang on; we'll get him around the next bend." Sahib pulled his truck beside the Mercedes to see the driver for the first time. He had slick blond hair, he wore a jacket and tie, and his eyes were like saucers—he looked petrified. The Nazi flag was fluttering. Sahib waited for a moment and yanked his steering wheel hard. The vehicles hit...there was a thud and a screeching of wheels, and the Mercedes flew off the road into a ditch and then, as if in slow motion, rolled over—once...twice...three times—and came to rest on its side, windows broken and covered in mud.

"A shame one had to do that to such a nice car, Rudi," said Sahib as he burst out laughing. "Good, ha, Rudi?"

Rudi was not laughing; he was quite shaken...much more so than the first time this happened...he was convinced that this time they'd get into serious trouble. *Probably when the police find the upturned car in the ditch. What if the guy is badly injured... or dead? Paint of the Mercedes must be on the bumper bar of Sahib's truck or vice versa... someone may have seen the truck push the Benz into the ditch... someone may recognize the truck... recognize Sahib or me.* Rudi was very worried when Sahib stopped the truck.

"Here we are...hope you can get the section completed today. See you this afternoon. I'll probably be a bit late...got to get the front bumper checked...has to be ready for the next time. *Ma'a salama.*" Sahib smiled and drove away, but it took several more minutes before the color returned to Rudi's face, and he remained worried for the rest of the workday.

"DID YOU HAVE a good day, Rudi?" asked Sahib about midafternoon, as he pushed the car door open for Rudi to get in.

"*Shukran,* Sahib."

"*Aafwan…*sorry I'm late, Rudi, but the bumper is ready for its next encounter."

Rudi paled as he recalled this morning's episode in vivid detail. Sahib lit a cigarette and was surprised that Rudi accepted one and lit up.

"Never known you to have a cigarette before, Rudi."

"I needed one ever since our meeting with the Nazi this morning. Are you sure we can't get into any trouble, Sahib, for—"

"Ah, forget about that. Didn't you notice we now have completely different number plates, Rudi?" Sahib smiled. Rudi's hands were trembling so much, he could barely find his mouth with his cigarette. There was a pause in the conversation.

"I suppose you didn't notice the article in the *Palestine Post* the other day about Germany's new eligibility standards for military service."

"No, what was that about, Sahib?"

"From now on, only thoroughbreds are allowed in."

"What was that?" Rudi found it difficult to focus on the conversation.

"Non-Aryans are no longer eligible for military service. Basically, Jews are barred from joining the German military."

"That shouldn't come as a surprise, given all the other restrictions on Jews," said Rudi.

"I think it's funny that some Jewish veteran organizations complained bitterly about this, Rudi. I'd be happy about not being obliged to be doing military service…guess I wouldn't want to be discriminated against, though."

Due to being delayed, Sahib missed his pre-*Maghrib* prayer beer, and Rudi had two. Rudi did not share the encounter with Lili and tossed and turned a lot during the night. While he despised Nazis as much as anyone, he didn't think it okay to drive them off the road, probably causing serious injury and possibly their death.

The following morning Sahib picked up Rudi, who was still very concerned about the previous day's episode and worried about possible consequences. Sahib sensed Rudi's concern, and their conversation was thin and strained. As they approached the spot where the

Mercedes had tumbled down the embankment, they were motioned to stop by a police officer.

"What's the problem, Officer?" asked Sahib.

"A Benz was apparently forced off the road…yesterday about this time."

"Oh!"

"Severe skid marks and evidence of impact from another vehicle… could be attempted murder. The driver's in pretty bad shape."

"Really?"

"Someone reported the attack and said there were two of them. Okay, you can proceed now…road's clear. Rudi turned as white as a ghost as Sahib drove toward Akko.

"Forget about it, Rudi," said Sahib, trying unsuccessfully to sound nonchalant.

"What if they find out it was us?" Rudi's high-pitched voice pierced the air.

"Settle down…we have different number plates, and this morning I'll have the whole bumper exchanged with another old one…and the bonnet of the truck while I'm at it…it'll have a different persona altogether."

Rudi remained very worried for days, and he had to try hard not to indicate to Lili that something was bothering him. At the back of his mind was the nagging thought that Sahib and he might yet be identified as the culprits.

SETTLED IN HAIFA

THE ANNIVERSARY OF their arrival in Haifa had come and gone without Rudi or Lili talking about it much. During the year, they had settled down in an apartment they enjoyed and that offered a splendid view; they both had good work, and they appreciated the Mediterranean climate. While they made new friends in Haifa, Rudi missed Joseph quite a lot, but not as much as Lili missed Tante Marianne and her former boss Mr. Schwartz, who had become an important confidant in her life. Lili also missed the lifestyle of Vienna. Though Lili didn't let on, she was deeply nostalgic. *Oh, how I miss the Kaerntnerstrasse; how can you compare shopping on Jaffa Street? Coffee at Hotel Appinger is quite good, but it isn't Landtmann or Central. The German bakery here is quite good, too, but it doesn't compare with Demel. I so wish I were with Hanna there right now, sharing a piece of Esterházy cake...even if we don't always agree about everything.*

Rudi missed certain cafés, especially Café Louvre, but he did not miss university life at all. He longed to visit his parents and would have loved to have another vacation with Tante Marianne and take Lili skiing again. There was never quite enough money to contemplate that, and Rudi soon developed itchy feet to perhaps gain better employment elsewhere. He regularly sifted through job advertisements and began to apply for positions in Egypt, London, and elsewhere in Europe. *Perhaps I wouldn't have the constant desire to go somewhere else if we had a child. Why doesn't Lili want to become pregnant? I know she doesn't because there's a pattern to her avoiding me. Does she not love me anymore? I think she's been different toward me ever since we landed in Haifa. Yes, I think she has...I guess that's my fault...still hasn't forgiven me for us fleeing Vienna.*

Haifa was now booming economically, due largely to the existence of the Iraqi Petroleum Company, a London-based firm consisting of many different oil companies. There was a great deal of construction taking place, including the development of the waterfront, warehouses of all descriptions, and housing for the increasing population of mainly Jews. There was a constant stream of news reports detailing the arrival of Jews, mainly from Germany and Austria, escaping the rise of Nazism.

The population was expanding in leaps and bounds, with people of different ethnicities and religions mostly getting on very well together. Rudi enjoyed working for a Jewish boss and was good friends with his manager, a Muslim Palestinian Arab, his Egyptian wife, and family. Lili worked in a health clinic beside Arabs and Palestinian and European Jews and enjoyed tutoring two German children. Rudi and Lili rented their apartment from German immigrants and were friends additionally with Austrians, Saudis, Persians, Lebanese, and British.

Nevertheless, some tensions had been developing. Some Arabs did not approve of the rapid increase of Jews coming to Haifa and buying up houses and land, and many disapproved of Palestine being governed as a British mandate. At the same time, some Templers were fighting the Nazi requirement from Germany that the Nazi pennant be flown from cars driven by Germans. And there were reported disagreements among teachers at the German school regarding the extent to which the school curriculum should be modified to ensure compliance with Nazi requirements.

———

RUDI AND LILI were moderately content with their life, frequently writing letters and sending cards to Rudi's parents and Tante Marianne in Annenheim and less frequently to Lili's mother, Mr. Schwartz, and Joseph in Vienna and to Lili's brother, Walter, in Paris. They were often disappointed by how long it took to receive return mail. Rudi and Lili visited with friends from time to time and read the newspaper on a daily basis.

It was now summer, and Rudi and Lili spent several evenings a week at the beach, enjoying the warm Mediterranean water and the cool ocean breeze. Lili commented several times how much easier it was to swim in the sea in comparison to swimming in the European lakes. They observed the considerable construction taking place on and around the port of Haifa, and they liked to watch the increasing number of boats of all shapes and sizes that docked in the harbor.

Rudi continued to do some drawing, sometimes arranging several kitchen items with flowers and fruit for a still-life composition, other times sketching outdoors while sitting at an outdoor café, on the beach, or in the adjacent countryside. He and Lili rekindled an earlier interest in collecting stamps and had all sorts of acquaintances bring them stamps they cut from envelopes.

Lili read avidly and began to do some knitting, not for the future, but for the next cool season—a cardigan for herself being on the needles at the present time. She often smiled as she reflected upon the times spent in Tante Marianne's kitchen as she knitted two plain, two pearl. Rudi continued to play violin from time to time, and this frequently led to some duet singing and dancing in the kitchen.

AROUND THE MIDDLE of September, Rudi and Lili were invited for dinner by Mr. Knopfelmacher and his wife at their newly acquired apartment, next to Rebecca and Arnold. Rudi and Lili had not spoken with any of the Knopfelmachers for months and were curious as to how they were getting on.

"Gruess Gott," said Rudi.

"Gruess Gott. How nice to see you, Lili and Rudi. You look so wonderfully brown; you must have been in the sun a lot, *Ja?*"

"Nice to see you, too. What a nice apartment you have…and right next to Arnold and Rebecca…how practical," said Lili, as Rudi smiled and shook hands with the Knopfelmachers.

"Very good, Lili, having them next door; I will need them soon, as you can see," said Rebecca, putting a hand on her enlarged stomach. "We will be lucky to have grandparents right next door."

"Have you been well?" asked Lili, looking at a woman who could give birth at any moment.

"Yes…I mean no…I was quite sick but am very well and quite big now, thank you, Lili."

"It could arrive before we've eaten if we don't get to the dinner table soon," said Mr. Knopfelmacher. "Rudi and I would like to enjoy our schnitzel first, Mama. Isn't that right, Rudi? Let's at least have a drink before I'm called to do an emergency delivery. Champagne, Lili? Mama? Rebecca, you can have a third." Arnold poured three beers while his father poured champagne for the ladies.

"*Zum wohl*," they said as everybody clinked glasses and settled down in the living room.

Lili became nostalgic, as this large room looked like a typical Viennese living room befitting a well-established, professional family. It reminded her of the home she had become used to as a child. There was a large mahogany dining table at one end and a grand piano at the other. The wooden floors were covered with several rugs that Lili identified as Balochistans and several beautifully carved pieces, including a wall of bookshelves and a desk. An ornate chandelier and half a dozen carved standard lamps and table lamps added to the decor.

Mrs. Knopfelmacher left a half-empty glass on a side table and went to the kitchen. The smell of frying butter soon filled the room as she came in with a large bowl of potato salad and left with her half-empty glass. No sooner had she left than Mr. Knopfelmacher assigned seats around the dining table, and his wife soon entered with a platter of schnitzel stacked high. There were many noises of approval but little talk during dinner, as the sounds of a thunderstorm broke the near silence.

"Arnold, will you please close the windows?" asked Mr. Knopfelmacher, "and bring me the paper I have on the desk. I didn't want to bring up the subject before dinner…would have ruined our appetite. Did you read yesterday's paper, Rudi?"

Rudi shook his head.

"Did you, Lili?"

"No, we missed yesterday's for some reason."

"Let me read just two lines: 'Berlin, September 15, 1935: Nuremberg Laws deprive Jews of German citizenship; Forbid Jews from marrying Aryans—for the protection of German blood and honor.'"

Rudi shook his head. "While this is a shock when you first hear it," he said, "it doesn't come as a surprise."

Arnold continued. "If you have just one grandparent who is a Jew, you are regarded as a non-Aryan, and you basically cannot work in Germany anymore...at all; you cannot belong to any sporting teams, groups...any associations whatsoever."

"It will soon be the same in Austria, Lili. I hope you have come to realize that we are lucky to be out of Vienna," said Mr. Knopfelmacher.

"I already know about the Aryan paragraph in constitutions of sporting organizations," said Lili. "Rudi wanted to take me skiing on the Grossglockner, and we couldn't because of the discrimination against Jews."

"What if you don't know who your grandparents are?" asked Rudi.

"My understanding is that you must be able to produce the papers to prove that each of your four grandparents are Aryan before you can be regarded as Aryan and therefore suitable for the German *Volk*—the superior German *Volk*," said Mr. Knopfelmacher.

"I know my father, of course," said Rudi, "but he doesn't know who his father was and his mother, my grandmother, didn't know either of her parents, as far as I know. I could be part Jewish myself."

"You'd be *ein Mischling*, a Jewish mixed breed, if that were the case," said Arnold.

"Did you know, too, that Germany has now officially adopted the swastika as its national flag, Rudi?" asked Mr. Knopfelmacher.

"Not surprised; they'll at least be easy to see, fluttering from a Nazi car that Sahib and his friends can run off the road," said Rudi. Lili and Mrs. Knopfelmacher rolled their eyes, and Rudi didn't mention the most recent incident of a new Mercedes ending in a ditch.

After a lag in the conversation, Arnold started up again, this prompting Rebecca to tug Lili on a sleeve and move to the far side of the room.

"The Nazis are making quite some headway with their preparations for the Olympic Games, according to an article I read the other day," said Arnold.

"I only remember that there's to be a vote by the American Athletic Union, or whatever it's called, in December, to determine whether or not the United States will boycott the games," said Rudi.

Lili chimed in from the other side of the room. "Isn't the head of the American Olympic Federation—what's his name—"

"Avery Brundage, isn't it, Lili?"

"Yes, he seems to support the games, and he has a lot of sway with the Athletic Union, from what I have read."

"He was obviously duped by the Nazis when he visited Berlin," said Mr. Knopfelmacher. "He belongs to an anti-Semitic club himself…in Chicago, I think. What is your take on that, Arnold?"

"He is clearly not worthy of a high position in the Olympic movement, Father…I just read that the Germans are building a one-hundred-thousand-seat track-and-field stadium and other smaller arenas. Hitler wants to outdo the Los Angeles games. He wants to promote the master race. He wants to prove German-Aryan superiority."

"Yes," said Rudi. "I also read a piece in the *Voelkischer Beobachter* that argued that blacks and Jews should be forbidden from participating in the games."

RIn the meantime, Rebecca explained to Lili that her pregnancy was quite unexpected. "I didn't really want to become pregnant so soon after arriving in Haifa; I would have preferred to have waited a year or two to see if I could really put up with staying here with all this sand. Why, may I ask, haven't you got any children yet, Lili? You and Rudi have been together for a few years already."

"Actually, it's a real dilemma for me. I feel I was torn away from Vienna. I didn't really leave under happy circumstances…I just followed Rudi, who had been very impetuous, unthinking…I don't think he took me into account at all when he made plans."

"But he really loves you, Lili."

"Yes, but I haven't totally forgiven him yet."

"*Ei yei yei.*"

"I'm not sure how responsible he is…thinks nothing about the danger of driving Nazis off the road. What if he were seriously hurt? And he's constantly looking for work elsewhere without discussing it with me. He said he would go to Europe to work without me to make more money."

"One can always do with more money, Lili."

"Yes, of course, but I would be left living here on my own. I don't want to be here at all…dammed heat, sand, and camel and sheep dung everywhere. I'd feel far too vulnerable…and lonely. I constantly worry about whether Rudi would be more responsible as a father."

"Of course…I don't know Rudi well enough…wouldn't he like to have children, Lili?"

"Yes, ever since we came here, he has said it would be great to start a family. I've been really careful avoiding becoming pregnant…and Rudi is not happy about that…if you get the picture."

"Come, Lili, let's get back with the others."

"But the threat to boycott the games put an end to that idea, didn't it?" said Rebecca when she heard the tail end of the conversation as she and Lili returned to join the others.

"You are right, Rebecca," said her father-in-law.

Mrs. Knopfelmacher just remembered something of interest. "Did you read, Lili, that Bronislaw Huberman will be giving concerts here in December?"

"No, I didn't hear that. Just in Jerusalem, Mrs. Knopfelmacher?"

"I'm not sure, but I think Tel Aviv was mentioned, too."

"Isn't he wanting to start a full Palestine orchestra here?" said Mr. Knopfelmacher. "Yes, I'm sure I read that somewhere and that Toscanini—"

"Arturo Toscanini?"

"Yes, he's apparently agreed to conduct the premiere when that happens. Wasn't there something also mentioned at the same time that Toscanini canceled his return to the Bayreuth Music Festival in 1934 in response to Hitler's policies?"

"I hadn't heard that, but it makes perfect sense that the many Jewish musicians all over Europe would come here to join an orchestra...to work as they had in their own country," said Rudi. "We should definitely try to get to see Huberman, if we can, Lili."

"Would you fetch the cognac and some glasses please, Arnold? It will leave a better taste in the mouth than thoughts about what Hitler is up to."

Everyone was now quietly sipping their cognac except Rebecca who had no sooner sat down before she fell asleep. The conversation continued quietly about less-political matters till a thunder clap startled everyone, including Rebecca, who just twitched and began to gently snore.

"We should go now," said Lili, looking at Rebecca.

"You can't leave now, Lili...wait till this storm is over," said Mrs. Knopfelmacher. "Do you plan to go to the camel races two weekends from now, Lili?"

"Yes, we must...our friends Sahib and Amelia are taking us. I think their eldest son, Muhsin, may be a jockey...though he's only nine years old."

"That wouldn't be allowed in Vienna...a jockey who's not even ten," said Mrs. Knopfelmacher.

"They wouldn't have camel races in Vienna either, Mother," said Arnold. Everybody smiled.

"I suspect there'll be some very young Bedouin boys riding, though," said Rudi as he took his last sip.

The storm passed. Arnold opened the windows he had closed earlier, and a cool breeze filled the apartment. Fond farewells were spoken, as Rebecca opened her eyes and waved to Rudi and Lili. They were home in a short time.

IT WAS A hot day in October when a few hundred people gathered near the finish line of the camel races in the desert a couple miles to the south of Haifa. Rudi and Lili, who traveled there with Sahib and his family, were relieved when they were told that Muhsin would indeed not be riding today.

"Don't sulk, Muhsin…that just proves you are not mature enough to ride yet…maybe next year," said his mother as she put her arms around her eldest son. He continued to sulk.

There was a lot of activity before and between the five races scheduled. Some Bedouins were greeting each other, not having seen one another perhaps for months, while others were trading animals. One extended family of at least twenty was sitting around a fire pit containing a whole sheep about to be cut up and put on a huge platter for a luncheon feast. Some camels were lying down, seemingly resting or thinking through race strategy, while others were just chewing their cud. Groups of men, young and old, sitting cross-legged, were sharing tales and hubble-bubble pipes. One young Bedouin boy, with his father not far behind, was trying to sell a calf still wobbly on its legs, while a couple of German boys were having more success selling slices of watermelon. Bookmakers were busy receiving bets before the commencement of each race.

Lots of cheering and dust accompanied the galloping hooves down the track, which ended with a few bursts of jubilation by those who had won their bet, while complaints could be heard from many. People turned their backs and covered their faces, as the dust caught up with the camels slowing down beyond the finish line. The dust had no sooner cleared, thanks to a gentle onshore breeze, than the next batch of camels was sent underway with a clear pistol shot. Rudi and Lili had five bets each. Rudi lost all five; Lili won three and ended up six pounds richer and happy.

"How did you do that?" asked Rudi, just as Sahib and family joined them barely beyond the finish line.

"The camels I chose had the best backsides," explained Lili. "My father took me to the races in Vienna once and told me you can tell the best prospects by their posteriors."

"Lili's right, Rudi; you can always tell a good camel by its rump, not its hump," said Sahib.

"You learn something new every day," said Rudi, as he jumped in the back of the truck beside four children, while the two ladies climbed into the cabin with Sahib. Sahib was about to drive off when two police officers approached the truck and asked him to step outside.

"This truck does fit the description," said one officer to the other.

"The description of what?" asked Sahib.

"Do you own this truck? Have you ever driven this truck to Akko?"

"Yes, I do so most workdays...is there a problem?" asked Sahib feeling a little uneasy.

"Several months back, a vehicle fitting this description was seen to drive a black Mercedes off the road...deliberately."

"Oh?"

"The driver has severe head injuries...unable to speak...may not survive. We require you to report to the Haifa Police Station at ten in the morning Monday with your truck...didn't get your name."

"Saleh Abdullah, but everybody calls me Sahib."

Rudi was able to hear the entire conversation from the back of the truck. He began to feel nauseous and to sweat profusely.

"Are you okay, uncle Rudi?" asked Muhsin.

"Yes, thank you, Muhsin...just a bit hot." Rudi turned his head and wiped his face.

"What was that about?" asked Amelia.

"They just want me to have a roadworthy check...noticed a couple of worn tires and a broken head lamp...wondered how old the truck was."

"It does look rather shabby, Sahib...different-colored bonnet and several dents...looks as if it's been in a war."

On Monday Sahib drove Rudi to work in Akko. Rudi, again sweating feverishly, expressed his deep concern. Sahib fobbed him off, dropped him at work, and drove back to the Haifa Police Station, arriving punctually at 10:00 a.m. Sahib was required to fill out some paper work while several officers inspected his truck.

"Seen better days," said one of the officers, looking at the truck. "We'll follow up with you if need be in the next week or so." Sahib drove around for a few minutes and went to mosque for the *Zuhr* prayers...*just as a precaution,* he thought.

THE LAST COUPLE of months of 1935 seemed to pass quite quickly and uneventfully. Rudi's birthday fell on a Sunday, so Rudi and Lili celebrated at Hotel Appinger on Saturday, December 7. Sunday evening, after a day's work for both of them, Lili made Rudi his favorite meal of Wiener schnitzel and *Kaiserschmarrn* and presented him with a stamp album, which he very much appreciated, and tickets for a violin concert by Huberman in Tel Aviv for the following Saturday night.

Rudi and Lili got all dressed up as if they were going to a concert in Vienna and drove to Tel Aviv in Sahib's car, which he had washed and had waiting for Rudi and Lili when they went to pick it up. The atmosphere at the concert hall was electric.

"It's nearly as exciting as waiting for a recital at the Musikverein in Vienna," said Lili.

"Yes, and Bronislaw Huberman should be wonderful," said Rudi. They took their seats near the middle of the hall, and the recital was indeed wonderful. Huberman, accompanied by Jakob Gimpel on a Steinway, played a very popular program that included pieces by Resphigi, Bach, Beethoven, and Chopin-Huberman. Rudi and Lili really enjoyed the concert.

"I loved the Beethoven piece," said Lili.

"I also liked the Bach sonata," said Rudi as he took Lili by the arm when they left the concert hall. On the way out, they heard various groups talking enthusiastically about the prospect of there being a Palestine orchestra in the future. Though it was quite late driving home, the excitement of the program kept them awake. They had no sooner arrived home, than Rudi went to get his violin. He carefully took it out of the case Lili had given him for his birthday several years ago.

"I love this case you gave me; I haven't played for quite a while."

"You can't play now, Rudi; it's too late."

"Of course. What a wonderful concert, Lili," said Rudi as he returned his violin to its case. "Thank you for getting the tickets."

Rudi returned the car to Sahib the next morning, a Saturday, and played violin till he made himself tired.

NEW YEAR'S EVE was celebrated with three generations of Knopfelmachers, Rebecca having recently given birth. This made for a very joyous evening, as Rudi and Lili were introduced to twin girls, Ariella and Talia.

"What beautiful girls," swooned Lili as Rebecca passed Ariella to her.

"It's contagious, of course, Rudi," whispered the proud grandfather who observed Lili adoring the baby in her arms.

"What do you mean, Mr. Knopfelmacher?"

"Womb ache, Rudi, womb ache…it won't be long before Lili—"

"Stop that, Father…it was so easy, Lili; I wasn't in the hospital half an hour, and there they were," said Rebecca.

"Popped out like a cork from a champagne bottle," said Mr. Knopfelmacher.

"Father, please…just get us a drink," said Rebecca.

Rudi smiled as he was passed Talia to hold. She gripped Rudi tight on one finger and looked up at him with a big smile.

"Just wind," said Mr. Knopfelmacher. "Could be an explosion any minute, Rudi. Don't be alarmed, though…it's quite natural." Mr. Knopfelmacher poured the champagne, and there was repeated clinking of glasses as everyone wished everyone well. Mr. Knopfelmacher tugged Rudi on the sleeve.

"Did you read that the American Athletic Union finally did approve of the United States sending their team to the Olympics?"

"Yes, I did read that," said Rudi. "Bloody disappointing…apparently, Mr. Brundage bullied them into that decision."

"Being an important figure in the Olympic movement and belonging to a club that forbids Jews…scandalous, just scandalous, Rudi!"

The evening continued joyously with much champagne and copious finger foods till the clock struck midnight, which led to more sharing of good wishes and one more glass of champagne for everybody except Rebecca.

"Couldn't have them getting inebriated through their mother's milk before they're even three months old," said Mrs. Knopfelmacher.

After many thank-yous, Rudi and Lili soon bid everyone farewell and meandered downhill, observing other couples in various states of happiness and steadiness.

As Rudi unlocked the door, he asked Lili, "Why can't we start a family, Lili? Those babies are beautiful."

Lili was a little taken aback and hesitated before she answered. "When it happens, it happens, Rudi. Yes, Ariella and Talia are certainly gorgeous."

"I've been noticing of late there's a pattern to when you avoid me, Lili."

"Oh, don't be silly, Rudi…it must be just in your head. When it happens, it happens. I promise you'll be the second person to know."

"Who'll be the first?"

"Me, of course." Rudi and Lili fell asleep in each other's arms, but soon Lili was recollecting the conversation she had had in Vienna just days after Rudi had first proposed to her. Dr. Schneider, a long-term family friend, was a retired medical doctor whom Lili sought out for advice. Lili shared her relationship with Rudi in great detail. She also shared the views that her mother, Walter, and Hanna held of Rudi. Lili wanted his advice as to the sense it made for her to marry Rudi. Lili could recall with perfect clarity the advice he gave her.

"Lili," she recalled him saying, "you should marry Rudi so that he may father you some children. If, for some reason, you lost Rudi due to his death or his running away, you'd still have the children you created together, and hence you'd never be lonely. Loneliness needs to be avoided at all costs. There is nothing worse, especially as you get older, than being lonely."

The advice had bothered her ever since. *I should only have children with a man if I were confident he loved me and would be a responsible and caring person for the children and for me.* At least for now, Lili wanted to prevent herself from becoming pregnant.

UNREST: 1936

FROM THE FIRST of January 1936, Rudi was promoted to foreman for the construction of an auto-repair shop in Akko and as an occasional driver for Mr. Finkelstein to run errands between Haifa, Jaffa, and Jerusalem. Rudi enjoyed his increased responsibility and especially having a car at his disposal full time. It was only a few years old: a two-door Ford, beige with dark-brown leather upholstery. Unfortunately, there was a broken spring on the driver's side seat, requiring Rudi to sit on a cushion.

HE TRAVELED SOUTH of Haifa a couple of times per month and only stayed overnight when he was obliged to drive to Jerusalem. Lili hated being left alone overnight, and Rudi didn't like being away from Lili, either. He and Lili would occasionally use the car on an evening and on weekends. Lili enjoyed these outings a lot, feeling most comfortable with Rudi's driving. There was an exception one Saturday morning as Rudi was driving Lili to Akko to show her the partially constructed auto-repair shop.

"You bastard," Rudi fumed, as a black Mercedes-Benz passed him.

"What's wrong, Rudi?"

He ignored Lili, clenched his teeth, changed gear, and took chase. "Didn't you see that flag? Nazi bastard," he said as he pushed the accelerator to the floor.

"Don't you dare…don't even think about it," Lili said tersely. Rudi took his foot off the gas and turned red in the face. It had been an automatic reponse.

"Sorry, *Schatzerl.*"

"You were just like a hound chasing a hare."

"No...just a Nazi." Rudi had temporarily forgotten Sahib running a late-model Mercedes off the road and being worried for some time that they might be caught. Rudi recalled that a policeman had told them that the truck had been seen, and Sahib was later required to report, with his truck, to the Haifa Police Station. *Perhaps we'll still be found out,* he thought.

After some silence and as Lili's heart rate returned to normal, she remembered her dream about being driven in a white convertible with red upholstery along the Amalfi Coast and being pampered by a very caring, handsome lover. *He wouldn't have taken off recklessly like that, not caring about the danger in that action, not caring how I might have felt... perhaps Mother and Hanna were correct, warning me that Rudi makes poor decisions. He has reckless tendencies...I wonder if he would be more responsible if I were pregnant. Would he be more caring toward me if we had children?*

WHILE THERE WAS little Nazi activity that people were aware of in Palestine, things were very different in Poland. According to the *Palestine Post,* anti-Semitic activity was increasing markedly there, including quotas being established in Polish universities, limiting the number of Jewish students.

"That would make Benjamin and Rivka sad...they spoke about returning to Poland if circumstances for Jews became worse in Vienna," Rudi said.

"Yes, Joseph and Ester would be upset, too. Poland was their original homeland...wasn't it, Rudi?"

"Yes, I guess Joseph will have a comment in his next letter...we should expect one any day now."

"I hope Joseph's mother and father have settled down well in Lyon and have found decent work," said Lili.

"They'd be very proud of the contribution of Bronislaw Huberman...to the music of Palestine...he's a Polish Jew, after all," said Rudi. "They'd be interested that we attended a concert of his recently."

While circumstances for Jews in Europe were continually worsening since Hitler's accession to the chancellorship in 1933, they were now, in 1936, also about to worsen markedly in Palestine. On a day-to-day basis, people from the various ethnic groups got on well together at this time—working together and often socializing together. This was, however, about to fracture.

Jews had been arriving in Palestine from Europe in increasing numbers since 1933 and now, in 1936, numbered close to four hundred thousand. As they bought up land and settled in increasingly expanding communities, resentments of various dimensions began to develop. Some Arabs claimed that their jobs were being taken by Jews and that some neighborhoods were dominated by them. Most Jews were aware of what had become known as the Balfour Declaration. It consisted of a letter from the British Foreign Secretary, Lord Balfour, to Lord Rothschild, supporting the existence of a national home for Jews in Palestine. It read:

> *Foreign Office*
> *November 2, 1917*
> *Dear Lord Rothschild,*
> *His Majesty's Government view with favour the establishment in Palestine of a national home for the Jewish people.*
> *Yours,*
> *Arthur James Balfour*

Arabs were against this determination of the British mandate. The Arab High Committee (AHC), led by Mufti Haj Amin al-Husseini, began a protest by calling for a general strike of Arab workers and a boycott of all Jewish shops and products in support of three basic demands: the cessation of Jewish immigration, the end of all further land sales to Jews, and the establishment of an Arab national government.

"I agree that we Palestinian Arabs should be responsible for our own affairs," said Sahib, who had stopped by to catch up with Rudi and Lili, whom he hadn't seen for a while.

"What about this call for a general strike, Sahib?"

"Most of us have to continue to work...how else can we buy the kids new shoes...they seem to wear them out every few months. It's mostly the fanatics and those who want an excuse not to work who are on strike."

"The Arab attack on a Jewish bus wasn't exactly the best tactic to win demands from the Brits, either," said Rudi.

"Terrorists, Rudi, terrorists...they are the ones responsible for the many incidents of harassment, violence, sabotage, and physical attacks, including murder."

"We read reports of Arabs killing Jews and Jews killing Arabs quite often now," Lili said. "It's terrible."

"Yes...now we have sniping, ambushing of cars and buses in desolate places...the railway bombed regularly...and gang violence...also quite common," said Sahib.

"I overheard a conversation at the Appinger Restaurant the other day, when I went to see Gudrun, that the small colonies of Templers are also suffering, as their Arab workers are no longer available on the farms, in the orchards, and in their homes," said Lili before heading into the kitchen to prepare some afternoon coffee.

Rudi asked in a whisper, "Have you heard anything from the police?"

Sahib shook his head.

"Did the driver die?" asked Rudi.

Sahib shook his head again. "He's not allowed to...the fuehrer won't let—" Sahib stopped as Lili reentered the living room.

SOON IT WAS Lili's birthday—Tuesday, June 16—when Rudi was on an errand to Tel Aviv. He was looking forward to taking Lili to Hotel Appinger later that day. She was looking forward to wearing a new summer dress that she had Hanna pick out and ship from Vienna. It had arrived only a few days earlier, and she was looking forward to opening the parcel, when Rudi came home. Lili was just about to head off for her tutoring commitment. Rudi was home early and was white in the face.

"*Servus*, Rudi, I didn't expect you till after six. Weren't you to drive to Tel Aviv today?"

"Yes, I'm lucky to be here at all. A bomb exploded, destroying the car in front of me."

"*Ei yei yei*. Are you okay?"

Rudi nodded. "The two people in the car are surely dead...their car completely destroyed...went up in flames."

"Rudi, are you sure you're okay? You're as white as a ghost...where did this happen? Come sit down," said Lili, grabbing Rudi tightly by the arm.

"Near Tulkarm...just near a bend in the road and some boulders behind which terrorists could easily hide. I'll be okay, Lili. You shouldn't be late."

"Please, Rudi, don't drive south again until there is peace. Promise me."

"I promise, Lili."

"It is far more dangerous here than in Vienna, Rudi. Why are we here? Really, why?" Lili hurried to see Ilse and Annemarie.

Several hours later, Lili tried on her new dress, and she and Rudi liked the way she looked. A touch-up with the iron, and they were soon on their way to the Appinger Restaurant.

"I can't blame the Arabs," said Lili, "to have us Europeans take over so much of their land so quickly." She took Rudi's hand. "Yes, there's certainly a lot of new construction going on, and it's mainly for residences for European Jews escaping...especially from Germany. European Jewish communities are clearly encroaching on Arab neighborhoods...even Sahib seemed to resent that...didn't you get that impression, Rudi?"

"I'm not sure, but the Arabs probably feel that their very culture is being threatened. Look who's ahead of us, Lili. He's spotted us."

"There goes a quiet evening with just the two of us, Rudi."

"Oh well, what can you do? *Guten Abend,* Mr. Knopfelmacher, Mrs. Knopfelmacher. How are you both? How are Arnold and Rebecca and the twins?"

"*Guten Abend,* so nice to see you both. Yes, everybody is well. Would you care to join us?" asked Mr. Knopfelmacher as a waiter indicated a table for four. The men pulled the chairs out for their wives and sat opposite one another.

"You look nice and tanned, both of you...and all dressed up. A special evening on a Tuesday?"

"Thank you, Mrs. Knopfelmacher. Rudi was rather pale a few hours ago. I'm glad he's got his healthy color back again," said Lili. Rudi explained his experience on the road to Tel Aviv earlier in the day and was immediately rebuked by Mr. Knopfelmacher.

"*Ja,* Rudi, under no circumstances should you drive south at the moment...much too dangerous."

"He upset me so, Mr. Knopfelmacher...and on my birthday," Lili said.

"*Ja,* happy birthday, Lili! Then we better have a bottle of champagne on two counts—one to celebrate and one to help us forget Rudi's close call," said Mr. Knopfelmacher as the waiter arrived at the table.

"A bottle of Monopole?" he asked. Lili nodded, and soon there were several toasts to Lili, to the end of Arab hostilities, and to the twins, Ariella and Talia.

"It is important to get away from the girls occasionally," said Mrs. Knopfelmacher.

"No...often," said her husband quickly. "Their screeching is sometimes so loud they're a danger to one's eardrums...and to one's sanity."

"Perhaps they'll become opera singers," said Lili. The champagne had nearly disappeared when dinner was ordered.

"So what else is happening with you two, Rudi?"

"Not much, really...but we are concerned about the level of hostility throughout Palestine and especially to the south between here and Tel Aviv."

"The Arabs are really fighting fiercely," said Lili. "The oil pipeline from the Port of Haifa has been blown up quite often and trains derailed. I won't mention the danger of driving." Lili threw Rudi a look.

"I haven't noticed much difference with the shops here in Haifa," said Mrs. Knopfelmacher, "you know...with the supposed boycott."

"No, life seems relatively normal here in Haifa," said Rudi, still feeling somewhat chastened. The meals soon arrived, and the waiter poured four glasses of white wine.

"From Bordeaux," Rudi said in surprise. "It's lighter than many but should have enough body for the schnitzel."

"Let's eat before the food gets cold," said Mr. Knopfelmacher, and for the next ten minutes or so, nobody spoke. Lili and Mrs. Knopfelmacher, catching each other's eye, got the giggles at the same time.

"Eating is a very serious business for my husband...you have noticed before, *Ja?*"

"I'm ready now for further conversation. Have you had any news from Europe, Lili?"

"Not really; there's been nothing special we have heard of since the German Army remilitarized the Rhineland...haven't heard from Mother for a long time," Lili said.

"Sorry to hear that. Yes, on the seventh of March, the German military forces apparently entered the Rhineland, violating the terms of the Treaty of Versailles and the Locarno Treaties," said Mr. Knopfelmacher.

"That was the first time since the end of World War I that German troops had been in this region...terrible...just terrible," said Rudi. "They're constantly increasing military power, and the Germans seem to be loving it."

"And they appear not to see the anti-Semitism that accompanies Hitler's every move."

"*Marillenknoedel* for anyone?" invited the waiter. "They're a special today." Everybody beamed, and four servings were ordered with four coffees.

Very early to have apricots, thought Lili. *Perhaps they have been preserved.*

"We'll have four cognacs, too, please, Herr Ober." The evening ended with more cheers and clinking of glasses and a reminder to Rudi to keep off the roads as far as possible.

"We'd never let Arnold drive south...the Arabs want to blow up everything and everybody, Rudi," said Mrs. Knopfelmacher.

ON THE MORNING of Saturday, July 18, Rudi and Lili were on the beach. It was already quite warm as it had been the previous few days, and they were walking along the water's edge after a swim, holding hands. They were very happy for the moment, despite the frequent news of disturbances throughout Palestine.

"Look, Rudi, another warship coming in."

"Yes, probably to support the British to try to quell the unrest." An Arab boy leading a donkey carrying two large baskets approached.

"*Sabaahalkhayr*...good morning, mister, ma'am...would you like some apricots? Apricots very good."

"*Shukran,*" replied Rudi as he exchanged a few coins (mils) for a large paper bagful.

"*Ahamdulillah...Aafwan...ma'a salama,*" said the boy as he joyously led his donkey to a group picnicking a little further up the beach.

"There are at least six warships out there," said Lili.

"Probably for some training maneuvers," said Rudi, as he broke an apricot in half and fed a half to Lili, eating the other himself. This was repeated several times.

"If you want me to make some *Marillenknoedel,* we'd better not eat them all now," said Lili. "Perhaps just one more; let's just sit here awhile."

"Okay." They sat for quite a long time, watching the newly arrived warship having its cargo unloaded.

"Rudi, look, your feet are beginning to get burnt, and you're already very red on top of your head. Let's go home." Even late morning, it was very hot with a clear sky and a searing sun. That night, despite it still being very warm, Lili made *Marillenknoedel*, which turned out exceptionally good.

"The apricots were never as good in Vienna," she said.

"By the time we'd get them, they were never as fresh, of course," said Rudi, picking up his serviette.

Over a coffee, Rudi and Lili shared the *Palestine Post*.

"They've blown up the oil pipeline again, Rudi. A couple of days ago, they attacked the railway. Now this...when will all this end?"

"Yes, it's awful...most of the hostility occurs within a triangle formed between the towns of Nablus, Jenin, and Qalqilya. Within the triangle are bare and rugged hills, a safe haven for armed Arab gangs."

"It says they're mainly involved in sabotage of the main railway between Haifa and Tel Aviv and the main road leading from the north to Egypt. Sniper attacks against nearby agricultural workers, villagers, and vehicles are also a common occurrence."

"The British are responding very forcefully now, though, using armored vehicles on the ground supported by aircraft from the Royal Air Force (RAF). It should be much safer now, Lili."

Lili was not convinced and was somewhat nervous about Rudi driving to and from Akko each day. She became quite alarmed when Rudi told her a week or so later about an important trip he was required to take.

"Mr. Finkelstein insists that I deliver a machine part in Tel Aviv."

"He can't expect you to do that, Rudi...no, Rudi, no."

"He can't carry it on his motorbike...and anyway, he's done the trip often and says it's quite safe."

"How can it be?"

"You go in a convoy."

"What convoy?"

"Each afternoon, cars travel in convoy...from Haifa to Tel Aviv, an armored car at the front and an armored car following behind."

"And a bomb can go off in the middle of the convoy, or a sniper can shoot you from the side of the road. Oh, Rudi, no!"

"I have to go, Lili, really. I'll be away only one night."

"What?"

"I'll come back next morning with the convoy again."

"You can't go, Rudi…I'll be worried sick…frightened to death. Are you being stupid like you were in Vienna? Our running away from there has changed our life…and not for the better. It's much more dangerous here than there…you mustn't go."

Rudi did go. Lili was angry and nearly beside herself. Rudi dropped in at the hospital clinic early afternoon to report his safe return. Lili hugged him very tightly and for a long time, tears streaming down her face, Rudi was reminded how much he meant to Lili. The trip, though slow, had been uneventful. Two women in the office sympathized with Lili.

"You mustn't let him go again…only a few days ago, a bomb went off in the middle of the convoy from Tel Aviv to Haifa, killing several people…they don't even know how many…there were body parts everywhere."

The general situation did not improve for some time, and the British responded with village raids, beatings, detentions, and the demolition of houses as punishment for acts of sabotage. House demolitions were the most successful deterrent to future Arab terrorist attacks.

Finally on October 12, 1936, the Arab Higher Committee called off the general strike. Rudi read the following in the *Daily Telegraph* a couple of days later:

PALESTINE RETURNS TO NORMAL

Smiles and cheers welcome end of six months strike. In Jerusalem it was reported that it was quite pleasant, after so long an absence of these features, to be jostled by donkeys, nearly knocked over by goats, importuned by peddlers, and drenched by water sellers as one descended David Street.

Joyous Holiday Season: End of 1936–Beginning of 1937

After a morning swim a few days later, Rudi and Lili were on the beach again, watching war machinery and supplies being loaded onto a warship, the same one they had seen being unloaded months earlier. They had just left the port area, when they heard someone yelling behind them.

"Rudi, is that you? Lili?" A little startled, they spun around to see two people running straight toward them, a small, stocky man with longish, dark, wavy hair blowing about and a slender, taller woman wearing a scarf.

"Moshe, Rachel—what are you doing here?" Lili and Rudi asked. The four shared feverish embraces that left everybody winded, and Rudi and Lili's eyes nearly popped out of their heads.

"*Shalom*, my friends. Did you not get our letter?"

"No. Why are you here, Moshe?"

"I've come to join the army." Rudi burst into laughter, and Moshe did, too, as he grabbed Rudi in a bear hug.

"Actually, we're pregnant...Rachel is pregnant...three months."

"*Mabrouck! Hamdulilla*," Rudi said automatically in Arabic.

"And we're even married," said Rachel, showing off her ring.

"*Hamdulilla*. Congratulations, Rachel."

"Thank you both; he was a hard fish to hook."

"When did you arrive?"

"This morning. We just went to collect our luggage, but it won't be ready to be picked up till five o'clock. We were just heading back to the Appinger."

"The Appinger Hotel?"

"Of course, if it's no good, we can blame you, Rudi," said Moshe.

Rachel said, "You said good things about it, and if it was acceptable to you, Lili, it'll be acceptable to us."

They continued their conversation at the Appinger Restaurant over drinks.

"And how is Vienna? How was life in Leopoldstadt?"

"It had become really untenable to stay there...too many anti-Semitic incidents in the neighbourhood. And when Rachel became pregnant, we just decided that we wanted to come here," said Moshe.

"Did you get married at the temple there? How are Joseph and Ester? Are Joseph's parents doing well in Lyon? Benjamin and Rivka...how are they?" Rachel and Moshe answered these and many other questions.

"We liked the idea of having our child in the Holy Land, Lili, and Haifa has been written about as a really desirable place to live and work," Rachel said. "And we are looking for an apartment somewhere on the slopes of Mount Carmel."

"You could be neighbors of ours; we'll help you find an apartment, Rachel."

"That would be great, thank you, Lili."

"I'd know where to go if our beer ran out," said Moshe. "*Oy vey*, is everybody deaf here?" he said as a call to prayer boomed out.

"It is very loud, Lili. Do you ever get used it?"

"Sort of, Rachel. For weeks it was very annoying; now I hardly notice it anymore. Come, let's walk up the hill to see if any apartments are advertised."

Several apartments were advertised, and Moshe and Rachel said they'd knock on some doors the following day after breakfast. Three days later they had decided on an apartment, and Moshe had found a job running a carousel in the middle of the main shopping area.

The owner offered Moshe the terms. "Half the money comes to me, and half the money you keep, Moshe—a deal?"

"A deal!"

———————

A COUPLE OF weeks later, Moshe and Rachel were well settled in a one-bedroom apartment on a street running parallel to Rudi and Lili's. Rudi had borrowed Sahib's truck, and he helped Moshe transport some furniture from the market and carry it into their apartment. The first-floor apartment was very similar to Rudi and Lili's and had a small kitchen with a large wood-burning stove, a living room with the main windows overlooking Haifa, and a bedroom not large enough to swing a cat, according to Moshe.

Lili and Rudi invited Moshe and Rachel to their apartment and a couple of days later, warmly greeted them at the door.

"*Guten Abend*; how are you, Rachel? *Guten Abend*, Moshe."

"*Shalom*, my friends."

"How is your job running the carousel, Moshe?" asked Rudi, being rather curious.

"It was touch and go at the start; the kids seemed to walk right passed it at first, so I changed the music."

"How did that help, Moshe? Let me get you a drink."

"A beer please, Rudi."

"Apple juice for me," said Rachel.

"They would at least stop," said Moshe. "I'd say something nice to their mothers, and soon they'd lift their kid onto a horse or a goose or something. I'd offer the kid a sugar lolly."

"With their mother's permission, of course, Moshe…right?" asked Lili.

"Of course, and now all kids want to come. After the first week, I had them lined up, mothers vying with one another to get their kid on a horse first…for the lolly as much as the ride, I suspect."

"Hasn't it become boring, Moshe?"

"No, actually it's a lot of fun. I see kids down the street screaming their lungs off as mothers want to do some shopping. Soon the kids are quiet and running toward the merry-go-round with much excitement and pulling their mothers along…like bees to a honeypot, they come, Rudi. And the other day, a little girl had a small brown-and-white dog sit beside her in a car. They were so happy…kids and dogs are often so much better than adults."

"Does it make you any money, Moshe?" asked Rudi.

"It does now. I get half of the takings from the whirligig—a good half if you get the drift—and I've set up a little side business."

"Oh, what's that?"

"I've got my chessboard on a table under an umbrella, and I play against myself. This created some curiosity, and I already have three students."

Lili served some latkes with lightly stewed apples, followed by stuffed vegetables—peppers, aubergine, and zucchini. Their thoughts soon went to Vienna, and Lili asked about the mood of the city.

Moshe thought for a moment. "The *Gemuehtlichkeit* is still there, Lili, but it is increasingly becoming tempered by a wariness."

"Oh, how is that?"

"Quite a number of Jews have lost their jobs under Schuschnigg, and he's generally considered to be weak. In various government departments, there is a push to reduce the percentage of Jewish workers to coincide with the proportion of Jews to the entire population."

"Yes, we have friends here," said Lili. "Jewish doctors who were dismissed from their hospital jobs in Vienna. One was a well-established clinical professor."

"A steady stream of Jews…exiting now, Lili. Anyway, you and Rudi were ahead of the game. No, Vienna is not really as it was," said Rachel.

"People have also become wary since Hitler marched into the Rhineland," said Moshe. "There is greater concern now than ever before that Hitler will want to move into Austria. Unfortunately, a lot of Viennese would welcome that. If anti-Semitism doesn't affect people directly, people seem not to care or remain ignorant of its extent."

"Everything hasn't been rosy here for some time either, has it Lili?" asked Rachel.

"No, it has not...Arab riots are very troubling this year, and even students and faculty from the Hebrew University were murdered by Arabs...we recently read it in the *Palestine Post.*"

There was a lull in the conversation as everybody finished their meal, and Rudi poured three more beers. Rachel went into the bathroom.

"Is Rachel doing well?" asked Rudi quietly. "No morning sickness?"

"No, touch wood...I've been having more symptoms than Rachel. Becoming a father can be nerve-racking, Rudi."

"It would have to be very exciting, too, Moshe, huh?" said Rudi as he threw Lili a glance. Rachel reappeared, declaring she was very tired, and requested that Moshe and she go home.

"Thank you for a wonderful evening, Lili, Rudi. I'm sure we'll meet again very soon. I just need to be horizontal. *Shalom aleichem.*"

"*Alechem shalom,*" said Lili.

"*Mazel Tov,* Good night."

———

RUDI AND LILI were very happy that Moshe and Rachel were in Haifa and so close that they were nearly neighbors. They saw each other quite frequently, and Rudi played chess with Moshe several times.

One evening at Rudi and Lili's apartment, Moshe asked, "Guess what happened last week, Rudi?" Rudi shook his head. "I was closing down the carousel...it was evening...a nice evening. Three men, one of whom I'd seen before watching me play one afternoon...wanted me to play against one of them for money. I said no, but they insisted.

"'We give you ten to one,' someone said. 'Abdullah plays against you. You lose, you pay one pound; you win, you get ten.' I shook my head, but this Abdullah guy started to set up the chessboard."

"What happened, Moshe?" asked Rudi.

"Weren't you a little frightened?" asked Lili.

"A little bit, Lili...I didn't trust them—they were very big men... from Africa, I think—but then soon there were four or five others standing around, waiting for the game to begin."

"And?"

"One of the African trio put ten pounds on the table; that's a lot of money, Rudi. I put one pound on the table. Someone else took the money and said, 'I'll hold it.' Abdullah said okay; I said okay, and we played."

"Well?"

"Well, there was some grumbling at the end. Everybody left, and I walked home with my chessboard and ten pounds. Rachel was happy I was late. What more can I tell you; *shul* was good for something."

DURING THE FIRST week of November, there were several letters, including one from Joseph, happy that his parents were happy in Lyon; one from Moshe, sent more than a month earlier; two rejection letters for Rudi, who had applied for jobs in London and Switzerland; and the following one from Mr. Henning.

> *Sattendorf am Ossiachersee, Kaernten*
> *Oktober 23, 1936*
> *Lieber Rudi, Liebe Lili,*
>
> *I hope life is treating you well. Here things are quite good, too.*
>
> *I followed the Olympics very thoroughly, and it was clearly quite a spectacle; I thought of you. Hitler wanted, of course, to show off to the world. I'm afraid most people were impressed. It was, indeed, a great propaganda success for him.*
>
> *The games were run very efficiently, and the German team performed really well. There were some interesting incidents where non-Aryan athletes refused to shake Hitler's hand, or Hitler refused to shake their hand. Jesse Owens, the African-American, won four gold medals and showed his superiority over Aryan competitors. Hitler was accused of snubbing him, but Owens was reported as saying, "Hitler didn't*

snub me—it was FDR (President Roosevelt) who snubbed me." Can
you imagine, Rudi?

There were also some mysterious cases of Jews withdrawing from
their event at the last minute.

Anti-Semitism was clearly present, and I'm sure it will get worse
now that the games are over.
With very best wishes to you both,
Henning

IN RECENT MONTHS, Rudi and Lili had, on several occasions, overheard Germans speaking about the Olympics with expressions of great pride and satisfaction. There were also conversations expressing pride as Germans in Haifa spoke of the upcoming concerts of a newly formed Palestine Orchestra with nearly half its members Jewish exiles from German orchestras. Indeed, most Europeans in Palestine seemed to be following the orchestra's preparation with considerable interest... following reports in the newspapers from time to time.

One evening in November, there was a knock on Rudi and Lili's door. It was Mrs. Knopfelmacher, her husband a step behind her.

"*Guten Abend*, Lili. *Guten Abend*, Rudi."

"*Ja, Guten Abend*. What a pleasant surprise. Come in," said Lili.

"Can I get you a drink?" asked Rudi. "Please have a seat."

"Today, yes, we have very exciting news...a glass of wine would be lovely, thank you, Rudi. Would you like to come to the Palestine Orchestra with us? The Palestine Symphony Orchestra. We can get a couple of extra tickets."

Lili was instantly excited. "Rudi, did you hear? We can go to the Palestine Orchestra. Mrs. Knopfelmacher can get us tickets."

"When is it?" Rudi asked.

"New Year's Eve."

"Oh, Rudi, that's so exciting; I used to go to the New Year's Eve concerts in Vienna all the time," said Lili.

"Yes, wonderful. That would be splendid, yes, thank you," Rudi said.

"Cheers. Isn't it exciting, a wonderful orchestra here in Haifa, at our own Armon Theater?" said Mr. Knopfelmacher. "It was a huge effort over a number of years to put this together, of course."

"Yes, we read...when was it, Rudi, that Huberman gave forty-two benefit concerts in sixty days?" said Lili.

"Across the United States," added Mrs. Knopfelmacher. "And did you know, too, that he had his Stradivarius stolen at Carnegie Hall this year...in February I think it was."

"Really? That's terrible," said Rudi.

"Did you know, too, Rudi, that Huberman asked Albert Einstein to host a fundraising dinner at the Waldorf Astoria Hotel in New York, raising at least eighty thousand dollars?"

"They've really worked very hard, haven't they?"

"Rehearsals have already begun, of course, here in Palestine," said Mrs. Knopfelmacher, "under a Wilhelm Steinberg, I believe...I had not heard of him."

"It should be absolutely splendid with Toscanini conducting," said Lili excitedly.

"Thank you so very much for thinking of us. Can we pay you now?" asked Rudi.

"We'll get the tickets first, Rudi," said Mr. Knopfelmacher. "Come, Mother, I think we are on babysitting duty tonight. By the way, Rudi, did you know that just recently Mussolini and Hitler became allies...the Berlin Axis...I think they called it. Fascists in cahoots with one another... cannot lead to anything good," he said as he was encouraged to leave by his wife.

"We did read it...enough to make you sick," said Rudi.

"You know, I think I read that Toscanini has chosen a Mendelsohn piece for the program just to make a point to those anti-Semitic bastards who drove all those wonderful Jewish musicians out of Europe."

"Good for him; thank you again so much for thinking of us." Rudi and Lili were really excited and looking forward to the concert.

A BUSY TIME lay ahead. Ramadan began on Sunday, November 15 in 1936. *Poor devils,* thought Rudi. *No eating and drinking during the day, and no smoking and no sex for twenty-nine or thirty days.* Sahib came around a couple of times after work for a beer, and he always seemed to go away feeling guilty. Rudi's birthday came and went with a quiet celebration at home, and soon it was Hanukkah—starting December 9. Rudi and Lili wished Moshe and Rachel Happy Hanukkah, and a couple of days later, Rudi came home with a small Christmas tree, which he and Lili set up in a bucket of moist sand in their lounge room. They decorated it simply with silver balls and angel's hair and red candles fastened to the tree with candle clips Rudi had asked his father to send.

"It looks beautiful, Rudi, and reminds me so very much of Vienna."

"It does…you'll just have to make some *Lebkuchen* to go with it."

"I'll just cry and think of Tante Marianne." And cry she did, as a parcel of Christmas cake and biscuits, including *Zimtsterne* and *Lebkuchen,* arrived from Tante Marianne, along with a tin of *Heisse Shokolade* powder a week later. It was accompanied by a note:

Weihnachten, 1936
Liebe Lili, Lieber Rudi,
    Froehliche Weihnachten. I hope the biscuits arrived on time and are not in bits and pieces.
    I look forward to news soon that I may resume knitting for the future.
Stay well,
A tausend Bussi,
Tante Marianne

She's persistent if nothing else, thought Lili. Lili wrapped some of the biscuits and took them to Gudrun's girls, to Sahib and Amelia's children, and to Arnold and Rebecca's twins. Soon it was Christmas Eve, and all of Palestine, it seemed, was abuzz with talk of the first performances of the new Palestine Orchestra. Just several days later, on

December 31, 1936, every second person seemed to have their nose in the *Palestine Post*. An article commenced with the following sentences:

> Toscanini Comes to Jerusalem
> Ovations for Conductor and Huberman; Palestine Orchestra's Brilliant Performance
> Ancient Jerusalem came of age musically last night with the third of the Palestine Orchestra's concerts under the baton of Toscanini.

Another article reported:

> The first Palestine Symphony concert, conducted by Toscanini in Tel Aviv on December 26, 1936, is attended by 3,000, including British High Commissioner Arthur Wauchope, Chaim Weizmann, David Ben Gurion, Golda Meier, and Tel Aviv's mayor Dizengoff.

"This is just so exciting," said Lili as she turned the page, sipping her morning coffee. "Did you read that tonight's concert is completely sold out, Rudi?"

"Yes, and they are closing Anaforta Street until ten thirty. I hope Mr. and Mrs. Knopfelmacher will not be late picking us up."

They were indeed so early, Lili was still in the bathroom when they arrived.

"Look at us all dressed up, as if we were going to the Musikverein or the Wiener Opera. You look splendid, Lili," said Mrs. Knopfelmacher as they wandered downhill to their destination.

"I'm just so excited. Thank you so much for having thought of us," said Lili.

And exciting it was. The Art Deco Armon complex took on a regal air, as concert goers, all dressed up, arrived for the first performance of the Palestine Orchestra in Haifa. The Armon Theater was the center of Haifa's entertainment district, serving as a movie theatre, a performance space, and a concert hall with eighteen hundred seats. Outside and inside the theatre, the atmosphere was electric. Lili got goose bumps with excitement and hooked her arm under Rudi's as they sat beside the Knopfelmachers in excellent seats. They locked around and read the program.

PROGRAM	
Overture: *La Scala di Seta*	Gioachino Antonio Rossini (1792–1868)
Symphony no. 2 in D Major op. 73	Johannes Brahms (1833–1897)
INTERVAL	
Unfinished Symphony in B Minor	Franz Schubert (1797–1828)
Nocturne and Scherzo movements for *MidSsummer Night's Dream* op. 61	Felix Mendelssohn Bartholdy (1809–1847)
Overture: Oberon	Carl Maria von Weber (1786–1826)

The orchestra settled, and Toscanini entered. There was enthusiastic applause...seemingly endless. Toscanini turned his back; there were a few final coughs and then complete silence as the conductor raised his baton. It was indeed a splendid concert, and no one moved till Toscanini, following several curtain calls, disappeared for the final time.

The Knopfelmachers, Rudi, and Lili were still highly energized as they walked under a full moon and went into Hotel Appinger for a coffee and cake. As they sat down, they changed their minds and ordered a bottle of champagne. The place was nearly full with many concert goers with programs in hand and faces still beaming.

"That was just wonderful. Thank you so much again," said Lili as they all clinked glasses and wished each other a Happy New Year.

"I just so loved the opening with Rossini," said Mrs. Knopfelmacher.

"I loved it all," said Lili.

"And did you know that Toscanini paid for his whole involvement out of his own pocket?" said Mr. Knopfelmacher.

"Yes, and we mustn't forget that this is all thanks to Huberman, who resigned his Vienna teaching post to manage the orchestra's development over a number of years," said Mrs Knopfelmacher.

"Yes, quite something!" said Rudi. Lili was beginning to tire as the excitement began to wane.

"You can't fall asleep on me, *Schatzerl.* I have a surprise for you. I have tickets for a midnight supper and dance at the Casino Bat Galim."

"On the Promenade?"

"And we must go to Arnold and Rebecca, who are expecting us," said Mrs. Knopfelmacher.

"Happy New Year."

"Happy New Year…please pass Happy New Year wishes from us on to Arnold and Rebecca."

Lili and Rudi went arm in arm to the Casino on the Bat Galim Promenade, where there was as much excitement as in the Hotel Appinger. Rudi and Lili admired the modern structure in the Bauhaus style.

"Did you know, Lili, this promenade area was the first point of Jewish settlement in Haifa?"

"I think I have heard that, yes, and several buildings, including this one, were apparently designed by that Richard Kaufmann…a German Jew who's been in Palestine since the twenties."

"He's the person who also designed many of the buildings we like in Tel Aviv, isn't he?"

Rudi and Lili danced all night to a range of music from a Russian orchestra—waltzes, polkas, and fox-trots. The music gave way to the New Year's countdown from five down to one. Lili and Rudi fell into a mighty embrace before Lili burst into tears.

"A wonderful, wonderful night, Rudi, thank you, but we should be with your mother and father at the *Gasthof* in Villach."

Lili had now come to the realization that she'd likely never be in Europe again. In the past, she had thought that there might be a chance. Tonight, she felt certain it would never happen. That realization made her very sad, though she tried not to show it. She thought she would never completely get over the feeling of being displaced. Although she had attended a truly wonderful concert this evening and enjoyed dancing with Rudi very much, Lili felt she was a transplant. She had been transplanted onto foreign soil in the latter half of 1934. Despite having work she mostly enjoyed, a very nice apartment, and a number of very good friends now, nearly two-and-a-half years later, she still felt that she didn't really belong in Palestine.

⸺

INSTEAD OF TAKING the bus to Tante Marianne's in Annenheim, as they had done years before, they wandered arm in arm to their apartment on Mount Carmel. They were soon asleep and didn't rise until they were woken by the Zuhr call to prayer. Rudi looked at his watch. It was after midday.

"We haven't slept in like this for a long time," said Lili.

"Happy New Year, *Schatzerl*; would you like me to make a coffee?"

"Happy New Year, Rudi; a coffee would be wonderful."

After coffee Rudi and Lili took a short stroll around the neighborhood and ended up at the Lebanese restaurant.

"Salam alekum. Happy New Year. Haven't seen you for long time; you are well?" asked the owner.

"Alekum salam. Happy New Year. Yes, we are, thank you...and you?"

"Hamdulillah! I am Hamoud, and my brother is Ibrahim. Music is from Syria," said Hamoud, as he brought Lili and Rudi a menu.

"Today we have three shwarma—lamb, chicken, and beef," said Hamoud. Lili and Rudi ordered lamb.

"Lamb is very good; lots of sheep here; more sheep in Australia. Australian lamb is good, but all sheep is very dumb."

Lili and Rudi both smiled as Hamoud disappeared, and they recalled Lili calling Rudi "ein bloeder Hammel" at the very start of their being in Palestine.

"Everything good?" asked Hamoud after they had started eating. "Any questions?"

"I have a question...nothing to do with food. Is skiing in Lebanon good?" asked Rudi.

"Hamdulilla...very good...especially in the north."

"Any idea how far it is?"

"Less than one hundred and thirty miles...you know miles?'

"*Naäam...Shukran.*"

"*Afwan.*"

"Are we thinking of going, Rudi?"

"It's worth looking into; we have our skis, and I'd love to do a little skiing."

Rudi and Lili enjoyed their New Year's Day luncheon, despite Lili thinking that they'd likely never ski in Austria again, never see their parents again, and not likely visit Tante Marianne again. She did not mention these thoughts to Rudi, as she didn't want to spoil luncheon, but he knew exactly what was on her mind. He also felt saddened by the same thoughts and by the memory of the freak skiing accident that took his friend Franz's life. Rudi didn't share this with Lili, either, for the same reason Lili had kept her thoughts to herself. They bid Hamoud and Ibrahim farewell and left the restaurant in a somewhat solemn mood.

"*Ma'a salama.*" Said Rudi.

"Shall we see if Moshe and Rachel are home?" asked Lili. *It could help cheer us up*, she thought.

IT WAS MIDAFTERNOON when they knocked on their door. Rachel and Moshe were home sharing yesterday's *Palestine Post.*

"*Guten Tag*, Happy New Year. How are you both?" asked Rudi.

"*Ma'a salama.* Happy New Year to you, too…how's my Arabic, Rudi?"

"*Hamdulilla*," said Rudi. "One can learn languages really quickly here, Moshe. People really do get on so well together…I have improved my English enormously, and our Arabic is coming on quite well, too."

"I find I speak mainly English and German here," said Lili. "How are you, Rachel? You're looking well…you're really glowing."

"I can't complain; I've only had a few days…early on when I was feeling poorly."

"How would you like to join Rudi and me in the next couple of days for a day-trip to Tel Aviv?"

"That would be excellent, thank you, Lili."

THE FOLLOWING DAY at eight in the morning, Moshe and Rachel were walking down the stairs, when Rudi and Lili arrived, and they were quickly in the car heading south.

"Was the concert with Toscanini wonderful, Lili?" asked Rachel.

"It was the best day I've had in Haifa. The concert was really splendid, Rachel."

"Toscanini must be a really good *mensch* to leave his post at the New York Philharmonic for a time to conduct here in Palestine."

"A good anti-Nazi, too," said Rudi. "Wanted to shove it right up Hitler, playing a piece by Mendelssohn." Lili winced.

"I see that he's conducting another performance," said Moshe. "Unscheduled...in Jerusalem, on the fourth...an all-Beethoven program, including the *Eroica*. What's this hilly, rocky area we're coming into here, Rudi?"

"We are close to Tulkram, where a great deal of the Arab activity against the British occurred," said Rudi.

Lili said, "Against everybody, not just the British! Rudi nearly had himself blown up along this road not long ago, Rachel...insisted he drive some errand for his unthinking boss."

"Lili is right," said Rudi sheepishly. "There were many ambushes around here, people shot, railway carriages derailed, and bombs blowing up sections of road. I should have refused."

"I read an interesting account of the orchestra's performance in Tel Aviv, Lili," said Rachel. "It was apparently held in the Italian Pavilion of the Levant Fair Grounds."

"That's pretty appropriate...Toscanini...he's from Parma...conducting the very first Palestine Orchestra there in the Italian Pavilion," said Lili.

"Yes, while all the muckety-mucks were inside, open-shirted Germans, who couldn't get in, were apparently gathered in rowboats on the adjacent Yarkon River."

"Good for them; about half of the members of the orchestra are Germans...Jews, of course."

"Speaking of Jews...you realize Tel Aviv, which we'll be coming into shortly, has become a largely European Jewish city."

"Since Hitler coming to power?"

"Yes, there's been a real Jewish population explosion. The last time I was here, I noticed a great deal of new construction taking place."

"Rudi, will we be there soon? I need to go to the bathroom," said Rachel.

"I wouldn't mind stopping, too," said Lili. Rudi headed straight for the Rothschild Boulevard. Almost immediately, a respectable-looking coffee house appeared before them, and they hurried in. The men waited for the women, and all were soon seated. They agreed it was too early for lunch, so the men just had a coffee and the women a juice. Back in the car, they drove the length of Rothschild Boulevard.

"Isn't it wonderfully wide with the big strip in the middle?"

"And I love the new buildings," said Rudi.

"Yes, they're very simple in design, very modern."

"I really like the curves in the design, especially with so many balconies."

"Most buildings seem to be built of concrete, rather than stone, Rudi," said Moshe.

Rudi drove to the side, stopped the car, and spent a moment looking out the window. They drove up and down a couple of times before they turned into Allenby Street, which had a great deal of activity with throngs of people shopping. They drove around for some time and found themselves at the fairgrounds, where the huge Levant Fair had taken place just last year and where that first Palestine Orchestra performance in Tel Aviv took place just days ago.

"I love that statue," said Moshe, pointing upward.

"Yes, it's called the *Hebrew Worker*, I believe," said Rudi.

They drove around somewhat aimlessly and were heading toward Jaffa, when they came across the Lorenz Café.

"I suggest we stop here," said Rudi. "It is very good café, and I learnt quite a lot about it from a local when I was here on that trip I shouldn't have taken."

"Where are we, Rudi?" asked Lili.

"We're on Eilat Street, about halfway between Jaffa and Tel Aviv. As you can see, it's very busy. It also has a dance hall, theatre, and cinema...on the second floor, I presume."

"It seems to be of German style...well built...solid furniture..."

"Table for four?" asked a well-dressed young man as he led them to the other side of the room. It was just after one in the afternoon, and service was in full swing.

"Is it a German establishment?" asked Moshe.

"German Jews?" asked Rachel.

"No, they are Templers."

"Can I take your order now?" the waiter asked. "The specials for today are *Schweine Braten mit Kartoffeln und Gebackene Ente mit Reiss und Salat.* We also have some new beers from Munich...just in." Everybody soon placed their oder.

"The Templers are an evangelical Christian sect," said Lili.

"A Lutheran offshoot," said Rudi.

"The sect was founded in southern Germany in the mid-nineteenth century...they yearned for the Holy Land, and their intention was to prepare people for the end of days," said Lili.

"There are two colonies, one here and one in Haifa, that were established in the 1860s," continued Rudi. "They are a very industrious people, started as agricultural communities—"

"Here are your meals," announced the waiter, as strong onion and paprika aromas flooded their table.

"*Zum wohl.*"

"*L'Chaim,*" they said to each other as they clinked glasses.

"Then they ventured out—building the railway, introducing electricity, and building roads...mostly good people."

"I get our bread from their shop in Haifa," said Lili. "They are easily identified, at least as soon as they speak. They have a strong Swabian accent."

"Why good people only mostly, Rudi?" asked Rachel.

"They are very German and are very patriotic and proud of their culture...can't hold that against them...but some are Nazis."

"I didn't imagine...when we came here, there'd be any Nazis," said Rachel with some surprise. Rudi described in great detail how some identified themselves with flags from their car and how Sahib delighted in driving them off the road.

"I'd be with Sahib," said Moshe, smiling.

"You can't even drive," said Rachel.

"He's like a hunter, running down prey," said Lili. The foursome finished their meal with hot chocolate or coffee, and they were soon on the road again and heading north.

"You know, Lili, I recognize that the Lorenz Café is not Café Central and that Hotel Appinger is not Hotel Sacher, but there are a lot of European Jews here, and though there are a few Nazis...I see a lot of happiness here...people aren't fearful," Moshe said. "People are now fearful in Vienna, Lili, and it's much worse in Germany...for the Jews still there. Vienna can only get worse. Joseph wrote recently that even Mr. Schwartz can now see the dark cloud that hangs over Vienna."

"I'm much better than I was, Moshe, but it's very difficult to contemplate never to be in Vienna again. Has Rachel fallen asleep, Moshe?"

"Yes, and she's so happy we are here despite all the sand, the camels, the donkeys, and those confounded calls to prayer. We are startled every morning with the call to the *Fajr* prayer at about five o'clock. How long did it take for you to be able to sleep through those prayer calls?"

"A couple of months, at least, Moshe."

Rachel woke up as the car stopped in front of Moshe and Rachel's apartment.

As Moshe helped Rachel out of the car, he asked Rudi, "Can you give me my first driving lesson tomorrow, Rudi? You have to make me as good a driver as I will make you when we play chess."

"It's a deal. I'll come here at ten thirty. *Ma'a salama.*"

"*Shalom.* Thanks, Rudi; thanks, Lili."

"GOOD MORNING, MOSHE," said Rudi the next day as he waved up at Rachel looking down from the window.

"*Shalom*, Rudi; I'm a little nervous…I don't know whether I can do this."

"Jump in; here are the keys. Okay?"

"Not really; I can barely see over the bonnet. Don't they make cars for short arses?" Moshe adjusted his seat and turned on the engine.

"Good. You've got it in neutral to start…good…throw the clutch and put it in first…release the clutch slowly as you give it a little gas."

"Ooh shit," exclaimed Moshe as the car began to do some bunny hops.

"Slowly, slowly…throw the clutch and let it out very slowly. Just a little gas…good…relax, Moshe…now throw your clutch again and put it into second…clutch out very slowly…great. Trick is that your left and right feet have to work in sync."

"That's a lot to expect from my feet," said Moshe.

"Always very gently…great, let's turn right here."

"Where are we going?"

"This is Ha'Carmel Street. Keep it in second for a bit."

"Nice street…wide, huh? And look at all the trees. Is this the Templer Colony?"

"Yes. Drop it into third…remember both feet working in sync. Super! All nice stone houses…with red-tiled roofs."

"This colony was built under the supervision of Jakob Shumacher, wasn't it?"

"I had forgotten that. This is their community hall, and just there is the school house. Drop it back into second a minute…excellent. Look at these farmhouses with stables."

"Everything is so very orderly and clean…very nice really, Rudi."

"Shit, stop the car, Moshe…back it up a bit. Reverse is a bit difficult to get in, I know…clutch out very slowly…stop…look, a bloody swastika, Moshe."

"Nazi bastards! *A feier zoll sie treffen*…shall we rip it down?"

"No, but Sahib or one of his mates will deal with it. Let's get out of here."

"Is that the post office, Rudi?"

"Yep. Can you imagine many of these people have never been to Germany…born here…and yet some are Nazis?"

"Yes, hard to believe. Thanks for the lesson, Rudi…hope I wasn't too rough on the gears," said Moshe as he wiped his brow with his handkerchief.

"You were great, Moshe…just need a little practice."

Moshe mastered driving without too much trouble and soon bought his own car. He wanted to have it on the ready in case he had to take Rachel to the clinic in a hurry.

A COUPLE OF days later, Rudi told Sahib of the Nazi flag in the front yard of a house on Ha'Carmel Street.

"Thanks for letting me know. These Templers may have been here since the 1850s, but we Muslims have been here a couple of thousand years longer. We don't much like Brits being here or the Jews coming here now in such great numbers and putting pressure on our land, and we don't like any display of offensive flags, either."

A week passed, and there was a knock on Rudi and Lili's door about half an hour before the *Maghrib* call to prayer.

"Come in, Sahib; we're about to have a predinner beer; will you join us?"

"*Masaa el kher*, I'd love to…thank you. I have some news. The Nazi flag is no more."

"How did that happen?" asked Rudi with a knowing smile.

"A friend and I went very late one night with a couple of gallons of petrol, doused the flag and a path back to the front gate, dropped a match near the gate, and drove away. We did a U-turn at the end of Ha'Carmel Street and drove back to see our handiwork."

"I don't think I'm hearing this," said Lili.

"There were people everywhere, scurrying back and forth with buckets of water and bashing the fire with wet towels. I heard they love bonfires…well, they just got one they hadn't planned on. Thanks for the beer. *Ma'a salama.*"

———

ONE COOL, DREARY April afternoon, Rachel and Moshe were having afternoon tea with Rudi and Lili at Hotel Appinger. Quite a few other people were doing the same. It was a hot-chocolate sort of a day, and Black Forest cake was on as a special. The conversation was very comfortably about nothing in particular, when Rachel suddenly became very uncomfortable and turned red in the face.

"I think my water's just broken."

"You sure? You weren't due for a couple of weeks yet, were you?" asked Moshe.

"Don't move," said Lili. "I'll get Gudrun to bring some towels." She got up from the table and moments later returned with Gudrun, who handed Rachel a towel and dropped one at her feet.

"I'll organize a taxi to take you to the hospital," said Gudrun.

"Not the clinic, Gudrun?" asked Lili.

"No, she is better off at the hospital…I know, I know it is a German hospital, run by the Templers."

"I can't go there, Gudrun."

"Yes, you can; it's very good…people from all over—British, Jews, Arabs all go there."

"I think it's coming."

"The baby?" asked Moshe, becoming a bit flummoxed. Gudrun ran out the door and called a cab.

"Come, it will be here any minute."

"The baby?"

"No, the cab, Moshe. Don't worry. Come with me, Rachel. Take my arm. Lili, come with me. Rudi, take Moshe home to get some things for Rachel and drive him to the hospital. Don't let him drive."

"It's all in that canvas bag, Moshe," said Rachel.

"*Mazel Tov,*" said an observant stranger, as Rudi took Moshe by the arm and dragged him uphill.

"*Oy Vei,* things can happen quickly," Moshe said.

While Moshe went inside to fetch the canvas bag, Rudi went to fetch the car. "I'll see you in front of the house in a few minutes, Moshe."

They drove to the hospital, where a nurse in an all-white, starched uniform, with a round, pink face, greeted them and took the bag.

"Wait there in the waiting room," she said briskly, as she pointed down the corridor. Lili was seated. Moshe began pacing up and down. Rudi had to drag Moshe down to sit beside him. There was much hand-wringing and little talking. A second nurse came out about half an hour later.

"It will not be so quick...baby is not ready...just wait."

It was not yet dark outside, and Moshe stood up and began to march around the room again.

"Moshe, sit down. Everything will be just fine," said Rudi. They sat and sat, and time seemed to move ever so slowly.

They were close to nodding off, when the same nurse appeared. "It will not be so quick...baby is not in a hurry...just wait."

"Do you think everything is okay, Lili? I haven't done this before."

"I haven't done this, either, but I'm sure all will be fine. Have you decided on a name for the baby, Moshe?"

"Daniella or Yasmin if it's a girl, and Daniel or Jacob if it's a boy."

"What lovely names."

The nurse appeared for a third time. "It will not be so quick...just wait." It was now past midnight and eerily quiet. Lili was asleep, Rudi nearly asleep,and Moshe was wide awake.

The *Fajr* call to prayer had just commenced, everyone was now wide awake, and the nurse returned, beaming from ear to ear. "Congratulations! It's a boy...six pounds, two ounces...his mother called him Daniel...ten times already. Come with me. Where's the father? You may come with me. You two may look through the window...just wait."

Moshe gave Rachel a big kiss and bit his lower lip as he was handed his son, red in the face and all wrapped up.

"Support his neck," said the nurse. "Looks just like you, with that black hair...congratulations, Mr. Rabinowitz." Moshe soon appeared at the window to show off his progeny to Lili and Rudi.

The nurse appeared again. "Wait for Mr. Rabinowitz. He is not allowed to stay. He may visit between eight and ten in the morning and four and six in the afternoon."

Rudi and Lili drove Moshe to their apartment. "Shalom, Moshe. That's really wonderful; we are so pleased for you both," said Lili as Rudi was about to open a champagne.

"Much too early, thanks, Rudi, but a coffee would be great." said Moshe. A generous splash of cognac was added.

"He looks like me...amazing, just amazing."

"Certainly does...with that shock of hair."

Unrest Returns: 1937

DANIEL RABINOWITZ WAS just three weeks old when much of Palestine was festooned with flags and banners to commemorate the coronation of Britain's George VI. It was a dreary sort of day, a Wednesday, May 12, as Moshe and Rachel took their young son for a ride in his pram. They had just walked under a commemoration banner across Ha'Carmel Street, when Moshe and Rachel stopped, nearly in unison, to observe a number of *Hackenkreutzer* flags in people's front yards.

"*Oy Gevalt!* The chutzpah of these people," said Moshe with both disappointment and venom.

"Let's turn around and go to the Bat Galim Promenade; I don't think it'll be too windy. Why do they seem to follow wherever we go, Moshe? First we get harrassed in Leopoldstadt, and now they are here."

"I guess a huge difference is that these Germans aren't harrassing anyone...just flying their flag. They feel very nationalistic... they are now compelled to fly the Nazi flag...now the official flag of Germany, but I hear they are not against Jews...not against Arabs, either, for that matter. Jews, Arabs, Germans, and everybody else here generally work pretty well together for economic reasons. Look how Haifa is booming—that can't happen if people don't get on together."

"I was certainly treated well in the German hospital, Moshe. Look, little Daniel's smiling."

"Why is he so red in the face at the same time?"

"Well, I think he's smiling."

"He's telling us something, that's for certain, but it isn't all that well timed," said Moshe.

⟡

A COUPLE OF weeks later, a small parcel with a note inside arrived for Rudi and Lili from Austria. Lili opened it, passed the note to Rudi, and with much laughter, held up a pair of knitted baby's booties.

> *Annenheim*
> *May 1937*
> > *Lieber Rudi, A reminder for you not to forget the thirtieth.*
> > *You should tie the little booties to the mirror of your car. Maybe that*
> *will help something happen.*
> *A tausend Bussi,*
> *Tante Marianne*

"Isn't she wonderful?" said Lili.

"Yes, she really is."

It was not long before Moshe saw the little booties swinging from the mirror inside Rudi's car. "I've meant to ask for a while, Rudi. Do you and Lili not want to have children?"

"Oh, yes. As Lili says frequently…when it happens, it happens. Until quite recently, Lili hated the idea of having children anywhere except in Vienna. I think she's changing her mind. She certainly adores your little guy. We'll see."

⟡

LILI AND RUDI celebrated their third wedding anniversary and Lili's birthday quietly at home. Subsequent months were busy with work, and weekends were spent visiting friends and on day-trips to places including Nazareth, Lake Tiberias, and Jaffa. Summer evenings were often spent on the beach and wandering along the Bat Galim Promenade.

— 139 —

Rudi made friends with several Arab fishermen, who frequently wanted to chat, and he and Lili stopped to talk to them one afternoon.

"Did you know the government is thinking of restricting our fishing on the sea? I think they want to give preference to Jews," one of the fishermen said.

"That doesn't sound right...it won't stop you from fishing here, though, will it?"

"No, they'd never stop us from fishing here. Would you like some? Rudi, isn't it?"

"Yes, and you remember my wife, Lili."

"Yes, and you're a lucky man. *Masaa el kher*, madam. We've caught a few too many this evening. Here, have some...I'll give you four small whiting...very sweet...and this one here...it's a *wrasse*...a spotted *wrasse*, to be precise. Wait, I'll clean them...better the mess ouside than in your kitchen," the fisherman said as he threw a glance at Lili. Lili smiled.

"*Shukran.*"

"*Afwan, habibi.* You carry them, Rudi."

"*Shukran. Ma'a salama.*"

ON A LATE summer evening, Sahib and his wife Amelia came to have dinner with Rudi and Lili. Their four children were on a holiday with their grandparents in Egypt, a quite infrequent occurrence. Amelia wore a floral dress in midcalf length with open sandals, and Sahib wore tailored black trousers and a khaki open-necked shirt. Lili and Rudi were pleased to have them in their home.

"It's so nice to be rid of the children," said Amelia. "They are so demanding. Even when they're at school, I am constantly doing things for them—shopping, preparing food, taking their shoes to be repaired, or cleaning their room...always something."

"She misses them, though, terribly, Lili," said Sahib. "I'm glad we actually got them away."

"Yes, we nearly didn't; there was some protest against the British on the wharf."

"The Haifa Wharf? What were they protesting about?"

"You know, same old, same old," said Sahib rather dejectedly.

"They were chanting against the *Peel Report*," said Amelia, "and making their position quite clear."

"Anything new, Amelia?"

"They were just really adamant…down with the mandate, down with Balfour, down with the *Peel Report*, and down with Jewish immigration."

Just then the doorbell rang, and Mr. and Mrs. Knopfelmacher appeared. They were both formally dressed. Mrs Knopfelmacher wore a subdued gray-green Thai silk suit and a large peacock broach. Her husband wore a gray suit, an open-necked shirt, and a floral handkerchief flowing from his jacket pocket.

"I'm sorry, we didn't realize you have guests; we were just walking the neighborhood."

"No, not at all…dinner is over, and I'd really like you to meet our very good friends Sahib and his wife, Amelia. This is Dr. and Mrs. Knopfelmacher. Their children and grandchildren are here, too. They were basically driven out of Vienna. Come, sit here."

"Oh, why were you driven out of Vienna, Dr. Knopfelmacher, may I ask?" Sahib asked.

"Rudi and Lili know the story. I was dismissed from my university post for being Jewish."

"And there are many in the public service and in academia who are being dismissed now. We know of some who went to Jerusalem, and one couple went to Jaffa," said Mrs. Knopfelmacher.

"We were just then mentioning the demands of an Arab protest group at the wharf last week, including a demand to limit Jewish immigration," said Amelia.

"Yes, perfectly understandable…they have a lot to legitimately protest about." Sahib and Amelia sighed a little sigh of relief.

"The July seventh *Peel Commission Report* would be untenable to me if I had lived here all my life. The British are bullies, and their ideas are not at all acceptable. What do you think of the idea of dividing Palestine between the Arabs and the Jews, Mr. Sahib?"

Sahib seemed to hesitate, and Amelia started to explain. "I am actually a foreigner, too…I'm Egyptian, but Sahib's family has been here for as long as the pyramids have been in Egypt. I think many young Arabs don't want a foreign power to tell them what to do, Doctor. If the British did not interfere, everyone would get on well here…if not by desire, then by necessity. This is a harsh land, and we all need to coop-erate with one another to have a decent life. The idea of partition would never work…would only set one group of people against the other."

"And limiting immigration, as some are demanding, is against basic decency," said Rudi. "But there are so many of us Jews coming to Palestine, I can imagine many Arabs resenting that."

"Yes, there is some of that, but there had been no strife or even any animosity till—"said Sahib.

"The middle of the month—that's when it started again," said Amelia.

"Yes, when a high-level British official was assassinated, right?" Said Rudi.

"Yes, there's been a lot of strife since then," said Amelia.

"You know, even if the rate of immigration were greater, there's enough land here for everybody," said Sahib. "The weather is good and the ground fertile. Look how well the Germans are able to tame the land, build nice houses, have nice farms, keep animals, and even produce crops they can sell, establishing a comprehensive commu-nity. They have even developed infrastructure to the benefit of us all."

"That's the first complimentary thing I've heard you say about the Germans. You generally want to run them off the road and burn their belongings. Rudi can attest to that," said Amelia, throwing Lili a glance. Mr. and Mrs. Knopfelmacher looked at one another.

"Save that little story for later," said Sahib. "I think Arabs and Jews can learn a lot from one another. We both have rich cultures and have lived well together, most of the time, at least, for hundreds and hun-dreds of years."

"There seems to be a lot of agitation behind the scenes," said Mr. Knopfelmacher. "The mufti and the Palestinian Defence Committee seem to be agitating a lot."

"Much of the Arab world is agitating and arguing over Palestine, as far as I can see," said Sahib. "There are ongoing power plays between the Arab states and various religious groups. Iraq, Saudi Arabia, Egypt, and Transjordania are all involved…yes, Transjordania is wanting to expand its borders and is making very aggressive overtures to the rest of the Arab powers."

"Isn't Europe also trying to play broker…Italy and Mussolini with a point of view, even the Americans stating their position."

"And…of course, the Germans are against whatever the Jews are wanting."

"That seems universal—well, not universal but across Europe. That's why so many Jews have been coming here and why so many more want to come."

"We must all get on well together," said Sahib, continuing from an earlier thread. "We have no option. When Arabs boycott Jewish stores and enterprises, and Jews, in turn, refuse to buy fruits, veg-etables, and other produce from Arabs…the whole economy grinds to a halt."

"All the violence must exacerbate things, too," said Lili. "Attacks on police posts, damaging oil pipelines, and blowing up trains and roads can only make things worse."

"And very expensive to fix," added Mrs. Knopfelmacher. "But the worst is all those terrorist acts, the killings, and the British reprisals, executing young men…some of them with children."

"To change the subject, Sahib, what have you been doing to the Nazis of late?" asked Mr. Knopfelmacher.

"Well, there seem to be fewer swastikas flying in the Templer com-munity now than before."

"Oh?"

"We burned a whole lot on May twelfth."

"Coronation night?

"Yes, must have been a dozen or so. Some at about eleven o'clock and some just before *Fajr* call to prayer. Cost us a lot of petrol. I think they've got the message now."

"Oh, and before I forget, Lili," said Amelia, "I read that Edith Wharton just died recently. On the seventh of July, I believe. She was a favourite author of yours, as I remember."

"Hm...I didn't see that. She must have been in her seventies."

"Yes, seventy-five, from what I remember."

"Yes, I really enjoyed her books, especially *The House of Mirth* and *The Age of Innocence.*"

"How about another round of drinks...all this talking can make you thirsty," Rudi said, as he poured some wine and beer.

"Did you see the reports about the Exhibition of Degenerate Art recently?"asked Mr. Knopfelmacher.

"*Die Ausstellung 'Entartete Kunst,'*" Lili said, repeating his words in German.

"I saw the reports," said Amelia. "A lot of people would want to see that...far more than would likely enjoy the Great German Art Exhibition that was shown at the same time."

"I think I read that the two exhibitions were actually housed next to one another."

"Hitler did that on purpose, of course," said Mr. Knopfelmacher, "displaying the Great German Art exhibits well spaced in a nice environment...the so-called degenerate art...fundamentally modern and experimental art...exhibited in a crowded space with pictures poorly arranged on purpose."

His wife said, "The venue was specifically chosen for its narrow rooms and it being particularly dark. Many paintings were displayed without frames, and some were apparently covered with derogatory slogans."

"Can you imagine, they raided all the museums and selected the art they perceived as decadent...and depicting racial impurity, and designated it as degenerate. There were thousands of pieces confis-cated," said Mrs Knopfelmacher.

"Yes, by German artists mostly but also works from artists of other nationalities," said Rudi.

"There were some from Chagall, Kandinsky, and Paul Klee," said Mrs Knopfelmacher.

"Foreign artists' works like those of Picasso and Mondrian were also looted from various museums," said Lili. "They could, of course, feature only a fraction of the pilfered art in this Degenerate Art Exhibition."

"I'm actually not all that fond of much of the modern art myself," said Rudi. "A painting consisting of one big blob and two smaller blobs can hardly pass as mother with two children...but then nobody should have the right to confiscate works from a museum and label them as degenerate...not worthy of being shown."

"I don't like it much, either...but that's actually the best adver-tisement for these pieces...to be on the list of confiscated art,' said Amelia. "That's why ove, a million people have seen the Degenerate Art Exhibition in the first six weeks, according to the paper."

"These exhibitions are running in Munich, aren't they?" asked Sahib.

"Yes, in Munich...*Entartete Kunst* opened on the nineteenth of May, and it is scheduled to end on the thirteenth of November," said Mrs. Knopfelmacher a second time.

"We could organize a tour to Munich perhaps...for all the Nazis in Haifa," said Sahib lightheartedly as he stood and looked at his wife, suggesting it was time for them to leave. The Knopfelmachers also had similar intentions, and soon Rudi and Lili were alone with some dishes to do and the need to get some sleep before the following day of work.

A COUPLE OF weekends later, Rudi and Lili arranged to go for a walk with Moshe, Rachel, and Daniel in his pram. It being rather hot and uncomfortable in full sun, they decided to stroll down Ha'Carmel Street, which was well treed, generally very pleasant, and provided some shade. It was quiet this late morning, and they were all engrossed in conversation, barely noticing the little activity that there was. A woman in an apron was raking up leaves in a front garden, a group of children was having a water fight in another, and a man on a small donkey rode past and said *Guten Morgen*. Suddenly from down the street they heard an orchestra playing, at first quite faintly and then becoming louder as they got nearer.

"Templers are playing in their community hall," said Rudi.

"They play very well, don't they, Lili?" said Rachel.

"They do sound very good," said Lili. "They are playing some Beethoven, but I can't quite recognize the exact piece."

Daniel became restless, so Rachel took him out of his pram and held him to her chest. "I think he's a little hot…I'll take off his booties and cardigan. Here, can you put them in the bag?" she asked, while handing the items to Moshe. "Do I hear a choir now? They sound very good, too…sounds like children."

Several musicians with instruments in hand came from the hall where they had earlier been playing and passed by.

"*Guten Morgen*," they said as they walked passed and smiled. "*Unser Kinder und Jugendchor*," (our children and youth choir), one of them said. "Listen to what they're singing," said Rudi.

"It's a march," said Moshe, becoming a little agitated.

"Are you all right, Moshe? You look pale."

"It has the same beat of Nazis singing when we were on the way to synagogue, remember, Rachel?" They listened to hear the lyrics.

Ich hatt einen Kameraden,
Einen bessern findst du nicht.
Die Trommel schlug zum Streite,
Er ging an meiner Seite
In gleichem Schritt und Tritt.
In gleichem Schritt und Tritt.
Eine Kugel kam geflogen

Gilt es mir oder gilt es dir?
Sie hat ihn weggerissen,
Er liegt zu meinen Füßen
Als wär's ein Stück von mir.
Als wär's ein Stück von mir.

(I once had a comrade,
You will find no better.
The drum sounded for battle,
He walked at my side,
In the same pace and step.
A bullet came flying toward us,
Is it meant for me or you?
It tore (swept) him away,
He now lays at my feet,
As if he was a part of me.)

"Germans love their marches and war songs," said Rudi, as the next song commenced.

"At least this one sounds more joyous," said Rachel, as they again listened to the lyrics.

Wenn die Soldaten
Durch die Stadt Marschieren,
Öffnen die Mädchen/Fenster und die Türen.
Ei warum?
Ei darum!
Ei warum?
Ei darum!
Ei bloß wegen dem
Schingderassa,
Bumderassasa!
Ei bloß wegen dem
Schingderassa,
Bumderassasa!

(When the soldiers march through the city
the young ladies open their windows and doors.)

"They do sing very well," said Moshe, "but I'd like us to move on before they sing 'Deutschland Uber Alles.' I think that would really unsettle me." Just then, several more musicians who had been listening to the choir walked out as two men walked toward them.

"*Heil* Hitler," they greeted each other, as they each thrust an arm out in front of them.

"Shit, Rudi, did you see that?" asked Moshe. Lili and Rachel both noticed, too, and were dumb struck, only able to cover their mouths with their hands.

"Yes, enough to make you vomit," said Rudi. "I haven't seen that before."

"I'd never have expected Nazis greeting one another like that in Haifa," said Lili.

"Please, let's turn around," said Rachel, and everybody turned around to walk in the opposite direction, Lili quickly taking Rudi's hand.

"I've never once seen that in Vienna," she said.

"Nor have we personally in Leopoldstadt, have we, Moshe? Though we know friends who have," said Rachel.

"Let's stop at Appinger Hotel to wash the bad taste away," said Moshe.

One drink led to another, and that led to lunch. On their way out, Gudrun was at the reception desk. "Hello, how are you? So nice to see you all. You should listen to the news tonight. Some high-level British officer has been assassinated, and violence is expected."

"There's always something to get in the way of a peaceful life," said Lili.

THE NEWS WAS soon read and heard all over Palestine: "On September 26, the British district commissioner for the Galilee, Lewis Yelland Andrews, was assassinated in Nazareth by a gang of armed Arabs. Britain responded by outlawing the Arab Higher Committee." This news was accompanied by various reports of Arabs being killed, Arabs engaged in reprisal killings of Jews, and sporadic violence—arson, theft, and bombings for instance, becoming widespread.

In early October, Rudi and Lili visited Sahib and Amelia to see if they could help them understand what was happening.

"Yes, it's all unfortunate…everything has gone downhill since the publishing of the *Peel Commission Report* in July," said Sahib.

"Is that because of the recommendation to partition Palestine into separate Jewish and Arab states?" asked Lili.

"Yes, we Arabs couldn't possibly accept any of our land being designated for the exclusive use by Jews…there is no sense in that for us. We've been sharing for a long time. Arabs and Jews have cooperated with one another in this harsh land for thousands of years, and I think most Arabs understand that there will be many more Jews coming here to escape the persecution in Europe…but partition—no bloody way.'

"What is this with the British authorities banning all nationalist political organizations?" asked Lili.

"The Brits are all too heavy handed as usual…they want to ensure control, exert their power."

"They even deported some of the leaders of the Arab Higher Committee, didn't they?" asked Amelia.

"Who's this Naj al-Suwaydi?" asked Rudi.

"He's the leader of the Palestinian Defence Committee, and the Brits see him as a thorn in their side, I think. If the Brits just left us alone, we'd work things out…you know my view."

"There are some pretty heavy rivalries among Arabs as well, aren't there?" asked Amelia.

"Yes. There've been rival clans in Palestine…in all Arab lands, for that matter, for a very long time, and that has never helped in showing a united front against non-Arabs. Even with the existence of clans… Arabs, Christians, Muslims, and Jews have lived quite well together for a long time…a very long time. The coming of the British has unfortunately changed this. The Germans aren't endearing themselves to anybody, either, at present." Said Sahib.

"Is that because of some Nazi activity?"

"Yes, I personally hate flag-waving, and foreigners waving flags on our land makes me more than unhappy. And there've been increasing reports of Arab agricultural workers being exploited and Jewish businesses being boycotted by some of them. The Germans make good bread, mediocre wine...and, more recently, lousy neighbours," said Sahib.

"Did Rudi tell you about the Nazis saluting one another we saw recently?" asked Lili.

"Yes, he did; it sent shivers down your spine, he said...time another one of those bastards was driven into a ditch. They should learn to know where they are...there is no place here for any offshoot of the Third Reich." Said Sahib.

IN THE MEANTIME, the sphere of influence of the Third Reich was clearly strengthening in Vienna, there being vague rumblings of Hitler pressuring Schuschnigg to agree to the annexation of Austria. Meanwhile, Jews were continuing to be sacked from their professional positions as doctors, lawyers, teachers, and librarians. Jews were fleeing their beloved cities, seeking refuge in Palestine, New York, Paris, and London, and even leaving for distant lands such as South Africa, Australia, and Argentina.

Mr. and Mrs. Knopfelmacher provided some evidence. "We have several more friends who have left Vienna," they said.

"Were they relations of yours?" asked Lili.

"N,, but longtime acquaintances...Mr. Rosenblatt lost his job as a dentist, so he and his family were headed to London, confident he'd find employment quickly...that was the last we heard of them," said Mr. Knopfelmacher.

"What about the Tannenbaums?" asked his wife.

"They were good family friends...he was a lawyer who found that some of his long-term clients would no longer work with him, and he was planning to come to Palestine or go to New York."

A letter dated November 3 arrived from Mr. Schwartz in Vienna that also provided a particular example of anti-Semitism. In it he wrote:

Recently three colleagues of mine have been barred from government con-
tracts they had had for many years. I am sure it is because of their names—
Brezwakowski, Jagonowitz, and Szulkovskaya. They all originally came
from Poland. They and their families are perplexed and distraught and do
not know what to do. They are reluctant to leave behind their well-estab-
lished homes and tear their children away from their schools and friends.

We have also noticed an increased incidence of signs saying
Juedishes Geschaeft appearing on doors of Jewish businesses.

Many Jews are now becoming a little edgy here in Vienna, and
some colleagues have emigrated to America and some to Palestine.

Rudi passed the letter back to Lili. "Perhaps he's finally seeing the light, Lili."

"Yes, as you predicted years ago, Jews in the first district would keep their heads in the sand till anti-Semitic acts occurred so close to them, they couldn't ignore them any longer."

SOON RUDI'S BIRTHDAY had come and gone, and it was the Christmas season. A beautifully decorated tree took pride of place in the living room, and many letters and cards were sent and received. Rudi and Lili exchanged moderate gifts, mainly of clothes they needed, and Lili baked Christmas biscuits for nearly a whole weekend.

"Will you roll out this dough, please, Rudi? My arms are getting tired."

"Sure."

"Would you now beat the egg whites for the meringues, please?"

"Tell me when you need more wood on the stove, Lili, and I'll—"
Just then there was a knock on the door.

"*Servus*, Moshe, what a nice surprise," Rudi said.

"*Shalom*, Rudi. *Shalom*, Lili," he said as he came into the kitchen with his son sitting on his shoulders. "I was just taking Daniel for a walk to give Rachel a break."

"*Servus*, Daniel," said Rudi, as he took his little right hand. "He's got a strong grip," he said." Daniel began to wave a chess piece about with his other hand.

"He took a liking to the king, and if I try to offer him the queen or a knight, he just throws them away."

"It looks as if he's teething."

"Yes, he's constantly chewing the king's ear...not sure what message he's sending...perhaps it's to tell him that the Brits are not really welcomed here in Palestine any longer." Moshe sat his son on the floor and held his free hand. Lili and Daniel exchanged smiles, as Lili continued kneeding, rolling, and creating biscuits, which were now beginning to come out of the oven and spreading appetizing aromas.

"Perhaps you should submit them to some quality control," said Moshe with a twinkle in his eye.

Lili smiled. "Rudi, you could put on a coffee, and we could heed Moshe's suggestion," she said. Moshe also took some biscuits home for Rachel.

"Remind Rachel of our luncheon with Mrs. Knopfelmacher and Rebecca next week, please, Moshe...thanks," sadi Lili.

Lili later packed small boxes of biscuits they took to friends they visited to wish them a Merry Christmas and a Happy New Year.

—•—

As HAD BEEN planned for some time, four women arrived, all wthin minutes of one another, at the Appinger Restaurant for a New Year's celebration. They were all elegantly dressed and in good spirits.

"Anyone would think we were going to the opera or something," said Mrs. Knopfelmacher, as the four greeted each other with hugs and kisses. "Motherhood obviously agrees with you, Rachel...you look splendid."

"Thank you...it's so much work. I don't know how you cope with twins, Rebecca."

"Thank God for grandparents; that's all I can say," Rebecca said as she cast a smile toward her mother-in-law.

"Are we going in for a drink, or what?" asked Lili.

"Let's go," said Mrs. Knopfelmacher, as she extended her arms around the three others like a mother hen ushering her brood beneath her wings. "This table over here, please…may we?" she asked the waiter.

"Of course. I'll get you your menus," the waiter said.

"Thank you. You can also get us a bottle of Monopole to help us." The waiter came with the champagne and carefully popped the cork while the ladies settled in their seats.

"Prost."

"*L'chaim.*"

"Chin-chin."

"Prost…to us," said Mrs. Knopfelmacher as glasses klinked all around. Perhaps today…the Appinger can be our Demel."

"Here's to Café Demel and to Vienna," said Lili.

When glasses were nearly depleted, the waiter gained the womens' attention. "Today we have two specials—"

"Please give us five minutes; we are not ready for the specials yet," said Mrs. Knopfelmacher. "How is Moshe enjoying his work, Rachel?"

"He's been extremely busy over the holiday period, of course, and he comes home too tired to be homesick for Vienna these days."

"Oh?"

"He was terribly homesick over Hanukkah…desperately wanted for Daniel to be in Vienna for this time."

"Does he generally miss Vienna a lot, Rachel?"

"Yes, he does, and I do, too…more than I thought I would…I miss all the people I worked with, and I miss our neighbourhood with the cafés we'd spend time at," said Rachel, as tears began to well up.

"Another bottle of Monopole, please, waiter," said Mrs. Knopfelmacher, as she touched Rachel on the shoulder. The waiter quietly refilled glasses.

"We have two specials today, ladies—Wiener schnitzel and *Kaiserschmarrn.* I'll be back in a few moments to take your orders."

Rebecca turned instantly red in the face. "If I have to eat one more Wiener schnitzel with Father in the next month, I'll be sick…that's all he wants to eat…Wiener schnitzel and damned *Kaiserschmarrn*…damn the kaiser."

"You know, Rebecca," said her mother-in-law, "it is the only way Father can cope with being away from Vienna. Wiener schnitzel and *Kaiserschmarrn* represent the essence of Vienna to him. He is a very proud man...and he doesn't want to show it...but he misses Vienna terribly...he is embarrassed about how he lost his job, and he hates it here with all the heat, flies, and animal droppings...as he reminds me frequently. He likes our apartment, but it is not like the one we had in Vienna. He can cope because of his family."

"Because of us?" asked Rebecca.

"Yes," Mrs. Knopfelmacher said, her voice quivering. "He is very proud of you and Arnold, and he loves...adores, absolutely adores his grandchildren...Wiener schnitzel to him is like a blankie to a child, a security blanket, something never to let go. And after dinner each night, he listens only to Strauss. Don't get me wrong, I like Strauss, but the same tunes each night—diddly dum, diddly dum, diddly dum, dum, dum—it's enough to drive you mad...literally. I'm even beginning to dream in three-quarter time." This brought a smile to everybody's face, and there was a spontaneous clinking of glasses all around.

"I'd be pretty depressed here, too, if I didn't have Ariella and Talia to keep me as busy as they do. I often feel very homesick, especially lying in bed at night while Arnold is asleep. I feel like a foreign object here," said Rebecca.

"I do, too," said Lili.

"The streets are still unfamiliar," said Rebecca. "The shops aren't where they're supposed to be, and especially around this time of year, I miss the snow and the smell of *Lebkuchen* and chestnuts. I even miss the toll of the *Stephansdom* bells." The waiter arrived at the table again without a word and topped up the glasses. He paused.

"Can we have a platter of assorted tea sandwiches for now, please?" asked Mrs. Knopfelmacher.

"Just like in Demel," said Lili. "It's Demel and other cafés I miss most and the music and gardens, of course...I have been transplanted...didn't have any say, really...it all happened so quickly... can't seem to take root here."

"I'm with Lili," said Mrs. Knopfelmacher, putting a hand on hers. "It's the whole culture of Vienna we miss…we've talked about it before. It's not as if anyone of us left without good reason."

"If it weren't for the rise of the Nazis in Vienna, we'd all still be there," said Rachel.

"Yes, we've all been uprooted…displaced from our homeland…we are all exiles," said Lili.

"Now, we mustn't get too maudlin at this time…here's cheers to good friendships in Haifa," said Mrs. Knopfelmacher, forcing a smile as glasses were again clinked. A platter of delightful tea sandwiches arrived at the table.

"You realize, Lili, you're the only one among us who's not a mother," said Rachel, emboldened by the champagne, "and you're older than Rebecca and me."

While Lili expected this topic to come up, it still caught her by surprise, and she nearly choked on a sandwich. She took a sip of water and made a little cough so as to clear her throat.

"Rudi is so good with children," said Rebecca.

"Daniel loves him, too," said Rachel.

Lili could feel three ladies looking directly at her. "That's good… Rudi can practice with your children before we have our own."

"That's an idea," said Mrs. Knopfelmacher with a smile and in support.

"We really wanted to start a family in Europe, of course," Lili said, "but we now realize that we won't likely get to Europe any time soon… so whenever it happens, it happens."

"Here's to Lili becoming a mother," said Rachel, becoming increasingly tipsy and pushing Lili a little on the arm. She raised her glass to offer another toast.

"To Lili." The tea sandwiches were all delicious and were soon depleted.

"I think I'll just have a piece of *Sachertorte* now," said Lili.

"I'll have the same and a hot chocolate," said Mrs. Knopfelmacher.

"I'll have the same, too," said Rebecca.

"Not even any *Kaiserschmarrn*, ladies?"

"No, thank you, I'll just have a piece of *Guggelhupf*, please, and a coffee," said Rachel. The waiter left the table, shaking his head, and everybody was pleased that there'd be no Wiener schnitzel or *Kaiserschmarrn* served at this table for now. There was some discussion about friends and acquaintenances who were still in Vienna, and hope was expressed that nothing untoward would happen to them.

"At least there was no political talk today...what a pleasure!"

"Yes, we'll have to do this again soon. Can be so much more fun without the men!" Everyone was in good cheer, and each one soon went their separate way.

A couple of weeks later, a letter came from Walter, and it took Rudi and Lili quite by surprise.

> *Paris*
> *January 1938*
> *Liebe Lili und Lieber Rudi,*
>
> *I am beginning to think that being in Europe is no longer a very good idea. Nazi encroachment in Vienna makes it highly unlikely that we will be able to return there with any feeling of security, and I fear ill winds from Germany may affect much of Europe sooner than we may think. Some acquaintenances from Vienna have lost their jobs, and some have already left. Some have even been arrested and carted off to concentration camps.*
>
> *I am thinking that I would like to emigrate to Australia or New Zealand to live. I hear that life is very peaceful there and is beginning to have the niceties that we have become used to in Europe.*
>
> *Let me know what you think.*
> *Alles Liebe,*
> *Walter*

Lili, with a slight nod of the head, passed the letter to Rudi and waited for a response.

"I think that would be a good move to contemplate for us, too, Lili."

"To join all those other *bloede Hammel*," she said with a smile. "I'd rather go to New York, which has a rich cultural scene like Vienna. They have excellent concerts there, and you can even get some *Gugglehupf* or *Krapfen* for breakfast."

"It would certainly be nice to explore another part of the world while we are—"

"Young...I know, I know, and you've got itchy feet."

"Perhaps we could at least do a little skiing this winter, *Schatzerl*."

"COME LOOK AT the map, Lili. It would be quite simple. We just take the road through Akko to Tyre, Sidon, and Beirut and head inland to Aley."

"How long do you think it will take, Rudi?"

"It can't be more than one hundred and thirty miles...just over two hundred kilometers. If we leave relatively early in the morning, we should be there in plenty of time to get above the snow line and find a bed for a night or two."

They tied the skis on a roof rack they borrowed from Sahib and set off while it was still dark one morning early in February. The sky was cloudless and the roads clear as they left Haifa and headed north.

"It'll feel strange to be on skis after so long, Rudi."

"Yes, I'm curious as to how well we'll manage." They had lunch in the car by the side of the road, overlooking the Mediterranean somewhere north of Sidon. Just short of reaching Beirut, they saw a sign, Skiing—Snow Chains for Hire, with an arrow pointing to the right. They drove for a good twenty minutes along a seldom-traveled and bumpy road. The car was beginning to skid a little due to snow, and Lili began to grimace.

"Any idea...oh good, there's a house ahead." They pulled up beside a sign saying Snow Chains just as a man came to greet them.

"*Bonjour*, madam. *Bonjour, monsieur.* The snow is very good. Do you wish to hire some chains?"

"*Oui, monsieur,* for tomorrow. Do you have accommodation available here, too, by chance?

"Ah, *oui.* Do you wish to have a look? My name is Simon Beauvrais. I would like you to meet my wife, Mathilde."

"I'm Rudi, and this is my wife, Lili; pleased to meet you."

"*Entrez.* Do come in." They were led to a small but comfortable room with two single beds and an outlook over trees. "The bathroom is here. If you wish to stay, breakfast, lunch, and dinner are included. We provide you some nice sandwiches for you for lunch." Rudi and Lili agreed.

"Come into the kitchen when you have unpacked. You can leave your skis on the car or bring them in...whatever you wish." Soon they were sitting in the kitchen, which reminded them of Tante Marianne's home, and a hot, spiced wine was put in front of them.

"Just wine with cinnamon and cloves. *À votre santé.*" Rudi and Lili nodded approvingly, recognizing the familiar winter *Gluehwein*.

"Prost."

"Chin, chin...tonight we have *coq au vin.* Saturday we always have *boeuf bourguignon,* and Sunday—*pot au feu* to make use of what's left over from the previous two nights," said Mathilde.

"Often the most delicious," said Simon. "We came here after the First World War with the French army and have never left. We run this small operation here in winter and a beach café in the summer."

Rudi and Lili enjoyed their meal and a little too much wine and found themselves under the duvet before eleven o'clock.

Home-baked bread and a good coffee greeted them for breakfast, and before long they were putting on car chains. Rudi, not having done this before, had Simon give a hand, and he cautioned them to drive slowly. Twenty minutes of climbing to the sound of the clattering chains found them facing a barrier and two other abandoned cars. Footprints guided them uphill, and they were both soon sweating.

"Are you okay carrying your skis, Lili?" Lili nodded with little conviction. They took off a layer of clothing each, had a few sips of water from a flask, and continued their ascent. At first there were quite tall trees—mostly cedars—but these soon became sparser and shorter, revealing a partly sunny sky. Some crows were squawking above as if to welcome them to the mountain.

"Any idea how far we're going, Rudi?"

"Haven't got a clue…till we get to the top or we fall over…whichever comes first." Lili made a bit of a face and trudged on a couple of meters behind. Rudi began to hum rhythmically in step, with his feet focused on making steady progress.

"I've never appreciated a *Kanzelbahn* as much as I do right now," said Lili.

"*Mit Geduld und Spucke.*"

"I know, I know…*faengt man eine Mucke* (With some patience and spit, you can catch a fly)." Rudi took Lili's skis and with both pairs crisscrossed over his shoulders, took care to stomp even steps in the snow to make it as easy as possible for her. After about an hour, they stopped for a breather and gazed west.

"The Mediterranean—what a great view," said Lili, puffing like a steam engine.

"I've never actually seen the sea from halfway up a mountain," said Rudi.

"Hope we're further than halfway, Rudi," said Lili, emphasizing the *half.* She soon fell in behind Rudi again, following the steps in front of her. They trudged on, hoping that the furthest point they could see would be the top. Lili wished she were on the Gerlitzen and would be able to have dinner this evening with Tante Marianne. She did appreciate Rudi carrying her skis and making nice steps for her to follow. She was also very pleased that Rudi was so happy here in the mountains. *But such a long trek really can become boring,* she thought. They were to be disappointed several more times before they finally reached the top of the Mount Lebanon ridge. Rudi stuck both pairs of skis in the snow and gave Lili a gentle hug. Arms around each other, they gazed seaward to observe a splendid view. It was quite cold with a slight breeze, and the sky somewhat overcast now, but the view to the Mediteranean was quite clear.

"For this, it's all worth it," said Rudi, quite red in the face and peering out toward the sea. "Shall we have lunch up here or a little further down out of the wind?"

"Let's ski a little…I want to see what I can remember…it's been so long." Lili skied a few tentative turns with Rudi close behind.

"It's not so easy, Rudi…the skis stick."

"Wet snow…I guess because we're so close to the sea. I'll put on some *Klister* (wax) after lunch, and that should help."

Lunch was excellent, complements of Mathilde, and the wax helped the skis glide. Rudi led down the untracked snow, and they soon fell into a comfortable rhythm. Rudi instinctively began to hum. They stopped quite a few times, and Lili took the lead on some gentler slopes. They both began to enjoy their skiing, as they had remembered it from years past. They reached the car park, and Rudi looked at his watch.

"It took just under two hours up and about twenty minutes down. Should we do it again?"

"Let's see how far we get." After half an hour or so, Lili was finding the uphill going rather tough.

"Let's see if we do better with skins," said Rudi, taking off his rucksack. He tied on the sealskin strips to the skis, and they were again soon headed uphill, Rudi's shoulders appreciating the change in climbing technique. It was easier going, not sinking into the snow shin-deep with every step. They sidestepped some of the way and herringboned on less steep inclines. They made headway more easily than before and enjoyed their second run, again with a thorough application of *Klister*. They were enjoying skiing between the cedars in a narrow valley, when the presence of an animal surprised them.

"What was that?" asked Lili as she unsteadily slid to a stop.

"Some sort of cat…yes, a wildcat…see it disappearing there to the right," said Rudi.

"I don't like cats,"said Lili. "I can only think of that green-eyed black cat meowing in the cargo hold."

They pointed their skiis downhill again and soon reached their car. With skins removed, skis tied on top, and the pack in the back, they were heading down the mountain and were soon cheerily greeted.

"*Bonjour. Ça va*, Rudi? *Ça va*, Lili? Did you have a good time?"

"*Magnifique…parfait*," said Lili, as she nearly fell out of the car. "Oops, I'm so sore."

Simon smiled. "Leave your skis on top; there's no snow expected overnight. Come join us in the kitchen whenever you are ready."

———

"I NEVER KNEW skiing could be so splendid here in Lebanon," said Lili as she grimaced and delicately inched her aching body across the bench. "And we saw a large cat cross our path."

"Yes, there are quite a few wild animals in these mountains. We see goats, bears, and foxes from time to time."

"I'm just so sore," said Lili again as she moved in her seat.

"Then you must have skied hard…perhaps this will help." A *Gluehwein* was thrust in front of her. "I am so pleased you enjoyed today. You know, people have been skiing in Lebanon since the twenties. It was introduced here in 1913 when Ramez Ghazzoui, a Lebanese engineer, returned from studies in Switzerland and introduced his friends to the sport. In 1934, *Le Club Libanais* was the first ski club to be formed in Lebanon. The following year, I think it was, the French army established the first ski school at *Le Grand Cèdre Hôtel* at the Cedars in the north of the country…about two hours from here. Just last year they moved the school higher up the mountain."

There were several newspapers on the bench, and when there was a lull in the conversation, Rudi asked if he could have a peek.

"Rudi finds it impossible to be without a newspaper for even one day," said Lili. Rudi smiled and leafed through several papers while still participating in the discussion.

"Oh, Lili, the French composer Ravel died."

"He couldn't have been that old. What a shame."

"He died on the twenty-eighth of December in Paris. He was just sixty-two."

"He wrote 'Boléro,' didn't he?" asked Mathilde, just as she took the lid off the *boeuf bourguignon*.

"I really like Ravel's arrangement of Mussorgsky's piano suite, 'Pictures at an Exhibition.' It's one of my favourite pieces of music, I think," said Lili.

"I like both Claude Debussy and Ravel's music...wonderful influence on impressionist music." There was a slight pause in conversation.

"With such splendid aromas, we must be ready to eat, Mathilde," said her husband. Dinner was excellent and the wine again plentiful.

SUNDAY'S SKIING, AGAIN under a cloudy sky, was as good as that of the previous day with the help of the sealskins and the *Klister* wax. They stopped for lunch not far from where they had seen the wildcat on the previous day. They enjoyed meatloaf sandwiches prepared by Mathilde, and Lili could only think of the lunches Tante Marianne made for her and Rudi to enjoy on the Gerlitzen. Lili missed Tante Marianne a great deal but didn't let on. She was at this time, after two full days of skiing, so sore she could barely make it out of the car and to their room. The next day they would drive home, again stopping to have lunch at a café overlooking the Mediterranean.

"What a wonderful few days, thank you, Rudi." Rudi just smiled a contented smile, concurring with Lili's sentiments. When they arrived home, they took their packs inside, leaving their skis on top of the car till the morning. Rudi pushed Lili upstairs, and they both fell into bed exhausted. They were both off to work the next day.

THEIR DAILY LIVES were now pretty settled, despite Rudi applying for jobs in England and Switzerland due as much to a general wanderlust as to wanting higher-paid work. Lili had virtually resigned herself not to be living again in Vienna in the foreseeable future. Collecting stamps, watching an occasional film, and visiting friends kept her relatively content. Communication with her mother and Walter was sporadic and infrequent, though letters were regularly exchanged with Rudi's father and Tante Marianne.

THE STORM FROM THE
NORTHWEST MAKES
LANDFALL: 1938

WALKING HOME ONE evening after visiting with Sahib and Amelia, Rudi and Lili were in very good spirits. They really enjoyed the children as well as Sahib and his wife. They were quietly heading uphill, when they noticed an unusual number of people huddled around a radio. Stern-faced individuals were craning their necks to hear, while someone was fiddling with a wire to an antenna to try to improve the quality of the audio. A father implored his children to be quiet. There was a precise statement.

"We announce this evening, on Friday the eleventh of March 1938, that Schuschnigg resigned as the chancellor of Austria."

"What was that?" someone asked.

"Quiet."

"We repeat—Schuschnigg has today capitulated to Hitler's demands. Seyss-Inquart has been appointed chancellor."

"Who is Seyss-Inquart?" someone with a Viennese accent asked.

"Arthur Seyss-Inquart is a Nazi. He's been minister of public security for a month or so."

"Why didn't we know that?'

"*Meine Guete*," said Lili. "What'll happen now?"

"It will only be a matter of time," said Rudi.

"What will only be a matter of time?"

"Hitler will claim Austria...he will annex Austria. The Anschluss will be complete. Austria will no longer exist."

Lili began to sob; so did the other woman with the Viennese accent. Her husband put his arm around her and tried to comfort her. Rudi was fixated on the news. Lili would have liked Rudi to comfort her, too; she was feeling very worried...after all, this was happening in her Vienna.

"Why are you women so bloody sentimental?" said a voice from beside the radio. "It will be good for Austria."

"Who are you?"

"I am Hans, and I have been praying for this for a long time. I, too, am Austrian, and this will be good for our economy."

"Who is that idiot?" someone asked.

"Oh, Rudi, what will happen to Mother...your parents...Tante Marianne?" asked Lili, still sobbing. As Rudi and Lili walked away from the sounds of the radio, another sound could be heard from a distance...the sounds of celebration in the form of songs from the *Gemeindehalle* (community hall) of the Templer society.

> *Deutschland, Deutschland über alles, Über alles in der Welt,*
> *Wenn es stets zu Schutz und Trutze, Brüderlich zusammenhält.*

(Germany, Germany above all, Above everything in the world, When always, for protection, We stand together as brothers.)

As they got nearer their apartment, both rather drained from the news, Rudi put his arm around Lili and quietly began to sing, "*Wenn der liebe Flieder wieder blueht.*" -when the lilac blooms again. Lili nestled her wet face on his shoulder as he took out the keys to the front door. Rudi and Lili slept little that night. Lili had terrible dreams of guilt about having abandoned her mother and wondered whether Walter would help her during what would clearly be difficult times ahead.

Newspaper reports, over the next few days, were full of varied explanations and contradictory reports but were generally quite neutral.

"Apparently what happened," said Rudi, explaining events to Moshe and Rachel, who dropped in on Rudi and Lili the following weekend, "was that Schuschnigg lost support of his own cabinet."

"Yes, you always said he was weak," said Moshe.

"Here, read this," said Rudi as he handed a newspaper to Moshe.

"We've read it, too. I'd like you to tell us what the report was over the radio. You heard it, right?"

"On March ninth Schuschnigg called a referendum for an independent Christian Austria...to better his chances at winning the plebiscite... he had the minimum voting age increased to twenty-four in order to exclude younger voters, who he thought largely sympathized with the Nazis."

"That seems to be going a bit far," said Rachel.

"Anyway, Hitler called the referendum a fraud. Goebbels apparently issued false press reports that riots had broken out in Austrian towns and that large parts of the Austrian population were calling for German troops to restore order...an ultimatum was sent by Hitler demanding that Schuschnigg hand over all power to the Austrian National Socialists or face an invasion."

"Not half bloody aggressive," said Moshe.

"We now know that Schuschnigg did resign as chancellor that same evening...as we heard. On the morning of the twelfth of March, the German *Wehrmacht* (army) drove into Austria, and the Nazis and Hitler were greeted with a great deal of enthusiasm. On the fifteenth of March, more than one hundred thousand people gathered outside the Heldenplatz in Vienna to celebrate Hitler's union of Austria and the German Reich."

"Hard to believe," said Lili, sobbing. "Hitler was apparently greeted with Nazi flags, Nazi salutes, and Austrian flowers." Lili was still teary eyed, and no one in the room could fathom why Hitler would have been so well received.

"Was there any fighting?" asked Rachel.

"Apparently not!"

"Who would've guessed that so many would support the Anschluss?" asked Moshe.

Rudi shrugged his shoulders. "Austria is no more," he said. "It is merely Germany's eastern most province now...Ostmark."

After a pause, Rachel asked, "Have you heard from your mother, Lili? I imagine she'll be beside herself."

Lili shook her head. "Have you heard from your friends Benjamin and Rivka and Joseph and Ester in Leopoldstadt?" she asked. Lili shook her head.

"*A feier zol sie treffen...die verdammten Nazis*," said Moshe, fuming. Rudi poured some more beers, and a deadly silence fell over the living room.

Rachel broke the silence. "What do you think will happen now, Rudi?"

"It's already happening...from what we see in the papers...Jewish businesses and homes are being ransacked and closed, and Jews are being harassed and are leaving as fast as they can."

"Where are they going?"

"Huge numbers will come here to Palestine. Many are apparently heading for either London or New York."

"Do you think your mother will come here, Lili?" asked Moshe.

"I have no idea; I really have no idea...we will try our best to get her here," said Rudi emphatically.

———— ∞ ————

RUDI AND LILI wrote a number of brief letters to family and friends, requesting news from Austria as soon as possible. A letter arrived first from Rudi's father at the end of April and written on March 15. It reassured them that he and his wife were okay, that Tante Mariane was thinking of them constantly, and most of Austria had become *narrisch* (crazy). A letter soon thereafter came from Hanna, Lili's school friend, informing them that she, her husband Michael, and their two daughters were planning to emigrate to London or New York within a week; they would make a definite decision over the next couple of days. Mr. Schwartz, Lili's boss in Vienna, and his family had apparently disappeared, the office and family home had been locked up, and there was no trace of them. Lili again began to cry as she had been doing a lot since March 11.

"Why would Mr. Schwartz up and leave just like that? It must have been unbearable for them…I can't imagine. And I am so worried about Mother, Rudi…what do you think could have happened to her?"

"We'll just have to wait a little longer…I'm sure there'll be news soon." Lili couldn't sleep much that night. She took her diary from her knickers drawer, and after quietly closing the living room door, began to write:

> *For Hanna and Michael to tear their children away from everything they know…things must be awful…really awful. And Mr. Schwartz just disappearing into thin air with his family…unbelievable! I am so fearful he may have been taken by the Gestapo and be somewhere on the way to a concentration camp. Perhaps he left for New York…that would be okay. And Mother…she'll be a right mess…there's not enough cognac in the world that could help her. She'll just have to come here. She has no option…she'll have to come stay with us.*

There soon was news from Vienna—and it was from Lili's mother.

Vienna,
March 23, 1938
Liebe Lili und Lieber Rudi,

> *I hope you are both well, and I presume you have heard that Hitler has taken over Austria.*

> *It is hard to believe that so many Viennese came out to support him and the German Wehrmacht. Walter tried to come from Paris to be with me but was turned back at the border. There is a great deal of confusion here. Actions against Jews are now occurring as I have never seen before…Jewish shops and businesses ransacked and closed, Jewish doctors, professors, and teachers driven from their posts, and Jewish businesses and homes appropriated by the Nazis.*

> *I do not know how to tell you what happened to me. I tried to write many times to tell you, but I just kept bursting into tears and developing the shakes. On March 18, I was listening to some music, trying to*

lock out reality, when there was heavy knocking on the front door. Two Nazi officers greeted me very politely, I must say, and with a formal document in hand, told me that I would be moved from our Ringstrasse apartment, as all these apartments would be taken over by the new administration. The officers came inside, looked into every room, and told me I was to begin packing immediately, as I would be moved at 8:00 a.m. the following Thursday. I would have all the moving done for me. I would need to leave behind the grand piano, the three large chandeliers, the Persian wall rugs, and all the paintings in the dining and living rooms. I was completely shocked...dumb struck. They left without further word. I tried to call Walter. I couldn't get through. I cried a lot.

Most of the time spent packing, I was crying. I had no one to talk with. I hadn't heard from Mizzi for a week or more, and she was probably trying to cope with the changes in Vienna herself. Everybody in the Ringstrasse apartments here were also packing and crying except for the widower Dr. Himmelwasser. There was no crying in his apartment. He had told me just last week that he'd been run out of his university office he'd occupied for forty-three years. Not five minutes after the Nazi officers visited him, straight after visiting me, he shot himself with his hunting rifle he had used to hunt pheasant and partridge.

All my things were moved, using three trucks with at least ten men, all polite and efficient. I am now at 9 Tuerkenstrasse 17/10 where I have two bedrooms, a dining room, and two sitting rooms occupying the second floor. It is quieter here than on the Ringstrasse, but the apartment here, though workable, is not special, and I miss my wall rugs, chandeliers, and paintings. And I miss having the grand piano because it was always a reminder of you, Lili, and Walter during happier times when my Alfred was still alive. Our dachsies—Kafka and Bela—seemed to have coped all right, as their barking and appetites haven't decreased.

I don't know what will happen next.

Please stay healthy and write straightaway.

Alles liebe,

Mutti

Lili couldn't contain her crying. She felt hugely guilty that she was not with her mother. She felt ashamed...felt she had abandoned her. She also became angry with her father again for having committed suicide, leaving her mother to cope by herself now during such a difficult period.

It took Rudi several days to console Lili, who wrote to her mother, imploring her to come and live with them in Haifa. She should come straightaway while so many Viennese were migrating to Palestine.

Days before the end of April, a letter also arrived from Joseph, Rudi's flatmate in Vienna from 1932 to 1934.

"It is no longer tenable to live in Vienna with its rampant anti-Semitism," Joseph explained. He and Ester would very soon leave for Lyon, get married, live close to his parents, and start a family. Benjamin and Rivka, the other couple of the "Leopoldstadt sextet of friends," had already traveled to London, where they had immediately found work in the clothing industry with jobs quite similar to those they had had in Vienna.

Lili remained quite concerned about her mother remaining in Vienna, and she had Walter agree to also try to convince her mother to emigrate to Haifa. In addition, after several exchanges of letters between Rudi and his father, it was decided that Rudi Senior would also try to convince Lili's mother, Hedwig, to join Rudi and Lili. Rudi's father spoke with Hedwig a number of times over the telephone and had even arranged to travel from Villach to meet with her in person in Vienna.

<hr />

FINALLY IN EARLY June of 1938, Hedwig Gruen joined the huge lines in Vienna to try to secure the necessary papers to emigrate. The lines being so long, she was turned back several days in a row and was asked to come back the following day. The lines seemed never to get any shorter, and on the third day, Mizzi, a long time friend, came along with her to keep her company. An ugly scene developed just in front of them.

A military vehicle screeched to a halt; officers jumped out and beat several men with truncheons and dragged several others into the back of the truck and sped away. The line just moved forward. No one said anything. Mizzi and Hedwig looked at one another in disbelief and left the line without saying a word. Right there and then, Lili's mother made up her mind that she would not leave Vienna...whatever was to happen to her would happen to her...this was all too much bother. Mr. Auer's trip from Villach to Vienna was canceled.

A letter written by Rudi's father at the end of June arrived in August.

Villach
June 6, 1938
Lieber Rudi und Liebe Lili,
I am very sorry to report that, despite considerable efforts over several months, I have not been able to convince Hedwig to leave Vienna and live with you in Haifa. Your sponsorship of her had been accepted by the authorities. In the end, she was not willing to give up everything...all the furniture, her furs, money, and jewelry and leave with just a suitcase of the very essentials. Somehow she seemed to hope against all hope that one day things would return to normal. I am really sorry.
We hope you are well,
Vater

Lili and Rudi were bitterly disappointed by the news, as they headed to the beach for one of their regular after-dinner strolls. Returning one such evening, they bumped into Sahib and his boys, who had been fishing.

"Uncle Rudi, look what we caught," said Khalid excitedly.

"*Salam*, Lili; *salam*, Rudi. Say 'hello,' Muhsin," said his father.

"*Salam Alekum*," said Muhsin, a bit dejected apparently, because his fish was a little smaller than the one caught by Khalid.

"They'll make an excellent dinner; the smaller one will be sweeter than the bigger one, of course," said Lili. Muhsin seemed to perk up at that revelation. "How have you and Amelia been, Sahib?"

"We are very well, thanks, Lili. *Hamdulilla*. Did you hear the outcome of the big fight the other night?"

"No, what big fight?"

"It was a very important fight...a boxing contest...a significant fight."

"Oh?"

"It was the Heavyweight Boxing Championship of the World held at New York City's Yankee Stadium. The whole world was paying attention—"

"Except us; we've never followed boxing, have we, Rudi?" said Lili.

"But this was different. Yesterday, Max Schmeling, a German, was fighting Joe Louis, a black American. Schmeling had defeated Louis the last time they had fought in 1936. Hitler followed that victory with many pronouncements about the racial superiority of Aryans. And now, with half the world expecting Germany to declare war soon, journalists were making a lot of this contest...I got up at three o'clock this morning to listen on my radio."

"Well, what happened?"

"It was all over in two minutes and four seconds...Joe Louis knocked the German out in the first round. It'll be headlined in the papers tomorrow, if it is not already in today's paper."

"Today's the twenty-second, isn't it?" Sahib nodded his head and continued. "I haven't looked at it yet today, but it'll make big headlines because all the Jews were cheering for the black man."

"Can we go home now to give Mummy the fish?" asked Muhsin.

"Of course, she'll be expecting us. Yes, must run. *Masaa el kher*, Lili, Rudi."

"*Masaa el kher*," said the boys.

"*Ma' a salama*."

Rudi and Lili reflected on the significance of this single sporting event on the other side of the world.

"This emphasis upon the superiority of one race over another, Lili, is very dangerous," said Rudi.

"Yes, Hitler is constantly spouting forth about Aryan superiority. Perhaps this outcome will cause him to rethink."

"Probably not…his entire *Weltanschauung* is that Aryan Germans are superior and deserve greater *Lebensraum* and can get rid of all peoples in German-speaking lands who are not pure Aryans," said Rudi.

LIFE AFTER THE ANSCHLUSS

"BUT WHAT CAN we do to get Mother to leave, Rudi? I hear they are ransacking Jewish homes. Mother would die of fright if Nazis arrived to take away her remaining beautiful things."

"We'll just have to keep trying, Lili...perhaps she'll come to her senses. Of course, the Nazis are making it increasingly difficult now for Jews to actually leave."

"How is that, Rudi...other than they have to wait in line to get their papers organized?"

"Just what Father wrote in his letter...Jews are required to leave behind all their valuables, including jewelery and cash. They even have to relinquish their bank accounts."

"How do you know that?"

"We read it in the paper...can't you remember?"

"Unfortunately, I can, and your father wrote it, too. No one would want immigrants, Rudi...if they have nothing arriving in England or wherever."

"Yes, there is a lot of sympathy for the plight of German and Austrian Jews around the world."

"So then?"

"But no countries are willing to increase their immigration quotas. Look at this report in the paper."

"What report?"

"Thr report about the Evian Conference."

"What does it say?

"Franklin D. Roosevelt—"

"The American president?"

"Yes. He convened a conference at Évian-les-Bains from July the sixth to the fifteenth in France, with thirty or more countries represented, to discuss the issue of the Jews wanting to emigrate."

"Well?"

"No country wants to take them...even the United States."

"Not even the United States?"

Rudi nodded. "Only the Dominican Republic is willing to take additional Jewish emigrants and use them as farm labourers."

"That's ridiculous. Can you imagine Viennese doctors, lawyers, or violinists working on farms in the sweltering sun?"

"Most countries expressed the fear that an increase in refugees would cause further economic hardship."

"And here...in Palestine?"

"The British are making it terribly difficult, too, as they are still dealing with the Arab revolt."

"But many are still making it here, aren't they?"

———⊶———

LILI AND RUDI continued to try to convince Lili's mother to join them in Haifa. They would soon—starting late October 1938—be living in a large two-bedroom apartment. Their present landlords, Felix Weber and his wife, needed the apartment Lili and Rudi were presently occupying for relatives from Germany who would come and join them. The new apartment, with more space, would be a perfect place where Lili's mother could stay with them and have adequate room for herself.

Lili and Walter exchanged several letters about helping Lili's mother emigrate, and they were becoming pretty confident that she would soon join Lili and Rudi in Haifa. Lili also implored Walter to see if he could find out what happened to Mr. Schwartz.

———⊶———

IN THE MEANTIME, however, Rudi, who had continued to apply for work in many different places, including Alexandria and London, soon received a letter that offered him a job with a British bank in Rämismühle, *bei Wintertur* in Switzerland.

The plan was for Rudi to go ahead of Lili and find an apartment, and if things worked out and they deemed it safe there for Lili, she would follow.

"I would love to get back to Europe to live, Rudi, but I don't want you to go ahead of me. You got us here in the first place against my wishes, and now you want to leave me here while you traipse back to Europe?'

Rudi was a little taken aback. "But it may not work out, and we'd have cut our ties here in Haifa."

Lili was quite unhappy about the prospect of being away from Rudi for at least some weeks. She returned several times to an earlier dream and wondered whether the prince who drove her around the Amalfi Coast in a white convertible would ever be so uncaring as to even contemplate leaving her on her own. Lili needed Rudi to be with her in Haifa. She'd feel too vulnerable and lonely without him.

Rudi was not deterred and, convinced that the plan was the right thing to do, wrote to his Onkel Roman, a tailor near Villach, and ordered a three-piece winter-weight suit to be made as soon as possible.

"Will you at least go and visit your parents, Rudi?"

"I will try and meet up with them in Trieste before I take the train to Switzerland," said Rudi.

Rudi gave notice at work, said a preliminary farewell to most of their friends in Haifa, took the boat to Trieste, and took the train from there to Switzerland. Though arrangements for Rudi and his father to meet in Trieste were quite advanced, the meeting never took place.

Rudi did not like his work very much and did not appreciate the frequent bitter cold. He did appreciate a better salary. He also became aware, from local newspapers, of the existence of anti-Semitic groups who seemed to relish in making Jews unwelcome.

Lili missed Rudi a great deal but was rarely alone of an evening, dining with the Knopfelmachers, Sahib and Amelia, Gudrun, and

Moshe and Rachel on a number of occasions. Weekends were also never lonely for Lili. Rudi and Lili exchanged letters a couple of times each week. Rudi expressed doubts about the situation in Rämismühle and declared he was missing Lili a great deal.

Lili sternly summoned him back to Haifa. "I want you to come back as soon as possible so that we can start a family." Having spent a great deal of time with Daniel, Moshe and Rachel's little boy, Lili had developed a severe dose of womb ache. She wanted Rudi back to proactively try to start a family. She was, after all, already thirty-three years old. And she was now convinced that Rudi would only begin to act really responsibly if he were a father.

Rudi was back in Haifa in late September just days before having to move from their one-bedroom apartment to a two-bedroom apartment. Sahib lent Rudi his truck, and with Moshe's help, they moved Rudi and Lili's belongings just a couple of streets further up Mount Carmel. Rudi and Lili were happy in their larger apartment, which they could use as further leverage to get Lili's mother to come and live with them. Mr. Finkelstein was pleased to have Rudi back working for him again at a slightly higher wage. The Rämismühle experience was quickly a distant memory, but Rudi's wanderlust still lurked in the background. It was imbedded in his subconscious.

"Do you realize what song you were just then humming, Rudi?"

"Humming? No."

Lili sang the words to the song.

Mein Vater war ein Wandersmann
und mir steckt's auch im Blut.

"Oh yes," said Rudi, completing the first stanza.

Drum wandr' ich flott, so lang ich kann
Und schwenke meinen Hut.

"Where does that restlessness come from, Rudi? Certainly not from your father or mother," said Lili. "A long-lost relation you've never told me about?"

Quite unexpectedly, Rudi received an invitation to work for the same British bank in Jerusalem that had employed him in Rämismühle. Lili was beside herself and frustrated that Rudi couldn't seem to settle down at all. They were invited to come to Jerusalem for Rudi to meet with the head of the bank there and for he and Lili to look at the apartment that would be made available to them as part of Rudi's package. Lili reluctantly agreed to travel to Jerusalem for the day. The meeting with Rudi's prospective boss went well, but that was all that went well that day.

The apartment offered Rudi and Lili was quite unacceptable. It was in a very narrow, dirty, and noisy street of mainly shops. It was on the ground floor, and the smell of garbage overpowered that of eastern spices. Lili had questions for the person showing them the apartment. It was tiny.

"Is this all there is to the kitchen? How do you do the dishes?" asked Lili.

"Yes, you'd have to get water from down the hall."

"And where is the bathroom?"

"Down the hall, too. It is shared with two other families." Lili turned red in the face.

"Thanks for showing us, but no thanks...Rudi, take me back to Haifa at once."

Not two days back from Jerusalem, Lili had barely spoken, and a letter arrived from Walter in which he expressed a desire to emigrate to Australia.

"I'd like for us to go to New Zealand or to Australia, Lili. I don't want to stay here," said Rudi.

"You've just arrived home from Switzerland and a stupid detour to Jerusalem, and you want to leave again—want to leave me again? No, Rudi."

"I hear there are such wonderful opportunities in Australia and New Zealand."

"Really? To herd sheep? How could we afford that...boat journey and you without a job?"

"I thought I'd go in a few months when I've saved enough money, get settled there, and have you come over to join me."

"Are you completely out of your mind, Rudi...Rudi Auer? Another one of your half-baked ideas?" *Bloeder Hammel,* she thought to herself. "You need to grow up, Rudi, really."

Rudi, feeling rather sheepish, was about to drop the idea. Loud instructions suddenly blared from a speaker mounted on top of a car driving the streets of Haifa: "A curfew is in place. Do not leave your home. Do not leave your home."

Just then Mr. Knopfelmacher burst in as Rudi was about to lock the door. "There has been some rioting, and bombs have gone off…I heard it on the radio. We are to stay inside…a curfew has been declared… oh, hello, Lili."

Mr. Knopfelmacher disappeared as quickly as he had arrived, and the instructions could be heard again from the next street: "A curfew is in place. Do not leave your home." The curfew stayed in place for the next day, and people were permitted to leave their home for two hours to do some shopping. People could not go to work.

SEVERAL DAYS LATER, a letter arrived unexpectedly from Lili's mother. It did not mention anything about the situation in Vienna. There was nothing in response to the pleas to have her come to Haifa. She just announced that she wanted to send Lili some furniture she no longer had any use for that was cluttering up her apartment and that they might like in their larger apartment. She wanted to send two cupboards, one armoire, two pairs of skis, books, and Persian rugs. Rudi's father had already kindly agreed to arrange the entire transaction.

"How weird," said Lili. "No mention as to what's happening in Vienna."

"No response to our pleas for her to come here."

"I guess she plans to just stay put," Lili said. "I don't understand her."

Sure enough, after several other letter exchanges, Lili received notification of the arrival of the consignment from Vienna. Sahib offered to help Rudi get it to their apartment using his truck. Lili was quite excited to receive some of her old furniture and a sewing machine, which had been included.

"What beautiful pieces of furniture, Lili!" Sahib said as he helped Rudi unpack the armoire and the cupboards.

"I have never seen them myself, Sahib," said Rudi. "I've seen these, though," as he recognized a pair of Lili's skis.

"This second pair is a pair of unwanted skis from Walter, I think," said Lili. "I guess he hasn't found a use for them in Paris."

LILI HAD OVERSEEN the movement of the items of furniture to their appropriate positions and busied herself rearranging the contents. She was looking forward to a few days' rest, having just left her work at the clinic. A well-to-do Viennese couple living just a few streets away asked her to work for them. Mr. and Mrs. Winzelmeier were both in their eighties and had, until recently, been involved for decades in the import-export business.

"*Ja*, Lili, we imported furniture, kitchen wares, radios, luxury cars…even ships, and we exported mainly olives, oil, and oranges… *a*, even sheep and camels," chuckled Mr. Winzelmeier.

"We need a little help keeping everything tidy in the house," said Mrs. Winzelmeier. "We have too many rooms, but we will not sell our home…this is our little part of Vienna, and even Hitler can not take it away from us…I might need a little help in the kitchen, and Mr. Winzelmeier always gets his newspapers in a mess." Lili enjoyed working for this old Viennese couple, though her early tasks were not seen by her as real work.

After her second day with this family, Rudi asked, "And what did you do at work today, *Schatzerl?*"

"You could hardly call it work…I helped Mrs. Winzelmeier draw out the dough for an *Apfelstrudel*; I took it out of the oven when it was ready. I beat some cream, and I made the coffee."

"You wouldn't have any trouble with those tasks. And?"

"I dusted some bookshelves…and I played mah-jongg with Mr. Winzelmeier when his wife got bored playing…very nice people, Rudi."

Within days of their first meeting, the Winzelmeiers introduced Lili to a writer who wanted someone for ten to fifteen hours a week to undertake some secretarial and research work. He was an Englishman, a freelance writer of nonfiction pieces. Lili gladly accepted this work and now found herself very busy, still teaching English to Ilse and Annemarie twice each week.

KRISTALLNACHT: NOVEMBER 9–10, 1938

RUDI AND LILI were quietly having breakfast on Thursday, November 10, getting ready for a day of work. It was barely light. They were sipping slowly, as the coffee was very hot.

A very excited and loud Mr. Knopfelmacher was at the door. "Come quickly. It's on the radio. Terrible things are happening in Germany and Austria. Come."

Rudi and Lili, glancing at one another, followed the doctor a couple of doors down, where his wife, Arnold, and Rebecca were sitting around the dining-room table listening to the radio. They listened intently.

"Jewish-owned businesses, Jewish hospitals, Jewish schools, homes owned by Jews, and synagogues are being attacked...ransacked and destroyed in many cities in Germany and Austria—"

"*Ach du liebe Zeit,*" said the doctor's wife.

"*Gott in Himmel.*"

"Still *bitte*, let us hear," said Mr. Knopfelmacher, as he turned up the volume. The broadcast continued.

"Gangs of Nazis are systematically going through towns, smashing the windows of these buildings using sledgehammers and pickaxes. There is chaos in the streets, which are littered with broken glass. There are reports of Jews being beaten and some thrown onto trucks and driven away."

"What brought this on?"

"Quiet. Listen."

The radio report continued. "It is particularly bad in Vienna—"

"Oh no! how terrible."

"Shush."

"Many synagogues have been destroyed and Jewish cemeteries desecrated. Signs such as *Juden Raus* and *Juden* Go to Palestine have been painted on footpaths. Jewish men have reportedly been rounded up in the early hours of the morning, bundled onto trucks, and taken off to concentration camps. This broadcast will continue after a short pause, when we can hopefully bring you some updates...in the meantime, a little music."

"What brought this on?" asked Rudi again. Nobody answered. There were a few shakes of the head. Rebecca went to the kitchen and quickly returned with a pot of coffee. Mr. Knopfelmacher got up and fetched a bottle of brandy, which he placed in the middle of the table. The music on the radio stopped. The report continued. Mr. Knopfelmacher added some brandy to his coffee.

"We have some further news. We report that most synagogues throughout the cities of Germany and Austria have been set alight and are burning as we speak. This systematic attack upon Jewish communities and the Jewish people came completely out of the blue. It was apparently in retaliation to the murder of an embassy official, Ernst vom Rath, in Paris. A seventeen-year-old, Herschel Grynszpan, with a personal grudge, apparently shot the official to death in his office."

The world seemed mainly shocked at the Nazi pogroms that continued for at least two days. The *New York Times* headline read, "NAZIS SMASH, LOOT, AND BURN JEWISH SHOPS AND TEMPLES UNTIL GOEBBELS CALLS HALT." It scathingly stated: "No foreign propagandist bent upon blackening Germany before the world could outdo the tale of burnings and beatings, of blackguardly assaults on defenseless and innocent people, which disgraced that country yesterday."

Hugh Greene, correspondent of the *Daily Telegraph*, wrote of events in Berlin: "Mob law ruled in Berlin throughout the afternoon and evening, and hordes of hooligans indulged in an orgy of destruction. I have seen several anti-Jewish outbreaks in Germany during the last five years, but never anything as nauseating as this. Racial hatred and hysteria seemed to have taken complete hold of otherwise decent people. I saw fashionably dressed women clapping their hands and screaming with glee, while respectable middle-class mothers held up their babies to see the 'fun.'"

The Templers of Haifa were also celebrating the Nazis rampaging against the Jews with the flying of flags, a bonfire within their community, and the singing of patriotic songs, including the "*Horst Wessel Lied*," the anthem of the Nazi party.

> *Die Fahne hoch! Die Reihen fest geschlossen!*
> *SA marschiert mit ruhig festem Schritt.*
> *Kam'raden, die Rotfront und Reaktion erschossen,*
> *Marschier'n im Geist in unser'n Reihen mit.*
> *Kam'raden, die Rotfront und Reaktion erschossen.*

> (The flag on high! The ranks tightly closed!
> The SA march with quiet, steady step.
> Comrades shot by the Red Front and reactionaries
> March in spirit within our ranks.
> Comrades shot by the Red Front and reactionaries.)

"They send shivers down my spine," said Lili.

"Just unthinking bastards—no sense of human decency," said Rudi. "I do suspect that many, however, would not approve of the actions against the Jews and the widespread destruction."

It transpired that this Nazi onslaught in Germany and Austria damaged, or completely destroyed, about two hundred synagogues in Germany, many Jewish cemeteries, more than seven thousand Jewish shops, and twenty-nine department stores. Some Jews were beaten to death, while others were forced to watch. More than thirty thousand Jewish men were arrested and taken to concentration camps, especially to Buchenwald, Dachau, and Sachsenhausen.

Only the pogrom in Vienna was completed, the others somehow having been called off early...by whom? Rudi and Lili were not sure.

Most of Vienna's ninety-four synagogues and prayerhouses were partially or totally destroyed. People were subjected to all sorts of humiliations, including being forced to scrub the pavement while being tormented by their fellow Austrians, some of whom had been their friends and neighbours. There was a lot of headshaking…a great deal of disbelief.

"I cannot imagine the Viennese turning on their neighbors like that," said Lili. "Have they all lost their senses, their decency?" Nobody could understand that.

During subsequent days, it also came to light that immediately after Kristallnacht, on November 12, the Exclusion Laws were passed. These laws excluded Jews in Germany from economic life altogether. And on November 15, Jewish children were excluded from German schools.

"That's just terrible that one group of human beings can behave like that toward another group of human beings," said Rudi.

"How can they discriminate against innocent children?" asked Lili. "How will Mother cope, Rudi? If only Father were still alive…so damned selfish…he would have managed to get them both out. "

"It's just too terrible to imagine. We'll have to increase our efforts again to get her here, Lili…get Walter to help convince her as well."

"Yes, it would be wonderful to have her here for Christmas. Perhaps Walter could bring her. Walter might stay a few days, and we could all celebrate together." Lili's face lit up…but only for a moment.

Changes, Treaties, Pacts, and Wars

CHRISTMAS 1938 CAME and went in Haifa without Lili's mother, despite strenuous efforts from every member of the family. With much of the news focused upon the progress of Hitlerism in Europe, the constant and relentless skirmishes between the Arabs and British government troops had been largely going unnoticed. There was constant pressure by Jews to have Palestine partitioned with a large area of land designated for their exclusive use. The Arabs resisted with all their guile and might, unfortunately suffering many casualities in the process. One of those casualities was Mohammad, a friend of Sahib and Amelia, a husband to Fatima, and a father to five children.

"It is such a tragic loss," said Amelia. "He was a great father, and the childrens' mother is now really concerned that her two teenage boys will run away and join the resistance…war is such a foolish enterprise." As Amelia began to sob, Lili responded with a comforting arm around her shoulders.

"Yes," said Lili. Amelia wiped her face with her apron and forced a smile.

"Have you been able to persuade your mother to join you here, Lili?" she asked.

Lili shook her head.

"I'm really sorry, Lili; I know you and Rudi have been trying so very hard to get her to come." After a pause, and with some further sniffling, Amelia asked, "Did you hear one of the Strauss dynasty died early in January?"

"Yes, Johann Strauss III...on the ninth of January, I believe. He was mainly a conductor," said Lili. "Not as well known as the other Strausses."

THE ACTIONS AGAINST Jews in Germany and Austria continued unabated, despite considerable condemnation from outside Germany and within. Increasing numbers of Jews were fleeing Germany and Austria. Following an hour-long speech to the Reichstag on January 30, the newspapers were headlining warnings by Hitler that if a war were to start against Germany, the result would be the "annihilation of the Jewish race in Europe."

"I don't think this is an empty threat," Rudi said to Moshe. He and his wife had come to visit with their son, Daniel, during the first weekend in February.

"Do you mean he would try to rid Europe entirely of Jews? There are millions of us," said Moshe.

"He stated this clearly in *Mein Kampf,* and it is often referenced in NSDAP publications, as you well know, Moshe," Lili said. "Some mainstream papers have mentioned what they referred to as the 'Jewish problem,' the idea that Germany and Austria belong to pure Germans... Aryans. Jews are regarded as an impurity...an impediment. Jews, part Jews, and gypsies—anyone who is not purely German...should be driven out."

Daniel began to cry, becoming upset at Lili's rising voice and apparent rising anger. He had only known Lili as soft spoken and happy. Lili tried to pick him up, but he hid behind his mother's legs. Lili went to the kitchen to make some coffee, and Daniel soon appeared sheepishly at the door. Lili picked him up, gave him a few noisy kisses on both cheeks, and with a smiling face, he hugged Lili as if he were a koala bear. Everybody was soon sitting down in the living room with afternoon coffee and almond stars and *Lebkuchen* Lili had made for Christmas. Moshe was beaming as he finished an almond star.

"I knew you'd like them, Moshe," said Lili. "I remember your fondness for anything made with almonds. Can you make these, Rachel?" Rachel shrugged.

"Just almond meal. No flour and a light lemon icing. Baked in a medium oven," said Lili, who had a different thought on her mind. "Hitler referred to 'annihilation' when he spoke about the Jewish question. That means something far worse than driving Jews from German territory."

"I'm sure he'd shoot all Jews in Europe, if he had half a chance," said Rachel.

"Yes, his desire is to rid all German-speaking lands of Jews…he wants these lands to be completely *Judenrein, Judenfrei* (free of Jews)," said Rudi.

"*A feier zol ihm treffen, des Arsch…*" Moshe's voice trailed off, not wanting Daniel to learn any swear words too soon. Everybody was somewhat depressed by the discussion, so Rudi offered a round of drinks to lift the mood. There were no takers, and soon Moshe, Rachel, and Daniel were heading home with a few almond stars in a brown paper bag.

"Just a little motivation for you to make some, Moshe!" Lili said. Everybody smiled as Rudi and Lili waved and closed the door behind them.

RUDI WAS BORED with his job supervising construction work mainly in Akko and driving between various locations, delivering machinery parts, tools, and equipment. He applied and was offered a job with the Haifa City Council. Mr. Finkelstein, though disappointed, bore no grudges and even sold Rudi the car he had been driving for very little money.

Rudi was no sooner settled in his new work, than they again relocated their home. For no more rent than they were presently paying, they moved into a farmhouse—House Schneider, Pine Road, Mount Carmel. It was a large house with a stable and was situated in an orange grove. It also had fig, plum, and lemon trees and a large vegetable garden. Lili and Rudi loved the house. There was ample space in the house and in the yard, and there was enough space to park four or five cars out front. A large pinewood table sat at the edge of the lemon grove...wonderful for *al fresco* dining, reading a book, or just whiling the time away and listening to the birds. Lili had never actually lived in a house with a yard before, though she spent vacations in a house...the house of Frau Stein in Annenheim and the home of Tante Marianne, especially, reviving warm memories. A family with small children must have lived here, for there was an overgrown sandpit and an old swing fastened on a branch of a very large eucalyptus tree.

It was the beginning of spring in 1939 when they moved, and Rudi prepared garden beds and planted and sowed seeds of all sorts of vegetables the very next weekend. They both enjoyed working in the garden, Rudi happy to do the heavy work. One variety of orange was already ripe, and Lili, with Rudi's help, made several batches of marmalade to consume and to give away.

RUDI AND LILI and Walter and Rudi Senior continued their efforts to persuade Lili's mother to leave Vienna and join her daughter and son-in-law in Haifa. Many letters were exchanged, and Walter phoned and visited his mother—all to no effect.

"I'm so sick of my mother...all the effort we make...others make...and she remains stubborn. Doesn't want to leave her precious things behind... but likely to be carted off by the Gestapo or SS."

"If you became pregnant, would your mother be more likely to want to come, Lili?" asked Rudi.

"Probably...maybe...who knows?"

"Hm."

"I didn't choose to leave Vienna, either...but now there's no choice, really...you either leave voluntarily, or you get driven out... carted off to some concentration camp...starved to death or just shot. I'm sick of her."

A letter from Tante Marianne arrived:

> *If your mother had a grandchild to love, she would surely go to Haifa*
> *What's wrong with you people? I haven't given up hope and am still*
> *knitting for the future. I want to remind you, Rudi, of you know what*
> *Tausend Bussi,*
> *Tante Marianne*

A few days prior to Rudi and Lili's fifth wedding anniversary, several more letters and cards arrived and thirteen red roses from Walter. On Friday, June 2, Rudi and Lili celebrated their anniversary, which had occurred on May 30. They were just settling in for a romantic evening at Hotel Appinger, when Mr. and Mrs. Knopfelmacher also came in for dinner as part of a group of five. Nearly two hours later, while Rudi and Lili were enjoying a coffee and sharing a piece of *Esterhàzy* cake, the Knopfelmacher party passed by their table on their way out and paused to share pleasantries. They also invited Rudi and Lili to their place for dinner in a couple of weeks.

"Thank you very much. Very kind of you, Mrs. Knopfelmacher," said Rudi.

A couple of weekends later, Rudi and Lili dressed for dinner and walked to the Knopfelmachers. They joyfully greeted Rudi and Lili at the door, and Lili presented Mrs. Knopfelmacher with a bunch of flowers and a jar of orange marmalade.

"Welcome; do come in. Lili, you look wonderful—radiant...glowing. Have you been on vacation?"

"Oh, thank you, Mrs. Knopfelmacher. No. That would be nice, though. We are actually exhausted with all our efforts to get Mother to leave Vienna and come here. We've all tried so hard."

"Will she not come, Lili?"

"I can't say we're optimistic."

Mrs. Knopfelmacher continued. "I'm sorry to hear that. The three people you saw us with a couple of weeks ago at the Appinger had just arrived from Vienna. They have a terrible story to tell. He was a physician...lost his job following the Anschluss. His wife and her sister...never married, were both teachers and were fired within days after Kristallnacht. They had their house completely ransacked of their valuable art and furniture and had the outside of the building defaced with ugly graffiti and terrible slogans."

"That's really awful," said Rudi.

"Signs like *Weg mit dem Judendreck* (Away with the Jewish filth) and *Juden gehoeren in Palestina* (Jews belong in Palestine)," said Mr. Knopfelmacher quietly to Rudi.

"That's dreadful, and they looked like such elegant people," said Rudi.

"Yes, the final straw for them was a terrible incident. You tell the story, Mama."

Mrs. Knopfelmacher let out a big sigh and paused. "The two recently fired teachers were enjoying some cake and coffee—"

"The doctor was running an errand," said her husband.

"There was loud rapping on their door. Two boyish-looking brownshirts in impeccable uniforms took two steps inside their front door and said, '*Unser* fuehrer is coming to Vienna, and all the streets must be spotlessly clean. Come at once with a bucket, soapy water, and cleaning cloth, and we will instruct you what to do. *Schnell.*' Petrified, the two women did as they were told. The brownshirts said, 'On your hands and knees, and clean this square with all the other women.'"

"Not really," said Lili.

"Yes, and after five minutes or so, the doctor returned with two shopping bags and wanted to ask what was going on. He was never able to ask a question. He was beaten with batons and when he crumpled to the ground, was kicked...suffered broken ribs and concussion."

"*Ach du liebe Zeit!*" Lili held her hand to her forehead.

"And now they are in Palestine...just as the Nazis wanted...bastards," said Mr. Knopfelmacher.

After a long pause and after Mr. Knopfelmacher thrust a glass in everybody's hand, Lili asked, "Are Arnold and Rebecca coming, Mrs. Knopfelmacher?"

"No, unfortunately; they had another obligation." Lili was so looking forward to seeing Ariella and Talia, as she found past dinners with the adult Knopfelmachers rather tedious. There were always similarities…always Wiener schnitzel, always served with potato salad, irrespective of the season…always an evening of political talk, dominated by the men.

"We were correct, Rudi, when last we met. We forecast that Hitler would destroy Vienna as we knew it and spread his evil beyond German-dominated lands. He wasn't satisfied with capturing the Sudetenland, he grabbed all of Czechoslovakia."

Mrs. Knopfelmacher came in, beaming with satisfaction and a platter of Wiener schnitzel.

"They look perfect," Mr. Knopfelmacher said. "Let's eat them before they get cold." The schnitzel were excellent and perfectly complemented by a Chianti. "I thought a Côte du Rhone or a Bordeaux would be too heavy."

Rudi and Lili also complimented Mrs. Knopfelmacher, and silence fell upon the table with the exception of the clashing of knives and forks and the cracking of Mr. Knopfelmacher's jaw each time he chewed.

"I know," he said. "I'm sorry…old joints need some oil. Can I have another one, please, Mama." Everybody had seconds.

"I hope you've left enough room for dessert. I made something very special for today. I know Rudi loves them. I bought some of the first *Marillen* of the season…from a boy with a donkey…and made some *Marillenknoedel*." Mr. Knopfelmacher produced a bottle of cognac and four liqueur glasses, while the two women went to the kitchen to make coffee and roll the *Marillenknoedel* in butter-roasted bread crumbs. Soon the room was filled with the aroma of Arabica coffee, and everybody's tastebuds feasted on the stewed apricot dumplings.

"Come with me, Lili," Mrs. Knopfelmacher whispered and led Lili back into the kitchen. "Look what I made yesterday."

"*Marillen* confiture…very nice," said Lili as she recognized the rich colour of the fruit.

"We bought ten pound of *Marillen*. The boy was very happy. You must take a jar. Lili, are you okay? You look as if you are not feeling as well as before."

"I think I might be pregnant."

"Oh, that would be wonderful," said Mrs. Knopfelmacher, her eyes lighting up. Becoming a little excited, she grabbed Lili by the arm.

"Everything okay in there?" Mr. Knopfelmacher said from the living room.

"I have had a little spotting and occasionally have cramps," Lili said in a whisper.

"Oh yes, Lili, that's it."

"My breasts feel a little fuller, too. I haven't told Rudi yet...but my body and my intuition tell me."

"Yes. You should have it confirmed. Oh, Lili, that's so exciting." Lili became a little somber.

"What's the matter? Are you not excited?"

"Rudi has this wanderlust...just wants to go here, there, and everywhere just on a whim. Do you think he'd become more settled if he were to become a father?"

"Yes, nothing surer. The thought of that responsibility helps the male's decision-making powers no end. I experienced that with my own husband. Arnold has settled down a great deal, too, since he has become a father."

In the meantime, Rudi and Mr. Knopfelmacher continued their discussion from earlier in the evening.

"Where were we, Rudi? Oh yes. Hitler invading the rest of Czechoslovakia," said Mr. Knopfelmacher, "in March this year."

"That was not surprising after he had so little resistance to occupying the Sudetenland."

"It was on the pretext of protecting German speakers in the area, wasn't it?"

"Yes, and there was not going to be any resistance, as Hitler had the British prime minister bluffed," said Rudi.

"Yes, Neville Chamberlain...and he had Mussolini...Benito Mussolini...in his pocket, too."

"Those two—Hitler and Mussolini—had been working toward a pact against Britain and France for some time," said Rudi.

"Wasn't the pact to include Japan?" asked Mr. Knopfelmacher.

"Yes, at first…Japan wanted it to be also aimed at the potential threat of the Soviet Union. That didn't come to pass, and Japan dropped out of the negotiations. Fascist Italy and Nazi Germany signed the pact aimed solely at France and Britain."

"That was called the Pact of Steel—the *Stahlpakt* or *Patto d'Acciaio* in Italian."

"Happened at the end of May, didn't it?"

"Have you two not finished yet?" asked Mrs. Knopfelmacher, making a statement from the kitchen.

"Soon, Mama. That's why there was no resistance to Italy wanting to flex its muscles, too, Rudi. It was feeling inferior to Germany, of course."

"Yes, at somewhat the same time…a little earlier or a little after Hitler taking the rest of Czechoslovakia, Mussolini invaded Albania…the Italians especially wanted the port of Viore, as I remember reading."

"Can you stop now, please. Lili isn't feeling well," Mrs. Knopfelmacher said, as both women appeared at the living-room door.

"I'm sorry, I feel a little sick in the stomach."

"I hope it isn't from something you ate, Lili?" asked Mrs. Knopfelmacher, with a subtle wink.

"You do look rather green, Lili," said Rudi. "I'll take you home and make you a herbal tea."

EVERYONE HAD BECOME used to the sporadic skirmishes between Arabs and British troops for several years, with sabotage and killings, curfews and warnings having been a part of the fabric of Palestinian life. All was suddenly quiet. Arab's persistence finally achieved the desired effect. British policy had now changed. In the White Paper of May 1939, the British government finally announced that the British rejected the establishment of an independent Jewish state.

"All that killing for nothing," said Amelia after welcoming Lili to a not-infrequent luncheon.

"From all observations, Jews and Arabs have lived well together in Palestine, haven't they, Amelia? Why would there need to be a separate state?"

"Yes, and especially here in Haifa."

Lili thought for a moment. "What effect might this have on future Jewish immigration?"

"I'm sure the authorities will now want to severely restrict it, but I think it will just drive it underground. Illegal immigration will just increase."

Lili sighed a big sigh, not sure how detrimental the White Paper might prove to become for Jewish immigration. "I guess that will make it all the harder to get Mother to come and join us here in Haifa."

"You've been trying so hard...eventually she'll come...*Inshallah*," said Amelia with a less than convincing voice.

Lili grimaced. "Yes, we can only keep trying." There was a long silence.

"Have you read *The Buccaneers* by Edith Wharton, Lili?" Lili shook her head, still a little upset, thinking about the diminished prospect of her mother escaping Nazi Vienna.

"It's about New York society of the 1870s...I really enjoyed it. I'd be happy for you to take it."

Lunch continued. The lamb and rice dish was splendid as usual, and a light Côte du Rhone slipped down easily. Neither Lili nor Amelia wanted to return to the previous serious discussion, so luncheon talk soon focused upon each other's husband, the children, and the weather. Lili didn't mention her suspicion about being pregnant before seeing the doctor. Anyway, she didn't seem to be having any symptoms so far this day.

After lunch, a melancholy Lili walked home, humming a familiar tune: "*Wenn der liebe Flieder wieder blueht*." And now she also began to feel a little queasy. *Could I be? After more than six years together, could I really be? I'll find out tomorrow,* she thought.

"Hello, Lili." It was Frau Weber, who met her on the street. "I haven't seen you for several months. How have you and Rudi settled into the farmhouse? You have lots of room now, *Ja*? Give Rudi my kind regards."

Lili trudged uphill and was about to prepare dinner for herself and Rudi, who would be home shortly. She was at a loss as to what she might make. She didn't feel like cooking. Her back hurt a little now, and she wasn't sure why. She could hear Rudi through the open window. He was whistling and obviously happy.

"Hello, *Schatzerl*, how are you?"

"Hello, Rudi; I was just wondering what to make for dinner."

"Weren't you going to make—"

"Can we go and have pizza, Rudi?" Lili said. "I just feel like pizza." Rudi burst into laughter.

"That sounds very strange, coming from you...but of course we can...at the Lebanese place?" Both Lili and Rudi enjoyed their evening with pizza, and Lili divulged nothing of her suspicion.

IT WAS A beautiful summer's day, and birds were twittering in the orange grove, as Lili locked the front door and headed for her appointment with the doctor.

"Good morning, Frau Auer. How are you? What's been happening?"

"I think I'm pregnant, Doctor."

"And what have been your symptoms?" Lili mentioned the spotting, the cramping, recent back aches, and the firming of her breasts.

"Yes, all good signs. Leave some urine. I will do some tests, and you should come back in two days, after ten o'clock, and I will tell you then."

Lili wanted to know now. She wanted to tell Rudi that evening. She didn't dare tell him till it was confirmed. Yet, she really did know. Her intuition told her she was pregnant.

Promptly at ten in the morning two days later, Lili got the news.

"Congratulations, Mrs. Auer, you are going to have a baby...not really sure when, but probably in late February or early March. Don't do any heavy lifting, please."

"Oh, thank you, thank you, Doctor."

"Don't thank me. Thank your husband."

As RUDI CAME home from work and entered the front door, humming a melody, Lili ran and leaped into his arms.

"Thank you, Rudi. Thank you."

"What for, *Schatzerl?* What's happened?"

"I'm pregnant, and you're going to be a father."

"Oh? Pregnant? Really? That's wonderful, Lili...wonderful! How do you know?" asked Rudi, beaming from ear to ear.

"I went to the doctor. I had this feeling for a couple of weeks now."

"You didn't tell me, and you didn't tell me you were going to the doctor?"

"I didn't want to tell you in case I was wrong."

"Wonderful. It must have been all the oysters I demolished when we were walking along the quay. How would you like to celebrate this evening, *Schatzerl?*"

"I've been so excited all day, I had to keep myself busy. I've already made dinner. I also made another batch of marmalade and a fig tart because we have so many figs we can't eat them all. Lets eat outside; it's a beautiful evening, and perhaps we could go for a walk afterward."

Bubbling with excitement, Rudi went about setting the table outside at the edge of the orange grove while Lili heated up the stuffed tomatoes, aubergine, and marrow.

"These are all from our garden," said Lili with a sense of pride. "They are the first vegetables I've ever grown. I remember well getting my fingernails all dirty, burying the marrow seeds in the soil. That was more than three months ago. Isn't it wonderful?"

The vegetables, filled with a mainly minced meat, onion, and rice mixture and various spices and served with homemade chutney, tasted delicious, as did the fig tart with ample whipped cream. Rudi whipped the cream and licked the whisk. They cleared the table. Rudi gave Lili a big, lingering hug.

"Thank you, Lili. I so look forward to being a father." Rudi took Lili's hand as they commenced their walk. It was a lovely summer evening with a slight smell of the sea breeze replacing the citrus smells as they headed downhill. They were about to enter the Bat Galim Promenade, when they met the entire Knopfelmacher family, returning from a summer stroll. Ariella was holding her father's hand, while Talia was trying to get something from her grandfather's pocket.

"*Ja, Gruess Gott.*"

"*Gruess Gott.*"

"Well?" asked Mrs. Knopfelmacher, looking directly at Lili. Lili nodded her head and smiled a big smile.

"Wonderful, Lili, wonderful…Lili is going to have a baby. Isn't that wonderful?" said Mrs. Knopfelmacher. Rudi threw Lili a quizzical look. There were congratulations all around, and everybody seemed very happy, except Ariella and Talia, who seemed a little confused.

"Mrs. Auer is going to have a baby," said their mother.

"But she hasn't got a tummy, Mummy?" said Talia.

"Not yet. I'll have a big tummy before your next birthday," said Lili. That seemed to satisfy the girls.

"When are you due, Lili?" asked Rebecca.

"Late February or early March."

"Oh, it'll be a fish…a Piscean," said Mr. Knopfelmacher Senior. "They are invariably imaginative, intuitive, and sensitive. Look after yourself, Lili, and don't lift anything heavy," he said. The Knopfelmachers headed uphill, while Lili and Rudi, still holding hands, continued along the promenade.

How good life is, thought Lili. *This is the best I've felt since leaving Vienna. We are living in a large house with lots of space and a wonderful garden…the perfect place in which to bring up a child, and Rudi seems so very happy.*

They stopped to say hello to some fishermen they recognized.

"Are they biting?" asked Rudi.

"Not yet...probably in another half an hour. *Inshallah.*"

"*Inshallah...Masaa el kher,*" said Rudi as they continued their walk.

"*Masaa el kher.*"

They walked down to the beach, where there were several groups still picnicking. Embers of a fire still glowed against a darkening sky, and food smells lingered. Rudi and Lili both slipped off their sandals and walked along the water's edge. Children were still frolicking in the water, and sea gulls scurried away as they walked. Lili and Rudi were very happy with the thought of becoming parents; they spoke little, but felt closer to one another than they had for years. Lili slept quickly and soundly that night, while Rudi tossed and turned due to excitement. Lili wrote briefly in her diary the following day:

> Oh, *how happy I feel. It will be wonderful to be parents...I'm sure it will make a huge difference to Rudi's attitude...and maturity. I wish Mutter would come; I fear she won't...and we have a wonderful home to bring up a family. I have not been so happy since the middle of July 1934 when we were still in Vienna.*

The excitement continued for weeks, as Rudi and Lili shared the news with friends in Haifa and wrote letters to inform Tante Marianne, Lili's mother, Rudi's mother and father, and Walter and Joseph and Ester. On his way home from work, Rudi went to tell Moshe and Rachel. Moshe was not yet home from work, but Rachel was most excited and pleased for Rudi and Lili. Rudi invited them for lunch on Sunday.

ON THE SUNDAY, Moshe arrived, holding Daniel by the hand, while Rachel brought a posy of flowers.

"*Ja,* what wonderful news! Congratulations. *Mazel tov,* Lili. Congratulations, Rudi," Rachel said, as kisses were shared.

"Thank you. We are very happy."

"Guess who is also pregnant. We received a letter from them only yesterday."

"Who?"

"Ester…Joseph and Ester."

"Oh, excellent. We must write to congratulate them, Rudi," said Lili.

"Let's sit outside for a little celebratory drink," said Rudi. They sat at the large table at the edge of the orange grove and discussed the trials and tribulations of fatherhood and motherhood.

Daniel soon spied the sandpit, recently cleared of weeds and the sand neatly raked. An old bucket and spade kept him busy when he wasn't playing hide and seek with his severely chewed king from an old chess set.

"How has your chess-teaching business been going, Moshe?" asked Lili.

"I now have five students, and this pays better than spending each day with the merry-go-round."

"Tell Rudi and Lili about playing three games at once," said Rachel. "He came home so late one evening, I was really worried."

"A group of about five chess enthusiasts came around as I was ending the last carousel ride for the day. They asked me, 'Are you tired?' and produced three chess sets and set them up on my little table…I was to play three games at once. They said, 'We pay five pounds per game, and you pay one pound. Winner take all.' One man, whom I'd seen before said, 'I will be referee and look after the money.'"

"How did you do?" asked Lili enthusiastically.

"A lot of people came around to watch. I became a little nervous. It was a very hot evening…I was sweating like a pig…I had to concentrate very hard…I had to be very quick…three games at once…phew! My brain was not functioning all that well after a day's work, and I knew Rachel would be worried."

"So what happened, Moshe?" asked Rudi impatiently.

"I put one guy out of his misery in five moves. I should have had him in three."

"Checkmate," said Lili.

"Yes, but the others knew how to play, and I had to concentrate very hard. I had my queen in real trouble a couple of times...anyway."

"Well?"

"I won."

"All three?"

Moshe nodded, a slight grin appearing on his face.

"That's excellent. Congratulations," said Rudi and Lili.

Rachel smiled proudly. "Yes. I put the money toward a holiday. Anyone want to play now?"

"No, but you could hold the ladder while I climb up and fix the swing."

"Aren't you getting ahead of yourself a bit, Rudi?"

"I thought you'd like a swing to demonstrate for Daniel."

"I'd likely get seasick."

"Rudi will make such a great father," said Rachel to Lili.

"I need to replace the ropes fastened from that eucalyptus tree over there," said Rudi, motioning toward a very tall tree. Moshe didn't seem that confident.

"Shall I hold the ladder and you climb up?" asked Rudi.

"You must be really joking," said Moshe. "I get scared of heights standing on a chair."

"Let's have another beer before you hold the ladder...the yeast'll give you strength."

They had their beers. Lili poured Rachel a glass of wine and retrieved a platter of finger foods from the kitchen.

"Oh, Lili, these look wonderful," said Rachel. There were *dolmades* (stuffed vine leaves), *sambousak* (meat-and-cheese-filled pastries), spinach-filled pastries, olives, and grilled vegetables (peppers, aubergine, and baby marrow).

"The veggies all came from our garden," Lili said proudly. "I've never had a garden before, and it's a lot of fun."

"Isn't it a lot of work?"

"As long as you keep on top of the weeding and do a little every day. Rudi does all the hard work...the digging."

"I bet he loves it."

"Yes, he does. You should take home some zucchini, peppers, and aubergine, Rachel, and don't forget to take as many oranges as you want. Look what we have in the sandpit."

"Three boys playing." Two of the boys soon stopped playing. Moshe held the ladder leaning against a large branch, about eight metres off the ground, while Rudi climbed up and replaced the fraying rope. Soon Daniel was sitting on Rudi's lap on the swing.

"It seems strong enough," said Moshe.

CONGRATULATORY CARDS SOON began to arrive from the relations in Austria and from Joseph and Ester in Lyon, and a baker's dozen of red roses arrived from Walter in Paris.

Sahib and Amelia also came to their house to offer good wishes. They were very happy for them. Lili went to show off the vegetable garden to Amelia, while Sahib ushered Rudi off in a different direction to recount an incident Rudi might be interested in hearing about.

"You remember us telling you about my friend Mohammad?"

"Yes, killed by the British."

"You will remember, too, there were five children, and the mother was really worried about the two oldest joining the resistance...well, I've been taking a bit of an interest in them and driving them around in my truck when I've been on this errand or that. They like to be with me and talk with me about things teenagers don't normally share with their mother. They were telling me about how they get rid of the smell after smoking hubble-bubble, what sort of girls they liked, and what they liked doing with them, when all of a sudden, one yelled, 'Don't let him get away, Uncle Sahib,' as a black Mercedes sped past. He said, 'Chase him. I want to get a closer look at him.' I thought that was harmless enough. But as quick as a flash, Issa, one of the two, climbed out the window and onto the back of the truck."

"That couldn't be too easy?"

"I couldn't do it...from a fast-moving car."

"What did he do that for?" asked Rudi.

"I didn't have a clue at that moment. Mohammad, with the same name as his father, kept yelling at me, 'Don't let him get away. Don't let him get away.' Before I knew it, shots rang out, and the Mercedes began to fishtail a bit."

"What was happening?" asked Rudi.

"There were more shots—seven or eight in all—till I saw a back tire blow out and the Mercedes plummet into a ditch...rolling over at least three or four times."

"*Ei yei yei.* What did you do, Sahib?"

"I was flabbergasted...I immediately slowed the car down and pulled off onto the side of the road. In the meantime, Issa climbed back into the cabin, hot and sweaty, and grinning from ear to ear. 'Good, ha!' he said, dropping a revolver at his feet. 'Please don't be angry with me, Uncle Sahib,' he pleaded. 'You saw the Nazi flag, didn't you?' 'Yes, but—' I said. He immediately interrupted me. 'You like driving them off the road, driving your car into theirs...that's more dangerous, and sometimes needs your car to be repaired. My technique is much better.'"

"You couldn't argue with that, Sahib," said Rudi with a chuckle as their wives arrived, and the men's conversation abruptly ended.

"Let's go back for some coffee." The aroma of the freshly brewed coffee overpowered the citrus smells of the orange grove. Lili served each person a slice of a freshly baked fig cake, which everyone seemed to like, and Sahib enjoyed a second. Lili gave Amelia back the Edith Wharton book she had borrowed and presented her with a jar of orange marmalade as they departed for home.

Later that evening Rudi reflected upon the conversation with Sahib. He wondered where else in the world there were Nazi groups adhering to the vile and perverted views of Hitler. *How safe will it be, even here, to bring up a child? When will war break out in Europe? For it surely seems likely, and how far will it spread?* Rudi wished it were a more peaceful time in which to bring a child into the world.

WAR, ARREST, AND GRIEF

FOR MONTHS THE daily newspapers detailed the existence of high-level meetings and deals made between various governments in Europe. Speculations were rife that commencement of hostilities could occur at any time. Rudi and Lili read about the pact the Nazis signed with the Soviets on August 23, 1939. They read about the Mutual Assistance Treaty between Britain and Poland on August 25. They heard on Mr. Knopfelmacher's radio that the British fleet was mobilizing for war, and civilian evacuations would soon begin from London.

On September 1, a Friday, Germany invaded Poland, and during the next two days, the radio and newspapers reported the events. The *New York Times* on that same day had the following headline: *"German Army Attacks Poland; Cities Bombed, Port Blockaded; Danzig Is Accepted Into Reich."*

On September 3, the BBC broadcast Neville Chamberlain's declaration of war, which was heard over the radio in many parts of the world: *"This morning the British ambassador in Berlin handed the German government a final note stating that, unless we heard from them by eleven o'clock that they were prepared at once to withdraw their troops from Poland, a state of war would exist between us. I have to tell you now that no such undertaking has been received and that consequently this country is at war with Germany."*

On the same day, September 3, 1939, France, Australia, and New Zealand declared war on Germany. News spread fast. The world was at war. Though it had been anticipated, it still came as a shock.

In Haifa, people were glued to radios at home, on street corners, and in cafés. There was much excited talk, but it wasn't upbeat. What would being at war mean? Many people there had friends in countries that were now at war. Palestine being under British mandate was probably at war, too. What would that mean?

Rudi and Lili visited the senior Knopfelmachers' home to listen to the latest war news and to invite them for Sunday lunch. Their children and grandchildren were there also. Everybody was invited for lunch.

"We have so many vegetables in the garden, we would love you to help us eat them if you have the inclination," said Lili. "I've already stuffed a whole lot of peppers, aubergine, marrow, and tomatoes and made a chutney to complement them...just need to heat them up."

"Sh! Let's listen," said Mr. Knopfelmacher, as he turned the volume of the radio up. There was a hush over the room; even the twins sat quietly.

War news dominated the airwaves, and everybody listened with a certain amount of disbelief and apprehension, though war had been expected and had been imminent. Faces were generally downcast. There was a lot of headshaking. There was much pondering. There were a lot of personal questions but few definitive answers.

Lili broke the silence. "Since Britain has declared war, will it mean that Palestine is also at war?"

"Will the Nazis here fight in Palestine?" asked Rebecca.

"They'll probably hurry off to Germany to enlist," said Arnold.

"Oh, Arnold, most of the Germans have already left to enlist," said his father. "That's why so many German businesses are already closed down and shuttered."

Trying to change the subject and actually wanting to go home, Lili got up and glancing at Rudi, said, "Well, see you all at about one this afternoon; we look forward to you coming."

THE KNOPFELMACHERS ALL arrived together just after one in the afternoon, and there were hugs and kisses despite everybody having been together only a little while earlier. Rudi had already set the outside table. There was a strong citrus fragrance in the air as Talia and Ariella made a beeline for the sandpit with its buckets and spades. The adults roamed around the large vegetable garden, everyone identifying the different vegetables. It was all so lush and healthy—green beans vigorously climbing up a teepee-type structure and yellow beans on smaller, squat bushes. Vigorous vines were carrying cucumbers, zucchini, watermelon, and cantaloupe. Peppers and tomatoes displayed fruit at various stages of ripeness. Carrots and radishes were planted together. Various lettuce plants were in neat rows, and clumps of different herbs were strategically located, as it was thought they would aid the growth of the vegetables. The garden appeared as a metaphor for life itself.

"What would you like as an aperitif?" asked Rudi as he glanced at the two Mrs. Knopfelmachers as they walked to the garden table.

"We'll leave it up to you, thank you, Rudi," said Mrs. Knopfelmacher.

He soon returned with well-chilled Kir for everybody.

"Prost."

"Prost. Very nice, Rudi…Chablis?" asked Mr. Knopfelmacher.

"Yes, I think Kir (Crème de Cassis) is better with Chablis than with Chardonnay or Veltliner," said Rudi.

Mrs. Knopfelmacher nodded. "It's harder to enjoy the finer things in life when you know a major war has just begun," she said. "What do you really think will happen, Rudi?"

"I really don't know, but I wouldn't want to be in Poland."

"I would certainly not want to be a Jew in Poland," said Arnold.

"We mustn't spoil Sunday lunch with talk about war," said Mrs. Knopfelmacher. "You look very well, Lili," she said, looking directly at her and touching her on the arm. She purposefully changed the subject. "How have you been keeping? It was all too upsetting this morning to ask you."

"Yes, I've been well…a little backache here and there, but otherwise—"

"Hasn't lost her appetite," said Rudi.

"Of course not…she has to feed two now," said Mr. Knopfelmacher, winking at Lili as she skipped away into the kitchen to check on luncheon. Rudi excused himself and quickly followed her. They both returned imminently to the garden table, Rudi carrying a huge, oval platter of assorted stuffed vegetables, while Lili carried a couple of bottles of Chianti.

"I thought this Chianti wouldn't overpower the vegetables as a Bordeaux might," said Rudi.

"Quite right," said Mr. Knopfelmacher. Rudi poured the wine, while everybody helped themselves to the stuffed vegetables.

"All these from your vegetable garden, Lili?" asked Arnold.

"Yes, and the tomatoes, onions, and peppers that went into a large batch of chutney as well."

Mr. Knopfelmacher was going to say something but refrained. Eating was more important to him at the moment. After a few moments, he said, "You don't seem to have lost any energy, Lili—working full time and doing all this gardening and cooking."

"Touch wood, I feel good."

The platter was nearly emptied as were two bottles of wine. Attention moved to the girls playing in the sandpit. They were barely speaking with one another. They seemed to just fill a bucket with sand, turn it upside down, and carefully lift the bucket to reveal a perfect sand castle. After a moment of apparently admiring their handiwork, the sand castle would be smashed by the single blow of a shovel. A smile of satisfaction followed, and the process would be repeated.

"Funny, aren't they?" said Arnold, just before helping Lili and Rudi take the platter, plates, cutlery, and emptied glasses back into the kitchen. Lili and Arnold returned to the table with a fresh set of dessert plates and cutlery, Lili carrying another platter with a freshly baked tart.

"A berry tart…mainly blueberries and mulberries. I hope it isn't too sour. I think I picked the berries a little too early. I didn't want to use too much sugar."

"Quite right, Lili. Too much sugar should be avoided during pregnancy," said Mr. Knopfelmacher.

"It looks splendid, Lili," said Rebecca. "Did you learn to cook from your mother?"

"No, Mother cooked very little. I learned from one of the servants," said Lili. Rudi arrived with a pot of freshly brewed coffee, a small bowl of sugar crystals, and a large bowl of cream.

"The tart is a little sour. I'm sorry," said Lili.

"A good dollop of cream will fix that," said Mr. Knopfelmacher with a smile. It did, and silence fell upon the group as everyone enjoyed dessert and coffee.

Mrs. Knopfelmacher soon broke the silence. "Mentioning your mother just before, Lili, I can't get it out of my mind that she didn't come here to join you."

"I don't understand it, either," said Rebecca.

"I can tell you why," said Rudi. "And I'm sure I'm right."

"Oh?"

"If someone else were Lili's husband…other than me, her mother would be here."

"What do you mean?" said Mrs. Knopfelmacher.

"It's easy to explain, but it hurts a little…Lili was meant to marry someone else…someone completely different from me." There was a brief, uncomfortable silence as Rudi slowly picked up his coffee cup and took a sip. He continued. "Lili married an agnostic, Catholic-born country boy from Carinthia…eight years younger than her…a mere university student, new to Vienna and green—inexperienced when it comes to sophisticated city living." Rudi took a deep breath and another sip of coffee, and Mr. Knopfelmacher poured himself a generous cognac. "Lili was supposed to have married an older, well-established, Jewish businessman well acquainted with the family and a member of the same Viennese social clique."

"Is that true, Lili?" asked Mrs. Knopfelmacher. Rudi poured himself a cognac and Mr. Knopfelmacher a second.

"Afraid so," said Lili. "I had to attend umpteen dinner parties at home and other homes, where supposedly eligible suitors were introduced to me with the hope that I would be attracted to one of them."

"You obviously weren't," said Arnold.

"No, none of them interested me. They were all into business, making money, and making a good impression...especially upon my parents."

"Not even one of them was interesting, Lili?" asked Rebecca.

"They would have just wanted me to stay at home, make babies, and dress them the way their father would have liked to have them dressed."

"Like ornaments,"said Mr. Knopfelmacher.

"And I was most shocked that, while they attended the opera and the Musikverein regularly, they were culturally ignorant," said Lili.

"How can that be?" asked Mrs. Knopfelmacher.

"They weren't watching the opera or listening to the music," said Mr. Knopfelmacher. "They were just checking out the members of the audience all the time."

"They honestly couldn't tell the difference between a waltz and a polka," said Lili. "And what's more...they didn't know the difference on the dance floor, either."

"Ouch, that would have hurt, as well," said Mr. Knopfelmacher.

"It did, yes."

"So here she is with me," said Rudi. "And we waltz and polka really well together."

"And did from the beginning," said Lili. "Rudi was my first love, and he courted me beautifully in Annenheim by the lake and then in Vienna."

"Red roses and candlelit dinners, Rudi?" asked Mr. Knopfelmacher.

"All the time," said Lili, swooning. "Sang to me and carried my skis uphill when I was tired. My mother fought against him for the entire time and wouldn't invite him into our home despite our two dachsies, Kafka and Bela, begging Mother to let him in...they barked like crazy every time Rudi brought me to the door."

"So you think your mother would've come here had you married a well-connected, well-bred Jew, Lili?" asked Mrs. Knopfdelmacher.

"Well-bred Jew...sounds like a horse," said her husband.

"That's exactly the situation," said Rudi.

"Yes, that's right," said Lili. "We've both come to that conclusion."

"You know, Lili," said Arnold, who had been sitting quietly but listening carefully, "perhaps there's a completely different explanation for your mother not being able to join you and Rudi in Haifa. Perhaps you blame yourself too easily, too, Rudi."

"How's that?"

"Well, perhaps…just perhaps, she couldn't tear herself away from her Vienna…psychologically tear herself away. Vienna has been the centre of her life—"

"All her life, really," said Lili.

"Perhaps she's been so enamored by Vienna that she has not been able to face the grim reality that has been unfolding in front of her. Perhaps she didn't believe all that was happening…perhaps she continued to hold out a thread of hope that things would return to normal. Perhaps she's been more anxious about leaving than about staying…and irrespective of what arguments are put before her or what reasons she is given, when it comes to making a decision to leave, she just can't, psychologically, and hence physically, she just can't leave."

Everyone was seriously considering Arnold's perspective. The men were helping themselves share the last of the coffee and cognac, when there was a loud rapping on the front door.

The three men dropped their serviettes as if in unison, left the garden table, and hurried to the front door.

"Open up. The CID (Criminal Investigation Department) here," said one of two uniformed officers carrying guns. The three men, who hadn't quite finished their luncheon dessert, noticed another armed, uniformed man standing at the back of a covered military-type truck parked in the drive.

"Yes, can we help you?"

"I am Officer Stanton, and my colleague is Officer Cohen. We are looking for a Rudolf Auer. Are you Rudolf Auer?"

"Yes, I am Rudi Auer."

"You are German?"

"No, I am Austrian."

"No difference. You have five minutes to pack a small case of clothes, and you will come with us."

"Where to? What for? For how long?" Just then the three women arrived at the front door.

"You can't take me away. My wife is pregnant...look...Lili, come here." The three women were made speechless by what they were witnessing. Lili began to sob.

"You can't take Rudi away from his pregnant wife," said Mr. Knopfelmacher.

"Where he's going, she at least won't be molested by him," replied an officer a little cheekily.

"Watch your tongue, Officer Stanton," retorted Mr. Knopfelmacher, turning a shade of red. His wife sqeezed his arm.

"Mr. Auer, you now have four minutes to pack some things before we put you into the truck...by force if need be," said Officer Stanton. Rudi left to pack.

"What's happening?" asked Lili. "You can't take my husband. He's not a German, and I'm a Jew," she said, hoping for some sympathy from Officer Cohen.

Goodness, thought Mr. Knopfelmacher fleetingly. *Imagine it could be a benefit here being a Jew.*

"It's orders, madam, just orders. Your husband will let you know where he is in due course." Lili burst into severe sobbing as Mrs. Knopfelmacher and Rebecca tried to comfort her.

"You could cause her to have a miscarriage...I know; I am a doctor," said Mr. Knopfelmacher. "You—" Just then Rudi arrived with a small case, dropped it beside him, and gave Lili a long embrace. He was gently tapped on the shoulder by Officer Cohen and shook Arnold by the hand. Before he could say any further good-byes, he was dragged off by Officer Stanton and shoved in the back of the truck. He observed about twelve other men sitting on benches around the periphery of the truck. They all seemed very different, seemingly having little in common except for the same smell. It was the body odor of fear. An armed officer had accompanied the men in the back of the truck. A screech of wheels and a cloud of dust, and the truck sped away.

"What took you so long? It's hot in this truck," said one of the men.

"My wife is pregnant, and she needs me to be at home," said Rudi, trying to offer a reason why he took so long.

"I have five children," said another man. "My wife does not work. How will she be able to put food on the table?"

"How long will we be away? Does anybody know?" asked another.

"I thought only Germans were being rounded up. I am a Jew."

"Do you have a German wife?" one man asked Rudi. He nodded. "That's why, then."

"Anybody got a cigarette? I gave up three months ago, but I really need one now," said a trembling, middle-aged man.

"Anybody know where they're taking us? Anybody say?"

"No, but we are definitely heading north," said the man sitting nearest the back of the truck, who was able to see out. The truck soon slowed down, drove up a long drive, and pulled alongside what seemed to be a farmhouse and stopped. Five minutes and some heated discussion later, another man climbed into the back of the truck.

"And who are you?" somebody asked.

"I am Mohammed Abdullah. I worked for a German man who left on the thirty-first of August on the Greek steamer *Paris*. I know; I took him there. There were more than two hundred other Germans absconding, I think."

"From Haifa?"

"Yes."

"Where was he headed?"

"I think he wanted to enlist in the German Army. He had lived here for decades. He grew the best *kusa* and melons in Palestine... good water supply. Anybody mind if I smoke?" he asked, pulling out a packet of cigarettes.

"Better than the smell in here now!" someone said. Mohammed Abdullah passed around the cigarettes.

―――

ABOUT THREE-QUARTERS OF an hour after Rudi had been picked up, the truck stopped by a double gate surrounded by a high barbed-wire fence. There was a watchtower, high on stilts, close to the gate. The gate creaked open, and the truck was driven through.

"Where are we?" asked one of the men.

"We are in the Akko prison camp," said the armed officer who had accompanied the men in the back of the truck and now spoke for the first time.

"Why a prison camp? We are not criminals."

"It is being turned into an internment camp."

"A concentration camp?"

"No, just an internment camp…you are here for your own protection," said the officer.

"Everybody out," said Officer Stanton. "Line up in twos; we British like order."

Another officer came to meet the new inmates. He was a tall, statuesque man. His hair was combed neatly back off his forehead, and he had a perfectly groomed handlebar moustache. He was impeccably dressed in a uniform Rudi did not recognize.

"I am Officer Halliday. Good afternoon, gentlemen," he said in a clearly British accent. "You are here for your own protection, so no harm can come to you…you are here at the invitation of and under the protection of His Majesty the King of England…excuse the noise and inconvenience of the construction being completed here…wooden barracks. There'll be more inmates like you coming over the next few days. Clear?"

"Clear."

"Rudolf Auer—step forward."

"Yes, sir."

"Bring your belongings. You are now Auer, internee two-nine-one. Don't forget it, or you won't get breakfast."

"Beg your pardon, sir?"

"Just kidding, Auer. Go with that officer with the limp and the red hair."

Rudi felt most uncomfortable, not at all sure as to what was happening. He was led into a dark, dank building with creaky doors and metallic echoes…down a long corridor. It was eerily quiet. They passed two cells; each had an inmate sitting on his bed, head in his hands.

The officer suddenly stopped. He selected a large, metal key from a collection on a chain, turned the key twice anticlockwise in the lock, and pushed open a heavy metal door that loudly creaked as if it were itself reluctant to open.

"This'll be home, Auer, at least in the short term till the barracks are completed. The door is not to be locked. There'll be an assembly in about an hour, Auer…in the quad."

Rudi half smiled at the red-headed officer as he limped away. He put his case on a metal chair and sat on the single, metal bed, causing some creaking from the rusty springs beneath a thin, not-so-clean mattress. The smell wasn't terrific. Rudi noticed a toilet hole with two footprints on either side of it and a hose dangling to the ground. A squat toilet, some might call it. There was a hand basin and a dripping tap, causing some discoloration. A couple of over-sized cockroaches scurried under the bed, causing Rudi to shiver and lift his feet. His new living space measured no more than three metres square. *This is not as good as the lockup I was in, in Vienna five years ago,* he recollected.

As if suddenly woken from a bad dream, Rudi's thoughts turned to Lili. *She'll be so upset…lonely; she won't be able to stay in that big house. How will she cope? Who will look after her? It's so important that she remains healthy for the baby. Who will look after the vegetable garden…at least water it? When will I be able to speak with her?*

Rudi was becoming increasingly worried for his wife, when his thoughts were abruptly interrupted by an officer stomping down the corridor and yelling, "Meeting in the quad; everyone out; everyone in the quadrangle."

Soon there were about fifty men in the quadangle, *an area large enough for a football field,* thought Rudi.

Commander Halliday soon stood before the men, whistle in hand like a football referee. "In twos…one behind the other now…on the double! Thank you…at ease. You are here at the pleasure of His Majesty. Within three or four days, there will be about two hundred and twenty men in this compound. Tomorrow, there will be a large contingent arriving from the German settlement of Sarona.

"You are free to go wherever you want inside this area. All your wants will be taken care of here. You will have three meals each day; you will be allocated two packets of cigarettes each week; a barber will be at your disposal each Tuesday morning; the *Palestine Post* will be delivered daily, and a post office will be set up as of tomorrow. Internees will be able to send one letter to each address in Palestine per week. Letters for overseas will be allowed one per month and limited to twenty-five words in a particular format and sent via the Red Cross of Switzerland.

"We will set up a common room where board games, including draughts and chess, will be made available. Once per month there will be an inspection by a CID officer. Note that fighting by internees is strictly forbidden. Firearms of any sort are strictly forbidden. Smuggling of any dangerous material, in or out of this compound, is strictly forbidden. The possession of a knife other than a pocketknife is strictly forbidden. Offenders will be subject to the due process of the law and severely dealt with. You will be responsible for your personal cleanliness and that of your living quarters. Any questions?"

"When's dinner?"

"In the dining room...at seven."

"Breakfast?"

"Seven...and lunch at midday. Men with any sort of cooking skills are to report to the kitchen immediately."

"Any further questions? Gentlemen, I wish you a good evening."

IN THE MEANTIME, back at House Schneider on Pine Road, Mr. and Mrs. Knopfelmacher, as well as Arnold and Rebecca, were trying to help Lili compose herself, just as there was another knock at the door. Arnold and his father answered the door.

"I am Officer McKenzie, and this is Officer Steinbach of the CID. Did Rudolf Auer live here?"

"Yes."

"We are instructed to search the property for any weapons or explosives."

"Come in, Officers," said Mr. Knopfelmacher. "There are no such things in this house."

The officers, followed closely by Arnold and Mr. Knopfelmacher into each room, opened armoires, cupboards, and chests, and looked under each bed.

"All clear," they said.

"Excuse me, Officers, would you be so kind as to tell me where Rudi Auer has been taken?" asked Arnold.

"Akko. The old prison has been converted to an internment camp. It is not a secret." Lili's quiet sobbing turned into wailing.

"Any idea how long they will keep him there?"

"No idea...sorry." With that, the officers left.

Lili was nearly beside herself. "Rudi's interned again, incarcerated, just like five years ago, and now I'm with child. What'll I do?"

"Lili, I know it's very difficult for you. We all really feel for you, but you must pull yourself together," said Mr. Knopfelmacher sternly.

"Yes, you must...for the baby," said Mrs. Knopfelmacher in a gentler tone.

"Rudi will be terribly upset himself, being dragged away like that, and he'll be so very concerned for you Lili," said Arnold.

"Yes, you have to be strong for Rudi, too." Rebecca put her arm around Lili.

"Why don't you stay with us, Lili?" asked Mrs. Knopfelmacher, looking at her husband for approval.

"Of course, you should," said Mr. Knopfelmacher. "You'd just have to get used to eating a lot of Wiener schnitzel and *Kaiserschmarrn.*"

A slight smile developed on Lili's face. "That's so very generous of you; I don't wish to be a burden on you; I should just stay here."

"But for tonight, at least, you must come with us, Lili...there is no question," said Mr. Knopfelmacher emphatically. "You would not even be able to cry yourself to sleep if you stayed here by yourself."

"Can I use your kitchen, Lili?" asked Mrs. Knopfelmacher.

Lili nodded. "Of course."

In a very short time, Mrs Knopfelmacher returned to the living room with a large teapot and five cups and saucers on a silver tray.

She placed the tray in the middle of the table and lifted the lid from the teapot. The perfumed smell of chamomile soon filled the room. Rebecca poured the aromatic tea for everybody except for her father-in-law, who put his hand over his cup.

"Chamomile will be very good to calm the nerves," said Mrs. Knopfelmacher. Her husband got up and took a few steps toward a sideboard.

"Oh yes, please help yourself, Mr. Knopfelmacher," said Lili, as he took a bottle of cognac and poured himself a double.

"Cheers. Half is for Rudi," said Mr. Knopfelmacher. "I'm sure he'd appreciate more than one himself right now." Everybody helped pack up dishes while Lili filled a small overnight bag.

Together they walked out to check the vegetable garden to see if it required any watering before the morning.

"It looks like it'll be fine till tomorrow, at least," said Arnold.

The girls looked up from the sandpit. "Can we stay some more, Mummy? I've got three more castles to make," said Talia.

"Yes, can we please, Mummy?" asked Ariella.

"Not really, we need to go home."

"Can't we please, Daddy? Please?"

"You heard what Mummy said...let's go." Everybody walked the short distance to the Knopfelmachers, Arnold and Rebecca each with a sandy child by the hand, while Mr. Knopfelmacher carried Lili's bag. Mrs. Knopfelmacher and Lili walked together a little behind the others.

"You know, Lili, you mustn't blame Rudi; he no more wants to be away from you than you from him."

"I know," said Lili, still sniffling.

"You can stay with us as long as you like, and you can count on us to help you with your house and garden."

"Thank you very much, Mrs. Knopfelmacher. How long do you think Rudi will be away?"

"I have no idea, but in the meantime you need to look after yourself and the baby. You should go to work as normal for as long as possible...don't lift heavy things or climb on chairs or anything like that, though."

Lili managed a little smile. As they arrived at the house, Mrs. Knopfelmacher suggested Lili join her in the kitchen and keep her company while she prepared dinner. She kept Lili busy peeling potatoes and tenderizing the veal.

Rebecca looked around the corner. "You know, Lili, Mother has never let me peel the potatoes, let alone handle the precious schnitzel. Is it okay if I give the girls a bath before they traipse all that sand around the house?"

"Of course, Rebecca. Now, where were we, Lili? Could you please pass me the flour on that shelf just above you? Thanks," said Mrs. Knopfelmacher.

The girls were quickly bathed, and dinner was soon on the dining table, as silence descended to allow Mr. Knopfelmacher to concentrate on his favourite dish. He noticed that Lili had not lost her appetite despite still being in a considerable state of shock.

"Lili, tomorrow I will make some phone calls for you," Mr. Knopfelmacher said. "I'll call Rudi's boss and Sahib, and I'll walk down to the merry-go-round to speak with Moshe. Would you like a ride on the whirly-gig tomorrow morning, girls?" he asked, addressing Talia and Ariella.

"What's a whirly-gig, Grandpa?"

"Uncle Moshe's merry-go-round."

"Oh, yes, Grandpa," came an enthusiastic reply.

It was not long before it was time for Rebecca and Arnold to take the girls home. There were kisses all around before the senior Knopfelmachers and Lili settled down in some easy chairs; Mr. Knopfelmacher took another cognac.

"I have a better potion for you a little later, Lili," said Mr. Knopfelmacher. "It's made from a mixture of Austrian herbs. It is good for the immune system, good for you and your baby, and it will help you sleep tonight."

"Oh, thank you so much. How long do you think they'll keep Rudi locked up?"

"We can't have any idea, Lili. We are registered as Austrians, too, of course...therefore, since the Anschluss, we are also regarded as Germans. On that basis, they could lock us up, too. The difference is that we and you are Jews. Rudi is not a Jew…in their eyes, he's a German and seen as being of the age where he can bear arms and be loyal to Hitler."

"Couldn't we explain he's been a supporter of Jews? He's more Jewish than many Jews themselves."

"They'd never understand that," said Mr. Knopfelmacher. "Realistically they'll keep Rudi for weeks, if not longer." Lili burst into tears again, which prompted Mr. Knopfelmacher to give her the potion. "Straight down, Lili; it doesn't taste very good. Wash it down with something else."

"You should try to get a good night's sleep; the bed in the guest room is very good," said Mrs. Knopfelmacher. "You should go to work tomorrow as usual. Arnold has already said he would water the vegetable garden tomorrow morning. In the evening we can plan a little further. One day at a time, Lili."

FIRST THING ON Monday morning, September 4, 1939, Mr. Knopfelmacher phoned Sahib. It was not yet 7:00 a.m., but Mr. Knopfelmacher figured he'd just be back from sunrise prayer.

"Sahib, this is Knopfelmacher here…friend of Rudi…Rudi Auer."

"Oh yes, *Salam Alekum*. Is something the matter?"

"*Alekum Salam*. He was arrested yesterday, his house was searched, and he was taken to Akko."

"Rudi…to the prison? That's a terrible joint. That's where they locked up scores and scores of Arabs during the uprisings against the British. Many were executed there, too."

"I believe it has been converted to an internment camp."

"Ah, of course, because of the war. He would have been taken away because they think he may be on the German side of the war. I will go there this morning and see what I can do. He dislikes Germans more than I do. Call me tonight between the *Ashr* and the *Maghrib* prayers, Mr. Knopfelmacher, okay?"

"*Shukran*."

"*Afwan*, bye." Sahib finished a coffee, now half cold, and drove directly to the Akko prison. A guard met him at the gate.

— 218 —

"Good morning, sir. I wish to see the commandant."

"He'll like being called that. May I say what it is in relation to?"

"I believe a grave injustice has been committed."

"Oh, and may I give him your name?"

"My name is Saleh Abdullah, but everybody just calls me Sahib."

"You may have to wait some time, sir."

To Sahib's great surprise, Officer Halliday appeared within minutes. "I am officer Halliday. How can I help you?"

"I believe you have a Rudolf Auer here, sir."

"Yes, internee two-nine-one, if I'm not mistaken."

"He should never be here, with all due respects, Commander Halliday."

"Oh?"

"He has been fighting against Nazis here in Haifa and in Vienna before he came. He is married to a Jew; they are expecting their first child."

"The papers say he is German."

"He is Austrian; he has fought against the Nazis...was even kicked out of Vienna by Nazi collaborators at the university there."

"Nothing I can do. Sorry. I just follow orders," said Officer Halliday as he turned his back.

"Any idea how long?"

"Sorry, I am very busy."

Somewhat dejected, Sahib drove back to Haifa.

In the meantime, Mr. Knopfelmacher phoned Rudi's boss, who was shocked at the news, and then went to check on Rudi and Lili's vegetable garden. It had been well watered. Lili went to work as normal.

Later in the morning, Ariella and Talia skipped toward the merry-go-round Moshe was in charge of, Mr. Knopfelmacher not far behind.

"*Shalom*, Talia. *Shalom*, Ariella; you want a ride?"

"Yes, please, Uncle Moshe. Grandpa's coming."

"*Shalom*, Moshe."

"*Shalom*, Mr. Knopfelmacher. What brings you here so early this Monday morning?"

"They've taken Rudi to Akko prison."

"*Oy Gevalt.* That's a dreadful joint…they keep breaking records for hanging people. We have to get him out of there. What did he do?"

"He was enjoying a piece of berry tart and a coffee yesterday afternoon, when armed officers of the CID came…gave him five minutes to pack some essentials and whisked him off in a truck."

"Why?"

"Because his papers say he's German. All Germans are being rounded up and shoved into the Akko prison, which has been converted into an internment camp, apparently."

"Idiots. What can we do? How can we get him out?"

"Sahib has already gone there this morning. If he can't get him out, we probably can't, either."

"How's Lili coping with this? Finally pregnant, and they're both so looking forward to being parents."

"She's a little in shock still. But she'll be fine…she is strong."

"Do you feel like a game of chess while the girls are on the whirlygig? Perhaps we'll think of a way."

INTERNMENT

ABOUT FIFTY TEMPLER Germans from the Sarona settlement arrived in a bus the next day, Monday, September 4, 1939, and there was considerable hubbub as men were allocated numbers and places in the newly constructed barracks. Over the following days, more than another one hundred and fifty men arrived, all under the age of fifty. They were allocated to barracks, virtually as the last bunks were being dragged in. Up to thirty-six men were alotted to each barrack, and each was assigned to a bunk and a public-bathroom complex.

Rudi was pleased that he was housed within the old prison. It was a solid, stone building and would likely keep cooler during hotter weather. He had his own space...a cell with his own toilet, water supply, and sink. After a few days, Rudi was able to get hold of a mop, a scrubbing brush, some rags, and disinfectant, and he spent half a day getting his space as clean as possible. It certainly smelled better than before. He turned the mattress over, so now most of the dirt was underneath. At least for now, the cockroaches were no longer to be seen.

Rudi could cope with the routines, the mediocre food, and the meager portions. He didn't even mind the goat meat served frequently as a main course. He thought it to be somewhat tough, but it wasn't all that different from venison, as far as he could remember. He was much more worried as to how Lili was faring. Within ten days he had a long letter from her. He read it over several times, and it made him feel very good.

Lili was coping well. She continued her busy schedule working for the elderly European couple and the writer and teaching English. After the first few days, she was doing all the gardening herself—watering, weeding, and washing off the aphids invading several bushes. She was never lonely. The Knopfelmacher twins, always accompanied by parents and/or grandparents, came a couple of times to help "Auntie Lili" with the harvesting but were more attracted to the sandpit. Lili never spent an evening at home alone. She had dinner at Sahib and Amelia's, Moshe and Rachel's, and at the Knopfelmachers—senior and junior. Mr. and Mrs. Knopfelmacher would also accompany Lili on evening walks on the promenade. Lili had written to all the relations in Austria, to her brother in Paris, and to Joseph and Ester in Lyon, providing minimum details.

That Lili was coping well compensated for all of Rudi's minor aggravations. He immediately set about writing a reply, which perhaps would make tomorrow's outgoing mail. He sat in the shade on the ground at the edge of the main building, leaning against a pillar. He had barely written two sentences, when a man chased another across the quadrangle, screaming and yelling.

"*Arschloch, verdammtes Arshloch* (arsehole, dammed arsehole)," shouted the man in pursuit as the man being chased stumbled and fell. The man in pursuit pounced upon him. Within seconds a dozen men were on the scene, and the pursuer was being restrained.

"That Jewish arsehole; look what he did to my hair." The barber got up, dusted himself off, and shrugged his shoulders.

"A normal haircut," he said, shrugging his shoulders again.

"A mess, a complete mess of my hair."

"Who the hell will see you in here, anyway…you expecting Marlene Dietrich? Didn't you know? She despises bastards like you…she hates Nazis."

"*Saujude* (dirty Jew)…can't even cut hair…shouldn't let them in here."

"What did you call him?" asked an onlooker as he took one step and punched the offender twice in the face, causing him to crumple instantly to his knees with two bloodied eyes.

"You look much more handsome now." Just then whistles were being blown, and three officers came running on the double.

"No trouble, Officers. We will not tolerate any Nazi behavior in this camp...this bastard should have left on a boat *fuer das verdammte Vaterland* last week."

"You can cut my hair next Tuesday," said Rudi, while looking at the barber.

"What time?"

"Ten. I am Rudi...internee number two-nine-one."

Rudi finished a long letter to Lili, saying little negative about camp life so as not to distress her. He told her he loved her very much, that he missed her every minute, that he was looking forward to being the father of their child, and was so very proud of how she was coping by herself.

RUDI WAS ON time for his haircut as arranged. He found the barber to be a very interesting and engaging character. A man in his sixties, he was a Palestinian Jew, recently from Jerusalem, who moved to Akko to be near the sea and near to his brother living in southern Lebanon. He was rather rotund, having such a large girth, he could cut hair only with outstretched arms. He had quite a mop himself—some black, some gray, a strand falling over his eyes, and a white beard...a scruffy Father Christmas look-alike. A lighted cigarette hung from his lips while he snipped away with his scissors. Occasionally he would also blow his hair from his face, cigarette still in place, and ash would periodically fall onto his beard and large stomach without distracting him from his task.

"Akko is a wonderful town, Rudi. The sun is warm, the fishing is good, and I can get cheap cigarettes."

"How often do you go fishing?"

"Every evening...my wife and I...married forty years next year... take our chairs, two beers, two fishing rods, and a bucket in case we catch something, and we watch the sun go down."

"And your cigarettes."

"Of course; without them nothing is possible."

"Do you ever catch anything?" asked Rudi.

"Rarely. We mainly solve the problems of the world over and over again." The barber picked up the mirror in his left hand, wiped some hairs from it with his hairy right arm, and was about to show Rudi his handiwork.

"Ah, don't bother...I'm sure it's good." Rudi gave him a couple of small coins, as the barber removed the cape from around his shoulders.

"*Shukran*; my name is Shlomo...see you in a month...unless you want to come just to chat, then come next Tuesday. *Shalom,* Rudi." Over the next couple of weeks, Rudi and Shlomo learned quite a lot about one another, Shlomo often having an hour or so between customers.

RUDI ALSO BECAME friends with a thirty-six-year-old Italian named Marcelo Moretti, who was quite tall, handsome, and athletically built but with a slight limp. He and Rudi struck up a conversation while walking along the beach on one of the internees' early outings.

"What brings you here?" asked Marcelo.

"I am Austrian, but since the Anschluss, I am regarded as a German."

"Where were you from in Austria?"

"From the south...Villach area."

"Just over the border. I worked in the Italian Alps...mostly in the Dolomites."

"Has a reputation for excellent skiing," said Rudi. "What work did you do there?"

"Si, si, skiing is excellent there. I have skied in Cortina a few times with Franz Zingerle and Anton Seelos."

"They were both Austrian champions, weren't they?"

"Yes, they came to train in Cortina...they were unbelievably fast."

"You worked in the Dolomites, you said?"

"I am an explosives specialist," he added quietly. "Worked on avalanche control. Once I didn't get out of the way quickly enough—hence my limp."

"No snow here," said Rudi, a little perplexed. Marcelo looked around to check that no one was within earshot.

"I helped the Arabs blow up bridges and oil pipelines during the Arab Revolt. They paid really good…I was able to buy a hotel in Positano on the coast…on the Mediterranean coast and much nicer than here."

"So why aren't you back in Italy now?"

"I lost all my papers during a raid."

The sound of two whistles turned everybody around and had them heading back into the compound.

"See you again, Rudi. Perhaps we can go skiing together when we get out of here. Perhaps we could blow our way out, Rudi," he said with a faint smile. "Can you think of anyone who would help us get some grapefruit? Let's use that word instead of explosives," said Marcelo, whispering. Rudi immediately thought of Sahib and his friends, who would very likely have access to explosives. Their conversation abruptly halted, as a man came running from one of the barracks with another two men in close pursuit and yelling.

"A thief…a thief…he is the cigarette thief."

Men had, for weeks, complained that cigarettes kept disappearing from their bunks, within their luggage, and elsewhere, especially when everyone was out of the barracks having a meal or were together on an excursion at the beach. The two in pursuit caught up with the likely cigarette thief and pinned him to the ground. Three officers were soon on the spot and handcuffed the alleged offender.

"Have you been stealing cigarettes?"

"Not many…I swear."

"Lead us back to your bunk," said one of the officers. They frog-marched the alledged offender, not so gently, back through a barrack. They suddenly stopped.

"Is this your bunk?"

"Yes, sir."

Two officers searched under the mattress, under the pillow, and under the bunk itself. There was a shoe box marked Personal Letters, tied up with twine. At least ten pairs of eyes peered at the shoe box.

"Open it," said one of the officers.

"It's personal, Officer."

"I bet. Open it." Without hesitating, one of the officers pulled on the twine that had been tied in a perfect bow. He lifted off the lid. It was full of cigarette packets.

"So it was you, you bastard!" Several men jumped on the thief and gave him a beating. The officers stepped aside, making no attempt to protect him.

"Alex," said one of the officers, "see to it that the cigarettes are returned to their rightful owners or distributed fairly. This bunk will remain empty for some time."

"Solitary confinement for you," said an officer as they dragged the handcuffed and now bleeding internee away.

RUDI AND LILI exchanged letters once each week, and occasionally Sahib was able to sneak in an additional letter for Rudi when he delivered several boxes of oranges that Lili picked from their citrus grove. Sahib could also sneak out a note from Rudi to Lili, and officers were aware of this indiscretion but thought it worth the extra boxes of fruit. On one occasion when Rudi had a quick word with Sahib on his way out, Marcelo noticed and, accompanied by another man, approached Rudi as Sahib disappeared through the camp gate.

"Rudi, I'd like you to meet Lacko. He's from Yugoslavia. I've already told him a bit about you." Lacko was dark haired, swarthy, and thickset and looked as if he'd be strong.

"Pleased to meet you, Rudi, Yes, I think I already know you. You're a skier." He shook Rudi by the hand, his grip being so tight, it caused Rudi to grimace.

"It is a passion of mine...yes...and you ski, too?" asked Rudi.

"Yes, I am from near Planica."

"Planica is famous for ski jumping, right? Mount Ponca is well known, as I remember? I think an Austrian, Seppi Bradl, was the first man to fly over one hundred meters there, yes?"

"Yes...impressive, Rudi."

"Lacko is a businessman, Rudi. He needs to get out of here before his businesses go broke," Marcelo said.

"What sort of business are you in, Lacko?" asked Rudi.

"The truth is, Rudi," said Lacko, "I'm really a smuggler."

Rudi was a little taken aback. "Oh, what do you deal in?"

"Anything from shoes and booze to fishing boats to guns...whatever people need and can't get through normal channels. I need to fulfill my contracts soon...otherwise, I will have to start my business from the beginning...problem, no?"

Marcelo broke in. "We've both noticed, Rudi, you have a friend who comes once a week and delivers oranges...sometimes a letter for you, too. Lucky, very lucky, man...could he not also deliver grapefruit, Rudi?"

Rudi turned red in the face, it being clear what Marcelo and Lacko were suggesting.

"We could be enjoying Christmas with our families far away from here, Rudi. Think about it," said Lacko. "We'll catch up with you after your friend has brought more oranges. Nice to have met you, Rudi." The three all walked away in different directions.

Whoa, thought Rudi. *What have I got myself into here? It would certainly be great to be out of here soon, but to blow our way out. No, no, no! I couldn't risk that. What if something didn't go according to plan? What if Sahib were caught bringing in the grapefruit? I wouldn't want that on my conscience. What if we got caught in the process? Worse, what if someone got in the way of the explosion? What would happen to us if we did get caught? I have had to run away from the authorities before. No, no, no...not any more! I'm about to be a father. And Lili deserves better than that from me. I've done the wrong thing by her before.*

Rudi made up his mind; he wouldn't entertain the idea. He would just have to tell Marcelo and Lacko directly as soon as possible. He wouldn't want them to be getting their hopes up of grapefruit delivered...grapefruit exploded...a wall knocked out...freedom... Christmas with their family in some far-off land.

Rudi kept an eye out for Marcelo and Lacko so he could tell them his decision. He didn't see them for several days, but he thought about them a lot. He also had some powerful dreams. One was that they blew their way out of the prison-internment complex only to be caught, flogged, threatened with the gallows, and thrown into solitary confinement for three years. Rudi's son would be without his father, and Lili would have run off with a respectable and responsible man. Rudi woke up in a lather of sweat. On another occasion, he had a more pleasant dream, which included meeting Marcelo's family and skiing with them in the Dolomites and overindulging in Sambuca. Rudi wrote to Lili about Marcelo and Lacko, mentioning their work and their common interest in skiing but leaving out any reference to grapefruit.

Marcelo and Lacko found Rudi early on Tuesday the following week, just after they had observed Sahib leaving with an envelope.

"Well?" asked Lacko.

Rudi pretended to play dumb. "Haven't seen either of you for a week or so. Everything okay?" he asked.

"Grapefruit, Rudi, grapefruit. Any news about getting us some grapefruit?" Lacko said insistently.

"I couldn't put my friend in that position."

"You didn't even ask him?"

"No."

"You weak bastard, I thought you were a man of character...with some spine, Rudi...weak bastard!" said Lacko, becoming louder and beginning to fume.

"Keep your cool, Lacko," said Marcelo, pleading. "We'll just have to find a different source for grapefruit."

"Rudi, you're a weak bastard...I'm half inclined to knock your block off," said Lacko, visibly angry. "We'll be out by Christmas, skiing with our families, and you'll be singing Christmas carols in here with all those Nazis and other lunatics."

Rudi turned his back and walked away. He was pleased that episode was over. He walked over to the barber shop to see if Shlomo had time to chat. He was sitting facing the door and reading the *Palestine Post*.

"Ah, Rudi, nice to see you...how are you?" he asked as he turned down the volume of the radio.

"*Ahamdulilla*. And you? Been catching any fish?"

Shlomo smiled. "A few here and there, Rudi. As you can see, I prefer to read in English...it's a good language...it gets to the point quickly. This *Post* is a little old, but I hadn't realized Sigmund Freud died some weeks ago in London."

"Yes, I had read that...on September twenty-third, wasn't it?" said Rudi.

"I recall in 1930 he was awarded the Goethe Prize, and then after the Nazis came to power in 1933, they burned his books," Shlomo said.

"Yes, I, too, remember clearly," said Rudi. "He was quoted as saying: 'What progress we are making. In the Middle Ages, they would have burned me. Now, they are content with burning my books.'"

"He was a good-quality person, Rudi...Rudi, you look white. Are you okay? Has something happened?"

Rudi recounted the exchange with Lacko and Marcelo, and a wry smile crept over Shlomo's face.

"This behavior is quite normal, Rudi. There are always some men, when they are first brought here, who develop a hair-brained scheme to break out of this establishment. A few actually try. They mostly don't get far and end up spending more time in here than necessary. You did the sensible thing. What's that they're playing on the radio?"

"I haven't been paying attention," said Rudi, now suddenly focusing on the music. "It's Wagner...'Tristan *und* Isolde,' I think, but I'm not certain."

"Yes, you are correct, Rudi. We don't listen to Wagner anymore...not since the Palestine Orchestra now refuses to play him because of his anti-Semitism...that's been their policy since Kristallnacht." Shlomo turned the radio off just as a client came in to occupy the barber's chair. "See you next time...*shalom*, Rudi."

"*Shalom*, Shlomo."

———

IT WAS NOW early November, and life as an internee had become somewhat tedious; most hours in the day were spent reading, listening to the radio, and wandering about and talking. Marcelo and Rudi had become quite good friends, despite Rudi not having delivered any grapefruit.

They talked most days about family and especially about skiing. Marcelo explained how he had set an explosive to bring down a wall of snow, and when he didn't get out of the way in sufficient time, a boulder, caught up in the snow, hit his leg and fractured it in different places.

"The doctors made a mess putting it together again, Rudi, and I now have one leg shorter that the other."

"Does it affect your skiing much?"

"I have a slightly built-up ski boot that helps a lot...ah. Skiing is okay...perhaps when we get out of here, you could take me skiing on the Grossglockner...I have always wanted to ski on that mountain."

"The Grossglockner is a great mountain to ski on. Unfortunately, it has brought so much anger to me and my wife, Marcelo."

"How so?"

"The authorities who have control over the mountain have included the 'Aryan clause,' which forbids Jews from skiing there and from staying in any of its huts." Marcelo looked puzzled. Rudi continued. "Lili and I were in Annenheim, skiing mainly on the Gerlitzen, when Lili got it into her head that she wanted to ski the Grossglockner. She was so terribly upset when I explained it wasn't worth us taking the risk of being evicted from the mountain because she is a Jew. I don't think she's gotten over it to this day."

"That's terrible. Rudi, I must get back. I don't want to miss out on my cigarette allocation. *Ciao.*" Marcelo limped uphill while Rudi headed toward the water's edge to see what shells he could gather for his collection or what pieces of driftwood he might be able to salvage for his carvings or making of picture frames. He had his eyes peeled, walking along the high waterline and quietly singing to himself, when he was stopped by two young men.

"*Guten Morgen.* You are Rudi, *Ja?*"

"*Guten Morgen.* Yes, I am Rudi."

"We have heard you singing many times, and you have an excellent voice. We would like you to join our *Gesangverein,* our choral society, and practice for a Christmas concert. Christmas is only six weeks away. We could make the fuehrer proud."

"You could make yourselves scarce right now, before I bash your heads together...ignorant idiots." Rudi's pulse rose appreciably for a few minutes. He skimmed several small stones across the water, composing himself, and reflected on his present situation.

Why should I be here with all these Nazis? They support Hitler and his war effort. I don't. I am married to a Jew and about to become a father to a child who will be a Jew...makes no sense that I would be in favour of Hitler's war. They regard me as their enemy. In any event, I have never been told why I am being incarcerated. It surely is a right, an obligation to be told of the reason for being locked up, and that reason would need to be proven. I learned that in law school in Vienna. I've done nothing wrong. I shouldn't be here. How could I get the commander to see the unfairness of my being here? How could I get out and be back with Lili?

Rudi was quietly returning for lunch and walking past one of the barracks, when he witnessed a skirmish.

"A pity they didn't get the bastard," one of the few Hungarian internees said, referring to a failed assassination attempt against Hitler. They had just heard a report about it on someone's radio.

Two Germans, who were part of the conversation, jumped the Hungarian. "*Gott sei dank* he was not harmed. You are the bastard. How dare you call Hitler that...how dare you wish the fuehrer—our fuehrer—harm?"

"They should've got him, and we should get you, too, you fascists." A melee quickly developed with a lot of shoving and fists flying. Whistle-blowing officers soon arrived and restored order.

It did not stop talk of the assassination attempt during the afternoon. It had been reported that Hitler had been addressing the Old Guard party members, when, just twelve minutes after he had left the hall, a bomb that had been secreted in a pillar behind the speaker's podium exploded. Apparently seven people were killed, and more than sixty were wounded. Rudi read a detailed report the following day.

BY MID-NOVEMBER, RUDI had amassed a huge collection of shells of all shapes and sizes and many pieces of driftwood. There were some pieces he thought were either pine or cyprus and others that were unmistakably olive wood. He began to be quite depressed at the thought that he and Lili would not be together over Christmas. For several weeks now, he spent many hours a day alone and brooding while crafting items, using mainly his pocketknife Lili had bought for him as a present a couple of years earlier. He used the various tools of his knife to whittle, cut, carve, and create a variety of items. With great patience and care, he whittled a couple of sets of buttons from olive wood. Next, he whittled a couple of belt buckles and a broach he hoped to give Lili soon.

Rudi was, however, most proud of a replica, about eight inches long, of an Arab boat, a *dhow,* that he made. It consisted of a carved-out hull, two masts, and two sails—a jib sail and a mainsail—and both a tiller and a rudder. There was also a small dinghy attached to the back of the *dhow,* tied together with camel hair. All elements were made from olive wood, the sails not more than one eighth of an inch thick. The forestay and backstay and tiny shackles were made from fine wire that had been scavenged from the inside of discarded pipe cleaners. Rudi also made a trestle-like frame the boat sat on. It was all held together by tight joints, as there were neither nails nor glue to be had.

Rudi also crafted several picture frames of different woods held together by matchstick pieces. Sahib arranged to have glass cut to order. Rudi framed the best of his drawings, some basic art supplies having been sent by Lili. His "*pièce de résistance*" was a creation of a vase, consisting of a half shell with flowers, made entirely from tiny shells. For this he was able to get some glue from the shoe repairer in camp in exchange for several cigarettes.

Many internees were engaged in similar craft-like enterprises, and just before Christmas 1939, a common display was arranged so that internees could admire each other's handiwork. There were some wonderful creations, including tiny carved animals, children's toys, and some board games. Rudi would have loved to have swapped any or several of his pieces for a chess set, complete with pieces carved from olive wood and pine wood to provide the contrast in colour. His *dhow* was particularly admired, as was his framed flower vase made entirely of shells.

Photo by Jacki Bisset

As CHRISTMAS APPROACHED, many of the men were becoming very agitated, as they desperately wanted to be with their family over the festive period. The thought of remaining incarcerated over this period was more than some could bear. Several men attempted to escape by climbing over the wall or digging underneath. This only had them end up in solitary confinement with an even worse holiday situation.

The camp authorities did their utmost to relieve the internees' mental dispositions. They offered additional cigarettes, and on Saint Nicholas Day, six Christmas trees were brought to the camp for decorating and keeping the men busy. Gingerbread men, in addition to other cookies, were baked and distributed at this time. There was also an announcement. Everybody was to meet in the quad.

"Good afternoon, gentlemen. I am here to give you some news," said a tall, statuesque man with hair slicked back and a perfect handlebar moustache. Rudi immediately recognized him as Officer Halliday, the commander of the camp.

"Do you wish to have the good news first or the bad?" Without waiting for a response, he quickly went on. "The good news is that most of you will be leaving here. The bad news is that you will all still be here over Christmas."

"Where will we be going?" asked several in unison.

"How soon after Christmas?"

"You will be dispersed to several locations. We have not as yet received any details regarding dates. Thank you for your attention, gentlemen."

Rudi immediately wrote to Lili and told her the news. He tried to cheer her up by expressing confidence that they would again be together soon. He was so looking forward to being with her. He was looking forward to feeling the baby turning and kicking. He was looking forward to being a father...to his and Lili being parents together. Rudi expressed his concerns to Sahib, as he handed him yet another letter for Lili.

"I've got to get back to Lili as soon as possible. I shouldn't be here with all these Nazis...they might be a real threat...but me? Look how I'm losing my hair...all the stress."

Rudi spent some very solitary few days over Christmas. He did not attend the several concerts held by the Templers, though sitting propped up against a pillar at the edge of the quad, he could only admire their excellent singing. He was not impressed by some of the songs they sang, which reminded him of those the troupe of Nazis sang in Leopoldstadt on a certain Sabbath in 1934. He had a game of chess with Shlomo, who also commented on Rudi's thinning hair, and he had a short conversation with Marcelo. Mostly he missed being with Lili. He remembered the Christmas periods in Vienna and the times he'd spent in Villach and Annenheim. He felt sorry for himself.

At this time he felt lonely...lonely without Lili. Here among so many Templers, he felt he didn't belong...he felt depressed. His mood was not helped by a brief notice that his father sent on to him. The notice was about his grandmother and was edged in black: *"On October 11, 1939, at age 85, Anna Auer (Rudolf Auer's mother) died (b. July 11, 1852)."*

He had not known his grandmother well and had not seen her for about eight or nine years, as she was confined to an old-people's home. Nevertheless, this news only added to his depressed mood.

LILI'S CHRISTMAS
IN HAIFA: 1939

THOUGH LILI WAS in touch with Rudi via the exchange of letters at least twice a week, thanks to Sahib, she missed him terribly. She had, however, little time to brood. She spent a very pleasant evening with Sahib, Amelia, and their four children; she joined Gudrun for a celebratory drink at the Appinger and spent several evenings, including the last night of Hanukkah, at the home of Moshe and Rachel with Daniel. Lili came with chocolate money and a beautiful set of candles. They played the dreidel game and ate too many latkes with applesauce.

One afternoon Lili went with Rachel and Daniel to visit his father operating the merry-go-round. Daniel sat on a horse, his mother holding on to him, while Lili observed the long line of children waiting for their turn. Moshe made good money during this festive period, as his carousel never stood idle. Once on the whirly-gig, the children received their lollipops and were soon seen to pester their mother...usually their mother...for another ride. Moshe was extremely busy.

Most time, however, was spent with the Knopfelmachers. One evening, Lili and the four Knopfelmachers, minus the children who were being babysat, attended a performance of the Palestine Orchestra.

"I really like the orchestra director, Leo Kestenberg, and I thought they played very well," said Mrs. Knopfelmacher to Lili.

"Yes, it was a wonderful program. But tonight took me back to the first concert of the Palestine Orchestra we attended...on New Year's Eve. Do you remember it well, too, Mrs. Knopfelmacher?"

"Oh, yes, I even remember the pieces that were played. They played an overture by Rossini and Symphony number two in D by Brahms. What did they play after the interval, Lili?"

"I think it was Franz Schubert's 'Unfinished Symphony' and Mendelssohn's *Midsummer Night's Dream* and a piece by Weber...I can't remember which one," said Lili.

"It was the Overture: *Oberon*. What a special night," Mrs. Knopfelmacher said, swooning. "And the conductor...Toscanini...so elegant and imposing...I could invite him...I won't be naughty," she said with a twitter as she grabbed Lili by the arm.

A couple of days later, it was Christmas Eve, and Lili was just getting dressed to go to the Knopfelmachers, who had invited her for a Christmas celebration, when there was a late delivery from the postman. She thanked the postman and finished getting ready. There were a number of Christmas cards from Austria, one from Walter from Paris, and one from Joseph and Ester from Lyon. And then there was a parcel.

What on earth could it be? thought Lili, noticing it was postmarked Annenheim. *It could only be from Tante Marianne,* she thought. She opened the parcel with her kitchen scissors and found a note:

> *Christmas 1939*
> *Liebe Lili and Lieber Rudi,*
>   *Still in the future I know, but it might come early. There are some items in blue and some in pink, so I have all eventualities taken care of.*
>   *Have a wonderful Christmas; I hope you are by now both together.*
> *Alles Liebe und a tausend Bussi,*
> *Tante Marianne*

Lili burst into tears. She had so hoped she and Rudi would be together again by now. She carefully took out the baby clothes one piece at a time and held them to her face. *What a wonderful, wonderful woman, but I have this awful feeling we will never see her again.* Lili went to the bathroom and washed her face before heading out the door to the Knopfelmachers with biscuits and presents in a basket. Both Mr. and Mrs. Knopfelmacher were at the door to usher Lili in.

"You look wonderful, Lili, same as the other night at the concert. Wasn't it splendid? But you've been crying...everything all right?" asked Mrs. Knopfelmacher.

"I have a little potion for you...nothing alcoholic but will bring on happiness within minutes, Lili," said the doctor.

It tastes just like a berry juice but with the effect of champagne, thought Lili. "Thank you, Mr. Knopfelmacher...very thoughtful." Just then the baby gave a big kick that caused everybody to laugh.

"Must be a girl," said Mr. Knopfelmacher. "I know it's counterintuitive—boys play football and are supposed to have a stronger kick, but just wait and see, Lili, I'll be right...girls can always give a mighty jab to the solar plexus."

"Yes, yes, Papa, if you say so," said Rebecca as she and Arnold came in with Ariella and Talia in tow, each carrying a thin folder.

"Hello, everybody."

"Auntie Lili, can you come with us?" asked Talia. "Can everybody else go in the kitchen, please...for ten minutes, please?" The room emptied out, and Ariella took Lili by the hand and walked to the grand piano.

"Grandpa got it not so long ago. Will you play four hands with us, please, Auntie Lili?"

"It might be too hard for me," said Lili with a smile.

"We'll help you...promise," said Talia. We've already decided. You'll play 'Hungarian Dances,' by Johannes Brahms with me. We'll go first, and then you'll play 'The Dance of the Sugar Plum Fairy,' by Tchaikovsky with Ariella."

"All right," said Lili with a smile. Talia and Lili practiced first and then Ariella and Lili. Lili had to be very careful to keep up with the beat the girls were playing at, as they played rather fast, she thought.

"You can come back in again," said Talia, with a raised voice. "Did you hear anything, Grandpa?"

"No, *Schatzerl*, of course not."

"Will you light the Christmas tree now, Grandpa, so we can get started?"asked Arnold. Grandpa and his son took some minutes to light the dozens of red candles on the elegantly decorated Christmas tree. The Knopfelmachers, though Jewish, had been assimilated into Viennese society for several generations and celebrated Christmas with considerable enthusiasm, just as Lili's family had done.

Arnold looked up at his father and asked,"Do you think they'll let Rudi out soon?"

"Not until the war is over, I suspect, and Hitler has only commenced on his war path...could be years...doubt if he'll be around when Lili gives birth."

"Daddy, will you please help move the chairs so they face the piano?" asked Talia. "We want to begin our concert."

Talia waited a moment, reached for Lili's hand, and commenced. "Shush...thank you for coming to hear our piano program for four hands presented by Miss Talia Knopfelmacher...that's me, Miss Ariella Knopfelmacher, her...and Auntie Lili. Auntie Lili and I will play first... here are the 'Hungarian Dances,' by Johannes Brahms."

The adults quietly giggled as Lili and Talia adjusted their stools. Talia nodded to Lili, and they played, Lili taking great care to keep to the same beat as Talia. When they got to the end, Talia took Lili by the hand and faced everybody, and they both curtsied in unison. There was much loud applause and several bravos from Grandpa.

"Now we are pleased to present Ariella and Auntie Lili playing 'The Dance of the Sugar Plum Fairy,' by Tchaikovsky. Ariella and Lili played effortlessly, turned to the audience, curtsied in unison, and were greeted by the same applause as before.

"Shall we play again?" aked Talia. The program was repeated as was the applause.

Mr. Knopfelmacher Senior stood up and said, "Time for dinner. I'm beginning to feel weak from hunger." The schnitzel was excellent as usual, and Mr. Knopfelmacher had an additional piece, saying, "This is for Rudi, who loves his schnitzel nearly as much as I do, and here's a toast to him and Lili that they may soon be together again."

A tear ran down Lili's face as she bit her bottom lip to prevent a flood."You must be very proud of your girls, Rebecca...how well they play the piano," she said, trying to remain composed.

"Here, Lili, have another drink," said Mr. Knopfelmacher as he handed her another glass of his secret potion.

"And they already read well, too," said Arnold proudly. "Ariella, can you come here, please, and bring your teddy-bear book?" Ariella came and read as her father requested.

"Can I read, too, Daddy?" asked Talia.

"Of course," he said, and in an instant, Talia was sitting on her father's knee reading confidently.

"I can smell the *Kaiserschmarrn* coming, children; don't make me eat it all by myself," said Mr. Knopfelmacher. Everybody enjoyed the *Kaiserschmarrn*, and Mrs. Knopfelmacher said, "You can have some more, Lili; you're feeding two, don't forget."

"Can we have some more for Uncle Rudi, please, Grandpa?" asked Talia. "You had some extra schnitzel." Grandpa nodded approvingly, and both girls helped themselves to seconds. The radio was turned up as a Christmas program was in full swing, and there was a very nice exchange of gifts between everybody...all simple gifts: slippers for Grandpa, gloves for Grandma, socks for Arnold, a scarf for Rebecca, and books for the three musicians. Lili received *The Grapes of Wrath* by John Steinbeck.

"It is set during the Great Depression," said Mrs. Knopfelmacher, "and is about one family that struggles to find work, land, dignity, and a future. I think you'll like it."

"Thank you, Mrs. Knopfelmacher, very much. I will leave now with Arnold, Rebecca, and the girls. I am feeling a little sore in the back."

"Lili, why don't you stay here?" asked Mrs. Knopfelmacher. "Your room is still made up for you; your toothbrush is still in its place, and I can lend you a nice, large nightie."

"It's not proper that you should be in your home alone on Christmas Eve," said Mr. Knopfelmacher. A hot bath may help a tired back, too, Lili."

"That's so kind...okay, then; thank you, thank you very much." Lili slept soundly and woke to the smell of freshly brewed coffee. She enjoyed breakfast of *Gugelhupf* and couldn't resist a piece of *Lebkuchen*. At around noon, Lili said farewell to the Knopfelmachers and spent the afternoon at her garden table, thinking about Rudi and the previous evening and writing in her diary:

> *I hope Rudi is okay with so many people in close proximity whom he finds objectionable. I am so lucky to have so many good friends who really care about others...Mr. K. is like a father I never had and has taken over from Mr. Schwartz in Vienna. I wonder what he and his family are up to...very strange to have left Vienna without a trace... I'd love to know. And Mrs. K. is like a mother...very perceptive and caring...much more caring than my mother. And Rebecca...really has it all. She is intelligent, a professional...has a husband who is loyal, as steady as a rock, makes good money, and they have intelligent, good-looking, and bright children...and she's younger than me... hmm, never heard anything about her parents, though. Are they separated, divorced, or even still alive? There's something that's perhaps not so easy for Rebecca.*

"AUNTIE LILI, *SHALOM*," yelled Daniel, holding his mother's hand and waving a chess piece around with the other. Lili locked her diary.

"*Shalom*, Daniel; *shalom*, Rachel; *shalom*, Moshe; what a nice surprise...just in time for some coffee; come in," Lili said.

"We wanted to be certain you weren't alone on Christmas Day," said Rachel. "These are for you," she said, handing Lili a box of almond stars...Moshe made them especially to show you he could do it."

"Thank you, thank you, Moshe."

"They're rather hard...you might want to dunk them in the coffee. How's Rudi...what's the latest news?"

"Sahib just brought a letter from him yesterday. He's feeling lonely and depressed...missing me a lot."

"That's good, Lili," said Moshe. "Wouldn't want him to be happy partying with those Templers and not missing you...of course, he's missing you. Any update as to when he'll be leaving Akko?"

"Early in the new year...but what does *early* mean? And where will he be transferred to?

"You'll be able to be with him then, of course," said Rachel.

"Don't know," said Lili. There've been no specifics about that...oh, I couldn't bear it if I had to stay here on my own, getting near to the baby's birth."

From Akko to Wilhelma

WHEN SAHIB DELIVERED oranges to the Akko internment camp on Christmas Eve and received a note from Rudi to bring to Lili, he was quite upset to see Rudi so depressed. So he decided to see the commander to make one more pitch to get a better deal for Rudi. After waiting for more than half an hour, he was finally granted an interview.

"Good morning, Sahib...very nice of you bringing all those oranges...much appreciated...vitamin C is very important to minimize the onset of scurvy. There was an outbreak here once, I'm told. But I'm sure you didn't come here to receive thanks."

"No, Commander Halliday, not to receive thanks but for you to consider the situation of internee two-nine-one—Rudi Auer."

"Oh?"

"Mr. Rudi should never have been brought here. He is Austrian... he is not a German. He has been fighting Nazis for years and was even run out of Vienna, where he was trying to expose Nazi activities being conducted at the university there."

"Go on."

"He is married to a Jew, and she is pregnant...six months already—"

The commander broke in. "And how is that relevant?"

"The child will be a Jew, and Rudi will be the father of a Jew, as well as the husband of a Jew."

"Go on, I'm listening," said the commander.

"Given those circumstances, Mr. Rudi would hardly be a Nazi or Nazi sympathizer, sir. And I have known him for years...he's a good man...no threat to anyone."

"Hm, I trust you, Sahib, and your judgments. I tell you what I can do. I believe I can convince the authorities to transfer two-nine-one to Wilhelma in the next few days, rather than him being reassigned there in February or later when, I believe, more than a hundred men will be disbursed to four different camps, one of which is at Wilhelma. There is a farmer there…a dairy farmer who needs help immediately, and the authorities have requested a man from here to be allocated to that farm."

"Do you think his wife could live with him there?"

"I believe so…it already exists as a camp where women and children belonging to men interned there live…I will need to handle this very delicately, as the transfer of two-nine-one could cause jealousies and anger…leave it to me, Sahib, but say nothing about this to anybody."

AFTER DINNER ON Thursday, December 28, Rudi received a message from an officer to be in the middle of the camp quadrangle at 8:00 p.m. He needed to be alone and not mention the meeting to anybody.

At exactly 8:00 p.m., Rudi walked to the middle of the quad, wondering what this could be about. There were a few other internees in groups, but none were close by. It was relatively quiet. There was a full moon, clouds moving rather rapidly to hide it and then again reveal the big white ball. Suddenly Commander Halliday was beside him.

"Let us keep walking as we talk, and if anybody approaches, we stop talking."

"Good evening…yes, Commander."

"You are internee number two-nine-one, yes?"

"Yes, sir."

"Rudolf Auer?"

"Yes, sir."

"You have lost a lot of hair since I first set eyes on you. You have been reassigned to the Wilhelma Camp, where you will need to show your ability to work with cows. You have been assigned to a dairy farmer, Herr Bauer, I believe...yes, I know...don't laugh. You will pack your belongings and will be escorted out at four o'clock tomorrow morning. We basically have to sneak you out, because there are many men who have a more rightful claim to be reassigned to Wilhelma. They have family there. You are, however, less of a threat than they might be. Is that clear?"

"Yes, sir. Thank you, sir."

"Your wife should be able to join you there the following day. You have Sahib to thank for this development. He came to see me yesterday. Clear?"

"Yes, clear. Thank you, sir."

"Good luck, Rudi," said the commander as he walked briskly away. Rudi was so happy he could barely stop himself from baying at the moon or letting out a loud yodel and doing a *Schuhplattler* dance. *Within a couple of days, Lili and I will be together again. I never realized how much I'd miss her.*

At precisely 4:00 a.m. on December 29, 1939, Rudi was led to an army vehicle; the engine was turned on, next the headlights, and then the vehicle rolled quietly out of the Akko prison compound. Though having slept barely two hours due to excitement, Rudi was wide awake, recognizing every turn in the road, for he had traveled it many times. As they drove through Haifa, he gave a little wave toward Mount Carmel, House Schneider, and Lili. Rudi would hopefully see her the following day. The drive took less than three hours, Wilhelma being just 13 km east of Jaffa.

A police officer greeted him. "*Shalom,* Rudolf Auer, internee number two-nine-one. Welcome to Perimeter Settlement, Camp V Wilhelma...I believe your wife will be joining you tomorrow."

"*Shalom,* good morning, sir. Thank you, yes, thank you," said Rudi.

"You should be aware that a number of people will want to know who you are and why you have been sent here, while their husbands or sons remain interned in Akko. Also be aware that some anti-Semitism exists within the settlement...I'm sure there was some, too, in Akko, but you will have a pregnant wife to protect here...good luck." And with that, Rudi was driven a little further to a large farmhouse with a number of outbuildings.

In the meantime, Sahib had been notified of Rudi's imminent arrival and was told he should inform Lili that she would be able to join Rudi in Wilhelma from noon the next day, Friday, December 29. Sahib and Amelia drove up to House Schneider to inform Lili and help her in whatever way they could.

"What a nice surprise, Amelia, Sahib. Come in, come in."

"We have a nice surprise for you, Lili."

"Really?"

"Can I put some coffee on, Lili?" asked Amelia. "You'll need to be sitting down when Sahib tells you what he came to tell you."

"Oh, how exciting...something good about Rudi?" asked Lili. "I'll get some biscuits to go with the coffee." Lili became quite flushed. Amelia poured the coffee while Lili sat bolt upright, her hands clasped in front of her like a schoolgirl in the headmaster's office.

"Tell me, tell me," she said, pleading.

"Rudi is no longer in Akko...he is at the Perimeter Settlement in Wilhelma...probably just arrived there a little while ago," said Sahib. "Near Jaffa—"

"And?"

"You can be with him from tomorrow...after lunch. We'll take you there."

Lili's eyes widened and filled with tears. "Oh yes, it's been so long... I've missed him so...thank you, thank you." Lili sat back. "How can I leave here by tomorrow?"

"Easy," said Amelia. "You don't have to take your belongings all at once. We'll have you come back a few days later to collect the rest you'll need. You'll be able to say good-bye to your friends this afternoon or tomorrow morning. In any event, you'll be able to come back here on occasions. It's Rudi they want locked up. You'll have some freedom of movement...probably not much, but some."

"How did you manage to arrange this, Sahib?" asked Lili. "I'm sure you had something to—"

"Just explained to the commander the situation in terms he could understand, and he arranged the transfer. My weekly orange delivery couldn't have hurt, either. Actually, Rudi was selected because of his ability to milk cows."

"He's never milked a cow in his life," said Lili with a smile.

"Never mind. He'll be milking twenty a day...twice a day," said Sahib, smiling.

"At least you'll have the best cream for your *Gugelhupf*, Lili," said Amelia. "And you and Rudi will be together." Lili gave Amelia a big hug and promptly sat down again. She needed to take all this in.

After lots of smiles all round, Lili stood up and said, "I'll go and pack, then...you could help me, Amelia, to make sure I'm being practical."

Sahib walked around the garden and orange grove, happy to have brought such joyous news and to see what needed attending to in the yard. *Nothing urgent,* he thought. *Can't do much gardening in winter.*

Later in the afternoon, Lili went to visit Moshe and Rachel and the Knopfelmacher half dozen. There was more coffee, much joyousness, a duet played, some tears, and some promises. Mr. Knopfelmacher promised to phone Lili's employers, who would surely understand and be happy for Lili, and Lili promised she'd be back to visit soon.

When she was confident that she had packed all she needed for Wilhelma, at least to start with, Lili went to bed and was soon asleep, as she had become exhausted from all the day's excitement.

As SAHIB AND Amelia arrived at the Pine Street House Schneider to pick up Lili at ten in the morning to drive her to Wilhelma, a lot of her friends were in the front yard to wish her well. There was Moshe; Rachel and Daniel; the entire extended Knopfelmacher family; Gudrun with a new man, Thomas, an Englishman, and her daughters, Ilse and Annemarie, and previous landlords; and Frau Weber and her husband, both deemed too old to be interned. There were many hugs, many good wishes, a few tears, and a dreidel charm from Rachel. As Sahib drove out the driveway, there was much waving and smiling.

During the journey to Wilhelma Camp V, which took just two hours, Lili reflected on leaving all these good friends with friendships that were years old and that made living in Haifa tolerable. She wondered how frequently she'd be able to visit them. She wondered how long the war would last, and she wondered whether she and Rudi would ever again live in House Schneider. Suddenly the car stopped at the entrance of Perimeter Camp V Wilhelma.

Rudi was standing inside the front gate, after having gained permission, when they drove through. Sahib stopped the car, and Lili jumped out and ran into Rudi's arms. There was a long embrace. Rudi rubbed Lili's tummy and with a big smile, greeted and thanked Amelia and Sahib. They drove to the far end of the camp, where a large farmhouse with barns and outhouses stood.

"Here we are," said Rudi, as the car came to a halt. "The property of Mr. Bauer...*farmer* in German...not sure whether that's a joke or not."

"Nice property," said Sahib.

"It is quite large, and I will surely have my hands full, responsible for twenty-five cows, three calves, two horses, several pigs, and a dozen or so chickens...and two workers," said Rudi as he took Lili's large case from the car.

"Arabs?" asked Sahib.

"Yes. They sign in every morning and go home each evening," said Rudi. "Come in and have a look around. The place was built by a German builder responsible for many of the homes in Sarona, the largest of the Templer communities. It's now also been turned into an internment camp. The house is very well built and with a practical layout, three bedrooms, a large kitchen with a wood-burning stove, and a large bathroom...a living room, of course...and a formal dining room."

"Not too much furniture," said Lili. "That's good."

"Then there are all the outhouses for the horses, the cow feed, a pigpen, a chicken shed, and a workshop. Shall I put a coffee on?" asked Rudi.

"Can we first look around outside?" asked Lili. There was a large, overgrown vegetable garden with various fruit trees near the house and a citrus grove leading to the back fence.

"Between two and three hundred trees, I was told, mostly orange trees," said Rudi.

"Look, there's a vineyard," said Amelia.

"Pretty overgrown, too, Rudi," said Sahib. "I think you'll be kept rather busy."

"All good work, Sahib, in the fresh air."

"Probably not so fresh in the cowshed," said Amelia. "Let's have coffee now, Rudi; Lili's been on her feet long enough."

The large kitchen included a table for four at which all made themselves comfortable. Rudi produced the required crockery and cutlery and placed a cake in the middle of the table.

"*Weihnachsstollen*...from a very nosy German woman, wanting to ask more questions than I was willing to answer."

"Can I ask you some questions about Akko before we leave you alone with Lili, Rudi?" said Amelia.

"Of course, Amelia."

"I'm very curious. What was it like living in such confined circumstances with strangers, I imagine with some people you didn't like?"

"There's a lot of tension—thirty-six to a barrack...a dozen or so different nationalities: mainly Germans but also Arabs, Jews, Italians, Yugoslavs, and Hungarians...little to do...boredom's a real problem."

"Most haven't done anything wrong, have they, Rudi?" asked Sahib.

"That's right. It's a real human tragedy—people locked up without cause. Everybody has family they desperately want to reunite with... especially before the holiday period...men got very edgy...lots of arguments...some fights and several futile attempts by people wanting to escape. I'm so grateful to you, Sahib, for getting me out of there."

"A pleasure, Rudi. That's what friends are for. Shall I pick you up next Saturday, Lili, and we can get the remainder of the things you want to have here from the Pine Street home?"

"That would be much appreciated, Sahib."

"Good, I'll pick you up at ten in the morning, Lili. I'll make arrangements with the gate officers as we leave now…shouldn't be any problem, as all the guards here are Jews; they'll be sympathetic to your circumstances. Come, Amelia…*Ma'a salama*, you two."

"*Ma'a salama*, thanks for everything." Lili spent the afternoon getting reacquainted with Rudi and acquainted with her new home. The property and home were large, though the upkeep could be somewhat daunting, she thought.

"I think the two farmhands, Abdullah and Mohammad, will handle the milking and care of the horses and pigs, and we'll look after the garden, orchard, and vineyard. Let's go and meet them before evening milking."

"SALAM, ABDULLAH; SALAM, Mohammad. This is my wife, Lili, expecting, as you can see."

"*Salam alekum*, ma'am…pleased to meet you, Miss Lili. You need not worry about anything…Mohammad and I very happy to look after property. We are very happy Mr. Rudi allows us grow our watermelons we have done for years. Watermelons sell well, Miss Lili."

Rudi showed Lili around the property and fed the chickens on the way. They settled in for a quiet evening, during which they shared the events that occurred while they had been apart.

Sunday morning Rudi got up very early to monitor how Abdullah and Mohammad went about their chores, including milking twenty-five cows and feeding the two horses and five pigs. He'd come inside for lunch at noon, he told Lili as he kissed her on the forehead.

Lili enjoyed some *Weihnachsstollen* with coffee for breakfast and took out her diary. She had a lot she wanted to write.

New Year's Eve, '39. Wonderful to be together with Rudi again. What a special send-off by friends at House Schneider yesterday. I will miss every one of them. I have really developed a deep friendship with them all. There is something weird about the present situation. I am leaving a town and friends somewhat reluctantly to be with Rudi. I am voluntarily moving from freedom to being incarcerated...following Rudi. We had similar circumstances leaving Vienna, where we ran away from Nazi encroachment, and I didn't want to leave Vienna then at all. Now Rudi, regarded as a German and possibly a Nazi, and I are locked up with real Nazis...probably dozens of them. Something ironic about that! Hmmmmm, I will likely be very uncomfortable here with all those fascists. It's wonderful to be together with Rudi, though.

LILI SETTLED INTO her new surroundings very quickly, planning the location of her furniture that would arrive the following Saturday and doing a little weeding in the garden each day, encumbered somewhat by a growing tummy and inclement weather. One day she nearly fell over when the baby suddenly lurched to one side. It rained heavily for several days, during which Lili spent reading and knitting, which always reminded her of Tante Marianne. Several evenings, Rudi and Lili bundled up and walked around Perimeter Camp V Wilhelma. A number of people peered out from their windows at them, and others walked by very close to have a good look, some with a "*Guten Abend*," others remaining silent. Rudi also found it very strange to be together with hundreds of Germans, not knowing who supported Hitler and who did not.

"What poetic justice here, Lili," said Rudi with a thought that had just come to him. "Throughout Europe there are dozens of concentration camps in which Jews have been herded together and guarded by Nazis or Nazi collaborators. Here, Germans, including a good proportion of Nazis, find themselves in camps watched over by Jewish guards who impose early nightly curfews."

"Yes, that is really ironic." Rudi and Lili quickly determined to keep mainly to themselves in Wilhelma, run the farm efficiently with the help of Abdullah and Mohammad, and maintain it well, while hoping for a quick end to the war.

—⊷—

As HAD BEEN planned, at precisely 10:00 a.m. on the following Saturday, Sahib arrived with his truck and oldest son, Muhsin.

"*Salam*, Lili. Muhsin will help me with the furniture."

"*Salam*, Sahib; *salam*, Muhsin; that's very nice of you."

They soon arrived at House Schneider. "You'll just need to show us the furniture you want to take and leave us to it. You could walk up the road and visit with some of your friends, Lili."

And that's how it was. Lili pointed out the furniture she wanted taken: a couple of rugs, the sewing machine, and some kitchen items to go, and she packed some more clothes, linens, and towels. She walked the short distance to the Knopfelmachers, where Arnold was visiting.

"Arnold, why don't you tell Moshe that Lili is here...he won't be working today, and bring the rest of your family as well," said his father.

"Oh, Lili, you look really well; how are you?" asked Mrs. Knopfelmacher. "Come to the kitchen with me while I rustle up some sandwiches." Everyone was very pleased to see Lili and overwhelmed her with hugs and questions.

"We must be careful not to exhaust the woman," said Mr. Knopfelmacher. They were nearly at the end of lunch, when there was a knock at the door.

"I am Muhsin, son of Sahib, and we have finished loading the truck."

"Do you think Father would like some lunch before driving back?"

"Probably."

"Go run and tell him to come; we will be expecting him momentarily." Sahib arrived, and he and Muhsin ate some freshly prepared sandwiches, while seconds were still being assembled, and they drank chai—strong, black tea.

"Lili should be able to visit quite regularly; the guards are all Jews and understand her situation well," said Sahib. There were many hugs and farewells, and soon the fully laden truck was on the road back to Wilhelma. Though it had been raining for most of the journey, the rain had now stopped, and the truck was soon emptied.

"I brought you a radio, Rudi, as your thirst for news cannot be solely quenched by the *Palestine Post*. I can't imagine you discussing major foreign-affairs events with too many of your neighbours, though."

"*Shukran*, thank you so much, Sahib. I appreciate that. Can I pay you for it?"

"*Afwan*, no, no...I was given a new one; don't need a second one...Muhsin and I must be off; Amelia will be expecting us for dinner. Happy New Year, Rudi, Lili! *Ma'a salama*."

THE FIRST COUPLE of months of the New Year were, from a weather perspective, pretty dreary. Rudi and Lili developed their daily routines. They developed a good relationship with the two Arab farm workers, completed the weeding of the vegetable garden, and covered the garden beds with lime. Rudi spent a great deal of time in February pruning the vineyard and several trees in the garden—apricot, plum, cumquat, and fig. Rudi and Lili snuggled up a lot by the open fire in their lounge room and read a great deal, as the house had a significant library. Most of Rudi's reading was of manuals that provided instructions on such matters as horse grooming, calf feeding, pig slaughtering, beekeeping, fruit-tree pruning, vineyard care, and determining the sex of chickens. That gave Rudi an idea that might interest the farm workers.

"*Salam*, Abdullah, *salam*, Mohammad. I have an idea you might like."

"*Salam*, Mr. Rudi. Anything you say, Mr.Rudi."

"You know when the hens get broody? Put a dozen or so eggs under them, and you'll have chickens in no time. You can fatten them up... we have plenty of feed...and you can sell the roosters when they are grown. Keep the hens for their eggs."

"Thank you, Mr. Rudi. We have one clucky hen now," said Abdullah enthusiastically.

———

READING THE *PALESTINE Post* regularly and listening daily to the radio clearly informed Rudi that the world was not a very settled place. On September 29, the previous year, the Nazis and Soviets had divided up Poland. On December 14, the Soviet Union was expelled from the League of Nations, and on January 8, food rationing began in Britain. There was little news from family, however. Other than formulaic Christmas greetings that were permitted, there had been no letter from any member of the family. Lili had not heard from her mother for almost a year.

At the end of February, Lili's pregnancy was getting close to term, so Rudi and Lili began to make inquiries as to which hospital Lili should go to, to give birth. There was apparently some indecision among authorities, because Lili was a Jew and Rudi was designated a German.

Early on Friday, March 8, Rudi was spreading manure from the stable over the garden beds, when Lili called him to come to her.

"I think I'm having contractions...I need to go to hospital."

"Oh, hang on, Lili...I'll run to the guardhouse, and I'm sure they'll arrange things for us."

"Quick, Rudi, please."

A still less-than-pleasant-smelling Rudi ran to the guardhouse. One guard took his car and drove Rudi back to fetch Lili.

"The other guard will find the most appropriate hospital. He'll tell us when we get back to the guardhouse on our way out."

"Go to the Jaffa Government Hospital; they'll be expecting you," the second guard said.

"*Schnell, schnell. Jalla, Jalla.* Please go quickly," said Lili. "I think the baby wants to come."

"It needs to hang on for about a half hour more, ma'am," said the driver.

A gurney was waiting as Lili arrived at the front door, and she was lifted on in a great hurry. Rudi was getting quite anxious, as Lili was grimmacing a lot, and her contractions seemed only seconds apart. She was wheeled in rather quickly, and a nurse pointed Rudi and the camp guard in the direction of the waiting room. Not ten minutes had elapsed before Rudi heard a scream of pain and about three seconds later, a baby's cry.

"I think it's here," announced the guard. Rudi smiled an awkward smile.

A nurse came to the waiting room. "Ten more minutes, and you wouldn't have made it. It's a boy, and Mother is very happy. *Mabrouk*, Mr. Rudi. Sorry, I am the midwife—Denise Haddod. I'll go and clean up, and you will be able to see your baby in a little while, Mr. Rudi."

"*Mazel Tov*, Mr. Rudi, congratulations...not much trouble really," said the guard.

The midwife soon reappeared and took Rudi to Lili and their child. Lili just beamed. They had spent a little time together, when the midwife came in again.

"You should leave now, Mr. Rudi. Driver, you can bring Lili and baby home next Wednesday. Be here at ten in the morning."

"I'll be here. *Shalom*."

And so it was that Rudi and the same driver arrived at the hospital the following Wednesday. Rudi and Lili witnessed the completion of the paper work:

Father: Rudolf Auer, Age 26, Religion Christian, Nationality German
Mother: Lili Auer, Age 34, Religion Christian, Nationality German
Name of Infant: Peter
Name of person notifying and registering birth: D. Haddod
Description of person notifying birth: Midwife, Jaffa
Date of Registration: 11.3.40.

Rudi and Lili both shrugged their shoulders.

"Didn't think I had converted to Christianity since last Friday," remarked Lili in the back seat, with Peter asleep in her arms. "Why was the birth not registered till the eleventh, Rudi?"

"Parden me for overhearing, ma'am; it's a custom here to wait three days before registering a birth in case the baby dies...baby Peter looks very healthy, ma'am."

"Thank you, sir," replied Rudi. Half an hour later, they were driven through the camp gate.

A Child Creates
Excitement; Hitler
Wreaks Havoc

"Welcome home, Peterle, son of Lili Gertrud Auer and Rudolf Auer, internee number two-nine-one of Perimeter Camp V Wilhelma," said Rudi. "I hope it won't be long before we are all out of here, so you can grow up without being surrounded by a high barbed-wire fence."

"Let's hope so, Rudi," said Lili as she leaned forward and gave him a squeeze on his shoulder. Rudi and Lili were very excited. They watched over their son much of each day for the next week or so. He was held a lot, he slept a lot, and he seemed to be on Mother's breast most of the time.

Rudi and Lili's next communication out of camp was not scheduled till the end of the month. Letters announcing the birth of their son were sent to all the relations in Austria, to Walter in Paris, to Joseph and Ester in Lyon, and to all their friends in Haifa. Rudi wrote the text in French. He and Lili were of the view that Swiss Red Cross censors might pass it more quickly written in French than if it were written in German. There was no logic in the idea; the decision was just made on a hunch. They also had no idea how long it would take for the news to reach its destination.

Rudi's parents received the form letter via the Swiss Red Cross on May 4. There was much excitement as Rudi Senior phoned Lili's mother and Tante Marianne, who shared the news with half of Annenheim.

COMITÉ INTERNATIONAL DE LA „CROIX ROUGE"
AGENCE CENTRALE D'INFORMATION
CENTRAL COUNCIL PALACE

GENÈVE
SUISSE

Monsieur le Directeur,

Je vous serais très reconnaissant(e), de bien vouloir vous renseigner sur

Monsieur RUDOLF AUER,

Madame MARIA AUER,

Mademoiselle

FAMILLE

qui jusqu'à présent habitaient à ANNENHEIM-KANZELBAHN,

AM/OSSIACHER SEE, POST SATTENDORF, KAERNTEN
AUTRICHE-ALLEMAGNE

et que vous m'informiez du résultat de vos recherches.

Je vous prie d'informer en même temps la dite personne, que me porte bien. **

Avec mes remerciements anticipés, je vous prie, Monsieur le Directeur, l'agréer mes salutations les plus
distinguées.

xx ET QUE MA FEMME
A DONNÉ NAISSANCE
A UN GARÇON PIERRE
MARS.

RUDOLF AUER,

PERIMETER SETTLEMENT

28 MARS 1940

WILHELMA,

PALESTINE

Ci-inclus: 2 coupons de réponse internationaux

— 257 —

On May 15, Lili received a knock at her door.

"*Shalom*, madam. I am Abraham, one of the guards. I have some flowers that just arrived for you…we do not know exactly how they got here, but they are from Paris."

"Oh, thank you, Abraham, *shalom*." Lili called Rudi, who was in the barn doing some repairs.

"Look—from Walter…isn't he always so thoughtful. Thirteen red roses and a note. It reads, 'Congratulations and very best wishes to the three of you. Walter.'"

Rudi put his arm around Lili, accompanied her into the kitchen, and got a vase from a high cupboard. He had some morning coffee with Lili and smiled at his son in his crib before returning to the barn with a piece of cake each for Mohammad and Abdullah.

Lili knew she'd be alone for some time now, so she fetched her diary and began to write:

> *May 15, 1940. What a wonderful experience to have a baby. Never dreamt it would be so marvelous. I now appreciate family and especially all our friends in Haifa more than ever. And Rudi is so caring…of the baby, of me. He seems to have become a very responsible person.*
>
> *Hitler seems to be taking over much of Europe. I fear for my mother. I fear I'll never see her again. I fear she'll be dragged off to one of those concentration camps.*
>
> *We have been so unsettled for years, being in places we hadn't intended being in—displaced, disoriented, and distressed. Nevertheless, we are very happy, but not as happy as we could be. We should be settled and very, very happy now, starting a family. These should be the happiest years of our lives.*
> *Thank God I have Peter.*

She went to pick him up as he began to stir.

THE FOLLOWING WEEKEND, as had been arranged at the front gate, Sahib and Amelia came to fetch Lili and Peter to spend a few hours in Haifa. Mrs. Knopfelmacher had arranged for all the usual suspects to come for a simple lunch, at which time they could meet the newborn.

Fingerfoods were passed around—some sandwiches, knishes, lamb kebabs, an assortment of vegetable fritters, and some spicy meatballs. Mr. Knopfelmacher steered Lili away from these, suggesting that they might not agree with the baby. With the aroma of coffee wafting in, Mrs. Knopfelmacher produced some halva, sweet dumplings, and a *Gugelhupf.*

"Especially for you, Lili. We know it's your favourite," said Mrs. Knopfelmacher. "Would you please fetch the cream, Arnold."

In the meantime, the baby was being passed around from person to person, adults and children alike, as though he were a jewel to be admired.

"Careful, don't shake him up too much, Talia, we wouldn't want any reappearance of his lunch," cautioned Arnold, keeping a watchful eye as the children passed around the baby with considerable confidence and care at the same time. Lili received many gifts for the baby, including a well-worn chess piece—the white king from an old chess set.

"Don't want it, Auntie Lili. I'm not a baby any more," said Daniel.

With many thanks, many hugs, and good wishes, Lili was driven back to Wilhelma with Sahib's promise he'd bring them both back at the same time a month from now.

"See you June fifteenth, Lili," said Mrs. Knopfelmacher, waving. Lili chatted with Amelia and Sahib during the entire return trip.

"I know you've been really busy with the baby, but have you been able to find out much about the people in the camp, Lili?" asked Amelia.

"We really try to keep to ourselves and enjoy our little family, but you can't help but hear things."

"Like what, Lili?"

"Well, every time there is news of some Nazi advance or conquest, like when the Germans bombed a naval base near Scotland exactly a week after Peter was born, there was loud, enthusiastic celebration by dozens of Germans. They can be quite noisy. The same happened on April ninth or tenth after we heard, on your radio, that the Nazis had invaded Denmark and Norway. Rudi loves the radio…listens to it all the time, even during the day when he's in the barn or the workshop."

"There must have been a heck of a hullabaloo the other day then, Lili," said Sahib. "On May tenth the Nazis invaded France, Belgium, Luxembourg, and the Netherlands."

"Oh yes, there was much jubilation…but I think the guards told them to be quiet. The celebrations seemed to stop earlier than on previous occasions," said Lili. The car slowed.

"Here we are, Lili. You certainly have a lovely baby. Congratulations again. We won't come in today; the children will be expecting us. See you in a month. *Ma asalama*."

"*Salam*, Rudi," they called as he appeared at the barn door.

"*Salam*, Amelia; *salam*, Sahib…*shukran*, thank you very much," he replied, smiling and waving as the car drove away.

LATE ON MAY 23, Rudi was in the workshop, repairing a door lock and listening to the radio, when there was a repeat announcement he hadn't heard before and that caught his attention: "Holland surrenders to the Nazis…we repeat, the Germans have taken over Holland. "

Rudi and Lili were having dinner that evening, lamenting all the successes Hitler had been having, seemingly taking over much of Europe, when they heard loud, celebratory singing. Shortly thereafter, one could hear loud yelling. Rudi ran out the door.

"Be careful, Rudi. Keep out of harm's way; don't do anything foolish." Lili locked the door behind him.

There was more than just yelling. There was a serious fight. A group of Germans was fending off four or five very agitated non-German men wielding weapons, including a hammer, a shovel, and an axe. A couple of Germans got hit and were bloodied before guards broke up the melee. A rumor spread the following day that three non-Germans had been taken to Akko.

Exactly a week later, in the middle of a rainy morning, two military vehicles screeched to a halt, and four officers stormed toward the farmhouse.

"*Shalom*, we are military police," they said, as Rudi, with a shovel in hand, suddenly stood beside them, having run from the barn.

"*Sabah el kheer*. What's the urgency, Officers?" he asked.

"We have orders to inspect all houses to check there are no firearms, no armaments, no cameras, and no radios."

"We have none of these," said Rudi calmly. "Not even a hunting rifle to keep foxes away. Please feel free to search the house, but be quiet; there's a baby sleeping." Rudi opened the door and let the men inside.

"*Sabah el kheer*, Officers. Can I offer you tea or coffee?" asked Lili. She felt she was outwardly calm, but within she was quite upset. *Can't one just be left alone? Four men with weapons...they're scary. I hope the baby doesn't wake...it could be a frightening experience for a little one...all those unknown noises they make.*

In the meantime, Rudi walked quickly back to the barn to see if he could hide the radio he'd been listening to.

"Go back to the house, Mr. Rudi," said Mohammad...radio safe." Rudi returned to the house to find the officers heeding his request not to disturb a sleeping baby. Rudi poured himself a coffee and soon followed the four men out of the house and into the barn, coffee still in hand.

"We will check all sheds," announced one of the officers. Mohammad and Abdullah quietly sneaked into the vineyard, conscious of the fact that not all Jewish officers were kindly disposed to Arab farm workers. The screech of tires soon announced the disappearance of the military police empty-handed and the appearance of Mohammad and Abdullah back in the barn.

"Radio in chicken feed, Mr. Rudi. Come." Rudi watched Abdullah digging in the wheat bin and pulling out the radio wrapped in a hessian bag.

"*Shukran*, Abdullah," said Rudi with a smile.

"*Afwan*, Mr. Rudi," said Abdullah, responding with a salute and a return smile.

———

THE RAINY SPELL of the recent couple of months seemed to have come to an end, and the likelihood of late frosts had passed. It was now time to transfer the seedlings that had been sown in the hothouse to the prepared garden beds. Abdullah and Mohammad helped Rudi construct a trellis for climbing beans and build mounds for the planting of vines, including watermelon, cantaloupe, cucumber, pumpkin, zucchini, and squash. These and other seedlings were planted in the one day. There were also onions, tomatoes, peppers, and aubergine. Rudi prepared rills for the sowing of carrots, radishes, and parsley. He finished sowing and could barely stand up, as his back was hurting so much. He tried straightening it.

"You become old man, Mr. Rudi?" asked Mohammad with a smile on his face. "Can we help you? You done a lot."

"Yes, plant garlic in between the plants where I tell you…keeps insects away." Rudi stepped back and admired the garden, hoping it would yield well in the coming months. He was just thinking, *I really hope we'll be gone by the time these vegetables can be harvested.*

"Come Abdulla, Mohammad; let's inspect the vineyard. Bring a pair of secateurs, Mohammad."

"All look good, Mr. Rudi?" asked Abdullah.

"*Ahamdulilla*; these weeds need to be kept in check with a hoe… probably once every two weeks. See these thistles?" asked Rudi, pointing. "The chickens really like them."

"We do weeding, Mr. Rudi," promised Abdullah.

"*Shukran*," said Rudi. "Could you hand me the secateurs, please, Mohammad?" Rudi cut off a few extra leaders on several vines. "How are your chickens coming along?"

"*Ahamdulilla*, Mr. Rudi. We have thirty-three now. Ten are nearly ready for kill. You and miss Lili should have some. Chicken kebabs very good."

"Save me one. See these grubs on the leaves?" asked Rudi, pointing. "Whenever you see them, squish them, like this," he said as he demonstrated. "Before summer, we will have to dig channels along each row of vines for irrigating. I will probably need your help, Mohammad. My back not so good anymore." Mohammad smiled as Abdullah gave him a nudge.

A couple of days went by, and Rudi went for a walk into the vegetable garden to check that the seedlings had all taken. There before him stood a scarecrow, about six feet tall, with a hessian body and a hessian head, big blue buttons for eyes, yellow wool for hair, and a floppy hat. A broad smile developed across Rudi's face. He also had the feeling he was being watched, and he spun around.

"Do you like it, Mr. Rudi?" asked Abdullah. "Mohammad's mother helped make it; she thinks it keeps evil spirits away and birds from eating vegetables. She learned it from her grandmother."

"Thank you, boys. Thank your mother, Mohammad."

The weather improved on a daily basis, and Rudi decided to make a garden table together with benches to put at the side of the house and under the large fig tree—similar to the garden table they had at the Pine Street house on Mount Carmel. Rudi showed Abdullah and Mohammad a sketch and told them what he wanted to do.

"Seven feet by three feet, Mr. Rudi? Will be big table."

"Please get me the wood together, take it into the workshop, and we'll make it tomorrow after morning milking."

"No problem, Mr.Rudi. We start milking a little early."

By ten o'clock the following morning, Abdullah and Mohammad had finished the milking, had the cans lined up for the milk-pickup truck, and had selected pieces of wood from which the table and benches were to be made. Mohammad was just sharpening a saw, when Rudi entered the workshop with the radio under his arm.

"I learned it from my uncle. Saw does better job when sharp," said Abdullah. The three of them worked together like a real team. Rudi liked both the young men, and they liked him. They measured, sawed, drilled, hammered, nailed, and bolted. They also sweated a lot. They had lunch, rested for an hour, and did more of the same.

Midafternoon, Lili, carrying Peter, walked into the workshop as the three men were proudly inspecting their completed product.

"*Salam*, Miss Lili. You have fine table and benches. Very good, very strong."

"You look so hot," said Lili. "Would you like something to drink?"

"Chai would be good, ma'am."

The men carried the table and benches and placed them under the fig tree. They moved the table around a bit to make sure it was in the best position. Lili returned, pushing Peter in a pram and carrying a tray of coffee, strong tea, sugar, and sandwiches. Rudi took the tray from her, placed it on the table, and invited Abdullah and Mohammad to join them.

"This is a very nice table, boys," said Lili." Everybody smiled. "Can I pour you some chai? Sugar?" They all sat for about half an hour, sipped, and ate, Abdullah barely able to take his eyes off the baby.

"I notice you are looking a lot at the baby, Abdullah. Do you like babies?"

"Yes, ma'am; my father and baby brother were killed not long ago."

"Oh, I'm so sorry, Abdullah," said Lili.

"How were they killed, Abdullah?" asked Rudi.

"Killed by British officers in a raid...they had the wrong house." There was an awkward silence.

"I will help you with the pigs, horses, and milking this afternoon," offered Rudi, looking at his watch, then at Mohammad and Abdullah. "I don't want to get you into trouble with the guards for leaving late."

"Thank you, Mr. Rudi. Don't forget next week we slaughter pig," said Mohammad.

That was a good cue for Lili to get up, return Peter to the pram, and head toward the house. Mohammad followed her with the tray. From now on, whenever the weather was fine, Lili would come to the garden table and serve the three men afternoon tea.

Rudi and Lili weren't really thinking about their wedding anniversary as it was approaching, when standard greetings arrived via the Red Cross from Rudi's parents, Walter, Moshe and Rachel, and the Knopfelmachers. There was nothing from Lili's mother. Lili became alarmed. *Why on earth does she not contact us? Is she still angry with me for running off with Rudi all those years ago? Is she angry with Rudi for all his stupid mistakes and taking me away from her? Is it perhaps that she can't write to us for some reason…perhaps she's too sick or has been taken away by the Nazis? Surely we would have heard… from Walter or Rudi's dad…perhaps she's just too caught up in her own world.*

There was also a box with good wishes from Annenheim. There were more than twenty items of baby clothing. The baby items all brought a smile to Rudi and Lili's face, and it spurred Lili on to preparing a celebratory meal. She spent several days preparing for it, including getting some veal from a German butcher in the camp. She was sure the butcher gave it to her reluctantly…it was only a feeling.

On their anniversary, Lili called Rudi to the table, lit a candle, and asked him to open the red wine.

"Where did you get that from, *Schatzerl?*"

"I smuggled it in with the furniture." Rudi opened a Chianti, neither being able to remember where it had come from, but it would certainly go well with the schnitzel. The schnitzel with lingonberries was as good as any they could remember, and they lingered over their wine. Lili surprised Rudi with *Kaiserschmarrn* she had made earlier in the afternoon and the *Apfelmus* made the previous day. The radio was playing some Strauss which prompted Rudi to take Lili in his arms and dance a couple of figure eights around the kitchen. There was a loud cry from the Moses basket sitting on a chair, so the dancing part of the evening came promptly to a halt, and Peter spent the next while on Papa or Mama's lap.

On the morning of May 28, Rudi read that Belgium had surrendered to the Nazis, and in early June he read that on June 3, the Germans had begun to drop bombs on Paris and that the Germans had entered the city. Lili was beside herself.

"What will happen to Walter? Perhaps something has happened to him already, Rudi," she said with anguish in her voice.

"I havn't heard this on the radio, Lili…I wouldn't want to guess. Walter's a very bright man. I suspect he's fled the city and is hiding out somewhere in the countryside. Perhaps he's crossed the border into Spain. Perhaps he'll join the resistance."

"I'm worried about Joseph and Ester in Lyon, too, Lili," said Rudi. "There was already more than a little anti-Semitism in Lyon six years ago. And now with a child and ageing parents…moving wouldn't be so easy."

Rudi and Lili became aware that on June 10, Norway surrendered to the Nazis, and on June 14 it was confirmed that the Germans had indeed entered Paris. Every day now, there was anxiety in the house as they read and listened for more bad news. It was as if the purpose of getting up in the morning was to turn on the radio to receive disturbing news of further advances by Hitler and greater attrocities inflicted upon mankind.

ON THIS DAY, death was also to come to a pig. It was not the designated day for the annual *Schweineschlacht* with all the tradition that went with it…that would not occur till the autumn. Today would be just a very matter-of-fact killing of a sow for sustenance. Not soon after breakfast, a German butcher from the camp came in his truck with his implements of death and other tools. Rudi led him to the barn, where he met Abdullah and Mohammad. Lili shuttered all the windows facing the barn so as to block out any possible noise of the activity there.

As the butcher was led to the *Schweinestall,* the pigpen, Rudi retreated to the vineyard. Today was a day when he couldn't witness a slaughter. He didn't have the stomach for it. Under normal circumstances, he believed, he would have been okay with the butchering of a pig, for it was, after all, for the provision of food for quite a few people for many meals. He wasn't sure, though, as he had never witnessed the killing of any animal larger than a hare. Today was different… he'd recently been having too many bad dreams of the SS killings in the streets of Vienna and elsewhere and even worse dreams about the butchers of the Gestapo.

Abdulla and Mohammad had indeed participated in such activity before. They had cleared the large barn table of various items the previous day, scrubbed it down thoroughly with soap and water, and let it dry overnight. They reconnected the block and tackle, which had been used for the same purpose on earlier occasions, and were now ready for the day's major activity.

There was not much resistance, not much of a squeal, as the pig was stabbed and strung up via the block and tackle, a bucket placed beneath to collect the blood. It measured over six feet from top to bottom and weighed well over two hundred pounds. It was soon being skinned, intermittently washed down, and divided up with skillful hands and sharp implements. Now, several hours later, the animal was all cut up and on display in pieces on the large table.

Neither Lili nor Rudi had become aware of the life-ending deed and were beginning to wonder how much longer the butchering process would take, when Abdullah came to the door and invited Rudi and Lili to inspect the butcher's handiwork. Lili took a close look at Abdullah's hands, which were clean, but declined the offer. Rudi went to look at the animal, all carefully dissected and laid out as if it were parts of a puzzle. He ordered a nice piece for roasting and six chops for himself and asked for a selection of prime pieces for a family of six, separately packed. The butcher was asked to bring back some prime ham and a string of sausages when the curing and smoking had been complete. Rudi was paid a sum of money he didn't bother to count and returned to have a late lunch with Lili. They were both pleased to hear the butcher's van drive away, and Lili entertained the idea of becoming a vegetarian.

— ⚬⚬⚬ —

THE FOLLOWING DAY, as had been arranged a month earlier, Sahib and Amelia came to pick up Lili and the baby for a short day with friends at the Knopfelmachers' home. Rudi felt disappointed that rules didn't permit him to leave the camp. Lili handed Amelia and Sahib the cuts of meat the butcher had selected for them the previous day, and they drove to their place to drop off the meat before proceeding to the Knopfelmachers' home. Sahib and Amelia were invited to stay for lunch and graciously accepted; a separate table was set up for the children. There was again quite a spread of finger foods—some Middle Eastern, some Viennese—and an appropriate selection of drinks. The men talked about international affairs and Nazi developments in various countries. They all knew some-one who was in harm's way and had empathy for their dilemma.

"Where on earth could Joseph's extended family go? Their original home was Poland...and now they're in Lyon. *Oy Gevalt*," said Moshe. Amelia was listening from the side.

"We are really worried for Lili's mother, too," she said. "Poor Lili hasn't heard from her for more than a year...not even anything after the baby was born. You'd think she'd have contacted Lili in one way or another if she were physically able."

"Lili did say that Rudi's father had spoken with her since the birth of the baby," said Arnold.

"Makes no sense to me, either," said Mr. Knopfelmacher. "You'd think having your first grandchild would spur you on to come and be here with it."

"It defies logic...for Rudi and Lili have tried so hard to have Lili's mother come here," said Sahib. "And now," Sahib lowered his voice so that Lili could not hear, "the Palestinian authorities have virtually stopped all immigration, even if there is a sponsor. I really fear Lili may never see her mother again." The mood in the room became very somber.

"*A feier soll si treffen—die* Nazis," said Moshe, fuming, as he got up to fetch a drink and join the children playing on the floor. There was further discussion about the German advances within Europe, and the somber mood did not improve for the rest of the afternoon.

Following good wishes, hugs, and kisses, Sahib and Amelia drove Lili back to Perimeter Camp V Wilhelma. There was relatively little talk on the way back, the three all being a little weary. Sahib did tell Lili that he and Arnold had been keeping an eye on the Schneider property and maintaining the garden to a minimum standard for the eventuality that she and Rudi might again live there some day. Lili hoped that Sahib's boys might want to sell the oranges for some pocket money.

BECAUSE OF THE uncertainty and general distress of the times, Lili's birthday passed with a minimum of fuss. Everybody seemed to be caught in a waiting game—waiting for what would become of Europe, waiting for Hitler's next move, waiting to hear what would become of folks that people knew, and always, always waiting for a letter from a family member.

"I am always waiting for a letter from Mother or Walter. Letters always arrive later than expected," said Lili.

"It's actually worse than that for me, Lili," Rudi said. "It is more than just constantly waiting for a letter...some news. Because you know all letters are being looked at...scrutinized, you can't express your real thoughts. I can't share with my father what's on my mind...especially within the measly twenty-five words we're allowed, I'm always careful with what I write."

"Who are these people who read our letters? Are they all Swiss? Are they all Nazis? Have they been drafted to do that work? Are there lots of them, or does a single reader read a number of letters from the same internee? Who oversees the readers, Rudi?"

"I don't really know, but I have to write in order to develop my thoughts...the act of writing to someone real is what's important to me...if I'm prevented from writing, I'm prevented from thinking... damn it, I am going to write a decent-length letter to Father soon and just post it and see if it gets there."

"You'll still need to be careful about what you say, Rudi. The last thing I need is for you to be taken back to Akko. Perhaps you should start keeping a diary...then you could write to your heart's content," said Lili.

On June 18, Charles de Gaulle made a powerful speech. In it he said, "The French have lost the battle. The French have not lost the war." He also implored all able-bodied men to enlist and help defeat the enemy. Most people just watched as Germany seemed to steamroll its way through Europe. Rudi and Lili followed the events closely in the *Palestine Post*, and on the radio it was announced, "On June 22, France signs an armistice with Nazi Germany, and on the next day Hitler tours Paris."

"Can you imagine, Rudi, all those soldiers on the Champs-Élysées, those foreigners invading...Walter will be aghast."

"He will have left Paris with his new wife, Lili...probably for the country or maybe for a town from where the resistance is organized."

"Do you really think he could fight for the resistance, Rudi? I don't think he's got it in him. I am really worried for him...I wish I could speak with him."

That, of course, was not possible under present circumstances. However, a couple of weeks later, a telegram arrived at the front gate of Camp V, and one of the police brought it to Rudi and Lili.

"*Shalom,* Mr. Auer, Mrs. Auer. Do not let this become a habit. Please let the sender know." Rudi and Lili gratefully accepted the telegram, which read:

> To Wilhelma Internee 291 Rudolf Auer and wife,
> Bordeaux
> Will resist sending flowers.
> Pierre Grun

"Do you think what I think it means, Rudi?"

"Your brother is just wanting to let you know that he changed his name to sound more French and that he's now in Bordeaux and that he's planning to join the resistance."

"That's what it means to me, too. He'll likely get himself killed, Rudi. Oh, I'm so worried."

"Don't worry, Lili. He won't necessarily be on the front line...he could be working for intelligence, clothing, or food supply or some underground newspaper...I can't imagine he'll be in an artillery unit or parachuting from a plane."

"*Gott in Himmel,* no!"

The restrictions and frustrations of the life of internees ground on. Rudi and Lili had little interaction with fellow Camp V residents, most of whom were German and many supportive of Hitler's rampage through Europe. Rudi and Lili were pleased they were quite independent of the internee community at large. There was plenty to eat from the property—pork, chicken, milk, and eggs providing sufficient protein—and sufficient vegetables, not only for home use but also for exchange to obtain butter, sugar, and bread. The sale of milk and oranges and the occasional sow and cow or heifer paid for the rent of the property with a little left over.

Positive communication via enfuriatingly brief letters from family was constantly overshadowed by the bad news of war, the ever-increasing advances by the German Army, and news of Nazi attrocities. Though there were other actions taking place at the same time, Rudi and Lili followed the war against Britain in some detail.

From July 10, 1940, there were frequent reports of the attacks of the German Luftwaffe against Britain. Early attacks were on ports and airfields along the English Channel and then moved to the interior of Britain, where the air battles between the Luftwaffe and the Royal Air Force (RAF) seemed to intensify during August. Huge casualties were reported. During early September, the British retaliated with a bombing raid on Berlin. It was reported that this infuriated Hitler. He, in turn, it was reported, turned the Luftwaffe on Britain's larger cities. For a couple of months, there seemed to be assaults not only upon London, but also upon a number of other cities, including Liverpool and Coventry. While the British loss of aircraft was reported to be very high, it was also reported that the Luftwaffe experienced even greater casualities.

"Look, Rudi," said Lili, "there's a report here that says that British fighters are shooting down German bombers faster than German industry can produce them."

"That's the best news we've had for months," said Rudi happily. "But Hitler has seemingly endless resources...nothing will stop him...in early October his troops invaded Romania. He just won't stop until—'

"Let's not talk about it any further, Rudi," said Lili, pleading. "It's making me feel physically ill...let's just have a pleasant day with the baby...perhaps we could have him outside beside us while we do a little work in the garden."

The summer had produced a spectacular harvest, vegetables and fruits being picked every day, plenty for doing well in this barter economy. Mohammad and Abdullah as well as Rudi worked very long hours, watering and irrigating, picking oranges and boxing these for the market, in addition to picking other fruit and vegetables daily. A truck would come and pick up the oranges twice per week. It was even more hectic during the grape harvest, for which Rudi brought in an expert who directed the operation. Picking often began in the early hours of the morning to ensure that grapes came off the vines in peak condition. Mohammad and Abdullah received permission to commence work long before sunrise.

Lili was also kept busy pickling vegetables and making preserves and chutneys. The vineyard expert also showed Rudi how to make his own *Moscht* (cider) from fallen fruit—apples, pears, and quince. Rudi and Lili drank it frequently on hot evenings. Mohammad and Abdullah were able to take home sufficient garden produce for their extended families. The two young men also spent countless hours in the evening selling watermelon they grew, with Rudi's permission.

In November a letter came with minimum words—fourteen, but it conveyed a great deal.

> *Bordeaux,*
> *Hope you are well*
> *Mother is well*
> *We are flying high*
> *Pierre Grun*

Lili opened it and called Rudi.

"Look, look, from Walter." Lili read the letter excitedly. "He's heard from Mother...she is well...what a relief, what wonderful news... oh, Rudi, Mother's safe. Walter's still in Bordeaux, and he must have become a pilot...flying high, he said...this is the best news we've had for months, many months. He wouldn't be a fighter pilot, Rudi, would he?"

"I wouldn't think so; he's probably flying supplies from here to there," said Rudi. This brief communication, however pithy it was, reminded Rudi of his perceived need to write to his father at length.

"If he doesn't get it, he doesn't get it, but I'm going to try." Rudi soon sat down and wrote to his father—more than five hundred words in very small writing on one sheet of small paper, double sided.

> *Rudolf Auer No. 291*
> *Camp No. V*   *November 17, 1940*
> *Liebe Eltern,*
>
> *We hope this letter finds you in perfect health. Lili, Peter, and I are always together and doing well. Peter provides us with much joy and happiness. He has black eyes, already talks, has three teeth, weighs about twelve pounds. We are economically independent.*
>
> *I have made Peterle slippers, a small bed, and other furniture for when he's a bit older. Lili has made him enough clothes.*
>
> *Our house is in a large garden with an orange grove.*
>
> *How is the weather? Any snow yet? How are Mizi and Tante Marianne?*
>
> *What is Lili's mother up to? Haven't heard from her for a year. Are you still sending her food parcels?*
>
> *Do you, dear Father, still get to go to Klagenfurt?*
>
> *Hope to get mail from you real soon. Hope you can answer all my questions.*
>
> *Sorry I couldn't write to your birthday, Mama. I wish Father a happy birthday.*
>
> *I will try to write again before Christmas.*
>
> *Please stay healthy.*
>
> *Your Lilirudipetale*

FRUSTRATION, THE TEDIUM OF WAR, AND DEPORTATION

NOT HAVING HEARD from his father for a long time, Rudi, feeling very frustrated, again wrote a full letter in small writing, double sided.

> *19. 1. 1941*
>
> *Liebe Eltern,*
>
> *Only just received your letter of 17. 8. 1940. I wrote again middle December.*
>
> *Petale is doing really well…round as a barrel, gold-blond hair, already standing, very lively, talks a lot, enjoys bread and butter, bananas, and orange juice.*
>
> *His mother has him visit in the cowshed. He rides on a small heifer's back and loves it.*
>
> *I have made him lots of toys—two cars.*
>
> *Still no news from (Lili's) mother.*
>
> *Feel that Petale will ski the Gerlitzen one day.*
>
> *How are Mizzi and Tante Marianne?*
>
> *Hope this letter finds you and Mama in the best of health.*
>
> *Eure*
>
> *Rudililipetale*

A few days prior to Peter's first birthday, Lili finally received a twenty-five-word communication from her mother. She was overjoyed, as her mother seemed in good health.

Wien 3
Ungargasse 4
Tuer 4,
Mezzannine bei Herrn Rudolf Mueller
August 1940
Dearest Lili, Rudi.

   Hope the three of you are well. I am also well, now living in a one-room apartment.
Alles liebe,
Mutter

Lili wrote in her diary:

Thank God Mother seems well. Why hadn't she written for so long, or did she get the address wrong? Did her letters not pass the censors? Why did she decide not to come to Palestine? She's now confined to one room only... oh dear. Will she survive the Nazis in Vienna? I am so worried about her

A letter also arrived from Rudi's father, dated January 16, that took only six weeks to arrive. He acknowledged receiving Rudi's first longer letter. A letter from Rudi's father, dated February 20, arrived April 10. Rudi replied again with a normal letter, small writing, double sided on a small sheet of paper on April 13. In it he wrote, "Hopefully the war will end soon so that we can all see each other again."

Rudi was really pleased that he had now sent several normal, two-page letters to his father that appeared to have been uncensored and delivered.

War rumbled on. There were daily news items in the paper and reports on the radio: "Half the world seems to be involved—Australians and British fighting in Northern Africa, British forces advance in Somaliland in East Africa; German general Erwin Rommel arrives in Tripoli, North Africa; British forces arrive in Greece; there's a coup in Yugoslavia; a pro-Axis regime is set up in Iraq; Nazis invade Greece and Yugoslavia, and both soon surrender; Deputy Fuehrer Rudolph Hess flies to Scotland. There is heavy German bombing of London, and the British bomb Hamburg. The Allies invade Syria and Lebanon."

"We skied in Lebanon not so long ago, Lili," said Rudi.

"I know...all these invasions, bombings, war everywhere, Rudi. When will it all end? We really need to be free."

RUDI AND LILI were having breakfast outside by the vegetable garden on a beautiful sunny morning. Birds were chirping in the tree above them, some feasting on figs; others were scratching in the garden in search of breakfast of their own—a worm or a grub, maybe. Mohammad and Abdullah were in one of the outhouses, completing chores after milking. A vehicle came to a screeching halt at the front of the house, and Rudi went to investigate.

"We are just having breakfast, Officers," said Rudi as he led two policemen back to their outside table. "How can we help you gentlemen?"

"We are police officers of Wilhelma Camp V. I am Captain Blaustein, and this is Sergeant Finegold."

"*Shalom*, gentlemen. This is my wife, Lili."

"*Shalom*, Officers," said Lili, putting down her coffee cup.

"*Shalom*. We have been tipped off that a pig has been stolen, and it is here."

"No stolen pig here, gentlemen."

"We have it on good authority that a large sow, with a triangular piece missing from her left ear, is on this property. Do you realize that thieving within the confines of the camp is taken very seriously?"

"Yes, we do."

"Do any other people work here...other than yourselves?"

"Yes, Abdullah and Mohammad."

"Aha, there you have it...Arabs...not to be trusted," said Captain Blaustein.

"I have told you there is no stolen pig here, and Abdullah and Mohammad are very trustworthy workers," Rudi said.

"We know Arabs...they are probably the thieves we are looking for."

"You are clearly mistaken, Officers, but come and meet them and search the piggery...and the rest of the property if you wish."

Rudi led the officers into the barn where Abdullah and Mohanmmad were working. "Mohanmmad, Abdulla, I'd like you to meet Captain Blaustein and Sergeant Finegold of the camp police. They are investigating the disappearance of a pig with a piece missing from one ear."

"*Salam.*"

"Do you realize the severity of stealing, Mohammad and Abdulla?"

"We understand; we steal nothing."

"I'm not so sure...lead us to the piggery. How many pigs do you have?"

"Four."

"I want to see their ears."

"No holes in ears."

"Go check out the other sheds, Finegold, while I interrogate these Arabs," said the captain somewhat gruffly and appearing a little frustrated.

"Where were you last night? Early in the morning? Who with? Are you sure? Did you steal a pig?"

Rudi answered the questions.

"We are still not convinced, Mr. Auerbach."

"I beg your pardon? My name is Auer, not Auerbach."

"You are Randolf Auerbach, are you not? We were told this was the house of Randolf Auerbach."

"No, I am not; I am Rudi Auer, internee two-nine-one...never heard of a Randolf Auerbach. Anything else we can help you with, Officers?" asked Rudi, trying unsuccessfully to hide his annoyance.

"We apologize. You can get back to your breakfast."

A couple of weeks went by. It was late July 1941, and there was another visit from the police. This was a very different visit.

"*Shalom.* Are you Mr. Rudolf Auer, internee number two-nine-one?"

At least they got my name and number right, thought Rudi. "Yes, sir. I am Rudi Auer."

"Good. I have some news for you and an offer. You may have heard some rumors. The internment camps in Palestine are shortly to be closed, and most internees will be deported."

Rudi nearly choked, and Lili visibly gulped as she sat off to the side with her son on her knee.

"Where will people be taken to?" asked Rudi.

"We cannot tell you. It is not general knowledge. We have only been told internees will need warmer clothes than here." He glanced at Lili, who didn't know what to say.

"*Oy Vei,* we were just beginning to settle down here...and now?" said Rudi.

"You are not like all the Templers; you are different. That's why I'm here. I was sent by my superior officer. Some men will be deported, while their families will be required to stay behind. You will be able to go together. Do you have a preference as to whether you leave sooner or later?

"We'll still be interned?" asked Lili, as she shrugged her shoulders.

"We'll leave on the first ship out," said Rudi, looking at Lili for confirmation. There was a moment of silence as if to confirm the decision. "Better to be far away as quickly as possible."

"I guess so," said Lili, somewhat apprehensively and a little perplexed.

"The first ship will be leaving in a matter of just days. You must not divulge this to anyone. Nobody else has been told yet. I will let you know more details later."

A flood of emotions swept over Lili. There were just so many questions.

"I can tell you now that you will be allowed forty kilograms of luggage each and thirty for the baby, and a reasonable amount of hand luggage." Rudi and Lili were somewhat shell shocked.

"*Mazel Tov.* See you again soon."

Lili put her son in the crib and enveloped Rudi in an enduring bear hug while conflicting emotions swirled within her that she could not fathom.

"We were in a situation once before when we were on a ship, not knowing where we'd end up...I'm so overwhelmed...I don't know what to think," she said.

Rudi and Lili talked for the next couple of hours, with a mixture of emotions—excitement, apprehension, hope...and many, many questions. The bottom line was they'd prefer to be further away from war, and hence they were keen to go, though the idea of such major disruption felt quite unsettling.

"Only a suitcase each and a smaller one for the baby...leaving everything else behind...oh, Rudi, I don't know how we'll manage. Where will they take us?"

"I don't know...we'll just have to go...it may offer us a new beginning. We will be okay."

"When? In how many years? Where?" After a sob-filled pause, Lili continued. "We'll have to let all our friends in Haifa know. They will be very unhappy...they all thought that we'd end up living in the Pine Street house again and see one another as we did before."

"I will particularly miss Sahib; he's been such a great friend—gave me my first job in Palestine. He was a godsend at the time," Rudi said.

"He loaned us his car very early on, allowing us to take a vacation to Jerusalem and Jaffa."

"He got us all that wine from the Côte d Azur, and he picked and delivered boxes of oranges to Akko."

"Then he gave us a radio, remember? And shifted all our furniture from the Pine Street house to here."

"Yes, and taught me how to drive Nazis off the road, too," said Rudi with a slight smile.

"Amelia has been a very good friend, too," said Lili. "She was so generous and loaned me all those books. We'll miss the Knopfelmachers, too, Rudi...those dinners and the concerts we went to together were all wonderful. I'll especially miss Mrs. Knopfelmacher, as she has really become my surrogate mother since before I became pregnant."

"Do you think Moshe and Rachel will stay or end up leaving here, too?"

"Maybe they'll end up wherever we end up. They followed us here from Vienna."

"I'll miss all the children, too," said Rudi.

Lili again had tears in her eyes. "And I'll probably never see Walter again."

———

THERE WAS MUCH gossip throughout the camp. It was rumoured a ship would take some people away to a distant land. Who would be selected, and who would stay? What were the criteria being used to make selections? Where exactly would people be shipped off to?

One of the British colonies, surely, thought Lili. *Maybe India, Australia, New Zealand, Canada?*

Would families be kept together? was a common and nervously asked question.

On July 31, 1941, a hot summer's day, Rudi and Lili hugged Abdullah and Mohammad among tears and with some of their family standing thirty meters or so away. They boarded a bus and were driven to the railway station at Lydda, where hundreds of people about to be deported restlessly waited for instructions. Some were from Jaffa, and a large number were from Sarona. Some people were sitting on suitcases, some were fanning themselves, and some were sipping water. It was early in the afternoon. It was already very hot and promised to become hotter. The smell of dirty feet in leather shoes was already in the air.

"Let's stay as calm as we can, Lili, and not expend too much energy. I feel that we could be in for a very long day," said Rudi, looking at his watch and changing the position of his son from one arm to another. "He can get quite heavy."

At night, with little to eat and drink all day, they made it onto a train to Kantara, in Egypt. Rudi felt very edgy; he sat close to their three pieces of luggage being jostled around by the moving train.

The sky was now pitch black with some stars. From Kantara, they were ferried across to Suez, via Ismailia. It seemed to take many hours. Peter slept a lot, Lili a little, and Rudi not at all. At Suez, they were ordered onto boats and headed out to sea. Several people were sick overboard, and many more fought against it as the swell-induced movement of the boat increased. A huge liner loomed in front of them. Rudi and Lili had never seen such a large ship. They were about to board it. It felt as if they were about to be swallowed up.

It was the Queen Elizabeth, which had been designed as a passenger liner—the largest passenger liner ever built—but she was now a converted troop ship ready to deport people to a far-off land. But where? People were anxious, not just curious. Everybody was ordered aboard as emotions were at fever pitch. Adults were yelling at each other, parents were disciplining children, and babies were crying, mainly from exhaustion. Rudi and Lili were led down a long corridor and shown to a cabin with narrow, double-decker bunks and a small port hole. They were too exhausted right now to be concerned about being without their luggage or about anything else. It would be brought to them later that day. They closed the door and fell asleep.

The next morning they were called to breakfast in a very large dining room. They were still at anchor. The next day seemed to go on forever among general commotion and consternation. The *Queen Elizabeth* finally left on August 2. Nobody seemed to know where they were headed. It was terribly disconcerting for everybody. Many people were on edge. Rudi and Lili settled into their tiny bunk room, which they thought was adequate. Lili also thought it was better here than being in the cargo hold, sitting on some creaky wooden crates or sacks of grain. There was no smell of oil, grain, or spices here. There was no black cat. It was somewhat stuffy, and they did wonder whether the lack of air conditioning would make things uncomfortable in the coming days. They also wondered how people would get on with one another at sea. *One soul won't have to worry about that,* thought Rudi, as they witnessed their first sea burial just a day after casting off. Soon thereafter, Rudi was taking in some air on the upper deck, and Lili took out her diary.

> *I hate war. I hate being an internee. Will this be our last journey as prisoners? Where on earth are we going—South Africa, India, New Zealand, Australia? Will I ever see my mother again? Rudi's parents? Tante Marianne? Will we ever see Moshe and his family, the Knopfelmachers, Sahib and Amelia? They have been all so good to me. Is Walter okay? Is he really a pilot? I miss them all so much. When will the war end? How will we all cope with what lies before us? Will I ever be able to have another child? A child needs a sibling. Will I ever again get to spend time in Vienna? I am sick of us perpetually being displaced persons. We so need to be free.*

PROLOGUE FOR THE NEXT BOOK

THE NEXT BOOK, about the lives of Rudi and Lili, commences with the following pages:

August 4, 1941

This, their third day at sea, it was still extremely hot, maybe 40 degrees centigrade. Rudi was on an upper deck taking in some fresh air. Lili, sitting on a lower bunk in their tiny, port-holed cabin, continued with her diary entry:

> *Living in another land could be a quite romantic idea … but not in internment. I don't wish to feel like a caged animal. No, no, please not. Why will we be interned again? … With whom? … Where are we headed … India, New Zealand, or Australia? Australia is huge, as large as all of Europe, I remember from school. It's very hot isn't it? … mainly desert too. I've had enough of sand. What will life be like in our new land? … will we live in a large farmhouse?… grow our own vegetables?… have some animals– for meat, eggs? Where will we get other supplies– flour, sugar bread? … or will I make our own bread? Will we live close to other people?… close to a doctor, in case we need one?… any Nazis in our midst?… Will we be able to communicate with family members in Europe?* She hid her diary between her clothes as she heard Rudi opening the door'.

They were aboard the HMS Queen Elizabeth which had been designed for the Cunard line as a passenger liner. It was the largest passenger liner ever built, but she was quickly converted to a troop-ship, then to a carrier of Prisoners of War (POWs) and enemy aliens, operating between Australia and Suez. She was 1031 feet long and 233 feet or twelve stories high and weighed 83,000 tons. She had on board about 550 Templers and other Germans, Austrians, Italians and a few people of other nationalities from Palestine; Germans from Persia and about 1,000 POW's from Rommel's North Africa Campaign.

The ship was guarded by British officers and auxiliary Jewish police and many of the German internees, mainly Templers felt they were being poorly treated.

"What an irony that is, Lili," said Rudi. "In Germany, Austria, and elsewhere in Europe there are thousands of Jews, as we speak, not just being ordered about, but dehumanized, brutalized and carted off to concentration camps or worse by Germans. And, the Germans here on the boat have a complaint … what bloody chutzpah."

There were huge dining rooms on the boat which also served as meeting places. The food seemed reasonable, but some people were displeased that there were insufficient fruits and vegetables and a lack of milk. Some deemed the food unsuitable for infants.

The Templers tended to find one another and congregate inside the dining halls and on the ship's decks. They were a largely cohesive group, mainly from Sarona and other internment camps in Palestine. Some people who had not seen one another for years were re-acquainted and new friendships were formed. People passed the time of day– walking and talking and reading, and there were a couple of small musical groups formed that sometimes provided entertainment in the evening. Yet, despite this seeming normality, there was always an air of disquiet.

At times during the day, music of a different type could be heard as groups of Hitler Youth marched around the decks, in military for-mation, singing Nazi songs to the applause of many Germans and to the dismay of non-Nazi Germans and the many other nationalities and racial groups, especially Jews who were acutely aware of what the

Germans had been and were still doing to members of their families and acquaintances throughout Germany, Austria and other European countries. Rudi and Lili thought that it would not be long before there'd be a reaction, possibly a violent reaction to what some saw as provocative behavior.

Indeed on the second or third evening of formation marching and singing of Nazi songs some passengers took offense, there was some name-calling and shoving before ship's police forced the singing marchers to disband.

ONE EVENING, ONLY a few days after they set sail, Rudi and Lili found themselves at dinner beside a couple whom they found very easy to like.

"I am Felix Schneider and this is Adina Schneider, my wife. We Are both from Vienna." Felix was a dark-haired man of medium build and rather handsome; his wife, an elegant lady with fine features.

"Oh, where from? We are both from Vienna too," said Lili. "Rudi spent just a couple of years there while I had been there all my life."

"We understand, before there were things that were happening in Vienna that became too uncomfortable for you to stay. You are from the Innere Stadt (inner city), am I right?" asked Felix.

"Yes, we lived in a small apartment on the Salzgasse in 1934 ... the last year or so, while Rudi was studying Law. But before we met, in 1933, I was living on the Ringstrasse with my parents and my brother. And you?"

"We lived just around the corner from the Musikverein and the Staatsoper so that I could be close for my performances and practice. I am a flautist and teacher... Felix would have preferred to have lived somewhere else with more garden and trees. And why did you leave Vienna, Lili?" Lili just wanted to say that Rudi made a series of poor judgments and found himself in serious trouble with the university administration. The administration, eliciting the support of the police, drove him, and therefore the two of them, out of the country.

Instead, Lili explained how Rudi wrote a series of articles for the university paper focusing upon activities of Nazis within the student body and exposing Nazi sympathizers within the teaching staff and administration. Accusing some within the administration and some within the teaching staff of collaborating with the Deutsche Studentenschaft (student association dominated by Nazis) was the last straw, especially because he intimated that the police were in cahoots with the university Nazis and their sympathisers. Felix and Adina scrunched up their face, understanding that Rudi had been hardly diplomatic.

"Yes," said Rudi, "I was charged with sedition against the university and therefore against the state and was sentenced to thirty days imprisonment. I spent one night in jail and escaped the next morning, knocking over some poor gardener and running away via underground passages just to the east of Wipplingerstrasse."

"Oh, and how did you get to Palestine?"

"You know, I don't even think our parents and most of our friends know the truth," explained Lili. "They took it for granted that we took the boat from Trieste."